THE
ALMOST
KING

Also by Lucy Saxon

Take Back the Skies

THE
ALMOST
KING

LUCY SAXON

BLOOMSBURY

NEW YORK   LONDON   OXFORD   NEW DELHI   SYDNEY

First published in Great Britain in June 2015 by Bloomsbury Publishing Plc
Published in the United States of America in August 2016 by Bloomsbury Children's Books
www.bloomsbury.com

Bloomsbury is a registered trademark of Bloomsbury Publishing Plc

For information about permission to reproduce selections from this book, write to
Permissions, Bloomsbury Children's Books, 1385 Broadway, New York, New York 10018
Bloomsbury books may be purchased for business or promotional use. For information on
bulk purchases please contact Macmillan Corporate and Premium Sales Department at
specialmarkets@macmillan.com

Library of Congress Cataloging-in-Publication Data
Names: Saxon, Lucy, author.
Title: The almost king / by Lucy Saxon.
Description: New York : Bloomsbury Children's Books, 2016.
Summary: After a taste of the brutality of army life, seventeen-year-old Aleks Vasin deserts and finds
love, adventure and a skyship full of technological discoveries, while pursued by vengeful soldiers.
Identifiers: LCCN 2015037734
ISBN 978-1-61963-627-9 (hardcover) • ISBN 978-1-61963-699-6 (e-book)
Subjects: | CYAC: Adventure and adventurers—Fiction. | Love—Fiction. |
Soldiers—Fiction. | Science fiction. | BISAC: JUVENILE FICTION/Fantasy & Magic. |
JUVENILE FICTION/Science Fiction. | JUVENILE FICTION/Love & Romance.
Classification: LCC PZ7.S27432 Al 2016 | DDC [Fic]—dc23
LC record available at https://lccn.loc.gov/2015037734

Typeset by Integra Software Services Pvt. Ltd.
Printed and bound in the U.S.A. by Berryville Graphics Inc., Berryville, Virginia
2 4 6 8 10 9 7 5 3 1

All papers used by Bloomsbury Publishing, Inc., are natural, recyclable products
made from wood grown in well-managed forests. The manufacturing processes
conform to the environmental regulations of the country of origin.

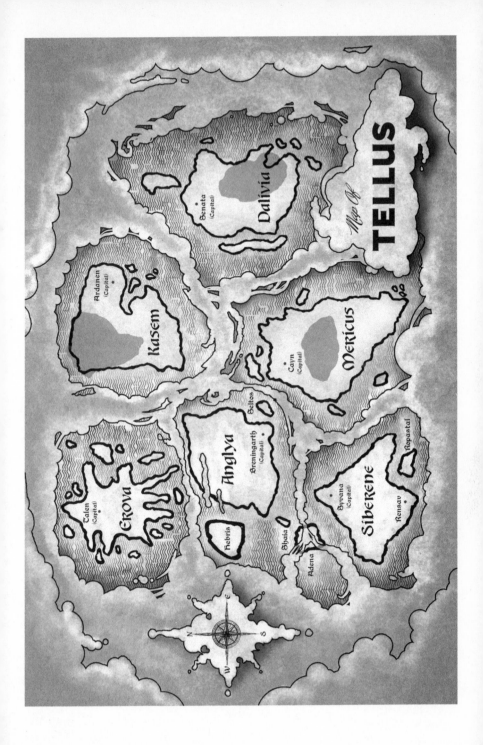

1

Now: Rensav

Aleks was woken by a deafeningly loud klaxon, and jolted up out of his narrow cot bed, blue eyes wide in alarm. 'Relax, new boy, it's just the wake-up call,' Jarek groaned from the bed beside his, plugging his ears with his fingers. The klaxon shut off, and Aleks relaxed even as he reddened in embarrassment, hearing a few men snigger at his overreaction. Not the best start for his first day as a cadet.

He moved to get back under the covers, but Jarek swung his long legs out of his own bed and reached over to swat him. 'No point in that – you're up now. The lieutenant will be here to get you soon, anyway. Better get dressed first,' he suggested. Aleks frowned, glancing around as several other cadets reached into their trunks for clothes and shaving kits, before heading to the washroom.

'Do I not get breakfast first?' Apparently that was hilarious, as Jarek laughed outright, green eyes glinting with cold amusement.

'Oh, you've got so much to learn, baby bird. They'll feed you when they're happy with you, no sooner.' Aleks gritted his teeth. Jarek was probably just teasing him, trying to make him scared. He should've expected it as the new kid.

He was lacing his boots when the door slammed open, and those still in the room hurried to stand to attention at the ends of their beds. Aleks hastened to do the same, face burning as he tripped over his unlaced boot, simultaneously trying to smooth his jet black hair down from its messy bedhead. The man who had entered strode down the rows, sneering at them all. He was fair-haired and pale, with a very impressive moustache and lieutenant rank white stripes on his deep blue uniform. He stopped in front of Aleks, who almost forgot how to breathe.

'You must be the fresh meat,' the man who could only be Lieutenant Shulga drawled, mud-brown eyes roaming critically over Aleks's form, taking in his untucked shirt and tangled bootlaces. 'Come with me.' Aleks bent to tie his laces, only to be dragged back upright by the collar of his shirt. 'I said come with me!' Shulga growled, spittle flying. Aleks nodded sharply, following the man out of the barracks and trying to ignore Jarek's muffled snickers. He could handle a little hazing; he was stronger than that. And it was only his first day, after all, though it felt as though he'd been here far longer. His arrival in Rensav felt like aeons ago, and his stomach was already knotted with anxiety at the thought of what lay ahead of him.

The Previous Morning: Rensav
He still felt half asleep when he poured himself onto Quicksilver's saddle, though after a good gallop with the wind in his face he felt

far more alert, finally able to appreciate the view up ahead of him. With very little to worry about in the way of storms or attacks, due to being so well protected by the mountains, the buildings in the Southern city of Rensav were taller than he was used to out West. The occasional wrought-steel spire pointed up out of a sea of grey stone houses and shops, making it clear where the temples were. The sparkling jewel in the middle of all the monochrome was the palace, built from what seemed like an entire mountain's worth of precious stones and metals, clearly visible even from so far away. Off to the West, he could just about see the Stormlands, a solid wall of raging black clouds; they looked angrier than usual, and he wondered if a big storm was going to hit soon. The Stormlands had been doing all sorts of strange things over the past year or so — he would miss the sight of them from his bedroom window.

Aleks stopped on the peak of a hill to take in the view, awed at the sheer size of the Rudavin palace, its rainbow of colours glittering in the morning light. The paintings and newscast pictures he'd seen of it did not do it justice. Who on Tellus needed a building that big? The king only had two children, but could probably fit three hundred in a palace like that. It was beautiful, but an incredible waste of space and resources.

Drawing closer to the city, Aleks was surprised by the quietness. The roads were wide and paved with dark stone, and several people were leading horses, pulling carts full of goods and going about their business. But no one waved to a friend across the street, or stopped to chat about the weather and other such trivialities. There were no street vendors loudly proclaiming their wares, no children laughing. It was a very sombre city, and it was eerie.

Dropping to the ground with near silent feet, Aleks kept a tight hand on Quicksilver's reins as he led the dappled grey *gelding through the city. Even his horse noticed the strange atmosphere, his pale ears flat to his head and his movements jerky. Aleks followed the wide street that seemed to be heading in the direction of the palace, ducking out of other people's way and hoping he didn't draw attention to himself. The walk felt endless; he could have walked from one end of his village to the other and back about nine times and gone the same distance. His pulse thudded in his ears and his palms grew damp inside his gloves, but he kept his stride as confident as he could, trying to channel Maxim. His eldest brother wouldn't let anyone intimidate him.*

The closer he got to the palace, Aleks began to notice blue-uniformed guards marching in pairs through the streets, guns clearly displayed at their hips. They didn't seem to be doing anything but patrolling, but their mere presence was daunting. Aleks tried to imagine himself in the stiff cobalt uniform, his messy black hair cropped short, back straight and marching in time with someone else's stride. It was a strange mental image, and it would take him a little while to grow accustomed to the real thing, should he get that far.

Walking past what seemed to be a large hospital with yet more guards surrounding it, Aleks found himself in the huge stretch of empty cobbled courtyard in front of the palace gates. Tugging Quicksilver to a halt, he eyed the gleaming multi-coloured panels of the palace walls in amazement. He couldn't imagine even beginning to build such a structure, and that it had been conceived three and a half centuries ago and still stood strong made it all the more incredible.

The palace probably covered more ground than the entire forest back home, going up at least seven storeys by his count, with neat square windows dotting the colourful façade. The boundary fence was over twice his height and crowned by painful-looking steel spikes. Wrought into the main gate was the Rudavin family crest, jewels embedded into the eyes of the eagle about to take flight, the dark metal feathers of its wings so realistic it took Aleks's breath away. The inner courtyard was full of soldiers running drills, the wooden practice rifles clutched as carefully as if they were the real thing, every single person completely in time with the others. It was like watching a machine of flesh and blood, each person one part of a whole, and the thought turned his stomach a little as he was reminded of the Anglyan newscasts of only a few years ago. That fateful day when images of massacre and destruction appeared on their screens with no warning, narrated by the voice of a young girl who would go on to become the queen. Aleks was twelve, but he'd been glued to the screen in horror even then.

He noticed several guards staring at him. He steeled himself and headed for the nearest one with the stripes of a commander. The man was standing to attention, though still managed to give him a dirty look with his otherwise impassive face. 'I want to enlist,' Aleks declared, wishing his voice would stop shaking. He heard a brief laugh before the culprit was silenced. One of the commander's pale blond eyebrows rose.

'What makes you think I can help you with that, boy?' he asked. Aleks shrugged.

'You're a commander. You have the rank to sign me up,' he explained simply. 'I wish to enlist in the military. Am I speaking to the right person, or do I need to go elsewhere?'

'Where are you from?' the commander asked, ignoring his question. 'And how old are you, brat?'

'I'm seventeen,' Aleks told him, bristling slightly at the condescending tone. 'And I'm from Baysar, out West.' The commander's other eyebrow rose to join the first, and he folded his arms over his chest, tilting his chin to look down at Aleks.

'Never heard of it. A Western lad? I should've known, with that horse. Why would a kid like you come all the way out here to enlist? You should be on a farm.' Another laugh broke out, and Aleks flushed angrily.

'Does it matter? I want to join the military – my motivations are my own. Now can you help me, or do I need to go elsewhere?' he repeated, holding his ground. He didn't want to look weak before he'd even started.

'No, I can help you,' the commander informed him, glancing to his side. 'Private Yanev, watch my position. You, boy, come with me.' One of the younger soldiers jumped to take up the commander's position as he left his post, catching Aleks by the scruff of the neck and pushing him towards one of the guard buildings set into the perimeter fence. 'A fine stallion you have there, brat. Did you steal him?'

'Gelding,' Aleks corrected sharply, blue eyes flashing. 'And no. I raised and broke him myself. I shan't part with him.'

The commander looked amused at his answer. 'Mounted infantry, then?' Aleks's step faltered for a moment; he hadn't thought past getting enlisted. 'Mounted will be the only way you'll get to keep your horse.'

'Then yes,' Aleks agreed instantly. 'What does that entail?'

'Basic training with the rest of the cadets, with separate training in horseback combat and the appropriate care of a military horse. He'll need to be vetted too to make sure he's up to scratch. But if you rode him all the way from the West, I can't see that being a problem. Good thing he's already gelded; makes them easier to control.' Aleks reluctantly handed Quicksilver's reins to the guard posted outside the building, following the commander inside.

The man gestured to the seat opposite the desk. 'Why are you here, lad? Not every day we have them as young as you, or from so far away. Usually the only Westerners signing up are the court-assigned enlistments,' he added with a vicious smirk beneath his neat moustache. Aleks grimaced; everyone knew that felons were given the choice between punishment or forced conscription, depending on their crime.

'I want to serve my king,' he said, making the commander laugh sharply.

'Try the other leg,' he retorted, perching on the edge of the desk rather than taking a seat himself. Reaching into a drawer, he pulled out a sheaf of papers.

'I also want to get out of the shadow of my older brothers,' said Aleks, bringing a satisfied look to the man's face.

'Much better,' he murmured. Aleks expected a further remark, but the commander merely thrust the papers at him, offering a pen from his uniform pocket. 'Fill those out. We'll put you and your horse up for the night and start on induction tomorrow.'

Aleks glanced down at the papers. It was all standard information: name, date of birth, place of birth, parents' names. It went on to ask about previous experience with firearms, blades and heavy machinery, as well as family medical history, school grades and then what seemed like a hundred other questions Aleks didn't know the relevance of but answered anyway.

When he was sure he had answered everything, he passed the papers back to the commander, who skimmed over the first page, then nodded in approval. 'Last chance to back out, lad,' he declared, *reaching for his stamp. Aleks only flinched a fraction when the stamp was slammed against his forms, officially accepting him into the Siberene military. No going back now.*

Now: Rensav

Aleks snapped to attention as the lieutenant marched him through the lines of squat concrete barracks towards an imposing stone building with a large blue four-point star over the door: the hospital. Not breakfast, then.

Nearly tripping over his loose laces on his way upstairs, Aleks tried to keep up the best he could, hoping he wouldn't embarrass himself on the first day. Or worse, fail his induction. Shulga rapped sharply on a door bearing the nameplate *Dr Anrep* in brass. It opened to reveal a weedy little man with a narrow face and high cheekbones, his expression like he'd smelled something particularly foul. He looked past the lieutenant to Aleks, who tried to stare back nonchalantly. 'Is this him?' the doctor asked. Shulga nodded. 'Young, isn't he? Bring him in, then.'

Shulga's large hand shoved Aleks's shoulder, pushing him through the door, then cuffed him round the ear. 'Do as you're told and you'll get fed after your physical. If we feel gracious enough,' he taunted, turning on his heel and walking away before Aleks could respond. Left alone with the unpleasant-looking doctor, Aleks felt his stomach turn to stone.

The medical exam was, in one word, traumatising. After making him strip to his undershorts, the doctor had examined every inch of Aleks's body, making snide remarks about his lithe frame. Aleks merely closed his eyes, praying desperately for it to end soon.

Finally, Anrep told him to put his clothes back on. Only then was Aleks allowed to eat, a tray having been brought up by an errand boy. It was just oatcakes and fish stew, but to his painfully empty stomach it may as well have been nectar of the gods.

Wolfing the food down, he gratefully accepted the chipped mug of water offered to him by the doctor, nearly choking on it when the door swung open. Trying to both swallow his mouthful and stand to attention, he succeeded in neither, doubling over as he coughed and spilled water all down his front. When he straightened up, still coughing, Shulga was eyeing him disparagingly. 'Gods, we've got another imbecile,' he muttered to himself. 'Come, boy.' Aleks followed obediently, cheeks red.

The next stop on their apparently busy schedule was to get his hair cut short, then off to the training ground, where Aleks could see the day had already started for his fellow cadets. Shulga took him towards what seemed to be an obstacle course, and Aleks's stomach churned with nerves. The course spanned the entire field, full of mud pits and high walls and climbing ropes, as well as plenty of things Aleks didn't recognise. He could see a small group of cadets who looked like they had just finished, covered in mud and practically crawling they were so exhausted. How well he performed would likely decide his fate.

Moustache twitching, the lieutenant patted him hard on the shoulder, forcing his knees to buckle slightly. 'Time to put you through your paces, brat,' he declared with a slimy chuckle. 'Let's see what you're made of.'

2

The Previous Day: Rensav

Enlistment forms filed, the commander led Aleks back outside, where the private was still standing with Quicksilver, back straight.

'Take the brat's horse to the mounted infantry cadets' stables, then put his saddlebag in barracks twelve.' The Private saluted, hurrying off to do as he was bid, and Aleks felt a stab of panic as he watched his horse being led away from him.

'We'll get you a physical and a fitness test tomorrow,' said the commander. 'Curfew is at nine, lights out and in bed at ten, no exceptions. You'll eat, sleep, train, shower, spend every waking moment with the men in your unit, and you'll like it.' He reached out, pulling Aleks's hat off his head, and frowned. 'You'll need a haircut too. No uniform until you've completed basic training, but I'll have one of the privates bring you some training clothes.' Aleks smiled at that, pleased with the prospect of wearing clothes that hadn't spent the past four days screwed up in his bag. 'And, of course, you won't earn a wage until you get your rank,' the commander told him, holding open the door to a large concrete building with a sign declaring it the Siberene Military Headquarters.

Everywhere around the building was fenced off, and Aleks assumed he was stepping into the army training ground. It surprised him how much of the city was taken up by military buildings; he'd seen the perimeter fence when he'd walked in, and it practically bisected the city. He couldn't help but wonder if that would change once the tunnel trains were up and running through the mountains; people from all over would head South to see the palace, and they'd definitely get a surprise once they reached the city.

His footsteps echoed in the narrow hallways of the building as he followed the commander, and he couldn't stop his eyes from drifting around in interest. The walls were covered with portraits of men in uniform and paintings of battle scenes, interspersed with large portraits of King Andrei looking proud and regal. Medals in cases sat on shelves and, as they entered a large room, Aleks saw a Rudavin flag spanning most of the back wall. 'This way, brat.' The commander led him back outside through a side door, and suddenly the world was a very different place.

Squat grey barracks lined the muddy road ahead, set in neat rows like the benches in a temple. Beyond that, Aleks could see some bigger, nicer-looking buildings that were probably for the higher-ranked officers, and then there was nothing but stretches of white snowgrass, turned brown in places with churned mud. The commander made a beeline for a barracks building set three rows from the front, knocking twice before opening the door. He led Aleks inside, the boy's heart racing as he saw all the men lined up at the ends of their beds, clearly having just jumped to attention at the commander's entrance. They all looked remarkably similar, dressed in their training clothes with identical haircuts and clean-shaven faces. The age range surprised him; some looked even younger than he was, despite the age limit supposedly being seventeen, and others looked almost forty. Aleks wondered if they were felons who had chosen conscription.

'Gentlemen!' the commander barked, his hand on Aleks's shoulder. 'I'd like to introduce you to your new room-mate, Cadet Vasin. Be gentle with him — he looks a bit fragile.' Aleks bristled, but the commander was the only one to laugh at the joke. 'Lieutenant Shulga will be here to pick him up in the morning for induction, so don't let him wander into the firing range overnight. Waste of enlistment forms,' he added in a mutter. He glanced down at Aleks, nudging him a little further into the room. 'I'll see you if you happen to be enrolled in mechanical combat.' There was a bloodthirsty smirk on his face, and Aleks resolved at that moment to do everything within his power to avoid being enrolled in mechanical combat. 'At ease, men!' With that last yell, the commander turned on his heel and left the barracks, the door slamming shut behind him and leaving Aleks alone in a room with twenty complete strangers.

'That's yours over there,' one of the cadets told him, pointing to a bed further back with his saddlebag draped on it. The beds had thin mattresses and navy wool blankets, each with a black leather chest at the foot. Aleks bit his lip; his saddlebag looked a lot lighter than it had when he'd last seen it. How much had they stolen from him?

'Thanks,' he murmured, crossing over to the bed. There was also a pile of training clothes in blue, white and black, looking to be about his size. They hadn't given him boots, but he knew his own would serve him perfectly well. 'I'm Aleks, by the way.' No one responded, and he didn't say anything more, shrugging his coat off as the rest of his room-mates went back to whatever they'd been doing before the commander had interrupted. A group of younger cadets, all about Aleks's age, were playing some sort of card game in the corner, betting cigarettes and round coins made of wood with lettering painted on them. Others were sitting on their beds, reading, staring at the ceiling, or in one case sharpening a knife. Aleks hadn't thought they were allowed weapons in the barracks.

'You forced or voluntary?' He looked up at the question, seeing the man in the bed next to his eyeing him inquisitively. His cropped hair was dark blond, almost brown, and his eyes were a bright shade of green. He looked older than Aleks, perhaps nineteen or twenty, and oddly slender for a military cadet. His accent sounded like that of an Easterner.

'Voluntary,' Aleks replied, stripping off his jacket. 'You?'

'Same. Barely, though. It was here or the streets, and I didn't really fancy my chances up East,' the man replied wryly. 'How about you?'

Aleks shrugged, shuffling on to the bed and leaning his back against the wall. 'My older brothers have all made something of themselves. Wives, kids, all that. I wanted to do something they hadn't already done.'

The man raised an eyebrow at him. 'And you chose this?'

Aleks bit his lip somewhat defensively. 'Yeah, why not? Learn new skills, serve my king and country, be part of something bigger and all that,' he reasoned, his tone a little dry as he practically quoted the recruitment casts. Truly, he was excited for the travelling aspect of serving, but that was a long way off yet.

The blond man gave him an almost pitying look, shaking his head. 'Where you from?'

'Out West, tiny little village called Baysar,' Aleks replied, and his companion snorted.

'Explains everything, then,' he muttered. Aleks wondered if he'd already been insulted by the first – and only – person in the

15

barracks willing to talk to him. 'Just . . . almost everyone here, we're here 'cause we've got nowhere else to go. Orphanages, prisons, the streets, death, they're the alternatives. And, well, it might be bad around here, but it's better than nothing. You're naive – it's refreshing.'

'Is no one here just because they want to be?' Aleks asked, aghast. This man was making the army sound like another sort of prison. All the soldiers he'd seen before, the ones who had come through the village during tax season or when there was a criminal on the loose, they'd all seemed honoured to be part of the army, encouraging young boys to enlist when they grew old enough, to make their king proud. It seemed like all the men of a certain age had been in the army at some point in their lives, and they spoke about their time with a particular fondness that only they seemed to understand.

'Yeah, the lords' brats who come in here at Lieutenant rank and don't do any real work,' his companion told him. 'Only cadets who really want to be here are the psychos who like having a gun in their hands and permission to use it. We get wide-eyed brats like you every now and then, but they don't last all that long before ending up in medical, begging to leave. Ration chips have probably already changed hands as to how long you'll last. I might bet a week, myself. Maybe ten days if you get decent enrolment.' Aleks glanced over at the cadets playing cards in the corner that the blond man was gesturing to, and one of them saluted mockingly with a fistful of wooden chips as he caught Aleks's gaze.

'A week! Do I really look that pathetic?' he demanded indignantly.

'Well, you didn't turn up in handcuffs or rags, so as far as we see it you've got better places to be,' the older man replied evenly.

'Not that it matters much now. You've signed your four years, you're stuck here. You should've paid the fee.'

'What fee?'

'They didn't offer you the enlistment fee?' Aleks shook his head, frowning.

'Hang on – the man who walked you in here, Commander Antova, was he the one who took your forms?' Aleks nodded, perplexed by the abrupt turn in conversation. 'Sounds about right. Grumpy bastard never lets anyone off.'

'What are you talking about?' Aleks pressed, but the blond man shook his head.

'Doesn't matter now, your forms are in, it's too late. But gods, you've got rotten luck.' His words frustrated Aleks, who gave up, deciding he'd find out what the man was talking about soon enough.

'What's your name, anyway?' Aleks asked, realising he'd never been given it.

The man's lips twitched, his green eyes glinting in the low lamplight. 'Do you really need it? I doubt you'll be around long enough to use it much,' he replied, but Aleks held his gaze confidently. 'It's Jarek.'

'Pleasure to meet you, Jarek,' Aleks replied, though pleasure was definitely not what his tone suggested.

Jarek smirked, getting to his feet. 'Try not to get eaten too early, baby bird.'

Now: Rensav

A week seemed too long to even contemplate, Aleks thought as he dragged himself through the door of his barracks, shivering violently and soaking wet, every inch

17

of his body aching. He'd learned as soon as he got to the communal showers that he was the newest cadet on base, which earned him the honour of last shower. The water was like ice by the time he could take his turn.

The obstacle course was brutal, there was no other way to put it. The first time round was bad enough, but the lieutenant wasn't happy with Aleks's time and insisted he do it another three times over before he was satisfied. Directly after that he was taken to the firing range, where his firearms skills were put to the test despite his inability to raise his arms. He'd barely been able to hold the gun, and had no doubt appalled Shulga with his poor aim, but as far as Aleks was concerned he hadn't shot a fellow cadet and that was a perfectly successful endeavour.

Crawling on to his bed, he turned his face to the pillow, wondering if suffocating himself would get him out of evening drills. Probably not; Shulga didn't seem the type to take death as an excuse.

'You're still alive, then.' He glanced up at the voice, seeing Jarek sinking down on to the next bed.

'That's a matter of opinion,' he retorted, earning a snort. 'Storms, I don't think I'll ever feel warm again.'

'You won't,' the other man replied. 'I've been here a year, and I'm still half-frozen from my first shower. I think they pump the water directly from the River Dynn.' Aleks winced, tugging his blankets up over his sodden form. 'At least you survived induction. That's half the battle.'

'Is it?' Aleks asked hopefully.

Jarek laughed. 'Gods, no. It's barely the beginning. Like I said, I give you a week.' Aleks scowled at him, making the man grin, but they were interrupted by the same ear-splitting klaxon from the morning. 'Ooh, dinner call. About time too. Think you can stand?'

After some exceptionally pathetic flailing, and a hand from Jarek, Aleks managed to get to his feet. Changing his wet jacket and shirt for dry ones, he followed Jarek and the others from the barracks to the cafeteria. He was still chilled to the bone, but at least his torso was dry. He couldn't help but think wistfully of the job he'd had back home; he'd thought it exhausting at the time, but it was child's play in comparison to this. Still, he was confident he'd get used to military life, in time.

Before: The Tunnels

His shoulders ached and burned with every swing of the pickaxe. Wiping a gloved hand over his sweaty forehead, Aleks glanced around, frowning at his fellow workmen. He wasn't the only one to have stopped, and the grimy clock propped up against a rusting bucket showed they were right on target. 'Y'know, I think we might actually be done with this,' Nikolas said, letting his own axe fall to the ground with a clatter. Aleks's frown deepened, and he surveyed the dark stone walls carefully.

'I think you might be right,' he agreed tentatively, unsure whether or not he was happy at the news. On the one hand, it meant no more slaving away for hours in the humid tunnels. On the other, it meant the end of his job, and therefore the end of his income.

'I'll go and ask the boss,' Nikolas said, heading deeper into the dimly lit cavern.

Creating a four-way tunnel beneath the Kholar Mountains was no small task, and crews had been working on it for years. Aleks had only been in the job for four months, since he'd finished school, but every day had seemed as long as ten. It could've been worse, though; one of his classmates had ended up shovelling dung on a cattle farm.

Nikolas returned, a grin on his face that had Aleks slumping in relief. 'You're free to go, gentlemen. It's been a pleasure working with you,' he announced. 'Our job here is done. They'll be bringing the mechanics in soon to start laying tracks.'

'They'll start paving the walkways too, won't they?' Kai asked, gesturing to the raised platforms off to each side that were to become the walkways for those too poor to afford train tickets. Nikolas nodded, nudging them both towards the pinprick of light that was the outside world.

'Maybe I can apply for that, then. See if they'll hire me,' Aleks wondered, earning a bark of laughter from Kai.

'Good luck. You know how they feel about these tunnels. Have to look perfect, and they can't do that with your clumsy hands paving the floors,' the older man teased. Aleks glared, half-heartedly bumping Kai with his shoulder. A job in the tunnels was the closest he'd get to leaving his village, and he wanted to keep that dream alive as long as possible.

3

Now: Rensav

After a meagre dinner, having been pushed to the back of the queue by every cadet until all that remained was the cold dregs of stew, Aleks took the opportunity to try and find the stables and see Quicksilver; a day's separation from his horse was more frustrating than he was willing to admit. It would be a weight off his shoulders if he could just see that his gelding was safe and cared for.

Walking straight past the rows of identical barracks, Aleks tried not to appear suspicious as he eyed the buildings further up the road. A lot of them were clearly administration and medical buildings, but he let out a triumphant mutter when he saw a low, long building that seemed to span miles, and could hardly be anything but stables. The door was open, and he was accosted as soon as he entered. 'What do you want?' the man sneered, wearing the blue riding breeches and tall black boots of the mounted infantry.

'I arrived yesterday, and brought my horse with me. I want to see him,' Aleks said evenly.

'Dappled grey gelding, fifteen-two, one white sock?' the Private checked. Aleks nodded, trying not to let his relief show. At least Quicksilver had definitely reached the stables.

'That's the one. Quicksilver,' he confirmed, making the Private roll his eyes.

'I don't care about his name, brat. Follow me.' Aleks stayed close at the man's heel as he walked past rows of stables. The horses didn't look starved; Aleks supposed that while starving the cadets could be considered character-building, starving the horses was cruelty however you looked at it.

Turning down a row near the end of the building, Aleks's face lit up. Quicksilver's head was hanging over the door of his stable, his ears back and his eyes narrowed but otherwise OK, as far as he could tell. 'Don't stay too long,' the Private ordered. 'I need to get them all fed soon and I don't need you in the way.' Aleks nodded, already halfway inside the stable, and he chuckled as a pale pink nose shoved hard into his side.

'Hello, you,' he muttered, smiling properly for the first time since he'd arrived in the South. Stroking the gelding's neck, he pulled the stable door shut behind him and reached over to flip the latch into place. Ignoring the young horse's playful nudges, he set to work checking him over, running his hands carefully over every inch of hair and muscle. 'Looks like you're getting better treatment than I am, boy,' Aleks murmured, pressing his forehead to the horse's warm neck. 'Oh, I don't like this,' he confessed in the barest whisper. 'I don't like this at all.' He couldn't quit yet, though. Not after only one day. Everything new was uncomfortable until you got used to it.

When he couldn't find a reason to stay any longer, Aleks pressed a kiss to the horse's nose, tugging playfully on his forelock as he left the stable and hurrying from the building before another stablehand could reprimand him.

Ducking round a group of men gathered by the door of his barracks, he headed straight for his bed, kicking off his boots and pulling the blankets over his shoulders.

'Where've you been, then?' Jarek queried nonchalantly, writing in a notebook balanced on his knees.

'Stables,' Aleks replied. 'Checking on my horse.'

Jarek looked up from his writing. 'You brought a horse? Gods, you're thick, aren't you?' Aleks scowled at him, making the older man smirk. 'You'll see. Just don't expect to be riding your own horse when you start training. Should've pegged you for a mounter – too scrawny for anything else.' Aleks thought that was a bit rich coming from the long-limbed Easterner, but wisely kept his mouth shut.

'I'll see tomorrow, won't I?' he retorted. He had his schedule, and his first training slot of the day was with the mounted infantry. 'What are you writing?' He knew Jarek had no family, so it couldn't be a letter home. Maybe he had a sweetheart in the city.

'None of your business, is it?' the man snapped defensively, shifting to cover the notebook from Aleks's gaze.

Aleks thought of his own family. Did they even miss him? Probably not too much; even when it had just been him and his three brothers in the house, Aleks had always been overlooked. He doubted they'd even noticed he was gone. They had the new baby to keep them occupied, after all.

Before: The New Arrival

He didn't know how long he waited, but eventually Lara's screams quietened, and his chest swelled at the sound of new screaming; infant screaming. The baby had been born. Hurrying to the stairs, he met Torell and Grigori on the way, all three brothers with matching grins on their faces. As the two older brothers pushed ahead of their sibling in the narrow stairway, Torell's wife Nadeah followed at a more sedate pace, a hand on her rounded belly. Aleks wondered how she could sit and listen to Lara's pain, knowing it would be her own in a few short months.

Their parents were waiting outside the door to Maxim's room when they reached the landing, both with smiles on their faces and tears in their eyes. 'It's a boy,' their father declared proudly. 'I have a grandson.'

'Can we see him?' Aleks asked hopefully, making his mother laugh softly. She stepped aside.

'Go on, but be quiet. Lara's had quite a time of it, and I think they've just got the boy to settle.'

Lara was propped up in bed, a bundle of blankets cradled in her arms and a radiant smile on her face. She was flushed, and her golden hair stuck to her forehead with sweat, but she still looked as beautiful as ever. Maxim was perched on the edge of the bed beside her, blue eyes glued to the bundle, oblivious to Dr Barsukov packing up his equipment. He glanced up for a second when his brothers entered, beaming at them. 'Come closer, look!' he urged quietly, beckoning them forward. Torell

24

was first, of course, his arm around Nadeah as they both looked at the baby.

'Oh, he's beautiful!' Nadeah gasped, awed. 'Looks just like his father.' Max grinned proudly, a hint of disbelief still in his eyes, as if he couldn't quite believe he'd created something so small and perfect. Peering over Grigori's shoulder to get a look for himself, Aleks couldn't believe it either; his brother's sprog was adorable.

'Well done, big brother,' he said. 'And well done, Lara. That didn't sound easy.' She laughed, smoothing down the wisp of white-blond hair on her son's head.

'I can't say it was, but it was definitely worth it.'

'So what's he called, then?' Torell urged, rocking on his feet with childlike excitement. Max and Lara shared a look, then turned back to their son.

'Daniil,' Maxim announced after a long pause. 'Daniil Anton Vasin.'

'A fine name for a fine boy,' said their father approvingly, his arm around his wife's shoulders. 'Now, I think we should let Max and Lara rest. You can all hold the baby tomorrow.'

Max and Lara had been trying for a baby for years, and had almost given up. Daniil was their little miracle child. For Torell too; he and Nadeah had waited, not wanting to upset the older couple by having children first, especially after Lara's many miscarriages. Things were finally working out for everyone.

'It'll be your turn next, son,' his mother told Aleks with a smile, patting his arm. Aleks looked horrified and immediately opened his mouth to splutter a protest.

His father laughed. 'He'd have to leave his own thoughts for more than ten minutes and actually talk to a woman first!

Don't worry, Aliya, he'll find a girl yet. He'd better do, anyway – you're not exactly getting any younger,' he added to his son, who grimaced. Both Max and Torell had been engaged by the time they were Aleks's age; as far as the family were concerned, Aleks was falling behind. As per usual. That lucky idiot Grigori had taken the Faith and was spared these awkward questions.

'I'm not in any rush, Father,' Aleks insisted, earning a roll of his father's eyes.

'That's what they all say. Leave it any longer and all the good ones will be gone.'

Aleks sighed, shaking his head, too weary of the argument to even bother making his point. 'I'll need to start looking for work before I look for a bride, at any rate. We finished in the tunnels today,' he explained.

'Already? You boys work fast!' Nadeah exclaimed.

'You can go back to the shop job,' his father informed him, as if he was an idiot for considering anything else.

Aleks stifled a wince; he'd had a job logging inventory and doing odd jobs for his father in their shop since the age of twelve, and the family business was exactly what he'd hoped to escape by taking the job in the tunnels. He didn't want to be his father's errand boy for the rest of his life!

'Well, I, uh . . . I was hoping for more,' he explained hesitantly, noticing the dark look that crossed his father's face.

'More? What more is there, boy? A steady job, a roof over your head, food in your belly, and the chance to find a nice girl to take you off our hands!'

Aleks sighed, tugging at his messy black fringe. He was seriously due a haircut.

26

'Never mind, Father. Now if you'll excuse me, I'm going to bed.' His father had never had the wanderlust he seemed to have developed. He'd always been happy exactly where he was, doing the same job, keeping his quiet life in their minuscule village. He'd never wondered what the cliffs in the East looked like, or whether the palaces were really as breathtaking as they were in the newscasts, or how it would feel to fly through a storm. Not like Aleks had.

Now: Rensav

Pushing away wistful thoughts of the family he'd left behind, Aleks shuffled to the end of his bed to reach into his trunk, sifting through his saddlebag for his notebook and pen. He should probably write to his parents and let them know he was alive. Settling back with the notebook balanced on his knees, he bit his lip and began to write.

Dear Everyone,

I'm safe, don't worry. I made it South in good time and without any problems; the workmen in the tunnels were very welcoming, and let me stay overnight and share their meals.

I'm in Rensav, and you'll never believe this: I joined the army. Yes, Max, I'm completely serious. It turns out enlisting is really the only decent work in Rensav, and I thought it sounded like a good idea; I'll learn a few new skills, and hopefully even get to travel if I make a good rank. Quicksilver is still with me, as I joined the Mounted Infantry. My first day of full training is tomorrow.

I hope things are well back home. Little Daniil is probably keeping you all busy, if he's anything like his father. Please don't worry about me; everything is fine, and I'm doing what I want to be doing. I look forward to hearing from all of you, but I'll be busy for a while so there's no need to rush your reply. Give my regards to everyone at home, and I'll write again soon.

All my love,
Aleks

Signing off with a messy flourish, Aleks looked up. 'Is there a post office around here?' he asked Jarek, who gave him a sideways glance.

'Writing home, are we?' Aleks nodded. 'Post office is next to the enlistment building. Big sign on the front, you can't miss it.'

'Thanks.' Carefully ripping the page out of his notebook and tucking the letter into his coat pocket, he locked his notebook and pen back in his trunk. Glancing over at the clock on the wall, he saw it was still over an hour until lights out. Aleks curled up tight under his blanket, willing sleep to come and praying to all three gods that tomorrow would be better. He reminded himself he was doing the right thing, that he was helping his family by being here and finally fulfilling his dream of travelling.

Before: The Decision
Exchanging his slippers for mud-crusted boots at the front door, Aleks shrugged on his thick fur-lined coat and headed for the

28

stables. No doubt in all the chaos of the baby's birth, the horses had yet to be tended to. Tiny flakes of snow drifted lazily to the ground and Aleks ducked his head to keep the cold off his face. Rounding the corner to their small stable yard, he paused at the sound of voices.

'We can't keep on like this, love, and we both know it. We can't afford to.' It was his father, his voice quieter than it usually was, his tone softened in a way it only ever did when he spoke to his wife.

'I know, I know,' Aliya replied, sounding distressed. 'But it's not permanent. We can afford to feed them all a few months more, at least.'

'Can we?' Olik asked plainly. Aleks shuffled closer, wincing as his boots crunched in the snow on the pathway. 'The shop isn't doing as well as it used to, we both know that. We could manage before the girls were about, but having both of them around – as much as I love them dearly – has overstretched us. The price to pay for four sons, I suppose.' It was custom when a woman got pregnant for her to move in with her husband's family for the duration of the pregnancy. Only when the baby was born were the couple expected to live on their own.

'If we cut some corners, we can manage it. Though I'll admit, Aleks finishing in the tunnels could have been better timed. We needed his income more than I care to say.' Aleks's stomach lurched, though he knew it was hardly his fault.

'I'll take him back at the shop, of course I will, but there won't be much money in it for him.' The man sighed, and Aleks imagined him running a hand over his thick grey beard, as he often did when in thought. 'Boy needs a real job sooner or later. But we'll figure something out.' There was the rustling of fabric, *like the pair were embracing, and Olik's voice was so soft when he spoke next that Aleks almost missed it. 'None of them have noticed in all this chaos, and we must keep it that way. When the other sprog's born and they've all moved out, it'll just be us and Aleks. We'll manage fine, the three of us, eventually.'*

Aleks bit his lip, creeping back towards the house, the horses still untended. If he'd ever hoped for a sign from the gods that he should leave his tiny little village like he'd always wanted, he wouldn't get a much clearer one than that.

Now: Rensav

Despite his prayers, Aleks's first official day of training was ten times worse than induction. For breakfast, he was given the tiniest, coldest bowl of porridge after spending almost an hour in the queue. With barely five minutes to eat, he was already lagging behind by the time he made it to his first mounted combat training session. His instructor was a tall, wiry man who looked very similar to the horse he rode. Jarek was right; Aleks wasn't allowed to ride Quicksilver, but was instead given an old nag he was quite sure was half lame already. He'd spent more of the session worrying about whether his steed would collapse underneath him than he did about listening to instructions. That had only resulted in him being told to get off his horse and run the drills on his own two feet for the remainder of the session.

Reluctantly emerging from the stables for his second training session of the day, Aleks found himself in a group of cadets who were all twice his size and at least five years older than him. They were clearly more interested in attempting to shoot each other than aiming for the targets, and one had even decided to prove he could swallow an entire clip of bullets in one go. He was sent straight to the medical centre, a smug look on his face as he crowed about having dodged another two weeks' training.

The obstacle course was just as brutal as before, if not more so because this time he had the added competition of several other cadets, and the last one to finish had to run the whole thing again. He was knocked over several times by cadets far bigger than he was, and one man had seemingly tried to drown him in the mud pool they had to wade through. It was only through luck that Aleks was able to reach out and grasp the man firmly around the ankle, tugging hard and sending him flying. He kept an eye on the cadet for the rest of the course, but thankfully lost him somewhere on his second lap. Either way, he was the last one to finish, and while everyone else went to shower and head to dinner, Aleks was covered in mud and restarting the course for the third time.

Shivering, chalk-white and covered in bruises, he lined up for his dinner, amazed when he finally got there to see a decent-sized portion still left. The gods were obviously taking pity on him. He sat in what he was beginning to see as 'his' corner, wolfing down the food as fast as he dared and then heading straight for the barracks after a quick detour to drop his letter off at the post office.

Ignoring Jarek's attempts to talk to him, Aleks tried to get an early night, praying for warmth and wondering how much longer he could cope before something in him crumbled.

4

Four days. Four days was how long Aleks managed to tough it out, each day progressively worse than the previous one. As much as he hated proving everyone in his barracks right, he was sure of one thing and one thing only: the decision to join the military was, hands down, the worst decision he had ever made in his life. But he'd made his choice now and he was determined to stick with it. The hazing would have to end eventually, surely?

A groan escaped his lips as he collapsed on to his bed. Jarek let out a low whistle. 'Gods. First hand-to-hand combat session?' Aleks let out another groan in confirmation. Everyone in his group was twice his size; he'd barely lasted a minute with each of them, and all the instructor did was laugh. 'The bruises will fade in time, don't worry. Just be glad you didn't lose any teeth.'

'I can't be certain of that, I haven't checked yet,' Aleks muttered, rolling gingerly on to his back.

'Who runs your session?'

'Lieutenant Dohma.'

Jarek winced, shaking his head. 'Storms, man. First Antova does your intake, Shulga's your CO, then you end up with Dohma – what did you do to get on the gods' bad side?'

Aleks huffed bitterly. He'd asked himself the same question a fair few times in the past four days. 'Don't think it would've mattered who did my intake,' he said instead. 'Still would've ended up here.'

'Anyone but Antova would've offered you the fee,' Jarek replied, shaking his head once more.

Aleks's brow furrowed. 'Could you *please* explain what you mean by that?'

'All right, but you won't be happy about it.' He sighed, shifting a little to face Aleks. 'Whenever a new cadet signs up of their own free will, the commander doing their intake is supposed to offer them the chance to pay the enlistment fee. Those who can pay end up in Pervaya, over in the Southeast. That's where the proper army types go, the ones who actually want a career in the military. The respectable ones. Anyone who doesn't have the money to pay ends up here. I think you can agree we'd all jump at the chance to pay the fee, if we had the money. The Pervaya base is the one you see in all the newscasts, the one that's supposed to teach you new skills and give you a better standard of living. Most folks don't even know there are two bases. All they do here is wait for us to kill each other or drop dead of exhaustion.'

Aleks felt sick to his stomach; he could have avoided all this? 'How – how much is the fee?' he asked.

'When I came in it was five golds. Can't see it having changed much.'

The news was a slap in the face. Aleks had had that money in his saddlebag when he'd arrived. He didn't any more, but at the time of enlisting he could have paid the fee. Storms, they had taken the money from him, anyway. Why hadn't they seen he could afford it and let him go to Pervaya?

'I'm guessing by the look on your face that five golds wasn't a problem for you,' Jarek said, sounding envious.

'How can they get away with this, right under the king's nose?' Aleks asked angrily, sitting up despite the protest from his muscles. 'How many others have ended up here when they could have paid?'

'A fair few – usually idiot country boys like you who don't know any better.' That was a bit rich, coming from an Eastern country boy. 'No one cares. Few people outside Rensav know that the two military bases are any different in their methods. Depending on who you ask, even the king doesn't know the difference.'

Rage swelled in Aleks's chest, and before he could stop himself he was shoving his feet into his boots.

'Where are you going?'

'To talk to Commander Antova.'

Jarek's eyes widened. 'Are you mad? You can't just march into the commander's office! You'll be on midnight drills for weeks!'

Aleks ignored him, shrugging his coat on and storming from the barracks, unable to think rationally due to the red-hot anger pounding through his veins. How dare Antova trick unsuspecting young men into signing their lives away and then steal their money for no good reason!

He didn't knock at the enlistment building. Shoving the guard aside and slamming the door open, he strode straight across to Commander Antova's office. The door was shut, but that didn't slow him; he wrenched it open, drawing the attention of several other men in the building. Antova was sitting behind a large mahogany desk, and he looked up with a dark gaze at the intrusion. 'What in the name of the gods do you think you're doing, boy?' he spat. 'I am your superior officer! How dare you walk in uninvited and unannounced.'

'How dare *you*!' Aleks retorted. 'How dare you not tell me about the enlistment fee! I could have paid it! I had the money, as you well knew when you had your men steal from my bag on my arrival. What gives you the right to consign me to this life when I could have afforded better?'

Antova seemed unimpressed by his rant, leaning back in his chair and folding his arms over his chest. 'You think I care, boy? Here or Pervaya, it makes no difference to me where you are. If anything, it's for your own good – those sissies up in Pervaya would only coddle you, make you soft. No one wants a soft soldier!'

'No one wants a dead soldier either, but that's all that'll happen to half the men in this bloody place!' Aleks snapped. 'And who gave you the right to make that decision for me, for anyone?'

Antova stood, pointing at the stripes on his shoulder. 'The king did, brat. You want to take it up with him?'

'I want to be transferred to Pervaya,' Aleks said sharply. 'You already took more than the fee from me when I arrived.'

'You can *want* all you like, boy, it's not going to happen. You're stuck here and the sooner you accept that the better. Shulga has your enlistment forms, so as far as the law's concerned you're our property.'

'I could go to the authorities,' Aleks threatened. 'The rest of the world doesn't know how it is down here, but I could tell them. Put you on the newscast as the man who treats even the legitimate recruits as criminals.'

Antova laughed, his moustache twitching. 'You daft, boy? I *am* the authorities! And you can bet your right arse cheek you won't find a newscast screen around here. Storms, those Anglyans have got a lot to answer for; that brat of a queen and her ilk have given everyone and their bloody mother ideas of rebellion.' He shook his head, giving Aleks a stony glare. 'You're not going anywhere, boy, and you're certainly not going to tell anyone how it is here. Accept your lot or do us a favour and go and throw yourself off a cliff somewhere.'

Aleks made to take a step towards the man, but before he could move he was grabbed tightly by the shoulder.

'Shulga,' Antova said with a nod, addressing the man holding Aleks. 'Take this cadet to the time-out room and remind him of his place.'

'Yes, sir,' Shulga replied promptly, dragging Aleks from the room. As the door shut behind them, Aleks glimpsed Antova's self-satisfied face, and his stomach churned. What was the time-out room?

Shulga marched him around the corner to a small, square concrete building, just before the rows of barracks. Aleks had never seen anyone come or go from this place;

it looked like he was about to find out why. Shulga took a key from his pocket, unlocked the door, then shoved Aleks inside. There was a single lamp hanging from the centre of the otherwise empty room, and the smell of soured blood made him gag.

'Maybe this will teach you to have a little respect for your betters, boy,' Shulga sneered, kicking Aleks firmly in the back with a steel-toed foot, sending him sprawling to the concrete floor. Aleks's eyes widened, pulse racing as he realised what was about to happen. Then all he could feel was pain.

Before: The Family

'Shouldn't you be out working?' Maxim asked, eyes flicking to Aleks. Three of the four Vasin brothers were in the kitchen, enjoying a rare moment of peace while Daniil slept; Grigori was busy praying. Their mother was cooking breakfast, humming quietly to herself, lost in her own thoughts.

'No, we're finished in the tunnels. I'm unemployed for now,' Aleks explained, sipping his tea.

Maxim frowned, scratching at his stubbled cheek. 'You'd better get about fixing that, then, before Father drafts you again.'

'Don't I know it,' Aleks agreed ruefully. 'Where do I start, though? There's hardly anywhere around here that's got a position open, especially for me.' As he spoke, Olik wandered into the kitchen, dressed and ready for a day of work. He passed by his wife, stealing a still-warm pastry as he kissed her on the cheek. 'I . . . I think I'm going to look a little further afield, now the tunnels are dug.'

'Why don't you try your luck down South?' Maxim suggested. 'They say that's where every man goes to make his fortune.'

'Don't go putting foolish ideas in his head, Max,' their mother scolded, smacking him on the shoulder. 'He's just a boy!'

Aleks wondered how his mother could consider him a boy and yet push him to marry and have children at every given opportunity.

'How would a brat like him survive in the South?' their father asked, laughing. 'He'd need money for food and board, and there's no telling how long it'll take to get a job!' Aleks felt himself flush in indignation.

'I could do it,' he insisted. 'I'd do brilliantly in the South. They'd call me the King of Rensav.' His father laughed even harder, giving him a look.

'There's already a king in Rensav, lad, and he's a darn sight more worldly-wise than you are. What do you know about cities? You've barely even seen one!'

That was true, but Aleks wasn't going to agree with him. He'd only ever been to Osir twice, and the city in the West was barely half the size of the Southern city of Rensav.

'I can learn,' he protested defiantly. 'Thank you, Maxim, that's exactly what I'll do. It's about time I made my way in the world.' Even just thinking about it, his blood rushed with excitement at the prospect of travelling, of seeing parts of Siberene he'd never seen before. And not having him around would solve some of his parents' financial troubles. 'I've got the money I saved up from working in the tunnels – that should last me until I get a new job, if I'm careful with it.'

'Storms, boy, you're actually serious about this, aren't you?' Torell asked quietly, stunned. Aleks nodded, jaw squared in determination. There was even a small skyship port in Rensav; maybe there he could finally fulfil his dream of flying.

'Might finally stop you yammering on about wanting to see the world,' Maxim said, shrugging. 'Good luck to you.' His tone was sceptical but Aleks ignored it, along with the looks on his parents' faces. One day his family would stop underestimating him.

5

Now: Rensav

Aleks didn't know how long he'd spent in the time-out room, but when Shulga let him go he could barely crawl through the door. Every inch of his body throbbed with pain, and he felt sticky with blood in places he didn't like to think about. Shulga had been careful to avoid the soft areas – his death from internal bleeding in the lieutenant's care would be hard to explain away – but that had left him with plenty of other options.

Drawing in a long, laboured breath, Aleks ran a hand through his blood-matted hair, clenching his jaw. Enough was enough; if he stayed at the army base any longer he'd be dead before the week was up. He had to do something, and he had to do it fast. And as much as Commander Antova would have liked it, throwing himself off the cliffs wasn't the answer.

When he dragged himself back to barracks it was to find everyone already at dinner. Sinking on to his bed, he resisted the urge to relax into the mattress and sleep. Forcing himself to his feet, Aleks opened the trunk at the end of his bed, pulling on as many layers of clothing as he could. It was going to be cold out overnight.

Slinging his light saddlebag over his shoulders and swallowing his cry of pain at the movement, he pulled his hat low over his forehead and made for the door. He needed his enlistment forms from Shulga's office; if he could find and destroy them, the army would have no record of him enlisting. Even if he did get caught after escaping – provided he escaped in the first place – there would be no proof that he was a cadet. Then all he had to do was reach the stables and get Quicksilver before anyone on the dinner shift noticed what he was doing. After that . . . he would find a way out. There had to be one somewhere.

Feeling a strange sort of strength build in him as the plan formed in his mind, he turned towards the enlistment building. He had no idea where Shulga's office was, but presumably it was somewhere near Antova's.

There were no guards at the door; the barracks was down to a skeleton guard for the dinner shift. Aleks silently retraced his steps from earlier in the day, making his way towards Antova's office. His eyes raced over every door's nameplate, frowning when none of them was the office he was looking for. He was incredibly short on time; he had to be on Quicksilver and heading for freedom before dinner ended.

Finally, he saw it. *Lt Shulga* was embossed on a name-plate three doors down from Antova's. Luckily, the door was unlocked and the room empty; Shulga had obviously gone straight from the time-out room to dinner. The office was decorated in the same way as Antova's, in blue and dark brown, with a large map of Tellus on the wall instead

41

of the royal crest the commander displayed. Darting across to a metal filing cabinet that took up most of one wall, Aleks wrenched open a drawer at random, ignoring the searing ache in his arms. Again, unlocked. Clearly Shulga was too cocky to think anyone would dare snoop around his office.

The drawer was full of neatly filed enlistment forms in alphabetical order; F–J. Aleks's form would come under V. Shutting the drawer, he reached for the next one, perplexed to find it containing M–P. The drawer after that didn't contain enlistment forms at all, but instead held a large stack of account books. Shulga didn't seem to have any sort of system whatsoever; how did he ever find anything he needed?

Growling in frustration, Aleks began to open multiple drawers at a time, rifling through stacks of papers and leather-bound books, his desperation growing with every unsuccessful attempt. Digging through a drawer of miscellaneous files and books closest to the desk, his fingers scrabbled at the bottom of the drawer and it tilted a fraction, sending three stacked files slumping against a small metal box. 'What the . . .' He trailed off, pressing harder on the base of the drawer, watching it dip under his fingers. The drawer had a false bottom!

Aleks glanced at the clock; he knew he shouldn't, but he'd always been the curious type. Emptying the drawer, he dug his nails under one side of the fake bottom, prising it up. The secret compartment was fairly narrow, containing only a thin file of papers and a battered leather journal. It was the journal that caught Aleks's eye, for it had the

Anglyan crest embossed in one corner of the cover. What on Tellus was Shulga doing with an Anglyan journal?

Aleks lifted the journal from the drawer, flicking it open to the front page. Immediately, his jaw dropped. *Property of Lord N Hunter* was scrawled across the header, and beneath it was a stamp in bright blue ink that read *EVIDENCE – CASE 13734* and a smaller stamp, this time in red, stating *CASE CLOSED – DO NOT REMOVE FROM MERICAN CUSTODY* and displaying a small Merican crest. Aleks's blue eyes were as round as dinner plates – Nathaniel Hunter was Queen Catherine of Anglya's father, the man who had tried to destroy the entire world with his horrific mecha-child creations. There had been rumours of private journals, blackmail logs and personal diaries, but nothing was ever confirmed to the public. Everyone had assumed Queen Catherine had kept them, along with the rest of her father's possessions.

Skimming a few pages, Aleks was stunned to see the journal was a personal diary, documenting Hunter's early ventures into mecha-human experimentation: lab reports written in his own hand, angry rants on the slowness of the process, theories on how to improve it; it was all there. Aleks had no idea how it had ended up in the enlistment building of the Rensav army base, but he could guess from the hiding place that Shulga definitely wasn't supposed to have it.

A door slamming somewhere in the building startled him out of his horrified trance, and a quick look at the clock nearly gave Aleks a heart attack. He barely had ten minutes until the end of dinner!

Stuffing the journal in an inner pocket of his coat, he hastily replaced the drawer's false bottom and contents, shutting it as quietly as he could. Tugging on the two drawers he had yet to check, he swore under his breath. Neither of them contained a V section, and Aleks felt dread creep over him at the realisation that his file was likely elsewhere. He didn't have the time to search any other rooms. Out of options, he straightened up, shoving all the cabinet drawers shut and sprinting for the door.

A quick glance through the glass panel showed the corridor to be empty, so Aleks slipped from the room.

Bursting through the door of the building, he turned for the stables, slowing his pace once he hit the cobblestone path, just in case anyone happened to look his way. There was nothing more suspicious than a lone cadet running.

While there was supposed to be at least one stablehand in the building at all times, Aleks couldn't see a single soul in the stables. Perfect. Hurrying to the tack room, he easily found Quicksilver's saddle and bridle, though carrying the heavy items in his current state nearly sent him crumpling to the floor. Still, he forced himself to ignore the pain, hefting the tack across the room towards Quicksilver's stall.

The horse whinnied when he saw the tack, knowing what it meant. Aleks shushed him, slinging the saddle on the door and slipping inside, easing the bridle on to the horse's head. Tossing the saddle on Quicksilver's back, he fastened it tightly and slung the saddlebag over the horse's rear, buckling it swiftly. He grabbed the reins, turning to press Quicksilver's nose to his chest for a brief moment. 'We need to be quiet, boy. No getting excited.'

Leading the horse from the stable and cringing at the noise of hooves on the concrete floor, he headed towards the back door. Night-time drills didn't run during dinner, so he was surely safe from being seen as he sneaked with Quicksilver out through the back of the stable building, letting the door shut gently behind them. Quicksilver's ears were pricked, his eyes bright and alert.

When he was clear of the stables, Aleks checked the girth strap once more, not sure he had the strength in his arms to pull it any tighter. It would have to do. Hissing in pain as he lifted his foot into the stirrup, the noise quickly became a barely stifled yelp as he swung up into the saddle, the leather pressing into bruises he hadn't even known he had. Gods, he hoped he wouldn't have to ride for too long.

His gaze was fixed on the treeline of the forest they used for training drills; if there was going to be any sort of escape route it would be there. Everything else was too exposed.

Aleks kicked the gelding into an easy canter around the back of the barracks. He couldn't help but grin as he heard shouts of alarm, urging Quicksilver on faster. The horse seemed eager to run, making Aleks wonder how much exercise he'd had since arriving in Rensav. Probably very little.

The loud klaxon started up before he could even reach the trees; a different sound to the usual wake-up and dinner klaxon. This one was continuous and obnoxious, spurring every lieutenant and commander into action. Aleks didn't care. His horse was fast, and he had a head start on anyone who wanted to follow him. He could make it.

It was through luck that Aleks stumbled on his ticket to freedom. He almost rode past it, then brought Quicksilver to a sliding stop as he spotted the gateway; a short, rusted section of fence between two rocky outcrops, too jagged for anyone to even think of climbing. But the fence itself looked like one good tug would bring it down, and the gap between the rocks was just about wide enough for, say, a horse and rider to go through. Jumping down and dropping the reins − he trusted Quicksilver not to run off without him − Aleks reached for the mesh of the fencing and tugged with all his strength. It shrieked horribly, but there was definite movement. He tugged harder, and with a loud wrenching noise the fence pulled free from its anchor, swinging aside with a screeching that made Quicksilver rear up in alarm. Still, the horse stayed put, and Aleks grabbed his reins, leading him through the small gap he'd created. It was a tight fit, but they made it.

Before he remounted, he turned and pulled the fencing back in place; hopefully if he covered his tracks it would give him a little more time to get clear of Rensav.

Leaping back up into the saddle at the dim sound of thundering hooves, he spurred Quicksilver on, and the horse needed no further encouragement to lurch into a gallop, easily darting around trees and jumping fallen logs. As far as Aleks was aware, he was heading in the direction of the city outside the military base, well away from anyone who might possibly recognise him. He'd go as far as he could, ride through the night to get to one of the towns outlying the city.

Squinting to see in the darkness, Aleks looked for what he thought was the edge of the woods, hoping he wasn't riding deeper instead. Finally, they broke the treeline, ending up on a grassy verge next to a cobbled path. The moon lit the path ahead, and when he looked back he saw the city walls looming behind a row of shrubs. Adrenalin coursed through his veins. He could hardly believe what he'd done. He was officially a military deserter. But it would all be for nought if he didn't move quickly; no doubt by morning they would have guards crawling all over the place in search of him, and he needed to be long gone before then. Once Shulga discovered what Aleks had taken from him, the lieutenant would be out for blood.

It wasn't long before he came to a small town, and exhaustion began to take its toll on Aleks's body. Everything ached, and after the third time he nearly slipped from the saddle he decided to walk. Quicksilver's reins in hand, he trod quietly through the rows of low stone houses, searching for somewhere that was concealed. He didn't want to leave Quicksilver out in the open.

'What in the Goddess's name do you think you're doing wandering about at this hour?'

He jumped at the voice, spinning round to see an elderly man standing in the doorway of what looked like an old farmhouse, a lamp in his hand and a coat over his sleepwear. The man stepped out from the doorway, lifting the lamp to get a better look at Aleks, and let out a soft curse at the sight of his bloodied face. 'Gods, boy, what happened to you?' He eyed him closer, his gaze landing on the dark blue trousers embroidered with the Rudavin crest. 'A cadet.'

'Please, sir,' Aleks stuttered hastily. 'Don't turn me in. I won't cause any trouble. I'll just find somewhere to sleep for the night and then I'll be on my way. Just don't call the guards on me, please. They'll kill me if I go back there.' The man frowned, bushy white brows furrowing.

'Looks like you're already halfway to it, with that face of yours. Come on, get your horse round the back, quickly now.' Aleks blinked, perplexed.

'Sir?'

'Come, boy, before someone else sees you!' The man beckoned him closer and Aleks did as he was told, following him to the back of the house towards three sturdy-looking stables.

'Why?' Aleks asked in a slight daze, allowing the stranger to take Quicksilver's reins from him and lead the gelding into the nearest stable. He could do nothing but stand and watch the man untack his horse, taking his saddlebag when it was thrust towards him.

'You don't look like a criminal – you barely look old enough to shave – so as far as I'm concerned you don't deserve whatever they've done to you in that accursed place. You escaped this far, least I can do is help you make it a little further. In you come, lad; I've got a cot bed down in the furnace room that'll do you fine.'

'I – I hardly have any money,' Aleks stuttered, making the man laugh as he led him back to the front of the house.

'I don't want your money, lad. Get in, quickly.' Ushering him into the house, the man shut the door behind them and locked it, turning to get a good look at the boy. He let out a low whistle, scratching at his salt-and-pepper beard. 'They really did a number on you. Storms.' He moved past Aleks, reaching for a door below the stairs. 'Furnace room is this way, come on.'

Aleks followed, a sigh escaping his lips at the warmth of the furnace room. He'd not felt this warm in days. The room contained a small cot bed pressed up against the wall opposite the furnace, and very little else.

'We can talk more in the morning. I'll wake you early so you can get off before the guards come calling. Yell if you start bleeding an unusual amount.' Aleks snorted, unable to help himself.

'Sir, I can't – I can't thank you enough for this.' He hadn't expected to be able to sleep indoors, let alone on a real bed.

'We'll talk more in the morning,' the man repeated.

Aleks let his saddlebag fall to the floor, sitting on the cot to unlace his boots. 'Well, goodnight, then.'

'Sleep well, lad. You look like you need it.' With that, the man turned out the lights and shut the door, leaving Aleks alone in the darkened room.

The blankets smelled a little musty, but they were clean and dry, and the furnace sent a delicious warmth deep into Aleks's bones, banishing the lingering cold from the army base. He couldn't imagine ever feeling that cold again; he'd begun to think his soul had frozen. Warm, safe and coming down from his excited high, Aleks fell asleep easily for the first time in a week.

6

He was dazed when he woke up, wondering why there was no klaxon, no Jarek mocking him from the next bed, no overwhelming cold. It was then he remembered where he was, and what had happened the day before. No wonder he ached so much. As his sleepy gaze focused, he realised there was someone standing over him, gently shaking his shoulder; the man from last night. His saviour.

'I left you as long as I could, but any longer and the guards will be about. They've already had a patrol through,' the man said gruffly.

In better light, Aleks could see that he was white-haired and about sixty. He was stocky, with a farmer's build despite his age, his skin wrinkled and weathered and his beard cropped short.

'What time is it?' Aleks asked blearily, sitting up with a wince as his many injuries made themselves known.

'Almost six,' the man replied, tossing several items on to the bed beside Aleks. 'Some bandages and disinfectant, as well as arnica cream. Thought you might need it. Stand up and take your shirt off, let me check your back.' Aleks didn't have the strength to argue, and let the man examine his back. 'You got lucky, lad. Whoever was punishing you knew where to hit. You'll be black and blue for a couple of weeks, but doesn't look like you've got any serious injuries.' He let Aleks put his shirt on, then stepped back. 'Washroom is the door opposite this one. Get dressed, tend to your wounds, make yourself presentable, and I'll have breakfast in the kitchen. It's at the back of the house. Quick as you can, lad, you're wasting daylight.' With that he left, and Aleks reached for his saddlebag. He was still in a state of shock; had he fallen from his horse and hit his head somewhere, and this was all a dream?

As promised, there was breakfast waiting for him when he walked into the kitchen. Toast, bacon and an enormous helping of eggs; more food than his entire week of breakfasts at the military base combined. He didn't know if his stomach could even hold that much food any more. Still, he dug in ravenously, making the white-haired man laugh quietly. 'Don't choke yourself, lad. What's your name, anyway?'

'Aleks, sir,' he responded after swallowing, taking a long drink of water. 'Like I said before, I can't thank you enough. The military base, they're horrible, the –'

'I know what they do, lad. We all do.' The man gave a wry smile. 'The South's best kept secret, that. Gods know what the rest of the country would do if they found out, but no one ever will. They don't want to know, anyway. Not as long as it keeps criminals and beggars off their streets and off their minds.'

'They stole my money and then wouldn't let me pay the fee,' Aleks told him. 'I didn't even know there *was* a fee until

51

yesterday. I asked my commander to let me pay it and he refused, so I decided enough was enough.'

'I'm sure you were very polite in your asking,' the man said drily. 'That's the problem with outsiders – no idea that they need to go through proper channels if they really want to serve. People slip through the cracks all the time. But the official word is that everyone in Rensav is a criminal or homeless, so they've no right to protest about their treatment.' He leaned against the kitchen counter, frowning. 'Your best bet is to get as far away as possible and lie low for as long as you can.'

'But surely someone should be told! They can't get away with treating people like that!' Aleks protested.

'They can as long as we're in peacetime, lad. No one cares about the military when there's not a war going on. Besides, the army will have to start cleaning up their act soon, anyway. When those mountain tunnels open properly, we'll get all sorts of visitors down this way wanting to see the palace. It'll be hard for them to keep going the way they are in that base with so many eyes around. Looks like they've managed to keep it from the king so far, but he's so busy now we're an independent country, gods bless him, you can't blame him for not knowing. Tourists, however, are a whole different matter.' That wasn't exactly a comfort. Visitors wouldn't be allowed within the gates – so long as everything on the outside looked legitimate, things could carry on as normal on the inside.

'They should be exposed,' Aleks insisted. 'The country needs to know, before more people make the same mistake I did.'

'Don't be foolish, lad,' the man returned. 'That base has worked like that since the Independence War; you're not the first, and you won't be the last. They have their ways of keeping people quiet. The smart thing would be to take the luck the gods have given you and get as far from here as you can.' Aleks bit his lip. The man was right.

'I'd better get going, then,' he murmured, pushing aside his empty plate.

'Smart lad,' the man said, nodding. 'I saw to your horse before I woke you. He's ready whenever you are.'

'Thank you, sir. I don't even know your name,' Aleks realised belatedly, making the older man snort.

'Bit late for that, isn't it?' he said. 'It's Vadik.'

'Thank you, Vadik.' Aleks got to his feet, offering the tub of arnica cream to Vadik, who waved him off.

'Keep it. You need it more than I do.'

'I wish I had some money to offer you for your hospitality. You no doubt saved my life,' Aleks said, buttoning his coat. He only had the money he'd kept in his trouser pocket while travelling, and as grateful as he was there wasn't enough for him to spend it so early in his journey.

Vadik gave him a lopsided grin. 'You can thank me by getting out of here and not looking back. Don't do anything foolish.'

Shouldering his saddlebag, Aleks offered a short bow to the man. 'I won't forget your kindness, and may the gods repay you for it.' Vadik inclined his head in response, clapping Aleks gently on the shoulder.

'Ride fast, and stay safe. If the guards ask, you were never here.'

Before long, Aleks was back out on the road with Quicksilver. If he hurried, he thought he could make it to the outside of the tunnels long before nightfall and stay in a village there. Every moment he spent in the saddle was painful, but he pushed through it, knowing that walking would be worse. His gelding didn't seem to have any objections to a hard day's ride.

Aleks made a point of stopping at a different village to the one he'd stayed in on his way in, renting a room at a small inn for the night with what little money he still had. He spent most of his evening close to the fire with his head down, a cup of hot cider in his hands, surreptitiously listening as an older man told fairy stories to an awed group of children. Aleks always liked staying in family inns; children underfoot were far more welcoming than the possibility of a drunken bar brawl.

He thought fondly of his first journey through the tunnels, before everything had gone to the storms. How different things could've been if he'd just listened then.

Before: The Beginning

It felt odd to him, riding the path he'd walked every day for four months, and he was surprised at how quickly he reached the mouth of the tunnels. Quicksilver shied away from the darkened cavern, ears pinned back in discomfort, but Aleks held his seat easily, leaning forward to scratch the horse's mane. 'Easy, boy. A little darkness never hurt you,' he murmured, nudging gently with his heels until the pale gelding took a tentative step into the tunnel. It was enormous, and Aleks could easily imagine it bustling with people and trains. There were wide concrete walkways on either side, and the plan was to have two sets of tracks in each tunnel, allowing trains to travel between all four of the main cities. All of Siberene was eagerly awaiting the day they would open, awed by the opportunity to finally explore other parts of the country, gushing with pride over their king's decision to create the tunnels. Aleks wondered if he'd bump into any other travellers on his way.

Uncomfortable in the silence, he hummed to himself, the sound echoing alongside Quicksilver's footsteps. He only noticed he was growing close to the central station when the number of workers began to increase and he could hear shouting and laughter echoing down the tunnel. He grinned to himself, yearning for the respite; it had been a long time since he'd spent a whole day in the saddle. Even Quicksilver's pace picked up at the sound of other people.

A gasp tore from his throat as he reached the opening to the central station; it was monumental. He wondered how the mountains could still be standing with a great cavern like this inside them, but the huge copper and steel support bars criss-crossing the high vaulted ceilings were clearly doing their job. The grey-tiled platforms were pristine and gleaming, and there were alcoves set up for merchants to sell food and other necessities to travellers. While the tracks had yet to be laid, there was a vast turnstile platform in the very centre of the terminal where the tracks would be able to rotate and direct each train to its desired tunnel. Bridges made of stone and twists of metal linked the platforms together, and Aleks could vaguely make out grates covered in metal mesh that led up through the ceiling, allowing air to circulate. It was all far grander than anything he'd seen before, even unfinished, and he wondered if it was the standard people in the cities were used to.

'Could anyone point me towards someone in charge?' he asked a group of workmen. His voice seemed louder in the open space and he almost jumped in surprise at the volume.

'There are dormitories through that archway on the other side of the North platform. If the bosses are around they'll be in there. You can hitch your horse over there too, if you like. Someone'll keep an eye on him for you,' an older gentleman with greying hair told him, his voice the gritty rasp of a chronic smoker. Muttering his thanks, Aleks dug his heels in and urged Quicksilver forward to the tunnel marked North, edging around the turnstile to cross over to the other tunnel.

He looped his reins around a horizontal bar in one of the bridge structures, patting the horse's sweat-damp neck. Tentatively hopping up on to the platform, he walked through the archway and into a narrow corridor with more rooms leading off it. 'Hello?' he called. 'Is anyone around? I'm travelling through and in need of a bed for the night. I can pay,' he added, peering into empty room after empty room.

'Not a problem, lad! You're a bit young to be travelling alone, aren't you?'

Aleks jumped at the voice, spinning on his heel. The man leaning in the doorway was taller than him and broad-shouldered, probably in his mid-twenties, with a scruff of dark stubble and equally dark hair cut close to his head. The sleeves of his grey shirt were rolled to his elbows and there were dirt smudges all over him, but he didn't seem to care.

'I'm seventeen!' Aleks replied defensively, making the man chuckle. 'I came from the West, and some of the men in the tunnel said you wouldn't mind putting me and my horse up for the night. Like I said, I can pay if need be.'

'We don't need your money, boy,' the man insisted, waving him off. 'You're welcome to join us; my ma always taught me not to accept coin from a traveller, as the gods'll pay you back in kindness. What brings you this way so soon, anyway? Weren't expecting many before the walkways are paved.' He offered a hand to Aleks. 'I'm Zhora, by the way. Come on, lad – your poor horse must be gasping and sore besides. Let's get you to the stables.' Aleks smiled gratefully, shaking Zhora's hand.

'Aleks,' he offered in return, following the older man back out to where Quicksilver was tied.

Zhora let out a quiet sound of approval, running a hand down the gelding's flank. 'He's a right pretty one, isn't he?' he murmured. 'And obviously a strong one if he got you here in a day.'

Untying the reins, Aleks followed Zhora through a smooth stone archway to a short corridor, finding a long stretch of concrete with stables lining both sides, most of which were empty. 'They're not meant for long term, but they do all right for a day or two,' Zhora remarked, nudging a door open. The horse went straight for the water trough, slurping noisily, and Aleks grinned.

'So you never said – what brings you here so quickly? Something urgent, if you can't even wait three weeks for the walkways to be finished,' Zhora asked, watching him tend to his horse. Aleks shrugged, rubbing Quicksilver's neck gently. He could groom him later, when he was dry and rested.

'Not urgent as such,' he replied. 'Just needed to get away before my family dragged me into a commitment that would prevent me from leaving.'

Zhora led him back towards the entrance, pausing to chalk a mark on a slate board with a series of numbers on it. It took Aleks a few moments to realise they were stable numbers and that the marked ones were occupied.

'They getting you hitched?' Zhora joked, making Aleks flush.

'No, no, nothing like that.' He shrugged. 'I just wanted to see the world, and I can't do that if I'm earning my keep in my da's shop and offering my services babysitting my big brother's new wee'un.' Zhora nodded knowingly.

'You've got the wind in your blood, hmm?' Aleks's nose wrinkled in puzzlement, and Zhora chuckled. 'That's what they call it where I come from. The kids who just can't sit still, need to ask questions and see things and travel. They leave to head wherever the wind blows them, so we say they've got the wind in their blood. Where's it taking you, then?'

'South, currently,' Aleks answered, absently looking around as Zhora took him through to a large cafeteria, practically empty at this time of night.

'I can tell you now, lad, you won't get much adventure in the South,' Zhora remarked. 'All that's Southwards is shop work. Unless you're planning on enlisting, I'd change your plans.'

'I could enlist,' Aleks retorted somewhat defensively. At least in the military he'd be taught enough skills to get a decent job once he left, and there were definitely travel opportunities.

Zhora gave him a sceptical look. 'You, an army brat? You don't seem the type.'

'What type is that, then?' Aleks asked.

Zhora's lips twitched. 'The stupid type. But if you want to try your hand at it, lad, be my guest. At least there's no better time to sign up. No chance of a war happening in your lifetime.'

Now

Being back in the tunnels the following morning was somewhat comforting in its familiar dimness. The workmen had been quick about paving the walkways, and there were already grooves cut in the ground for the tracks to be laid. He wondered if Zhora was still working around there somewhere; he hoped so. As much as it would sting having to admit the man had been right about how poor a decision it was to go South, he'd enjoyed his company.

The central station was now even more spectacular; the tracks were mostly laid, and a breathtakingly beautiful mechanical design was being painted across the domed ceiling. Wooden boards that would show arrivals and departures had been mounted on the walls of each platform, and there were newscast screens in the four corners of the station.

Heading towards the nearest workman, Aleks tapped him on the shoulder. 'Excuse me, sir, I was wondering if a man named Zhora was working in here, and if so, where I might find him?' he asked. The worker blinked at the sight of Aleks's bruised face.

'Oh, aye, Zhora's still about. You'll need to get over to the North platform; that's where we're all living, he'll probably be around there. Looks like I get to show you the horse crossing,' he said, sounding excited. Aleks watched the man practically bounce over to a lever in the floor. 'Watch this – genius bit of machinery, it is.' He pulled the lever and there was a whirring noise like rapidly spinning gears. Before Aleks's eyes, a slab of solid steel began emerging from the side of the platform, reaching across to the North side. It slowly stretched out across the train tracks, resting neatly on top of them, fixing into place when it reached the walkway on the other side.

'That's brilliant,' he murmured, and the workman's face lit up.

'Isn't it just! Go on, take your horse across, it's perfectly safe,' he instructed.

Aleks smiled at him, nodding. 'Thanks for your help.' His first step on to the platform was tentative, but once he was sure it was sturdy he crossed with Quicksilver easily.

Wandering through to the stables, he looked about for a stablehand but couldn't find one anywhere. Shrugging to himself, he picked a free stall and let Quicksilver inside, checking it for fresh hay and water, every movement still causing him pain. 'You need a hose down,' he muttered, eyeing the horse's mud-browned legs and belly.

With his horse happily resting, Aleks left the stables, heading through to the dormitory corridor. Surreptitiously peering through the open doorways as he passed them, a tired smile tugged at his lips when he spotted a familiar head of short dark hair.

'Zhora!' he called, watching the man turn, dark eyes widening when he spotted Aleks.

'Well, there's a sight for sore eyes!' he exclaimed, quickly crossing the room to bring Aleks into a half-hug. Aleks couldn't stifle his cry of pain, and Zhora stepped back, eyeing him closer. 'Storms, lad, what happened to you? You look like you've gone ten rounds with an angry bull.'

'Let's just say going South wasn't the best decision I ever made.'

Zhora's eyes widened. 'Come on, let's go somewhere a little more private, let you sit down before you fall down.

Your horse safe?' Aleks nodded, allowing the man to lead him through to one of the back dormitories.

It wasn't until he was sitting down on one of the spare beds that Aleks let himself relax, shoulders slumping in exhaustion. He pulled his hat off his head, and Zhora let out a quiet gasp.

'You enlisted.' Aleks nodded. If there was anyone he could trust around here, it was Zhora. He gave the man a quick summary of his time in Rensav, a lump growing in his throat as he spoke. He hadn't realised how much of a toll his journey had taken on his emotions. When he was finished, Zhora gave a long sigh.

'Well, you *have* been busy,' he muttered, and Aleks huffed out a laugh. That was an understatement.

'I don't know what to do, Zhora,' he admitted, hating how young and pathetic he sounded. Zhora's frown deepened. 'I can't go home. It'll be the first place the guards come looking – my address was on the forms – and I can't tell my family what happened. They'll never let me out of the house again.' They would be so disappointed it would kill him. And he couldn't put them in danger by bringing guards about.

'The bloke you stayed with was right – you need to get as far away from there as possible. Go North, lie low, find a job and a place to kip, keep your head down. If guards come up this way looking for you, I'll tell them you went East. Keep them away from your family.' Aleks looked up at the man's words, surprised.

'You'd do that for me? Why? You hardly know me.' Zhora gave him a smile.

61

'Truth be told, you remind me of my little brother. Heart of gold, head of stone, and a brain of little more than air,' he added teasingly, making Aleks scowl despite the smile that threatened to break through. 'You got in a bad situation, but you've done nothing wrong. I had no idea the Rensav base was that bad. Sounds like you're lucky to have got out like you did. Least I can do is help you stay lucky.'

'You're a good man, Zhora,' Aleks declared solemnly, making the mechanic laugh.

'So they tell me. Now come on, let's get you some food before the dinner shift ends, and then you can get washed up.'

7

The Northern tunnel passed in a blur of stone walls and dim lamps, the monotony only broken by an overnight stay in the rest stop.

His first two days out of the tunnels took him through several small villages. The Goddess was smiling on him, he thought, allowing him to get so many free meals as he passed through.

It took just under a week of travelling before the villages started becoming towns; he was getting close to the city of Syvana. Suddenly, a man passing through on a horse was an oddity instead of the norm, and he found himself interrogated almost everywhere he went, particularly after his bruises started to turn an ugly purple-green as they healed. He almost wished he'd stayed in the country; at least there the people were more welcoming to travellers. Closer to the city, everyone treated him with the same regard one might treat a particularly irritating tourist. He hoped the people in Syvana itself weren't of the same mindset. Aleks kept his head down and his eyes alert for guards, never truly letting himself relax. He hadn't yet dared take the journal he'd stolen out from his coat pocket;

it was safest there, and he dreaded to think what would happen if someone found him with it.

He first saw Syvana from the clifftop, and it took his breath away. Rensav had *nothing* on the city in the North. It wasn't much to look at, truthfully; the buildings were all rather uniform, low and grey and sturdy enough to withstand the harshest storms. But they sprawled out for miles and miles in their neat rows, and the shipyard sent his blood pumping just that little bit faster, its beautiful ships docked or rising into the sky like gigantic birds, catching the nearest updraught and soaring off into the clouds.

Unsurprisingly, the city was guarded, with straight-backed soldiers in blue uniforms and white caps visible even in the dimming light. Aleks cursed as he watched them stop another traveller, asking for documents and demanding an entry tax. Of course, for security purposes they would need official documents from everyone who wanted to get into the city. His documents were currently somewhere in Rensav; they too had been taken from his saddlebag when he'd enlisted. And if they went to check the records, they'd find out he was a wanted man.

He turned Quicksilver away from the main path, taking to the grass in the hope of finding a side entrance he could slip through. It wasn't until he was almost at the cliff line that he saw it; a dirt path that passed by the shipyard, clearly used by the workers. It was out of the way enough that anyone coming in from the main road wouldn't see it; Aleks would bet it was only used by locals. He turned towards it, keeping Quicksilver at a walk.

Despite the late hour, the brightly lit streets were bustling with people. The city was amazing! Technology the likes of which he'd never seen before seemed to be taken as standard; the newscast screens were still on, and between news updates from all over the world there was footage of extraordinary circus acts, fire jugglers and ballet dancers and trapeze artists performing for the cameras. Aleks had heard rumours that the newscasts in the cities were being used for more than just news, but the entertainment casts didn't reach as far as his village – they only had one newscast screen, in the corner of the tavern, where it went ignored for most days of the year, barring international disasters. Villagers had no use for the news of the cities.

The trams were gleaming machines, trailing faint plumes of purple smoke as they rolled smoothly through the city, the tracks clearly marked on the streets so that no one was hit. Strange automated carriages piled high with goods and cargo were pulled not by horses, but by people, who guided the machines as they propelled themselves along. No wonder they seemed to have very little use for working animals in the city.

As much as Aleks would have liked to stay and explore, he knew he had to find a place to sleep for the night. 'Excuse me, sir,' he said to an elderly gentleman. 'I don't suppose you know of a place with stables, where I could stay the night? I just arrived in the city.'

The man eyed him, a shrewd expression half-masked by a bushy moustache and a thick fur cap. 'There's an inn about three streets over. They still have a couple of stables, if memory serves. Food's not bad either,' he replied with a sharp Northern accent, pointing over his shoulder.

Aleks grinned. 'Many thanks, sir.' With a quick bow, he turned in the direction the man was pointing. The inn was, like everything else in the city, well lit, proudly proclaiming itself to be *The Brass Compass* in wrought iron letters that melted into an intricate design of cogs and gears framing the door. There was a hitching rail outside, and Aleks hesitantly tied Quicksilver to it, wary of leaving his horse alone so late in an unfamiliar city. He reassured himself that it would be easy to track Quicksilver down if anyone tried to steal him, as he was the only horse he'd seen since arriving. Aleks entered the inn, pulling his cap from his head.

His senses were immediately hit with the familiar pub smell of good food and good ale, and it brought a smile to his lips as he made a beeline for the bar. A tall man with greying black hair and a beard to match was pulling pints with ease, while a smiling brunette woman worked the other end, her elbows propped on the bar as she chatted with some of the patrons.

'Excuse me, sir,' Aleks called, voice barely audible over the chatter of a busy evening. 'Have you any free rooms?'

'Aye, lad, I've a couple. You wanting a night or longer?' the landlord asked.

'Longer, if you'll have me. I just got in. I've travelled from out West and I'm looking to find a job here. My horse is tied up outside; I heard you're one of the few inns in the area with stables.' At this, the landlord cracked a smile and reached over the bar to shake Aleks's hand.

'The name's Bodan, lad, and the wife over there is Ksenia,' he said, lifting the partition to join him on the other side of the bar. 'We'd best get your horse locked up safe for the night. Come on.' They headed back outside, where Quicksilver was looking slightly disgruntled at the unfamiliar city smells and sounds.

'My name's Aleks,' he said, quickly untying the reins so Bodan could lead him round to the stable block at the back. 'And this is Quicksilver.'

'The name suits him,' Bodan replied, unlocking a stable door. Quicksilver clearly had no complaints, dropping to his side and rolling in the straw as soon as Aleks had removed his tack.

'That's quite the colourful face you've got there,' the landlord noted as they returned to the inn. Aleks winced.

'I had a bit of a rough journey,' he admitted. 'I was mugged on my way up.' Giving a heavily altered version of his story, he explained to Bodan about his travels. 'So, you see, I don't have much money to my name. But I'm looking for work, and I'm not too fussy about jobs, so I should start making wages fairly soon if the gods shine on me.'

'We've a room up in the roof that we don't usually rent out to customers. It's a bit small, see, and most of the folk round here only want a week at most. Tell you what – how would you feel about working for your bed and board? Always things to be done around here, and if you work hard enough we'll let you stay for free until you get wages in from a real job. I'll have to talk it over with the missus, of course, but I can't see her objecting. She wouldn't leave a brat your age without a roof over his head.'

'I'll take it,' Aleks said instantly. 'If your wife doesn't object.'

Bodan smiled, turning towards his wife. 'Ksenia, love, come meet our newest tenant!' he called, making the woman look up in surprise. She was pretty, her dark hair braided neatly down her back, her honey-coloured eyes twinkling.

'Evening, lad. Are you travelling alone, then? No parents, or older brothers?' she asked, extending a hand, not batting an eyelash at his bruises.

He nodded. 'No, ma'am, just me. I'm from down West. It's a pleasure to meet you, and thank you kindly for giving me a room.' She smiled at him, patting the hand that still held hers.

'The pleasure's all ours, lad. Which one's he taking, dear?' she asked her husband.

'The attic room. He had a bit of a run-in with highway-men on his way up, and is a little strapped for cash. I said he could work down here for his supper until he can get a real job,' Bodan added.

'Oh, that is good news! Our boys have both grown and left and it's been awfully quiet without them. Go and put your things away and I'll have a nice hot dinner waiting when you get back down,' Ksenia assured him kindly.

'This way, lad.' Weaving easily through the gathered patrons, Bodan led Aleks up a narrow staircase right to the top, where there was a dark wooden door. The landlord unlocked it, nudging it open, and with a flick of the switch a lamp overhead flared with light, startling Aleks. He wasn't used to switch-lamps, having grown up with lamps that needed setting by hand.

The room was small, but he doubted he'd spend much time in it; all he needed was a place to sleep safely at night.

'It's not much, but it's clean enough,' Bodan remarked, staying in the doorway as Aleks crossed the room, dropping his saddlebag on the bed and peering through the narrow window set in one wall. He could see half the city, the tall masts by the shipyard towering high over everything else, and once again he was amazed by how brightly lit the city was at this late hour. His father always said the city folk had no sense of time; out in the country, you rose when the sun did, and you went to bed not long after it got dark. Aleks supposed that when artificial light could make it bright enough to work by, little things like daytime hardly mattered.

'It's brilliant,' he said firmly, perching on the bed.

'I'm glad you like it. This is yours,' said Bodan, tossing the door key at him. 'We lock the front door at midnight, so if you're out any later you can sleep in the stables. You're welcome at every meal, but if you're here you'll be expected to help clear tables with our kitchen girl. You'll meet her later, my niece – she's about your age I should think. How old are you, anyway?'

'Seventeen,' Aleks replied, shedding his outer coat and gloves. As had become his norm, he kept his hat on to cover his military haircut. He only took it off to sleep and bathe these days, too scared of getting caught out.

'Then she's a mite younger – just turned sixteen a month back.' At Bodan's prompting, Aleks got up and left his new room, locking it behind him. 'Bathroom's just down there. Takes a while for the pipes to heat in the mornings, so if you're wanting an early shower you'd best prepare for a cold one,' the bearded man told him.

Downstairs, Ksenia had set up a meal for Aleks at the end of the bar. Fish stew, with green beans, bread and a tankard of sweet-smelling mead.

'It smells lovely, thank you,' he said, picking up his cutlery. A small, suspicious part of his brain wondered if he was being too trusting, if he was letting his guard down too early, but he resolutely ignored it; he didn't have the luxury of being wary right now, not when he was more bruise than flesh and half-starved. If it turned out later on that Bodan and Ksenia weren't all they seemed, he'd deal with it – unless, of course, it was too late by then.

As the night crept on and the men began to leave the inn, Aleks found himself chatting with Ksenia. She started compiling a list of places for him to start looking for work; reputable places that didn't require previous experience and paid adequately. Despite the many new pubs and taverns opening up in the city, it seemed that the locals preferred to stick to their familiar haunts; some of the men frequenting the Compass had been doing so for thrice Aleks's lifetime, back when Ksenia's father ran the place. As such, she knew half the decent businessmen within a ten-mile radius, and knew which ones were looking for employees or could point him in the direction of someone who was.

Finally up in his bedroom for the night, Aleks didn't go to bed right away, instead dragging his rickety desk chair to the window to sit and peer out at the city that was now his home. For a while, at least. There were still plenty of people out despite the late hour, though his attention was drawn to the blinking dots of light created by the tiny thunderbugs fluttering about the stable block. He could hardly believe how quickly his life had turned around; just a few days ago he'd been stuck in the Rensav army base with no expectation of surviving his four years. Now he was relatively safe and sound at the other end of the country, with good people around him and countless options for the future ahead of him.

Aleks just hoped he could keep his new-found luck for as long as possible.

8

Armed with a list of places to look for work, Aleks went out almost as soon as the sun rose, fully prepared to spend the day knocking on doors. He was well rested, and there was a spring in his step as he started down the street. He felt better than he had in a long while, possibly even since he'd left home, and he could only hope his high spirits would help him find an employer. Every flash of blue, black and white made him want to hide, but he avoided any guard-heavy areas and resolutely told himself that news of his escape couldn't possibly have travelled faster than he had. That didn't stop him from having a near heart attack at the sight of a man with strawberry blond hair and a moustache, believing momentarily that Shulga had arrived with plans to take the journal back and Aleks with it.

Now the sun was up, he could get a look at the city in all its glory; and it definitely was glorious. Old-fashioned Siberene architecture mixed with the new designs that were clearly influenced by Mericus and Anglya, and even Erova, and a few daring people had gone for the Anglyan mix of brick and wood rather than the sturdier stone buildings Siberene was famous for.

Aleks's first stop was near the shipyard, an enormous warehouse full of all kinds of goods brought in on the trade ships. According to Ksenia, the owner of the warehouse was looking for a new boy to haul and sort stock. It didn't sound like much to start with but it offered the opportunity to move up in the ranks, possibly even to the point of travelling with the stock back and forth between countries. That was a job he would enjoy.

The warehouse owner was a squat, slightly greasy-looking man with a distinct Southern accent and the white-blond hair to match. He was curt with Aleks right up until the moment when he explained Ksenia had sent him, at which point the man couldn't have been kinder about rejecting him; apparently he'd already filled the position. Aleks wasn't disheartened; he had this long list of prospective jobs for a reason. All it required was a little perseverance.

By late afternoon Aleks was still unemployed, and his spirits were starting to dampen. It seemed that no one was hiring, or they wanted someone a little burlier for the job they had in mind.

Still, he refused to give up after only a day, folding the list away neatly and deciding to take a break to explore the city. He picked a random direction and set off with his gloved hands shoved in his coat pockets, eyes taking in everything they could.

It quickly became clear that if he wanted to get around the city he'd have to become very familiar with the tram system. Syvana was much too large to even contemplate walking everywhere. With that in mind, Aleks made his way to the nearest tram station, spending a good while staring at the map in utter confusion. To him it was just a series of lines and place names that meant nothing.

Eventually, a cheerful blonde woman took pity on him, helpfully explaining how to go about purchasing a ticket and which tickets allowed him access to which parts of the city.

'It took me a while to get used to it when I moved here too,' she said with a smile, having already mentioned her relocation from Erova earlier in the conversation. 'But once you get into the routine you hardly have to think about it. Good luck!'

Aleks thanked her, buying a ticket to a random district on the opposite side of the city. Riding the tram was strange, the floor moving under his feet in a way that nearly toppled him several times, and he was very glad of the metal bars overhead for people to hold on to.

After wandering for a while around a district full of what seemed to be office buildings, he successfully navigated his way back to the shipyard. Leaning against a railing with a mug of hot tea cupped between his hands, he watched the ships dock and take off, letting the strange sounds wash over him. Some of the shouting sounded familiar, if he didn't listen to the words – men calling out in the fields had been the background noise of his childhood – but the sea crashing against the concrete pillars and the creak of sails catching wind were new to him. He wondered how the men didn't feel anxious, working so close to the water's edge and being splashed by the spray of the high waves. Didn't they worry that one wrong step would send them flying over the edge? He shuddered at the prospect, feeling new respect for the dock workers. He wouldn't like to end up in that water, and he didn't doubt it happened at least a few times a year. Especially with the number of sprogs running about, doing errands for their captains and masters.

Shaking his head, he dragged himself away from the shipyard, deciding to start heading back to the Compass. He'd missed lunch, but he could still make it back to help with dinner. He needed to prove to Bodan and Ksenia that he was good on his word to work for them.

Proud of himself for not getting lost on the way back, he offered a half-hearted smile to Ksenia as he entered, slumping on to a bar stool opposite her.

'No luck, lad?' she asked.

'Nothing yet, but I'm only halfway down the list,' he replied, brandishing the paper pointedly.

Ksenia's frown lifted and she patted his arm. 'That's the spirit. Dinner service isn't technically for another fifteen minutes or so, but if you're hungry I can start early for you.' He shook his head at the offer, tugging off his gloves and putting them in his pocket.

'No thanks, I can wait. A drink of water wouldn't go amiss, though?' he asked hopefully, making her smile. She turned away to get him his water and Aleks took the opportunity to survey the rest of the tavern. It was fairly empty, which made sense for the hour, though there were a few men grouped in one corner whom Aleks could have sworn he'd seen when he'd left that morning. Had they been there all day?

Draining his tankard, he slipped out of the building and round the back to the stables, where Quicksilver's head was peering out over the stall door. Pale grey ears pricked when Aleks approached and the gelding let out a soft nicker. 'Not going anywhere today, my friend. I thought you'd appreciate the rest,' he said by way of greeting, allowing the horse to nose against his jacket. 'Not sure when we *will* be going anywhere together next. The city is hardly the place for a horse.'

There was a box of brushes in the tack locker and Aleks picked out a few, shoving lightly against Quicksilver's shoulder so he could enter. Lining his brushes up carefully on the top of the stable door, he picked one and got to work, the repetitive motion helping him clear his head. He really ought to write home; it had been a while since he'd sent the letter back in Rensav, and he'd promised to write frequently. He would have to be careful about it, though; his family needed to believe he was still in the army. He resolved to write after dinner, and to ask Ksenia where the nearest post office was.

Before he knew it, it was supper time, and his stomach was rumbling fiercely. Patting Quicksilver's flank, he gathered his brushes and left the stable, quickly filling a feed bucket to drop over the stable door before locking up and heading back inside. Bodan took one look at him and directed him upstairs to wash before dinner. Aleks obeyed with a smile on his face; it was almost like being back with his parents. His mother had hated it when he'd come in from the stables with dirt on his hands and silver-grey hairs clinging to his clothes. With a horse like Quicksilver it could hardly be helped.

Settled at the bar with his dinner, Aleks glanced up at the sound of plates clinking together, seeing a girl emerge from the kitchens who could only be Bodan's niece. She looked just like her uncle, with the same coffee-brown eyes, the same clever-looking smile. Shorter than Ksenia and somewhat stocky, she was pretty, her dark brown hair tied back in a long ponytail to keep it out of the way as she worked. She was carrying several full plates of food and seemed to be having some difficulty.

'Here, allow me,' Aleks said, easing a few of the plates out of her grasp.

'Oh, no, sir, it's no trouble, really,' she insisted hurriedly.

'It's fine. I'm finished eating, and I promised your aunt and uncle I'd work for my keep around here,' he said with a smile. Her eyes lit up in understanding.

'Oh, all right,' she relented. 'Those are all going over to the gentlemen on table six,' she told him, nodding towards the table in question.

'Thanks,' she said on his return. 'I'm Raina, by the way.'

'It's good to meet you. I'm Aleks. I'm hoping to be staying here for a while, if I can find a job.' Her smile brightened at the news.

'Oh, how wonderful. It's been a long while since we've had a regular tenant around here.' At a shout from Ksenia, Raina sighed and looked at him apologetically, ducking back into the kitchen to continue her work.

Aleks helped her until the end of dinner service, when he went to lean against the bar. He didn't know how to pull a pint, so he couldn't really help with that.

'So, new boy, what brings you up this way, then? My uncle said you wanted to get away from your family, which I understand, but why come North?' Raina had reappeared at his side.

'Apparently it's the best place to look for a job,' he said wryly. 'My original plan was to head Southwards, but I was told there was nothing down there for me.' If only he'd actually listened.

'You really are a country boy, aren't you?' she remarked with amusement, making him blush. 'There's not been decent work down South for months. They stopped sending out expeditions to the Stormlands once it started getting too rough, and now the only thing going for a lad your age is the military. Something tells me that's not really your style.'

'Definitely not,' he agreed, shaking his head and trying not to grimace. He was surprised at the news of the Stormlands, though. Of course, he knew they were getting rough; in the West he could see them from his bedroom window on a bad day, and there were more and more bad days now. There were rumours that the Stormlands were growing, that the gods were in conflict and it was making the storms bigger, and that soon enough they'd touch land and the entire city of Osir would be blown apart. Aleks had thought it all a load of rumours for the most part, exaggerated beyond use. Storms changed all the time, it was just how nature worked. But if even the expedition teams were taking heed, maybe there was something to it. 'They're praying almost every hour of the day back home, trying to appease the gods and get the storms to slow. I don't think it's doing much, though. Some folks are saying there's a reason for the storms getting so big, and we just need to wait it out and see what the gods bring.'

'And what do you think?' Raina asked, one dark eyebrow raised.

He shrugged. 'I think that if the storms really are getting that big so quickly, praying won't do much to stop it. And if it is the gods fighting, well, isn't that how the world began in the stories? Could be something like that all over again,' he mused, casting his mind back to the scripture. Legend said that when the world was young, the Sky God and the Sea God couldn't stop fighting, covering the world's surface with their storms. Eventually, the Earth Goddess got so sick of the brothers' fighting that she constructed the six countries in an attempt to break up their disputes. It didn't work, only causing the storm barriers to form between the countries, so the Goddess populated the land that would become Anglya. This finally got the brothers to calm down. They still fought wherever they could reach, creating storms all over the world, but the Goddess kept them in check in order to protect her children. When those children started spreading to the other countries, until there were six different nations all born from the same blood, the gods finally came to an agreement that their storms would only hit at sea, where people couldn't be hurt. And that was how the world was born.

'What, you think we'll be getting a new country out of all this? Don't be daft! If there was any land out there we'd have found it by now, and as much as I believe in the legends I doubt a new country will just spring up out of the sea. There's hardly room, anyway — where would they put it?' she asked. Aleks shrugged, scratching at his chin where stubble was beginning to grow.

'No one's ever been to the other side of the Stormlands, so for all we know it could be there. Maybe the Goddess will calm the storms enough for men to sail through,' he suggested, hoping he didn't sound too eager about the prospect. He'd spent half his childhood climbing trees to get a better look at the far-off storms, imagining what might be on the other side. Even Torell, the most patient of his brothers, had grown tired of joining in his make-believe adventures to beyond the Stormlands.

Raina giggled, shaking her head. 'You country folk and your crazy dreams,' she said with a sigh. 'Come on, new boy. If Uncle Bo says you're working for your board, I've got a huge stack of dishes that need washing.' Not giving him a choice, she hooked her arm through his, leading him through to the kitchen. He caught Ksenia's eye as he passed, and was given the distinct impression that she was laughing at him. Life at the Compass was definitely going to be interesting.

★ ★ ★

It was fairly late when Aleks finally made it up to his room, his gait weary but a smile on his face. Kicking off his boots, he turned to the door he'd just locked behind him. It looked pretty secure. Drawing the blind on the window just to be safe, he reached into his coat, hand going straight for the tightly buttoned inner pocket; the pocket containing the small journal he'd stolen from Shulga in the Rensav base. He hadn't dared get it out before now, too worried someone might see it. For Shulga to have hidden it so well, it had to contain important information, and Aleks didn't doubt he'd be in a lot of trouble if he was found with it on his person.

Fingers shaking, he perched on the end of the bed, journal in his lap. Flipping it open past the title page stamped with evidence markers, he came to several pages of text in scrawling cursive written with an expensive ink pen. It took him a while to make it out – he wasn't used to reading Anglyan, especially not in such messy handwriting – then he bit his lip as he began to decipher the words. It was just as he'd thought; pages and pages of notes on the inner workings of the Anglyan government, before its destruction at the hands of Queen Catherine. Lists of people Aleks had never heard of, each with crimes listed beside them. Some were fairly minor: embezzlement, cheating on spouses, buying from the black market. But others . . . other crimes made Aleks's stomach turn. No wonder Nathaniel Hunter had had so much power, if this was the kind of blackmail he'd wielded.

Skimming over some of the pages, not particularly caring about the sordid lives of people who were now dead or jailed, Aleks began to wonder why Shulga would bother keeping the journal in the first place. Then a sketch caught his eye, making him freeze. His jaw dropped. In the centre of one of the pages was a rough sketch of a figure, neither male nor female, with machinery protruding from their limbs and other body parts. It was clear the person who'd drawn it was no artist, but they didn't need to be for Aleks to understand what he was looking at; the very first musings of the plan that had brought Anglya to its knees. Around the sketches were scribbled little notes – things like 'Possible? Ask Thomas' and 'Must remain conscious'.

The sound of the clock chiming startled Aleks, and he winced when he realised how late it was. He needed to sleep, or he'd be useless trying to find a job in the morning. The rest of the journal could wait, preferably until a time it wasn't likely to give him nightmares. At least now he knew why Shulga had hidden it so carefully. If it contained Hunter's early workings on the mecha children, it could well contain the secret to recreating them. Did the lieutenant know Aleks had it? He could only hope not.

Wedging the journal beneath his mattress, the safest place his tired mind could think of, Aleks changed for bed and crawled under the thick blankets, trying to force his thoughts away from what he'd read, and the hazy memories it dredged up of newscast images of butchered children, their limbs replaced with grotesque machinery. Storms, he was going to have nightmares.

9

Once more, morning found Aleks sitting on what he was starting to think of as 'his' stool by the bar, an omelette in front of him and Bodan perched on the bar to his left. 'You could always sell him,' the older man mused, a frown on his face. 'There are a few stud farms about; kingsguard horses, you know the like. They'd take a horse like him off your hands quite happily.'

'Even if I were willing to sell him, he'd be useless to stud farms – he's gelded,' Aleks revealed, watching Bodan's eyebrows shoot up to his hairline.

'You mad, boy? What did you have him gelded for? I know all sorts who'd pay to have him mount their mares!'

Aleks shrugged, swallowing his mouthful before replying. 'He was a scrawny little thing when he was a colt, and stayed that way until he was two. My da insisted on it before he got too old, saying I'd have hell to pay if my runt horse mounted one of the farmers' mares when they could've got a decent stallion to do the honour. Then 'Silver filled out and got about two hands taller, and Da nearly shot himself.'

Bodan shook his head. 'Serves him right; wasted potential, that is. But even if turning him out to stud is out of the question, I'm sure someone would take him. He's still young yet.'

'I'm not selling him,' Aleks insisted stubbornly. 'I'd rather turn around and head back home. All I need is somewhere to give him a good run every other day until I can figure something out.'

'You can take him outside the city walls. There's a decent pasture outside Sarkov that's not private land.'

'Fine by me,' said Aleks with a shrug. 'I'd better get a move on, then – jobs to find, people to talk to.' He nudged his empty plate to the side and pulled his gloves on.

Bodan nodded, hopping off the bar to take his plate. 'Good luck, lad.'

Aleks grinned at him, heading to the other end of the bar where Ksenia was.

'You off, dear?' she asked.

He nodded. 'I was wondering if you could point me in the direction of the nearest post office? I've got to send a letter home.'

'Turn left from here, head down two streets, then turn right on Ormova and keep walking until you see the post office. There's a huge pony express sign on the front, you can't miss it, not that they use pony express any more. It's all about trains these days,' she added with a sad sigh. 'Now, go on, off with you. Good luck.'

Aleks offered a brief bow, already turning towards the door. The cold hit him like a brick to the face, however much he might be used to it, but he slipped easily into the flow of people going about their daily business. It was oddly reassuring how much he blended in with the crowd up North, his blue eyes dark enough to look grey or black in most lights, and his hair as black as anyone else's. He had stuck out like a sore thumb among all the pale-eyed, pale-haired people in the South. There were enough people in Syvana to represent a good mix – and not just from various regions of Siberene, but foreigners as well. He was sure he'd seen a group of women with the telltale dark skin of Kasem earlier on, and the shipyard had been full of people from all over.

He found the post office without too much trouble, and despite the disapproving stare from the cashier he managed to get mail redirection set up, so that it would appear to his family as if his letter was coming from the South. The cost made him wince, however; he couldn't keep that up for too long without a job. He left the post office, unfolding the list of prospective employers as he walked towards the trading district.

After three rejections over the next two hours, Aleks was beginning to question Ksenia's definition of 'available work'. The list of remaining names was growing worryingly small, and he finally had to admit to being somewhat disappointed. Deciding to give himself a bit of a break, he pocketed the list and set out to explore the commercial district. Not that he could afford anything, but it was interesting to see what was for sale. Shop windows displayed things like Siberene furs and wool, jewellery and clothing, books and tools that were of more use to tourists and upper-class people than the working-class men the trading district catered to. His eyes were round at the price tags on some items; that sort of money could feed a family of six for a month at least back in Baysar.

He paused at the sight of a mechanic's workshop. Large struts of metal that would look more at home in a skyship melded with the sturdy stone of the walls, the structure protruding a little, as if the contents of the shop had altered the building itself. The sign above the door was lopsided and weathered with age, hardly legible. Aleks pulled out his list to confirm what he already knew; the name wasn't on it. Still, it surely wouldn't hurt to look?

A bell rang above his head as he opened the door, and he whipped round to see the gear shift back into place once the heavy door had closed. Turning back to the shop, his eyes widened; it looked more like a junk sale than a workshop, pieces of metal intertwined in mysterious ways, gears and chains turning steadily on most of them, thin copper wires joining pieces together. Some of them looked half-finished, as if they'd been forgotten and abandoned mid-project.

His boots heavy on the metal floor, Aleks tried not to make too much noise as he walked up the aisles of machinery. Some of it he vaguely recognised, either from the shipyard or the farms back home, but these models seemed slightly different, almost bastardised. Perhaps they had been altered in an attempt to make them more efficient; he knew mechanics valued efficiency above all else. Pausing at what seemed to be a broken steering mechanism – from a train or tram perhaps – he reached out to run his fingers over the smooth wooden steering wheel.

'What do you think you're doing, boy?'

Aleks jumped, flailing as he looked about for the source of the voice.

'Over here!'

There was a rattling of metal, and Aleks finally spotted a man perched high up on one of the shelves, a harness around his waist supported by hooks in the ceiling as he worked on something Aleks couldn't even begin to describe. 'Didn't your mother ever teach you not to touch things without permission?' The man was old, his hair a dishevelled shock of white, his dark brown eyes and thick-set features those of a Northerner born and bred. His clothes were baggy on his thin frame and he was missing a tooth in the front of his mouth.

'I'm sorry, sir, I just . . . it looked so interesting, I couldn't help myself,' Aleks apologised quickly, lowering his hands to his sides. The man rolled his eyes, and with a tug of the rope attached to his harness he was able to jump off his shelf, landing easily on the shop floor.

'You could have, boy – you just didn't want to,' he said. 'Now, what did you want? Who sent you?' His slightly rheumy eyes fixed unnervingly on Aleks.

'No one sent me, sir. I was just looking around. I didn't want anything.'

'Nonsense, lad. Everyone wants something. Especially everyone who walks in here.' He laced his fingers together, eyes not moving from Aleks's face.

'Well, I mean, I want a job, but I've no experience with mechanics whatsoever,' Aleks replied, fiddling with a button on his coat.

'A job, hmm?' the man enquired, pulling a wrench from the pocket of his grease-stained overalls. 'Come, boy.' He immediately set off down the aisle, and Aleks blinked for a moment before realising he was expected to follow.

'Sir, I don't mean to be rude, but I have to go. I have places to be,' he stuttered awkwardly as they hurried along.

'Don't be ridiculous – you're exactly where you're supposed to be,' the man replied. He stopped in front of a shelf loaded with machinery. He pulled out an item, presenting it to Aleks. 'What is this?'

'I don't know, sir. I'm not a mechanic,' Aleks responded, keeping his tone polite. The sooner he humoured the man, the sooner he could get back to looking for work.

'You seem to have a brain between your ears, lad. Figure it out.' The man pushed the device at Aleks, who sighed but took it and looked it over. It was small and narrow, with a web of intricate chains linking its fragile gears, wires emerging and leading to nowhere; it was part of something bigger. There didn't seem to be anything remarkable about it, as far as he could tell. It could be anything. Glancing up at the man, Aleks knew he wouldn't be able to leave until he'd given an answer, so he turned the object over once more.

'Is it part of a newscast screen?' he guessed helplessly. The man raised an eyebrow so high that Aleks worried for a moment it would escape and disappear into his hair.

'Why? What makes you say that?' the old man asked, lips spread in a grin that showed his yellowed teeth.

'Well, it's small and delicate, so it's probably not from a vehicle of any sort. It's also not farm equipment, I know that much. Nothing this fragile would last ten minutes in a field when the snow is thick. It's probably part of something with a sturdy casing, that isn't likely to take much of a beating. Newscast screens are complicated technology, but they're stationary and pretty well protected from the elements and things,' Aleks reasoned slowly, feeling very much like he was back in school, having to answer a question in front of a class of twenty other children.

'Wrong, wrong, and wrong again,' the man told him. 'It's the wrist joint of a mecha. It would be useless in a newscast screen. And they aren't complicated technology, boy! A sprog with a box of scraps could build one given enough time,' he said, tapping Aleks on the forehead with his wrench. It hurt more than expected, and he rubbed the spot with an irritated frown. 'You start tomorrow, seven sharp. Don't be late.'

'Excuse me?' spluttered Aleks, wondering if the man was truly as insane as he seemed. 'But I got it wrong! I don't know a single thing about any of this!' He gestured to the workshop at large.

'Exactly! Means you've got a lot to learn, and won't expect to be any good at it,' the man replied. 'I do hate those brats fresh out of an apprenticeship – or worse, the Academy – who think they know everything about everything and are doing me a favour by gracing me with their presence. You, my lad, will only expect to get everything wrong, and *that's* what makes all the difference. So, seven on the dot. Do we have a deal?'

'I don't even know your name,' Aleks argued pathetically.

'Can't you read, boy? It's on the sign! I'm Luka,' he said with an impatient roll of his eyes. 'I can pay twenty silvers a week, with bonus commissions for any sales you make.' Aleks blinked; that was far more than he'd expected from any job. It wasn't like he was qualified for something of that pay grade; he hardly knew the first thing about mechanics.

'Deal,' he agreed impulsively, causing Luka's face to split into a wide smile.

'Knew you'd see it my way. Now get out – you're interrupting my work.'

Aleks didn't hesitate, offering the man a short bow before practically running to the door. He waited until he was a whole street away before stopping, replaying what had just happened and half wondering if he'd imagined it. He snorted to himself; even his imagination couldn't come up with a man like Luka.

10

With a free day ahead of him, Aleks sought out the city's main courtyard, wanting to see if the sketches he'd seen of the place in books lived up to reality. It was easy to find; not only was it signposted everywhere, but the enormous clock tower was a bit of a giveaway. It surprised him to see snow-grass this close to the coast – it usually only grew near the mountains, where the temperatures were coldest – but he soon realised it had probably been planted there on purpose, for the tourists.

The courtyard was a veritable hive of activity, and Aleks loved it on sight. The shops lining it were beautifully kept and selling expensive wares of all shapes and sizes. Many of them boasted 'traditional Siberene crafts', and Aleks realised the courtyard was probably as far into the city as most visitors got, especially if they were only staying for a short while. It was close to the shipyard, and seemed to have everything one might need for a good day in the city. His eyes lingered on a squat little shop selling handmade jewellery, the window displays sparkling in the bright daylight, and he wished he were rich enough to afford something to send home to his mother and the girls.

The only downside of the courtyard was the many guards; there were two at the Rudavin fountain and several more wandering about to keep an eye on things. With his hat on and his hood up, Aleks doubted any of them would look at him long enough to think him even vaguely suspicious – if, indeed, they knew to be looking for him in the first place – but their presence still set him on edge.

Squinting through the falling snow to look at the clock tower, he realised he needed to start finding his way back to the Compass if he wanted to eat before Bodan took him out to run Quicksilver. Reluctantly dragging his gaze away from the pretty trinkets in the jewellery shop, he set off in the direction he'd come, hoping he could remember the way.

The lunch rush was just starting when Aleks arrived, but Raina managed to grab him a plate from the kitchen, a grin on her face as she poured him a mug of hot apple cider.

'Oh, that smells wonderful,' he murmured. She smiled at him then darted off to do her job, reminding him of the stoats in the countryside; there one moment, gone the next.

Happily digging into his food, Aleks didn't take long to eat, then helped with wiping down tables and depositing empty plates in the kitchen ready for cleaning.

When service was over, Bodan beckoned Aleks out to the stables, where he tacked up a fidgeting Quicksilver, the gelding pawing the ground in his eagerness to get going.

As much as he wanted to swing up into the saddle as soon as he had Quicksilver out of the stable, Bodan told him it would be best to walk alongside him until they got out of the city; the only people within city walls who rode horses were the kingsguard.

'How'd your morning go, then, lad?' Bodan asked as they walked, cap pulled low over his ears and gloved hands in his coat pockets.

'Fairly well, I think,' Aleks replied, still somewhat dazed from the experience. 'I got a job, at least.'

'Oh, aye?'

Aleks nodded, describing the interesting man and his workshop.

Bodan smiled, an amused expression on his face. 'Oh, that Luka's a funny old soul,' he said wryly, directing them down a small street. 'As old as the city itself, so he'd tell you. No one around to argue otherwise. He seems to have been here for as long as anyone can remember. Harmless bloke, even if he is as mad as a rabbit in a hurricane.' Aleks smiled; he hadn't heard that expression in a while, but it was apt. 'Very clever man, so he is. All sorts of genius ideas rattling around in that brain of his, but a fair few idiotic ones too. Takes him a little while to figure out which is which.' Aleks wondered if he'd turn up for work in the morning only for Luka to decide hiring him was one of his idiotic ideas, not one of his genius ones, and then he'd be back to square one.

'You think I should keep the job, then?' he asked hesitantly.

'Oh, you'd be mad not to. Luka might be a few gears short of a mecha, but he knows what he's doing and he'll teach you all sorts. He'll pay what he promises too – no underhand scheming from our Luka, which is more than you can say for most around here. Rumour has it his da was

93

some rich lord, and Luka inherited a fortune when he died. Has to be something along those lines, or he'd not have the money to keep the shop going. He's got a few regulars, but they hardly make him tax money, and apart from that he makes a sale about as often as the skies are clear.'

The two men stayed out as long as they could, Aleks jumping into the saddle and taking off as soon as they hit grass. But soon the sky grew a little darker, the air a little colder, and Aleks knew he had to bring Quicksilver in for the night. Working him down through a stretched trot and walk, Aleks eventually got out of the saddle, legs aching in a familiar way when his feet hit the ground. No one accosted them for tax on their way back into the city, and Aleks tried to follow the route directions more closely, mentally noting street names and turnings so he could find his own way there. He hoped he could make enough time in his week for excursions with Quicksilver to become a regular thing, until he could settle on something more permanent. He might even be able to keep his horse with him in the city, if he was particularly lucky.

As promised, Aleks turned up at Luka's door at seven in the morning, slightly trepidatious about what his first day of work would entail. Luka seemed surprised to see him, leaving Aleks to wonder if the man had forgotten he'd hired him, but he soon recovered and set Aleks to work sweeping the floor. It was the menial sort of task Aleks had expected, though it was made infinitely more challenging by the sheer amount of dirt and dust. As he swept Aleks had to listen to Luka ramble on about whatever it was he was making – despite him talking endlessly on the subject, he hadn't actually told Aleks what the object's function was – as well as any other thoughts that popped into the old man's mind.

It was only after Aleks had swept and mopped the floors that Luka allowed him into his little corner of the workshop, showing him the workbench littered with scraps of metal and coils of wire, charred blueprints buried under veritable mountains of half-finished works. He handed Aleks an intricate metal puzzle comprised of gears and chains, then wound an alarm clock and challenged him to solve it before the alarm went off. Aleks stared at the object. It seemed to be an incomplete gear plate, and he presumed solving it would require making it work. From there it was just a matter of common sense, connecting gears that turned each other and moving chains so they didn't tangle. It moved quite happily on its own when he set it down on the workbench, well within the allotted time, and Luka beamed widely at the sight of it. He didn't say anything, however, soon turning back to his own work.

Luka let him leave at five, when the floor was absolutely pristine and some sort of typewriter-like device had been half-built by the elderly mechanic. As Aleks left he wondered what task he'd be set next. Washing the windows, maybe, or polishing the finished pieces? Were there even any finished pieces? He'd find out, he supposed.

11

Aleks joined Bodan, Ksenia and Raina at temple the next morning, dressed in the nicest clothes he owned, feeling very much out of place despite the familiarity of the service. It featured the same scriptures and songs they had back home, and he knew most of them by heart thanks to Grigori, but the huge, tightly packed temple with its elaborately painted walls was very different from the small, shabby temple in the centre of his village. It made him uncomfortable in a way he'd never felt before during a religious service. At least the service was similar; he'd worried the North might have adopted some of Anglya's practices of letting the service deviate from scripture. Or worse, incorporating Mericus's views of the New Religion. He hoped he'd get used to it; temple was one of the few places he found peace, and he didn't want to lose that.

With no work on temple days, Aleks left Bodan and his family talking to some of their friends after the service, and decided to do a bit of exploring. He found himself in the city's main courtyard once again. It was emptier than it had been the last time, but it filled up as temples all over the city emptied out and people made their way there. He bought a small bar of chocolate for two coppers from a stall set up by the grass, nibbling on the treat as he watched the crowds move around him.

A glint of silver and a female cry caught his attention as a particularly fierce gust of wind blew through the court-yard. A girl selling jewellery reached out fruitlessly as several of her finer wares blew straight off the table, scattering on the cobbles. Aleks jogged over, dropping to his knees to help her pick them up, and she smiled in surprise when he offered her a woven silk and silver bracelet.

'Oh, thank you, you are kind,' she said emphatically, gathering her skirts with one hand as she tried to grab a necklace and another bracelet with the other.

'It's no trouble,' he insisted. 'Here, let me help.' He rescued a few more pieces of jewellery, giving them back to the girl. She studied one bracelet carefully, a forlorn look on her face. Aleks took a moment longer than he should have to tear his gaze away from her bright hazel eyes.

'It's ruined!' she mourned, showing him the crack running down a large sapphire-coloured bead. 'Father's going to kill me!'

'It wasn't your fault. You can't help the wind,' he pointed out.

'According to him, I can,' she replied wryly. 'I keep tell-ing him that setting my table out this far is just asking for trouble, but he won't let me bring it any closer to the shop. Says anyone already walking that way will see the shop itself, and I need to pull in customers from elsewhere. Thank you so much, sir, you didn't have to.' She counted the pieces he passed to her, smiling in relief when every-thing was accounted for.

'I could hardly leave you scrabbling about on the cobbles there, could I? Wouldn't be very gentlemanly of me,' he told her, earning a sly smile.

'And are you a gentleman, good sir?' she asked, one eyebrow rising as she curled the end of her honey-blonde braid around her finger. Now that Aleks could get a good look at her, it was hard for him not to stare; she was about a head shorter than him, with fine features and a smattering of freckles across her cheeks. When her eyes met Aleks's a second time, he forgot to breathe for a moment.

'I like to think so,' he replied cheerfully, drawing a laugh from her lips. 'Is that everything?'

'Yes, thank you again – your kindness is very much appreciated.' She offered him a shallow curtsey, which he returned with a quick bow. 'I haven't seen you about before, and I pride myself on remembering faces. Especially faces like yours.' Aleks wasn't sure if he'd just been complimented or insulted.

'I'm new to these parts,' he replied. 'Travelled in from the West, and hopefully staying for a while. I'm still learning my way around, to be honest.'

She smiled at him, laying out her jewellery neatly on the table. 'And how's that going for you, then?' she asked lightly.

'Not as well as I'd anticipated,' he admitted ruefully. 'I'm a little fearful of wandering too far from the inn I'm staying at, in case I can't find my way back in due time and get locked out for the night.' The girl laughed, shaking her head in amusement.

'Well, that won't do at all,' she declared. 'How do you fancy having a tour guide? I've spent my whole life in this city. I'm sure I could get you back home before nightfall. And it's the least I can do for the gentleman who stopped to help a girl pick up her beads.'

Aleks looked at her, surprised. 'You'd do that? I mean, you don't have to. I'm sure once I settle in I'll start learning my way around.'

She laid a hand on his arm. 'Please, it would be my pleasure,' she insisted.

'But don't you have to work?' Aleks questioned, gesturing to the table of jewellery. She smiled and shook her head, already beginning to pack the jewellery away into padded boxes.

'Oh, no. I do this on Sundays just to pass the time. My da doesn't expect much business on temple days. He won't begrudge me a day off,' she assured him.

'Well, if you're sure it's no trouble, I'd be delighted for you to accompany me,' he told her, bringing a wide grin to her face.

'Brilliant. I'm Saria, by the way. The little shop over there belongs to my father. I'll just need to take these over,' she added, gathering the case full of jewellery boxes. She reached to grab the table too, but Aleks got there first, lifting it easily.

'Allow me,' he insisted. 'And I'm Aleks.' She gave him a look but then relented, allowing him to carry the table to her father's shop, though the man didn't seem to be around.

When everything was put away Aleks smiled, offering her his arm. 'Shall we?' She giggled, dancing around to his side of the counter and slipping her arm through his.

'We shall,' she agreed. 'Maybe I should head West for a while, if all the men there are such gentlemen,' she joked, before giving him a sideways glance. 'Unless you're just a special case?' Aleks felt his cheeks flush but tried to maintain his composure.

'I, uh, think my ma would insist we're all such gentlemen, or it would imply she's failed to raise my three older brothers just as well,' he told her, hating how he stuttered. He'd never been good at talking to pretty girls.

'You're the youngest of four?' He nodded. 'That must be nice. I'm an only child and it can get awfully lonely at times.'

'Oh, I don't know – there are times I wish I was an only child. While having three brothers is nice, being the youngest means being bottom of the pack. I love them dearly, but they didn't half torment me growing up. Still do, really. It's partly why I left.'

Saria shrugged, her shoulder bumping against his. 'I suppose it must be difficult,' she acquiesced, though she didn't look convinced. 'So where do you want to see first?' Aleks brightened at that, looking around.

'I don't really know,' he mused. 'What are the best tourist spots? I can hardly write home to my family without something interesting to tell them!' Not that he could really tell them about any of it, of course. But he wasn't going to pass up Saria's offer of company – it seemed like the kind of offer that didn't come twice.

Saria laughed and tugged him over towards a long street that wound away from the shipyard.

'I know just where to take you, then.'

Not only was Saria charming company but she was startlingly intelligent, able to tell him the history of almost every building in Syvana. She wanted to show him the kingsguard stables, but Aleks made up a hurried excuse; going to the Northern military base was just asking for trouble. They went to the First Temple, where all royal religious ceremonies took place, and then the Central Library, which had the largest collection of books in Siberene.

They didn't have nearly enough time to go round the whole library together, and Aleks carefully mapped the path there in his mind, resolving to come back in future. The enormous building contained more books than he'd seen in his entire life, and he planned to spend the odd day there reading to his heart's content.

After that was the Academy, though they couldn't enter as neither of them were students. Between the three buildings they'd walked halfway across the city and back, though with Saria leading the way through streets full of interesting shops and pretty little courtyards, occasionally detouring to show him something she thought he might enjoy, Aleks hardly noticed the distance.

'I should get home. Da will be putting supper on soon, and he'll worry if I'm late,' Saria said, checking the timepiece above a newscast screen as they walked past, a stock market report playing out with no one stopping to watch.

Anyone who cared that much about the stock market was probably rich enough to have a screen in their home.

'Yeah, I should get back too. I'll starve for the night if I miss evening service hours,' Aleks joked.

'Would . . . would you care to do this again?' she asked tentatively, a rosy flush coming to her cheeks. 'I mean, there's still so much of the city I haven't shown you. You'll need to know all about it if you're going to live here permanently,' she added, her smile returning.

Aleks grinned, his confidence growing. 'My own personal tour of the city? How could I possibly say no?'

'Great.' Saria's smile widened. 'I'll have my table out again on Tuesday, but I only usually sell between nine and four. I could take you round the fabric district before supper?'

'I should finish work about the same time, if I'm lucky. Meet you by the clock tower?'

Saria nodded, beaming. 'I look forward to it. Can you find your own way back to your inn, or would you like me to walk with you?' she offered.

'I'm quite sure I can get back without too much trouble, and in any case, I should be walking you home. It's getting late, and a girl shouldn't wander the streets alone,' he fretted.

She giggled. 'You're sweet, but I assure you, I've been wandering about alone later than this for most of my life,' she said. 'So I suppose I'll bid you goodnight.'

Aleks offered a short bow, which she returned with a curtsey.

'Until Tuesday,' he confirmed, reluctantly turning away from her and towards the street that would lead him back to the Compass. He glanced over his shoulder, unable to help himself, but she had already gone. With a sigh, he continued on his way, shoving his hands in his pockets and trying to compose himself. It wouldn't do for Ksenia or Bodan to find out he'd spent the whole afternoon gallivanting about the city with a pretty girl; they'd never let him hear the end of it. He couldn't keep the grin off his face, however; for the first time since leaving home, he felt *normal*.

It quickly became clear that Luka's work hours tended to be 'You can leave as soon as you finish this task,' with the occasional additional task thrown in if the old man thought he was finishing too quickly. Aleks didn't really mind, however tedious the tasks occasionally were; sorting inventory, organising the contents of the shelves, cleaning the tools. Every now and then he was rewarded with a more interesting job. Luka would sometimes give him a pile of assorted parts and challenge him to make something functional. Mostly he ended up replicating a device he'd watched the eccentric man build days before. Other times his work resulted in something completely different, surprising even himself and sending Luka into fits of laughter. When that happened, though, Aleks was sure he could see a pleased glint in the old man's dark eyes.

These hours meant that nine times out of ten Aleks could head to the main courtyard and meet up with Saria after work. He would spend several hours with her most evenings, wandering about the city until they had to get home for supper. Sometimes she had something specific to show him, either a tourist spot or just an interesting part of the city she liked to frequent. A lot of the time they picked a random direction and simply started walking, too caught up in conversation to really care about where they were going. The two evenings he took Quicksilver out instead of meeting Saria, he found he spent half his time thinking about what she might be up to without him around.

Just over a week after Aleks first met Saria, he finally got a letter back from his family. A notice turned up at the Compass, and he went down to the post office to pay his redirection fee, pocketing the thick envelope to read as soon as he got back. Aleks nearly tore the letter itself in his haste to open it, spreading the papers out on the bar surface. There were two of them; one from his parents and one from his brothers. He skimmed the one from his parents, rolling his eyes at his mother's protective worrying and repeated questions about whether he was eating enough. His father's pride at his enlistment in the army caused nerves to coil in his gut, strengthening his resolve to not tell them that he'd left. So long as he kept paying the post office to have his mail redirected, he was confident he could keep up the ruse. He was relieved that no guards had turned up at his home; maybe they weren't looking for him as desperately as he'd thought? Perhaps he'd got lucky and they didn't care about one escaped cadet – or perhaps they thought he was dead in a ditch somewhere. And perhaps Shulga hadn't found out about the journal.

Aleks folded the letters neatly back into the envelope, tucking them in his coat pocket and taking his breakfast plate through to the kitchen. He'd read his brothers' letter later. 'I'd better get to work,' he told Ksenia.

'Have a good day, lad. Will you be back late?' Her eyes were knowing, and it made him flush; he'd probably talked about Saria more than he should have.

'I, uh, don't know yet. Possibly. But I'll be here for evening service,' he promised.

'See you then, Aleks. Don't let that girl of yours keep you out past dark.'

'She's not "my" girl,' he insisted with a glare, and Ksenia laughed.

'Well, you've only yourself to blame for that, haven't you?' she retorted, shooing him out of the door.

Luka was well into his latest project by the time Aleks arrived, and the teenager glanced curiously at the half-finished piece his boss had been working on the day before. 'What's the matter with this one? Is it not working?' he asked, resting a hand on the machine. He was quite sure it was meant to be a device to cook eggs in, but considering it was of Luka's invention it could just as easily have been some sort of explosive, or worse.

'Oh no, it'll work perfectly well when it's finished. But this model's going to be better,' Luka replied, gesturing haphazardly to what he was building. Aleks didn't see how it bore any resemblance to the first item, but if Luka said they had the same function, he'd take the old man's word for it.

'No reason why you can't finish this one first, though,' said Aleks. 'Just because it's not the best doesn't mean it's useless.' Luka rolled his eyes, tongue between his teeth as he carefully soldered a tiny gear peg in place.

'Waste of time, lad. Why work on inferior machinery when you know you can do better?' he said distractedly. Aleks sighed. That explained why Luka's workshop was full of half-finished inventions.

'Where should I put it, then?' he asked, lifting the piece of machinery. Luka shrugged, waving a hand vaguely at the rows of shelves behind him.

'Wherever it fits in with the system.'

Aleks frowned. 'What system?'

Luka looked up, incredulous. 'You haven't designed a system yet?' he asked. Aleks shook his head, and the white-haired man tutted in annoyance. 'Useless boy, honestly. Looks like you've got your job for the day, then. Organise that mess over there.' Aleks gaped. How in storms was he meant to organise it when he didn't know what half of it was?

'It'll take me far longer than a day, sir,' he said.

'Good; the longer it keeps you busy, the better. Now hop to it or you'll not finish in time, and then your lady friend will be heartbroken.' Aleks spluttered, eyes wide. He hadn't said a single word to Luka about Saria; how did he know? 'Oh, don't give me that. You've got that look about you, it's obvious,' the man insisted.

Aleks felt himself turn bright red for the second time that day, taking the half-finished egg-cooking device with him as he went to the opposite end of the workshop, as far away from Luka as possible. It was as good a place to start as any, he supposed.

12

Almost a month later, Aleks was quite happily settled in Syvana, wondering why he'd ever doubted he'd find happiness here and gone South instead. His heart still pounded and his mouth went dry at the sight of a blue and black uniform or a guard's white hat, but he was learning to curb his instinct to duck and run. Even Quicksilver seemed happy enough, though Aleks constantly felt guilty about how little time he had to exercise the gelding.

He was also far less happily falling even deeper for Saria's charms – not that she seemed to notice. She often told him how refreshing it was to have a man around who wasn't trying to court her, telling him of the suitors her aunt sometimes brought round to dinner. Regardless, he listened sympathetically to her stories and wished he could regale her with a few of his own, but his life was terribly boring compared to hers; the parts he was willing to tell her, anyway. She had laughed when he told her as much, insisting he tell her what it had been like growing up in the village. He'd talked for almost half an hour before he realised he'd been speaking exclusively about his three brothers rather than himself.

Though he and Saria had grown close, he had yet to work up the nerve to tell her how he felt; she was far, far out of his league, being both the daughter of a wealthy, respectable shop owner and the kind of woman who turned heads wherever she went. Aleks doubted her father would approve of her dating him, providing she was even interested to begin with, of course. But there were times when he caught her eye and couldn't help but feel she was waiting for something – for him to kiss her, maybe?

He shook his head to clear his thoughts of Saria – Luka would never shut up if he caught him daydreaming again – and returned his attention to the alarm clock he was trying to build, leaning his back against the wall with the clock resting precariously on his knees, balanced on a sheet of steel. Everything on the shelves was finally organised and catalogued in his notebook, allowing Aleks to quietly work his way through the list of half-finished devices he thought he had a fair chance of completing. Luka would probably appreciate him clearing some shelf space, and if he could make some commission money, all the better.

'Lad, what in *storms* are you doing down there?' Aleks nearly dropped everything in his lap as he jumped in fright, head snapping up to see Luka eyeing him in bemusement.

'Working,' he replied, holding up the half-gutted clock. It just needed a few gears and a chain or two and he'd be finished. All the real work had already been done for him.

'But . . . why? I made that clock months ago. I've already made six better ones since then!' Luka protested, shaking his head. Aleks raised one eyebrow, jerking a thumb at the small pyramid of six alarm clocks, all in various states of progress.

'No, you *started* six better ones since then. You never finished them,' he pointed out. 'Since you weren't doing anything with all this, I figured I might as well see if I can sell these and clear a little space around here. You're running out of room for all the new things you're abandoning.'

'I don't abandon, brat – I *redesign*. I wouldn't expect you to understand,' Luka retorted. Aleks stifled a laugh, carefully reaching for the small box of spare parts he'd appropriated from Luka's workspace.

'Yes, well, redesigning doesn't make the previous designs useless, just inferior. Someone will still buy them. It's not bothering you, I know – I've been doing this for a week and a half already and you've only just noticed. But I can stop, if you have something else for me to do?' he asked, words dripping with politeness. Luka gave him a long stare, his slightly fogged brown eyes unnerving Aleks, as they always did when he went so long without blinking.

'You've organised the shelves?' he queried.

'Organised, labelled and catalogued. All in here, if you're looking for something in particular,' he added, reaching for his notebook and tossing it to the man. Luka caught it easily, flipping it open and skimming the pages, glancing up only once to give Aleks a grudgingly impressed look.

'Thorough,' he said simply, bringing a flicker of a smile to Aleks's face.

'I like to be.'

Luka huffed, giving him a look. 'Don't get smart about it, lad.' He passed the notebook back to Aleks, then leaned back against the edge of a shelf. 'You know there's another workbench in the basement – you can bring it up if you want. Working on the floor is all right for clocks, but you'll lose a leg once you start needing a little more heat for soldering. When you finish the devices, set them up in the display case by the door. Might as well let people know we have things to sell.'

'Will do, sir,' Aleks replied with a grin, getting to his feet. Apparently satisfied, Luka wandered back to his workspace and Aleks made for the door to the basement. His eyes went round when he flicked on the light; the basement was in an even worse mess than the shelves upstairs. But he could see the workbench buried under a small mountain of parts and half-finished machines. Sighing to himself, he pulled out his notebook and pen; he had a lot of work to do before he could even think about dragging out that workbench.

He made fairly steady progress through the chaos in the basement. Instead of moving the workbench all the way upstairs, he decided to keep it down there and use the small basement as his workspace. The elderly mechanic didn't seem to mind, as long as Aleks kept the door open so he could hear when Luka called.

As he worked on a half-finished typewriter, Aleks heard the faint tinkle of the bell above the door of the shop. He set down his tools and made for the stairs; Luka didn't have the patience for customers. Reaching the top of the stairs, he peered through the open door to see who was there, and froze. He could only see the man's back, but he would recognise a military uniform anywhere, the cut distinctly different from a kingsguard uniform. Quietly, he edged back from the door, far enough that he could still see through but wouldn't be noticed if the man happened to turn. What on Tellus was a soldier doing in Luka's shop?

'Excuse me, sir,' the soldier barked, making Aleks forget to breathe for a moment. He knew that voice. Lieutenant Shulga. His heart sped up and his stomach squirmed so violently he thought he would be sick. There was only one reason Shulga would be here; he knew Aleks had the journal, and he wanted it back. How had the man caught up with him? How had he tracked him all the way to Luka's? It had been over a month since Aleks had escaped. Did the entire army know? Did they want him back in Rensav, or worse? Panic rising, Aleks glanced towards the front door of the shop; he wouldn't be able to make it out without being noticed. He was trapped.

'I'm busy,' Luka replied. 'If you're looking to buy something, come back another day.' Aleks doubted he'd even looked up from his work to notice there was a soldier in the room.

'I'm not here to buy something. I'm here to ask you some questions about a particular person of interest to the Crown,' Shulga said curtly.

There was a clink as Luka set down whatever he was working on. Aleks bit his lip so hard it bled, mentally praying to all the gods for some sort of saving grace.

This was it; Shulga would ask about him and Luka would tell the man exactly where he was.

'What makes you think I have any knowledge about what interests the Crown?' Luka sounded irritated, and while his attitude might have amused Aleks in any other situation, now it only unnerved him. He'd seen what Shulga could do when he was angry.

'We have evidence of a young man repeatedly visiting this building. A Western lad, dark hair, blue eyes, about five foot ten, scrawny. He's wanted on the charge of military desertion, and I warn you, old man, the Crown always gets what belongs to it. If you know of this man, a Cadet Aleksandr Vasin, I insist you tell me where he is immediately.'

Aleks held his breath, eyes squeezed shut. This was it. He could say goodbye to his freedom, and probably his life. Shulga wouldn't let him live, not when he knew Aleks had the journal.

'Does this look like the sort of place a brat might hang about?' Luka snapped in reply. 'Let alone a Western one. Bloody farm boys don't know a pipe wrench from a spanner.'

Aleks's eyes snapped open. *What?*

'Sir, this is no joking matter. I demand you tell me the location of Cadet Vasin. I don't want to have to . . . coerce you.' Shulga's tone was deadly, but Luka simply snorted.

'You can coerce all you like, my friend. I can't tell you things I have no knowledge of, no matter what you do to me. Now if you'll excuse me, I have work to do, and you're in the way.'

'Si—'

'Are you deaf,' Luka interrupted, 'or just stupid? I said I don't know anything. So are you going to stand here all day and harass a poor old man into giving up information he doesn't have, or are you going to bugger off and let me get on with my work?'

'I, well, sir, are you accusing me of lying about evidence of this man's presence in your shop?' Shulga demanded, clearly flustered.

'I'm accusing you of being an idiot,' Luka replied bluntly. Aleks had to bite the sleeve of his jacket to stifle the laugh that threatened to escape. 'I told you, there are no young men in my shop, military deserters or otherwise. I have a girl who delivers my groceries once a week, but she's blonde as sunshine, so I doubt she fits your profile.'

'I know what I saw,' Shulga said through clenched teeth. 'And I saw Aleks Vasin entering and leaving this building multiple times. He is somewhere in this city, I know that, and I will find him. Now, if you don't step aside and let me search your shop I'll have to do so by force.'

'Do you have a warrant for that?' Luka asked. 'If your search is sanctioned and legal, then by all means you should. And if your search were legal, you'd have arrested this boy on the street if you'd really seen him.'

Shulga's silence was answer enough, the lieutenant's face turning an angry red.

'I thought as much. Come back when you've got the king's permission to search for this cadet you're so obsessed with, though you still won't find him.'

'I am not *obsessed* with Vasin,' Shulga hissed, slamming his fist into one of the shelves and knocking half the contents to the floor. 'I am determined to bring him back and make sure he pays his dues. And I have some . . . personal grievances with him to straighten out. Bloody brat's going to cost me my rank if I can't find him soon. So, if you see him, *old man*, you tell him that I'm watching him. He'll slip up eventually – he's not clever.'

'That seems to be the common theme with you military types,' Luka replied, unimpressed by Shulga's blustering. 'Now, you've threatened me, you've broken my wares, and you've shouted at a senile old man. Anything else you want to tick off the list? Because I assure you, I will be reporting you to the kingsguard office. Maybe then you won't have to worry about dropping rank due to a lost cadet.'

Shulga stiffened, the effort it took him not to hit Luka almost palpable. He was clearly infuriated by the old man's lack of fear. 'No, sir, I'll be leaving now,' he said. 'Thank you for your time.'

'Might I ask your name?' Luka queried. 'So I know what to put on the report, you see.'

Shulga sighed. 'Lieutenant Pietr Shulga, sir,' he said tersely, before turning on his heel and storming from the shop.

Aleks stayed where he was, his hands shaking and his heart hammering against his ribs. 'You can come out now, lad. I've locked the door, and he's long gone,' Luka called a few moments later. Aleks let out a long breath, rising on unsteady legs, and emerged from behind the door. Luka was standing by his workbench, arms folded over his chest. 'Wanted for desertion, hmm? You neglected to mention that little piece of information.'

114

'It never came up,' Aleks replied drily. 'You lied to Shulga for me. Why?'

'Can't say I have much respect for the military,' Luka mused. 'Especially not soldiers like him. More ego than sense. But it sounds like you, lad, have a lot of explaining to do.' Aleks tensed and Luka's expression softened. 'Come upstairs. I'll put the kettle on and you can tell me everything. If I'm going to be denying all knowledge of you, I want to know exactly what I'm denying.' Without waiting for a reply, the mechanic turned to the stairs that led up to his flat. A grateful Aleks followed; stumbling across Luka's shop really had been a stroke of luck. Maybe the gods were trying to apologise for letting him enlist in the first place. Still, as much as he wanted to trust Luka, he couldn't tell him about the journal. He couldn't risk it.

As soon as dinner service ended that evening and Quicksilver had been taken care of for the night, Aleks made his excuses to Raina and sprinted up to his room, locking the door and scrabbling under his mattress for the journal. Shulga had tracked him all the way across the country in order to get it back, and from the sound of things he wouldn't be happy just to take it and leave. If the lieutenant ever caught up with him again Aleks was a dead man. He'd only read part way through the journal – he hadn't been able to bring himself to continue any further. It had sat under his mattress for the most part, as if he could forget about it by keeping it out of sight, and eventually it would disappear. If only. Maybe he could take the journal to the kingsguard, try and turn Shulga in . . . but then they'd find out how he got it and arrest him for desertion.

If he kept it, however, Shulga would find him sooner or later. Aleks didn't know which fate would be worse; the lieutenant killing him, or dragging him back to Rensav for the rest of his service.

Cracking the journal open to where he'd left off, Aleks's eyes were glued to the pages, the blood draining from his face. It was clear, the point at which Hunter had truly latched on to the idea of creating the mecha-human soldiers. Pages and pages of theories on how to get the perfect balance of human and machine, plans to implement testing without the public catching on. There was a whole section devoted to Hunter's strategy for creating his half-mecha army.

As the journal continued, Hunter wrote more and more obsessively about the mecha experiments he'd already carried out. It made Aleks sick to read about the many ways in which the early experiments had failed, and the subsequent 'adjustments' the scientists had made. The process used to decide the optimum age at which to start modifying children was horrifying at best.

Closing the small book with about a quarter left to read, Aleks took a deep breath, pinching the bridge of his nose. His hands were shaking. The information in that book was easily enough for someone to start repeating the process if they wanted to. It was just one step short of the actual lab reports themselves. Was that why Shulga had the journal? Storms, Aleks hoped not. Siberene was still scraping itself back together after the Independence War; they didn't need what had happened in Anglya to happen to them.

It was pitch black when he looked out of the window and the clock declared it to be nearing midnight. As tempted as he was to read on, Aleks didn't think he could stomach it; he'd reached the part where Hunter started describing the 'further experiments'. Replacing limbs with weapons was one thing, but entire bodies and brains . . . he couldn't take it. Maybe he'd finish the journal one day, but not today, not if he wanted to keep his dinner in his stomach. Journal securely back in place under his mattress, Aleks tried to keep his mind off the things he'd read, but sleep didn't come easy for him that night. One thing was certain; he was living on borrowed time.

13

The day after Shulga's unexpected visit, Aleks turned up at the workshop only to be ushered straight out again. Luka had a bulging satchel slung over one bony shoulder and was grinning widely. He looked almost demented, and Aleks eyed him warily. 'Turn around, lad, you're coming with me.' The elderly man already had his thick coat and gloves on and was pulling a hat over his bushy white hair. He had hardly reacted to Aleks's tale the day before, merely calling him a stubborn fool. But it was clear that he wasn't going to turn Aleks in, which was all that mattered.

'What? Where are we going?' Aleks asked, perplexed. The satchel looked like it contained some sort of awkwardly shaped device, possibly the machine Luka had been working on sporadically for the past couple of days.

'Doesn't matter, you'll find out when we get there. Now hurry up – you're wasting daylight!' Despite his apparent age, Luka was incredibly sprightly and Aleks found himself jogging to keep up.

They arrived at the nearest tram station, and Aleks's brow furrowed. Where could they possibly be going that was so far it required a tram journey? They weren't all that far from the shipyard, and Luka had barely left the shop in all the time Aleks had been working there. Still, he kept his questions to himself and obediently followed his boss to buy a ticket, then joined the queue to board.

Luka's knee bounced impatiently throughout the journey, his eyes flitting about nervously, and Aleks couldn't help but wonder at the man's strange mood. He cradled his satchel like it held the secret to the universe, his suspicious gaze landing on anyone who got even remotely close to it.

Finally, Luka stood up, gesturing for Aleks to follow him towards the tram doors. Aleks squeezed between two people in order to get out when the tram came to a steady halt, running a few steps to catch up with Luka. 'Could you not slow down for two seconds and explain to me where we're going?'

'What? Can't you keep up with an old man?' Luka retorted playfully, slipping behind a low stone building and taking a narrow alley away from the main part of the city. As far as Aleks was aware, they were in the storage district – judging by the many warehouses surrounding them – but Luka was heading away from it, towards the very edge of the city's walls. 'We're almost there, anyway. Just a bit further.' Aleks huffed, but kept walking, ducking his head against the fierce winds; were they near the coast?

As it turned out, there was no actual wall at the border of the city. The only distinct difference between the city and the land outside was the abrupt transition from paved streets to grass and dirt paths. The old man took off without hesitation down a rocky path, leaving Aleks no choice but to keep chasing after him. Worry was starting to gather in his mind. Luka finally stopped in front of a tall, slightly haphazardly built warehouse and pulled a key from his pocket. 'Come on, lad – get in before you're blown off a cliff, for storms' sake.'

Aleks glanced back over his shoulder, well aware that Luka's words were less of a joke and more of a probability. He'd never been this close to the sea before. It was a deep grey-green colour, and while he wasn't near enough to the edge to see, he could hear the waves crashing violently against the rocky cliffs, smell the sharp tang of sea air. His pulse quickened in equal parts nerves and excitement, giving him a brief urge to head closer to the cliff edge for a better look. A couple of ships flew through the thick clouds above, heading away from the city. As Luka unlocked the door, Aleks wondered where those ships were going.

The warehouse was pitch black, and Aleks blinked several times as he tried to adjust to the lack of light. Suddenly, Luka turned on bright lights without warning. White spots dancing in his vision, Aleks squinted until he could see properly again, at which point his jaw dropped. Sitting in front of him was the smallest skyship he'd ever seen; it didn't even look flight capable, it was so small. The sails were slack and bunched against the mast, the wings were bound tightly at its sides, and the viewscreen was so low down Aleks could see into the control room. It was tiny, with only one seat and consoles piled high around it. Still, the ship was beautiful, polished until it was almost a mirror, the seams between the wood barely even visible.

'What on Tellus is this?' he breathed, turning to Luka, who was grinning proudly.

'Don't be daft, boy. Don't tell me you've never seen a skyship before!' he barked. The old man pulled the warehouse door shut behind him and grabbed the ladder propped against one wall, carefully shifting it to lean against the side of the skyship.

'Yes, but it's so *small*, surely it can't actually be flown?' Aleks eyed the vehicle warily. A little ship like that was sure to be blown around like a feather in the storms.

'You'd think so, wouldn't you?' Luka agreed, scurrying up the ladder. He hoisted himself on deck, peering down at Aleks. 'Are you coming or not?' Aleks didn't hesitate, climbing the ladder with ease and swinging over the railing to stand beside Luka. The deck seemed to contain everything a full-sized skyship had – not that he'd ever been on a full-sized skyship to compare – but Aleks could probably walk from one end to the other in about fifteen strides. He wandered over to the mast, running a hand up the shining wood, and absently wiggled the boom slightly. 'Don't do that, you idiot!' Luka protested, darting over to slap his hand. 'You don't touch the boom while a ship is stationary – you'll ruin the directional propellers! Don't you know anything about skyships?'

'Not really,' Aleks replied.

'Well, that's going to make my plans significantly harder to implement. But never mind, never mind, it's only theoretical aerodynamics. You're a smart lad – you'll pick it up quickly enough,' he said, waving a hand dismissively. 'Come on, I'll show you round inside.' Aleks wondered how much there could be to see, but followed Luka through the trap-door anyway. They dropped down into a corridor that was so narrow it was almost uncomfortable, and Luka headed straight for the end opposite the control room, nudging open a door on the left. 'Captain's quarters,' he announced, showing Aleks a room that was barely bigger than a cupboard, a narrow bed squeezed in one corner and a stor-age trunk at the foot of it.

'Not meant for long voyages, then?' Aleks presumed, making Luka snort.

'Not particularly.' Shutting the door to the tiny room, Luka then showed him the door opposite, which was a marginally bigger bedroom, with two beds and trunks inside. 'Crew's quarters. A ship like this isn't meant to fly with any more than three people – one pilot, one mechanic and one backup pilot to switch shifts with the main pilot.'

'Is that even possible?' Aleks asked, shuffling backwards into the corridor as Luka shut the door.

'Technically, yes. Bathroom, nothing special.' He didn't even give Aleks a chance to look inside before shutting the door and moving to a fourth door. 'Galley.' It was the biggest room in the ship so far, with a basic stove and some cupboards on one side and a rickety table with three chairs on the other. The galley didn't look like it could store much food, and Aleks said as much to Luka. 'Storage is downstairs, lad,' he retorted, jerking a thumb back at the main corridor. To Aleks's surprise, there was a trapdoor in the floor at the end of the corridor next to the bedrooms, the trap opening to lean against the wall and reveal a small hole with a ladder.

Luka went down first, Aleks following, and he was amazed once more as he found himself in the ship's engine room. The underbelly of the ship was split into two rooms, the small one, Luka told him, was merely for storage, and the larger one was the engine room itself. The two of them could hardly move for all the pipes and gears and chains spanning the room, connecting the propellers and the wings and everything else in the control room, linking all the mechanisms to the steel furnace against the back wall. It looked about the same size as the average household furnace, which was ridiculous when you considered how much more power was needed to fly a skyship than power a home.

'This is incredible,' Aleks murmured, eyeing the complicated systems. He wouldn't even know where to begin. 'Where did you find this ship?'

'Find it?' Luka replied, amused. 'I built it, lad, with my own two hands. Best eight years of my life, designing and building this beauty.' Pride was heavy in his tone. 'Come on, I'll show you the control room.' Aleks eagerly followed Luka back up the ladder and to the opposite end of the corridor, the older man allowing him to go first into the control room. There was barely space for two people in there, and Aleks couldn't resist the urge to sit in the pilot's seat, peering out of the viewscreen and imagining endless skies in front of him instead of the blank walls of the warehouse.

'This is unbelievable,' he declared, grinning as he looked around at the controls.

'I know,' Luka agreed. 'She's just about ready, just needs a last finishing touch. Then she'll be good to get airborne. That's where you come in.'

Aleks frowned, perplexed, as Luka clapped him on the shoulder. 'What do you mean?'

'I'm old, lad. I can't fly the blasted thing myself. These hands might be good with small gears, but the strength is gone. I'd lose her in a storm within ten minutes,' Luka told him. 'You, on the other hand, are young, smart, fairly strong. Not going to lift a cow or anything, but strong enough.' Aleks eyed him expectantly. 'You might not know how to fly her yet, lad, but you will. If you're willing to learn, of course.'

Aleks's eyes widened. 'You want to teach me to fly?' he breathed excitedly. Luka nodded.

'Don't want her going to waste, do I?' he reasoned, shrugging. 'You're a fast learner, and don't have any preconceived notions about flying. She'll be a bit different to a regular skyship due to her size and weight, so it's easier to start with a fresh mind than try and retrain someone who thinks they already know what they're doing. So, what do you say, lad – are you willing to learn?'

Aleks laughed – as if there was even a choice! 'Of course!' he said eagerly, grinning. 'I've always wanted to be able to fly a skyship.'

'Hasn't everyone, lad,' chuckled Luka. 'Shall we get started, then?'

Aleks froze. 'What, now?' he asked. Luka nodded, giving him a pointed look until he got out of the pilot's seat. 'I thought you said there was a last thing to do before she was finished?'

'There is – it's in my bag. Once we put that in, she's ready to fly. No time like the present. It's a beautiful day for teaching a seventeen-year-old to fly in a previously untested illegal skyship of dubious structural integrity.'

'When you put it like that, it sounds so risk free,' Aleks muttered under his breath. 'What do you mean by illegal?'

'Flying a skyship without having it registered with the Department of Vehicular Transport and Safety is illegal,' Luka explained nonchalantly. 'But I couldn't let those money-hungry blockheads near my design – it'd be all over the market before I even got her back with a certificate of safety.' Aleks winced; there was nothing worse for a mechanic than having their designs stolen before they could properly market them themselves.

'So, basically, you're using me as a laboratory rat,' Aleks surmised, climbing up on to the deck after Luka.

'That's about right, yes,' the old man confirmed, already halfway down the ladder to the ground, his eyes set on his satchel. 'Any objections? You've broken one law already – surely you can't be afraid of breaking another?'

Aleks looked at the ship as he climbed down the ladder; it was unlike any other skyship he'd seen before. And he was being given the chance to fly it. 'None whatsoever.'

Luka grinned at him, pulling a many-pronged object with a plated gearbox in the centre out of his satchel. 'Excellent. Let's get to work.'

14

Luka's tiny skyship quickly became the focus of most of Aleks's attention; the pair of them spent more time at the warehouse than the workshop, Luka guiding Aleks through the basics of skyship flight and mechanics. Aleks took to the whole thing like a duck to water, exhilarated at finally being able to pursue childhood dreams he'd never truly expected to fulfil.

Despite not seeing any sign of Shulga for several days after his appearance at Luka's shop – and the mechanic's assurance that he'd filed quite the report at the kingsguard office, where they'd been utterly fooled by his 'poor senile old man' act – Aleks couldn't help but be nervous outside the warehouse. He took long and winding routes back to the Compass to avoid being followed, and didn't go to the main courtyard; the last thing he wanted was Saria getting caught up in his problems. He missed her company more than he cared to admit, but she was safer without him around. He would lie low for a while longer, then maybe go back to the main courtyard and see how she was doing. If he left it much longer, she'd no doubt forget about him. Perhaps that was for the best.

Friday nights were always busy at the Compass, meaning Aleks didn't have much time to dwell on thoughts of Saria. Darting from table to table, taking orders and depositing plates and glasses, he settled easily into the work that was becoming second nature to him now, keeping up an easy banter with Raina as he did so. For once, Aleks wasn't wearing his hat – his hair had finally grown out of its military style and into something a little more ordinary – and Raina was teasing him, remarking that she was amazed he wasn't secretly bald.

'Aleks!' Ksenia's voice called from out in the bar. 'There's someone here to see you!' Aleks froze, brain immediately summoning Shulga. He ignored his instincts and squared his shoulders as he stepped out of the kitchen.

'Saria?' he said, surprised, his heart rate slowing in relief. She was wrapped up in a dark fur coat and looked somewhat disgruntled. Disgruntled and very, very beautiful.

'So, you are still in the city, then,' she remarked, a hint of steel to her tone. Aleks winced; so much for her forgetting about him.

'Why wouldn't I be?' he asked, playing dumb. She raised an eyebrow at him, arms folded over her chest.

'Well, I've not seen you in over a week, so I was beginning to wonder.'

'Do you want to take a break, Aleks?' Ksenia asked. 'Raina can cope for twenty minutes or so.'

'Thanks,' he said, stepping out from behind the bar. 'Saria, why don't we go out the back? We can talk where it's quieter.' Saria didn't look impressed, but followed him out behind the inn towards the stables, pausing for him to grab his coat from the hook in the kitchen. 'Look, I can explain,' he began, making her scoff.

'I'll bet you can. Did I do something to offend you?'

'What? No, of course not! You've done nothing wrong, nothing at all,' he insisted quickly. 'I've been busy with work, and I just . . .' He trailed off helplessly. There was nothing he could say that was convincing enough to cover the truth. Except . . . 'I've been trying to make a decision.' That seemed to catch her off guard.

'About what?' she asked. He bit his lip; he wouldn't ever get a more perfect opening than this.

'About whether or not I'm brave enough to ask you to go out to dinner with me. On a proper date,' he clarified. He hadn't planned on asking her out any time soon, but it was better than admitting why he'd been absent. She didn't need to know about Shulga.

Saria's jaw dropped, and Aleks felt his pulse quicken, wondering if he'd just ruined everything. At least, if he had, it would keep her away. Keep her safe.

'Oh,' she murmured, making him grin despite himself. 'A difficult decision, was it?'

'Very.'

She moved closer to him, the barest hint of a teasing smile crossing her lips. 'And what did you decide?'

His grin widened. 'I would've thought that was obvious,' he said, feeling his cheeks flush.

'Well, you haven't asked me yet.' Saria's tone was playful, though she too was blushing.

'Will you go on a date with me, Saria?' he asked, summoning his courage to look her in the eye as he spoke.

She smiled properly, reaching up to tuck a strand of hair behind her ear. 'I would like that very much,' she said, startling him. For all her teasing, he hadn't actually expected her to say yes. Well, there went his plan to stay away until Shulga was gone. He could only hope Saria didn't pay the price – he was being selfish, wanting to keep her in his life, but he just couldn't bring himself to let this opportunity pass. Couldn't bring himself to let her go.

'But that doesn't excuse your avoidance of me.'

'Of course not,' he agreed quickly. 'I am sorry for that.' He was grinning like an idiot and he knew it, but he couldn't stop. Saria had agreed to date him! 'Brilliant,' he breathed, making her laugh. 'I, uh, when?'

'I'm out of the city all weekend,' Saria informed him, leaning closer to him. If she just tilted her head a little further, it would be resting on his shoulder. 'My cousin is getting married tomorrow. But I'll be back on Sunday evening, so . . . Monday?'

'Monday is perfect,' he replied. 'Meet you by the fountain at six?' He doubted Ksenia and Bodan would mind him missing evening service, especially when they'd both been telling him to make his move for weeks.

'I look forward to it,' she said.

He opened his mouth to say something but was cut off by a loud, irritated whinny from the stable block, followed by several short bangs in quick succession. Saria jumped at the noise, and he closed his eyes briefly.

'Shut up!' he called, fond irritation in his voice. Saria's eyes widened, and he realised how that had sounded. 'Not you, him.'

'Who?' Bravely, he reached out to take her hand, leading her closer to the stables, over to where Quicksilver was kicking at his stall door.

'Honestly, you are such a baby,' he said to the horse, shaking his head even as he reached over to scratch his nose. Quicksilver stopped kicking, nuzzling him in satisfaction.

'Oh, he's lovely!' Saria murmured, stepping closer and tentatively reaching out to stroke him. The young gelding preened under the attention, making Aleks roll his eyes.

'He's a brat,' he insisted lightly, scratching the horse's ear. 'Saria, this is Quicksilver.'

'A pretty name for a pretty boy,' she said, grinning. Quicksilver tossed his head, setting his nose on Aleks's shoulder and snuffling his neck, making him jolt at the sensation. Saria laughed, delighted. 'He likes you!'

'I should bloody hope so – I raised him,' Aleks muttered, peering over the stable door; Quicksilver was out of hay. That was why he was causing such a fuss. 'Oh, for storms' sake, you are going to be enormous if you keep this up,' he told the gelding, tapping him on the nose in reprimand. Aleks hadn't managed to take him out as often as he was used to, but that didn't seem to slow Quicksilver's appetite any.

'He's yours?' Saria asked. 'I thought you said you weren't one for horses?' He winced; yes, he'd said that back when they'd first met and she'd suggested going to the kingsguard stables. He hadn't thought she'd remembered.

'I'm not one for the kingsguard,' he clarified sheepishly, tossing a bale of hay over the stable door. 'Horses suit me just fine.'

'I can see that,' Saria replied with a grin, plucking a stray piece of hay from his lapel. 'Look, I need to get back before Da worries, but . . . no more avoiding me, all right? And I'll see you on Monday.'

'No more avoiding,' he promised. 'Have fun at your cousin's wedding.'

'I don't doubt I will,' she assured him. There was an awkward pause, neither of them sure how to say goodbye, before Aleks smiled and gave a short bow.

'Go, before the snow comes down. Goddess guide you home safely.'

'Goodnight, Aleks.' She left, soon becoming a dark blur at the end of the street, and Aleks absently patted Quicksilver's neck before heading back inside, a grin on his face.

Raina was waiting in the kitchen, and she smirked at the look on his face. 'Kissed and made up, have we?' she teased, laughing when he flushed brightly.

'Quiet, you,' he growled lightly. 'And for your information . . . Saria and I have a date. On Monday.'

Raina's eyes widened for the briefest moment, before she beamed, hugging him around the shoulders. 'Awww, I'm so proud of you! Aunt Ksenia!' she called, dragging him through to the bar. 'Aleks has got himself a girlfriend!'

He sighed; he was going to regret telling her that.

15

Aleks arrived at the courtyard early for his date with Saria, a bouquet of snowdrops in his hand. He grinned upon seeing Saria already perched on the fountain ledge, looking anxious. Her hair was down for once, lying like spun gold over her shoulders, and she wore a pretty dark red coat over her ruby-red dress. As he got closer, he realised she was wearing make-up too, and his heart beat even faster. He was very glad he'd decided to buy some proper clothes, or he'd look like a street rat next to her.

She smiled when she saw him, getting to her feet, and he couldn't help but beam back. 'Hello,' he greeted her. 'Uh, these are for you.' He thrust the flowers at her somewhat awkwardly.

'Oh, they're beautiful,' she murmured appreciatively. 'Thank you very much.' She tucked them in the crook of her arm, offering her other arm to him. He looped his own through it, grinning when she leaned into him.

'Shall we?' he said, turning them in the direction of the South side of the courtyard. Saria fell into step beside him, and he couldn't keep his eyes from drifting to her every few moments. 'You look beautiful,' he told her.

Her cheeks flushed to match her dress, but her smile was radiant.

'Thank you. You clean up very well yourself,' she added with a smile, smoothing a hand down the lapel of his new coat. Aleks wouldn't tell her he'd needed Raina's help to pick his outfit. 'Where are we going, then?'

'You'll have to wait and see, won't you?' he teased. Saria huffed playfully, but allowed him to lead her through the streets, clearly trying to work out where they were going. The restaurant Aleks was taking her to was a little place that Raina had recommended. She had never been herself, but several of her friends had gone there on dates, and it offered good food at prices that wouldn't leave Aleks broke. 'Here we are.' He let go of her arm in order to pull the door open for her, and resisted the urge to hold his breath and pray. He'd never been on a date before; he could only hope he turned out to be good at them.

Luckily, Saria seemed happy; the food was wonderful, and though she led most of the conversation, Aleks managed to keep himself from getting too tongue-tied.

'As much as I'd love to stay for dessert, I don't know if we'd be able to get home if we stay any longer,' he said with a frown as the waiter took their plates, eyeing the thick-falling snow in the lamplit street outside. Saria turned to see what he was looking at.

'Oh, it looks awful out there! And it's late too. My aunt will be terribly mad if I'm not home soon – she doesn't exactly approve of this as it is. We'll have to do dessert another time,' she told him, smiling sweetly. He blinked, ignoring the remark about her aunt; did that mean she wanted to go on another date? Saria had already told him about her Aunt Anastasia and her very strict ideas about the kind of man Saria should aim to marry. Aleks definitely did not match those ideals, but that was a bridge he'd cross later.

He flagged down the waiter and paid, then helped Saria with her coat, tugging on his gloves on the way to the door. He couldn't help but shiver as they stepped out into the cold evening air, snow immediately settling on their heads and shoulders. Saria linked one arm through Aleks's, huddling in close to him as they walked, telling him which streets to take to get to her house. He glanced sideways at her, frowning at the pinkness of her cheek.

'You must be freezing,' he muttered. She shifted her flowers to the crook of her arm and swept gloved fingers through her hair, brushing off the snow.

'I'll be fine. I just wish I'd remembered a scarf,' she added ruefully. Aleks rolled his eyes, a faint smile tugging at his lips as he took off his hat, placing it on her head. It was a little big for her and came down almost past her eyes. 'Oh, but now you'll be cold! I can't!' she protested, reaching up to take the hat off, but he stilled her hand with his own.

'I'm trying to be a gentleman here, Saria,' he told her. She laughed, but released his hand and left the hat on.

'If I must, then,' she relented playfully. She reached up, brushing her fingers through his short fringe. 'By the way, I do love that you're not wearing your hat all the time now. I was beginning to wonder if I'd ever see your hair.' Her smile was coy, bringing heat to his cheeks and

134

butterflies to his stomach. 'You should go without it more often.'

They walked quickly to Saria's house, and Aleks wasn't surprised to see she lived in one of the high-end areas of the district; not obnoxiously affluent, but upscale for a shop owner's family. Obviously the jewellery business did well. 'This is me.' She tugged on his arm, pointing him towards a house with a lamp above its blue door. Saria slipped her arm out of his, giving him a smile. 'Thank you for tonight,' she murmured. 'I had a lovely time.' He grinned, flushing with pleasure.

Saria took a small step closer, and Aleks's heart skipped a beat. She was looking at him like she wanted to kiss him. Was she going to kiss him? He'd never kissed a girl before – and he desperately wanted to kiss Saria. Aware that his arms were hanging uselessly at his sides, Aleks lifted one hand and tentatively rested it on Saria's waist, feeling the curve of her corset under the thick wool of her coat. 'Will you be in the courtyard tomorrow?' she asked him, not reacting to his hand placement.

'I should be,' he confirmed. 'Unless Luka decides to keep me late to make up for letting me out early today. But I doubt he will. I'll see you tomorrow?' He didn't dare move, not wanting to upset her should he be reading the signs wrong.

Her smile widened as her eyes fixed on his. 'See you tomorrow,' she agreed, and then she was kissing him.

It wasn't a particularly long kiss, and he didn't really participate much, too shocked to even register the contact until Saria was on the verge of pulling away. But he managed to pull her closer and respond to the kiss, assuring her it was definitely welcome. When they parted they were both burning bright red. 'Goodnight, Saria,' he murmured, watching her step away and open her front door. It was only when she was safely inside and he was already walking away that he realised she still had his hat. He grinned to himself, jogging in order to get back before his ears got frostbite. Definitely worth it.

As was usual now, Aleks found himself ensconced with Luka in the engine room of the ship, the old man methodically teaching his employee about each part of the ship's mechanics and how they were all connected. It was still strange, having Luka so actively involved in his learning process; usually he just gave Aleks a challenge and waited for him to figure it out himself. Obviously, he understood that a skyship was a sight more complicated than a lamp with a timer switch or a mecha's arm. Aleks liked it, though; even the smallest insight into the intelligent chaos that was Luka's brain felt like a privilege, and to learn how the man had invented and created everything in front of him was incredible.

Having been told that he wasn't going to get to take the skyship off the ground until he could name and describe the function of everything in both the engine room and the control room, Aleks tried his best to memorise it all. Luka wouldn't let him take notes, wary of them being stolen.

He watched Luka point out each section of propeller and wing control, amazed at how closely they were linked.

Luka took great pride in telling him that in ordinary skyships they functioned independently, but his design connected them to allow better control in the smaller vehicle. 'Otherwise you'd be putting too much power into one side at a time,' the old man explained, 'instead of giving equal power to both sides and keeping her steady. Not much of a difference in a large ship – it needs that much power just to stay upright. But in a little thing like her, you'll capsize with a regular steering system.' Aleks winced, imagining flipping a skyship completely. He hadn't thought it was possible.

'Makes sense, I suppose.'

'Good, good. Let's move on, then. The sooner you learn to fly this thing, the better. While you could probably keep her stable through weather that would ground most ships, it's looking like a harsh winter ahead and I don't want you crashing her. Eight years of work down the drain.'

'Surely it'd be too dangerous to take her out in harsher weather, though?' Aleks asked, confused.

Luka scoffed, moving to another section of the engine room. 'Haven't you been listening to a word I've said, boy? She'd be useless if she couldn't handle harsh weather – it's what I built her for.'

'I thought you built her because you wanted a smaller, faster skyship,' Aleks said. Actually, he'd thought Luka had invented the ship just to prove he could, but he wasn't going to say that.

'Don't be daft, lad. If that was all I wanted, I would've been finished years ago!' Luka told him, shaking his head. 'No, this little beauty is designed to face the kinds of storms normal skyships are too heavy to survive. While they'll be battered by wind and rain to the point of splintering, she'll just rocket around in them and make it out the other side. She was designed to do something that no ship has done before.'

Suddenly, it clicked. 'You want to fly her through the Stormlands,' Aleks said, stunned. Luka smiled ruefully, shaking his head.

'Once upon a time, I did,' he confirmed. 'But you've seen the newscasts. You know what they're saying about the Stormlands getting bigger. No, I've missed my chance, lad. Now I'd just like to get her up in the air where she belongs.'

Aleks frowned; he had indeed seen all the reports on the Stormlands, and seen first-hand how much more tempestuous the storm was growing. But it wasn't that much worse than it had been a few years ago. And if Luka had designed the ship to take on the Stormlands, Aleks didn't doubt it could manage even now.

'So you think there's something on the other side, then,' he asked eagerly, glad there was someone else who shared his views. Everyone else he'd brought it up with, even Saria, thought he was crazy, or being fanciful.

'There's got to be, hasn't there?' Luka reasoned. 'When you look at how little distance there is between most of the countries, and how much of a space is estimated between the two sides of the Stormlands, it can't be solid storm the whole way through. There's no way anyone in Dalivia would be able to get past – their side of the Stormlands is even worse than ours, and it's far too hot – but here . . . well, it doesn't matter now.'

'I want to do it,' Aleks blurted out, the words rising unbidden. But he didn't want to take them back – he'd always dreamed of flying to the Stormlands, of discovering what might lie on the other side. Sure, it was a risk; hundreds of expedition ships had gone to the Stormlands and never returned. But none of them had been built by Luka.

'You what?'

'I want to do it,' Aleks replied. 'I want to fly through the Stormlands. You've spent all this time building this ship, it'd be a shame for her to go to waste. It's not too late, Luka. She'll make it to the other side. If you'll teach me to fly her.'

'Are you mad?' Luka spluttered. 'Or do you just have a death wish? I told you, the storms are too rough, it's too late now.'

'What if it's not, though?' Aleks persisted.

'Then we'll leave finding that out to someone who doesn't have as much to lose as you do. What about your family, lad? And that girl of yours – you really want to risk losing all that just for a bit of adventure?'

Aleks bit his lip, thinking of all the people he cared about. Luka had a point. But if he could make it, if he could fly through the Stormlands and return successfully, he'd go down in history. This appealed to Aleks more than he was willing to admit; to the guilty, selfish part of him that wanted to do something that would finally place him above his brothers.

'I trust your work, Luka, and I don't think the Stormlands are as bad as you think they are. I can do this,' he insisted.

Luka sighed, folding his thin arms over his chest. 'I'll think about it,' he said eventually. 'One step at a time, lad. Learn to fly her, then see if you still want to throw your life away on a pipe dream.' Aleks grinned; that was probably the best he was going to get.

'Regardless of whether you take her to the Stormlands or not, you'd still be doing me a favour by helping me get her in the air. So I thought I'd do you one in return.' Aleks raised an eyebrow at the mechanic's words. 'I talked to a friend of mine in the records department. His name is Kir. You do this for me, Stormlands or no Stormlands, and Kir can make that little arrest warrant of yours disappear, along with your enlistment file. There'll be no record of an Aleksandr Vasin ever joining the army. You can get your apprenticeship, get married, do whatever you like. Even if that obnoxious little Lieutenant comes sniffing around again, he'll have nothing that'll hold up in court.'

Aleks gasped. Luka could get his record clean. He could make it so Aleks was free to do whatever he wished, without constantly looking over his shoulder in fear of being caught out and dragged back to Rensav to serve out his four years.

'You would do that? For me?'

'If you're going to risk your life in one of my contraptions, the least I can do is reward you for it when you're done,' Luka retorted, glancing up at Aleks. 'It'll have to wait a while, until the records department starts the annual overhaul. No one will notice a few missing papers in all that chaos.'

'Still, that's . . . that's more than I ever expected,' Aleks said, stunned. 'Thank you.' He was now even more determined to fly the ship through the Stormlands; if Luka could give him his freedom, the least Aleks could do in return was fulfil his dream. 'So when do we start flying?'

Luka beamed, clapping him on the shoulder and nudging him closer to the furnace.

'That's the spirit, lad.'

Winter was well and truly on its way, and Aleks was worried they would soon miss their window of opportunity; if the weather got much worse than it already was, there was no way he would be able to fly. As usual, the snow was falling thick and fast as he hurried through the streets to meet Saria, still in his tyrium-smudged clothes from work.

She was waiting under the awning of her father's shop, bundled up in a thick fleece-lined coat. 'Not the best day for it, is it?' he remarked as he approached, leaning in to kiss her briefly. She laughed, dusting snow off his shoulders with gloved hands.

'This? This is nothing! You wait until the storms really get going!' she replied. 'Come on, I want to show you something.' She took his hand, tugging him back out into the blizzard. Aleks had no choice but to follow, his head ducked away from the icy flakes. He now understood why so many people wore flight goggles as part of their everyday clothing in the North.

'Where are we going?' he asked, not recognising any of the streets they were taking.

'It's a surprise,' Saria said, still leading him by the hand. 'I think you'll like it.'

Digging his work goggles out of his pocket and putting them on for better visibility, he glanced up at a street sign, his step faltering. Now he knew why he didn't recognise where they were; Saria had led him right into military territory. The small military base that held the kingsguard was barely three streets away, and they seemed to be walking right towards it. 'Saria, really, where are we going?' he asked, a hint of panic creeping into his tone.

'I told you, it's a surprise!' she said laughingly, not noticing his growing alarm. He had to leave, but he couldn't do so without alerting Saria to the fact that something was wrong, and that was opening a whole other can of worms that he just didn't want to deal with. 'Now, come on, before we're too late!'

Heart beating fast, Aleks had no choice but to follow, letting Saria take him closer and closer to the barracks. He could see the base now; much cleaner and nicer looking than Rensav, but a military base all the same. Even the sight of the uniform rows of barracks made him flinch.

'It's just around here,' Saria urged, heading over towards a large building at the front of the base. Suddenly, everything made sense: the kingsguard stables.

'Should we really be doing this?' he asked, trying and failing to keep his voice even.

'They haven't started drills. It's fine,' she assured him. 'Oh, good, they haven't covered it over yet. I was worried they would because the snow is so bad.'

As they rounded the corner, Aleks saw the stable yard was open, ringed by stalls full of tall, gleaming horses of all colours. He had to admit it was impressive. Two stablehands were doing hay rounds and another was sweeping snow from the concrete, but it was clearly too cold to have any of the horses out in the yard. He could imagine the place was quite popular in the summer, when the horses could be on full display. He wondered how they kept all the horses fit and healthy with so little land to run them. Quicksilver was already starting to pack on some fat beneath his thick winter coat.

'Maybe we should come back another day when the weather is better,' Aleks suggested. The stablehands didn't worry him – they probably didn't care about much but the horses – but at any moment Shulga could come around the corner, and then he'd be in deep trouble. And while Aleks had no proof that there were any soldiers other than Shulga looking for him, it wasn't a risk he was willing to take. 'There'll be more to look at, then.'

'There's plenty to look at now,' Saria insisted. 'We just have to wait – they'll bring them out soon. The mounted guards always run drills on Wednesday afternoons.' That didn't make Aleks feel better; did it mean the area would soon be filled with guards and soldiers? He and Saria were in plain view. They had to leave now. Before someone saw him, before he was arrested and tried as a deserter, sent back to Rensav, or worse. But there was no excuse he could give Saria that wouldn't sound pathetically flimsy.

She seemed enraptured as the stablehands began to bring the horses out ready for saddling. Aleks might have been too, if he weren't so on edge; the Syvana kingsguard truly did ride the best horses in all of Siberene.

'Come on, it looks like the snow is getting worse,' he said once most of the mounted guards had ridden out of the yard, off to do their drills. They were the only ones around, and the silence made him nervous. 'We should get inside.'

'It's only snow!' Saria protested. 'We can stay a little longer. Aren't the horses amazing?'

'They are, truly,' Aleks agreed. 'But there's not much point in staying now, and I'm starving.' Saria huffed. She seemed annoyed that her little surprise hadn't gone down as well as she'd hoped.

'Oh, fine,' she relented, reluctantly turning away from the stables. 'I only thought you might enjoy watching, but if you're bored . . .'

'No, no, it's not that!' he insisted, trying not to look too happy about the fact that they were walking away. 'I've just had a long day at work, and I've hardly eaten since break-fast.' The excuse fell flat and he sighed in frustration. 'I did enjoy watching.'

Ignoring the urge to run, he stopped in the street, pulling Saria close. 'Thank you for showing me,' he murmured, trying to slow his racing heart now he was out of sight of the base. 'I liked seeing the horses.' He leaned in to kiss her, trying to draw a smile to her face, and he grinned when it worked.

'I'm glad,' she replied, huddling closer for warmth as the snow fell thickly around them. 'I didn't mean to get cross with you. I just want to show you all my favourite parts of the city, so they can be *your* favourite parts too. So you might see everything this city has to offer, and decide to stay here a while longer.' Aleks couldn't imagine wanting to leave any time soon, and told her as much, wrapping his arms around her waist. He ducked his head, pressing his lips to hers as one hand moved to her hair, then froze at the sound of footsteps crunching on snow.

'Oh, how sweet.' The sneering voice sent shivers down Aleks's spine. 'I almost feel bad about what I'm going to do. Almost.'

Aleks let go of Saria and turned, facing the uniform-clad man who had emerged from the adjacent street. There was a gleam of triumph in the lieutenant's eyes. 'I told you I'd find you, brat. Though I have to say, I didn't expect you to just walk right up to base.' He paused, barking out a laugh. 'Getting homesick, are we?'

16

'Aleks, who is this?' Saria's voice snapped Aleks out of his panic, and he realised that she was eyeing him with a mix of confusion and fear. He had unconsciously stepped between her and Shulga, protecting her from the man.

'Yes, *Aleks*,' Shulga mocked. 'Introduce me to your little girlfriend. Haven't you told her about me yet?'

'Let her leave,' Aleks urged. 'Whatever you're about to do to me, she doesn't need to see it.'

'I'm not going anywhere,' Saria argued, her voice wavering. She tried to step out from behind Aleks, but he moved with her.

'So you *haven't* told her, then?' Shulga said, taking a step closer. 'That's rather rude, isn't it? Not that it'll matter soon.' He moved closer again. 'I told the commander I'd find you here – asked him to transfer me to Syvana and everything. He advised me to give up, to let you get away, but I was sure I'd find you eventually. I was put on probation thanks to that report the stupid old man filed, and banned from that section of the city. You got cocky, coming here. One would almost think you wanted to be caught.'

Had Aleks not been taught to evade attack as a child he would have taken a fist straight to the face, but he saw Shulga preparing to move and ducked, darting forward to ram into the man's chest and punch him in the stomach. 'Saria, run!' he yelled, unable to turn back and check if she'd obeyed. Shulga was on him now, gripping him tightly by the coat, and Aleks had the air forced from his lungs as the man threw him to the ground, pinning him to the snow-covered concrete.

'Thought you could get away with it, didn't you, you fool!' the lieutenant growled, punching Aleks in the face so hard he was sure his nose was broken.

'Then take me in,' Aleks muttered, ignoring both the pain and the blood trickling down his cheeks and lips. 'Sending me back to Rensav has got to be more satisfying than killing me.'

Shulga's eyes widened as Aleks attempted to knee him in the groin, but he dodged it easily, pinning him tighter. 'Oh, far more satisfying. But no one will care if you get a little . . . *damaged* in transit. Besides, I can't kill you until you give back what doesn't belong to you.' He reared back, raising his fist once more, and Aleks closed his eyes in anticipation of the blow. But the blow never came, and instead there was a loud crack and Aleks felt a heavy weight on his chest. Opening his eyes, he was sure Shulga had knocked him out and he was imagining things. There was no way it could possibly be Saria standing over Shulga's unconscious form with a half-shattered flowerpot in her hands and a vindictive expression on her face. Hadn't he told her to run?

Aleks blinked, but the image didn't change. Finding it difficult to breathe with Shulga slumped over his torso, he shoved the man off with some difficulty, staring in astonishment at his beautiful Saria, who looked stunned at her own actions. 'Saria,' he murmured, still sitting in the snow.

'I broke the flowerpot,' she declared in annoyance, looking at the piece of pottery. 'I didn't mean to do that.'

Aleks scrambled to his feet, only to sway dangerously, blood gushing from his nose. He pinched it, yelping in pain, and Saria dropped the flowerpot to hurry to his side. 'Are you all right?'

'He broke my nose,' he muttered, grimacing. 'Gods, Ksenia is going to kill me.'

'Forget Ksenia, I have half a mind to kill you myself,' Saria retorted, looking furious even as she gently pulled his scarf aside to tend to his nose. 'What on Tellus was that all about?' Aleks winced, and not because of pain.

'I . . . haven't been entirely truthful with you. It's probably best if you don't know, to be honest,' he added, glancing nervously at Shulga as the man's uniform became dusted with snow. How long would he be out? By the sluggishly bleeding lump on his head, Aleks assumed it would be a while.

'No,' Saria said firmly. 'I just knocked a man unconscious because he was trying to kill you. You can't expect me to simply ignore that and move on!'

'It's not safe for me to tell you!' he argued, making her glower.

'Clearly it's not very safe for you to leave me in the dark either! Tell me what's going on, Aleks, or I'm leaving. I mean it.' She stepped away.

'Saria, please,' he started, but trailed off at the look on her face. He couldn't evade this one. 'Fine. But you're not going to like what you hear.'

'That's for me to decide, don't you think?'

'We should leave first,' Aleks insisted. 'Our friend here is going to wake up at some point, and I need to be as far away as possible when he does.' Not giving Saria a chance to argue, he grabbed her hand and took off at a jog, leaving Shulga in the snow. The man could get frostbite for all he cared.

He didn't speak until they were back in familiar territory, wandering narrow streets that were deserted at this time of day. Saria tugged on his hand. 'We've walked far enough – now I need answers. That man, that soldier, what did he want with you?'

Aleks took a deep breath, dread curling in his stomach. 'He wanted to take me back to Rensav,' he started, 'where I can serve out the rest of my four-year commitment.' Saria's hazel eyes widened in shock.

'Wh– what are you saying?'

'It's complicated,' he said, trying to think of a way to explain properly. 'Gods, I didn't want you to find out, especially not like this. When I first left home, I went South to Rensav and enlisted. Only the military wasn't what I expected at all. I had to get out before they killed me.' Saria gasped, connecting the dots for herself.

'You deserted,' she said softly. Aleks nodded.

'Grabbed my horse and ran for it,' he confirmed, not mentioning his little detour to Shulga's office. It wasn't safe for Saria to know what he'd already told her, let alone anything else. 'Made it up here through luck and the will of the Goddess.' Only he clearly hadn't had *too* much luck, to have been followed so diligently. Shulga was like a bloodhound! It only cemented Aleks's conviction that the lieutenant wasn't supposed to have Hunter's journal.

'And you didn't think I might want to know that my boyfriend is a criminal?' Saria asked indignantly. 'Gods, Aleks, I was so scared. I thought he was going to kill you! You're telling me that he's just under orders because you broke the law?'

'No, you don't understand!' he said hastily.

'I think I understand plenty, thanks,' Saria said, cutting him off. She pulled her hand from his, stepping away. 'I can't do this, Aleks. I'm sorry, I just . . . this is too much.'

'Saria, wait!' Aleks called, but it was too late. She disappeared in a flurry of snow and a swish of dark red fabric. Aleks's shoulders slumped, his nose throbbing painfully. He cursed; could his day possibly get any worse?

He didn't think Ksenia believed his story about getting a piston to the face while working in the shipyard with Luka, but she bandaged his nose all the same. 'It might look all right, once the swelling goes down,' Raina remarked from over at the bar, where she was wiping the surface down. 'Roguish, or something. You never know, Saria might like the bad boy look.' Aleks stiffened, and the dark-haired girl frowned. 'Wait, she didn't do this, did she?' Aleks almost snorted, before he realised how painful it would be.

'No, no, Saria didn't break my nose. Though I don't doubt she could if she wanted to. Especially at the moment,' he added bitterly.

'What did you do, lad?' Ksenia asked bluntly.

Aleks feigned obliviousness. 'What do you mean?'

'Don't even try it,' Raina said with a roll of her eyes. 'What did you do – stand her up? Insult her? Make an idiot of yourself in front of her?'

'What? No! We had a little disagreement, that's all! But thank you, ladies, for the vote of confidence,' Aleks said wryly. 'I don't really want to talk about it.' Ksenia finished wiping the blood off his face and tossed the cloth in the bin, along with Aleks's scarf; Ksenia had declared it a lost cause.

'Ooh, it must be bad,' Raina mused, frowning. 'Is everything all right?'

'Everything is fine,' he insisted. He wished he could believe his own words. He didn't know how long he would have before Shulga woke up and got back on his trail again. He needed to talk to Saria, before she did anything rash – like never speak to him again.

First, however, he needed to talk to Luka. They would have to speed up the timeline on their little adventure if Aleks was going to get his record cleared before Shulga caught up with him again. There were only so many times he could escape before his luck ran out.

17

Aleks was distracted as he worked, despite Luka insisting that if they were going to speed things up he would have to work even harder than before. He couldn't stop thinking of the look on Saria's face when she'd found out the truth; the hurt in her eyes had made him feel physically sick.

'Oh, for storms' sake, lad, just go and talk to her.' Aleks looked up at Luka's words, seeing the old man frowning at him. 'You're useless right now. I bet you haven't listened to a word I just said.' Aleks smiled sheepishly, unable to deny it. 'Go, talk to your girl, get this whole mess sorted out before it escalates. If she reports you to the kingsguard I'll have to find another bloody pilot, and then I'll have to wait until after winter!'

'You almost sound concerned for my well-being,' Aleks remarked drily. Still, he smiled in thanks at the mechanic, getting to his feet. Luka waved him off, already turned back to the ship's furnace.

Aleks got the tram back into the city and made straight for the courtyard, keeping his eyes peeled for familiar honey-blonde hair. Saria's table wasn't set out and she was nowhere to be found. Gathering his courage, he walked straight to her father's jewellery shop, the bell over the door ringing as he entered. It was quiet inside the shop, and a man with greying blond hair who could only be Saria's father was behind the counter, arranging necklaces in a glass case. He looked up when he saw Aleks, a curious expression on his face. 'Can I help you, young sir?' Aleks swallowed, his throat suddenly dry, and belatedly pulled his hat off when he realised he hadn't already. Saria's father was enormous, tall and muscular, and looked very much like he could crush Aleks without a second thought.

'I, uh, I'm looking for Saria,' he croaked, watching the man's blue-grey eyes narrow in comprehension.

'You are the boy,' he said. 'Aleks.'

Aleks tried not to look surprised that Saria had told her father about him, nodding even as he stood up a little straighter.

'Yes, sir. I wanted to talk to her. We had a bit of a . . . disagreement yesterday.' Saria's father continued to eye him, and Aleks tried not to squirm under the man's piercing gaze.

'My daughter was most upset last night,' he said conversationally. Aleks winced. 'She would not say why, just that you caused it. I do not believe she has any reason to talk to you.'

'No, she doesn't,' Aleks agreed, 'but I would very much like the opportunity, anyway.'

'She's not here,' Saria's father finally told him. 'She stayed at home with her aunt today. But I shall let her know you came by, and you wish to talk. If she is willing to listen, she will be by the fountain selling our wares tomorrow evening. If she is not there tomorrow, it means she does not want to see you, and you will not bother my daughter again.' His accent had the curt formality of higher-class Northerners, and it sent shivers down Aleks's spine.

'I understand, sir. Thank you. I . . . I'll be going, then.' The man nodded, turning back to the jewellery case, and Aleks presumed that was the end of their conversation. Storms, Saria's father was terrifying. Still, he'd agreed to pass Aleks's message on, which was the important thing.

Finding it incredibly hard to focus on Luka's lessons in the warehouse the day after, Aleks let out a sigh of relief when an alarm went off in the middle of a thorough and complicated explanation of the emergency landing system, indicating it was time for Aleks to leave. The alarm wasn't there usually, but after impressing upon Luka how important it was for him to be on time, Aleks had been allowed to set one.

His heart was pounding rapidly in his chest as he walked to the tram station and he could feel his palms sweating. He tried to calm down, breathing steadily and reminding himself that Saria was a lovely, rational young woman who surely would at least hear him out before leaving him. He hoped.

He froze when he reached the edge of the courtyard, instantly spotting Saria behind her table of jewellery. She was selling something to a young couple, and Aleks took the opportunity to watch her. Her smile didn't meet her eyes and she looked paler than usual; was that his fault?

After a few minutes the couple walked away, a paper bag being slipped into the woman's handbag, and Aleks had no excuse to stay away. Taking a deep breath and sending up a quick prayer, he started walking. He could tell when she spotted him, as her whole body tensed and her gloved hands clutched the edge of the table. But she stayed put, and Aleks felt a flutter of relief.

'Hello, Saria,' he said softly. She folded her arms over her chest, eyeing him warily.

'Aleks,' she replied, her tone verging on icy. 'My father said you wanted to talk. I suppose it's only polite for me to let you.'

'Please,' he requested, taking a tentative half-step closer. 'Saria, let me explain. But . . . not here. It's too public.' His eyes darted towards the two guards at the fountain.

'Is it safe for me to go somewhere private with you, or will you be attacked again?' she asked sharply.

'That's hardly fair – it's not like I planned that,' he said. 'But we should be safe.' Aleks hadn't seen Shulga around since the other day, and could only hope the flowerpot had done more damage than he'd initially assumed. All Shulga knew so far was where Aleks worked, and he wouldn't put the kingsguard on alert while he still needed him to give the journal back. Thanks to Luka's report, the lieutenant couldn't get anywhere near the workshop himself.

Saria didn't take his hand as they walked, and Aleks didn't dare reach out to her. They found a small, unoccupied courtyard, and went to sit on a bench in the corner. Bracing himself for her reaction, Aleks explained himself, telling

Saria everything that had happened in Rensav, and Shulga's appearances since. She listened patiently, horror on her face as he explained the truth behind the enlistment fee and his confrontation with Antova. When he was finished he looked down at his lap.

'Oh, Aleks,' she murmured. 'Gods. When you said, I never expected . . . I never thought it was like that. I thought our army was noble.'

'You thought I would break the law just because I didn't feel like being a soldier any more?' he asked incredulously. Saria blushed, ducking her head.

'Well, no, I jus– what was I supposed to think?'

'You were supposed to trust me!' Aleks exclaimed. 'You know me, Saria. I thought you knew by now that I don't do things without good reason.'

'I did trust you! If I hadn't, I would have gone to the kingsguard to report you as soon as I left you!' she argued. 'I think you can forgive me for being shocked.'

Aleks opened his mouth to respond, then closed it again. Arguing wouldn't get them anywhere.

'Thank you for knocking Shulga out with a flowerpot,' he said eventually.

She smiled, reaching to take his hands in her own. 'I suppose suggesting you take the matter to the king is a foolish idea? He certainly wouldn't let it stand if he knew the truth.'

'Because an audience with the king is so easy to arrange,' Aleks said drily. 'The corruption in the army goes against everything he stands for, everything he's worked to make this country represent. But the fact of the matter is, he's never going to find out about it. Anyone who cares to tell him would have to go through the kingsguard, and they're in on the whole secret.'

Saria sighed, leaning against his shoulder. 'You can't keep running forever, Aleks,' she pointed out. 'Sooner or later, he's going to catch you, and you won't be able to escape. He already knows where you work. What if he brings guards to Luka's?'

'I'm working on it,' he assured her, not wanting to explain why Shulga wasn't likely to get the authorities involved yet. If they arrested Aleks now, he'd never get the journal back. 'Luka has a plan.' Saria gave him a sceptical look. 'I'm serious; he's going to sort it out. Trust me, OK?'

She bit her lip, but eventually nodded. 'Just promise me you'll be safe. And don't do anything stupid.' He grinned at her, leaning in for a kiss to avoid having to answer, sliding closer to her on the bench. None of what he was planning on doing was safe, and it would definitely be considered stupid, but it was necessary to gain his freedom. For her.

18

Several days later Aleks was deep in conversation with Raina, walking from the market after picking up the groceries for Ksenia before he had to go to work. Suddenly he saw a face that made him break off mid-word and stop dead in his tracks, colour draining from his face. Wandering through the crowd several feet ahead was none other than his brother Torell, looking very much out of place as he glanced around. In his old, weathered leather coat and work trousers, he looked like a stereotypical wide-eyed country boy. Had Aleks looked like that when he'd arrived?

'Aleks, what's wrong?' Raina asked in concern.

'We need to go now –' It was too late. Just as he started heading in the opposite direction, Torell's blue eyes landed on him, widening in pleased surprise. 'Storms,' Aleks muttered under his breath, hanging his head. Torell could see Aleks had noticed him; there was no point in running now.

Torell was grinning by the time he reached them and pulled Aleks into a rib-crushing hug. 'Knew I'd find you sooner or later! The city might be big, but it's not that big!'

he cried. 'Oh, it's so good to see you! What happened to your nose?'

'What are you doing here? You should be at home with your pregnant wife,' Aleks exclaimed in annoyance. How could Torell just abandon Nadeah at a time like that? 'How did you even know I was here, anyway?'

'The others might be a little dense, but I noticed the Syvana postmark on your letters. The first one definitely came from Rensav, but every letter after that?' Aleks groaned under his breath; how could he be so stupid? Of course, there were postmarks on his letters! The redirection only worked one way.

'No one else noticed?' he checked, panic gripping him. Torell shook his head, an easy smile on his face.

'I made a habit of getting the mail first and removing your letters from the envelope before passing them on,' he replied. Aleks sighed in relief, bringing an arm around his older brother in a brief hug.

'Thank you,' he murmured. 'But that doesn't explain why you left Nadeah alone when she's as pregnant as she is.'

'Aleks, I don't mean to be rude,' Raina cut in tentatively, looking between the two men in confusion, 'but we really have to get these back to Aunt Ksenia before lunch preparation starts, and you need to get to work.' She held up the bags of groceries pointedly, and Aleks nodded.

'Oh? Who's this, then?' Torell asked curiously, the faintest of smirks tugging at his lips.

'This is my friend, Raina,' he replied, giving his brother a meaningful look at the word friend. 'She works in the inn I'm staying at – her aunt and uncle own it.'

'I believe introductions are supposed to go both ways,' Raina said.

'All right, nosy,' he teased her, earning an affronted look. 'Raina, this is my big brother Torell, who I hadn't the slightest clue was coming to visit, and should be back home with his *pregnant wife*.'

Raina frowned slightly as they began walking once more. 'And is his visit . . . a good thing?' she queried.

Aleks paused, glancing sideways at his brother. 'I'm not sure yet. I'll let you know.' Torell snorted, taking one of the bags out of Raina's grasp. 'I'm insulted, little brother. Here, allow me.'

Raina didn't protest, and Torell grinned at her. 'So how long has my brat brother been staying with your family, then?'

'About a month and a half? Give or take a few days,' Raina replied. Aleks blinked, surprised. Had he really been there so long already?

'So, taking into account the travelling time, that still gives you . . . a week, in Rensav? Possibly ten days – I know how fast Quicksilver is,' Torell calculated with a faint frown on his face. Aleks shook his head frantically at his brother, but Torell had never been good at reading non-verbal cues.

'When were you in Rensav, Aleks?' Raina asked, confused. 'You said you came straight to Syvana from Baysar.'

Torell's brow furrowed, and he gave his brother an enquiring look. 'You haven't been bragging about your stint in the army, however short it might have been?'

Aleks cursed silently, and Raina's eyes narrowed. 'Army?'

Aleks wished the ground would swallow him up, wished a snowstorm would sweep in and make everyone forget about what had happened, but the ground stayed solid and the snowfall remained pathetically minimal.

'Can we talk about this later? Back at the Compass, after work, where there aren't so many people around?' he asked sharply, eyes darting about for any glimpse of blue and black fabric. There were even more guards around than usual on market days, and if one of them happened to overhear him talking, it could spell the end for him.

'Seeing as Aunt Ksenia will have both our heads if we're not back soon, that's probably for the best,' Raina agreed, though she didn't look happy about it. 'But when you get home from Luka's, you're telling me *everything*.' Aleks winced, glaring at his brother. Why did he have to barge in when things were going so well?

'There you both are. What took you so long?' Ksenia asked when they entered the inn, only to pause when Torell slipped in behind Aleks. 'Oh. Who's your friend?'

'Ksenia, this is my older brother Torell,' Aleks introduced reluctantly. 'Torell, this is Ksenia, the lovely landlady of this establishment.' Ksenia's gaze grew inquisitive, but thankfully she did nothing but hold her hand out to Torell, allowing him to press a kiss to it. 'Now I'm afraid I need to get to work, or Luka will have my head. Tor . . .' He paused, running a hand through his hair in frustration. 'Just stay here, all right? I'll explain everything when I get home. Ksenia will take good care of you.' *And keep your mouth shut while I'm gone*, he prayed silently, hoping he didn't come back to even more confusion. Torell nodded, then turned to Ksenia with his best charming grin.

'Need any help anywhere? My wife would never forgive me if I didn't at least offer.' Aleks sighed, pulling his hat back on and squeezing Raina's shoulder as she rushed past him with a bowl of peeled potatoes.

'We can talk later, I promise,' he murmured, before turning for the door. He was already late; hopefully Luka would let him off.

They had moved up to the control room of the skyship by now, Aleks having learned to name and use every part in the engine room with his eyes closed. Luka taught him the basics first, explaining how each part differed from a regular skyship, and Aleks begged him to go further in depth; anything that might get him closer to being airborne. Still, to avoid disaster, Luka insisted that Aleks get a proper foundation on skyship mechanics and flight before he could start on the complicated stuff.

Aleks didn't dare broach the subject of flying through the Stormlands, not wanting to push his luck too early. He'd ask Luka about it again once he'd actually flown the ship and knew how difficult it was likely to be.

All too soon, Aleks was walking through the door of the Compass and hanging his coat on the hook, his eyes immediately finding his brother in the busy dinner run.

Torell was happily digging in to a bowl of thick stew, but Aleks could feel the man's storm-blue eyes watching him as he started to take orders, rushing back and forth from the bar. Anything to postpone the inevitable.

Only when the majority of orders had been taken did Ksenia force him on to a bar stool and set a plate down in front of him, reminding him that he'd hardly eaten since breakfast. 'You can go and sit with your brother if you like, but the look on your face tells me you'd rather not,' she remarked. He glanced over his shoulder at Torell.

'Is it that obvious?' he asked, and she nodded.

'He did mention you had a lot to talk about. A conversation you don't want to have, I presume?'

Aleks grimaced. 'You could say that.'

Ksenia nodded in understanding. 'Well, you're welcome to take him up to your room if you want the privacy.'

'No, he's not,' Raina interrupted on her way past. 'Because I want to hear what's going on, and I'm not allowed in his room.' Aleks winced at the look on Ksenia's face after her niece's words.

'That much to talk about, hmm?' she said, giving Aleks a pointed look that made him want to both hide and spill all his secrets to the woman.

'I haven't been entirely truthful with you,' he admitted reluctantly. 'Or Torell. I wasn't expecting him to notice, or call me out on it, if I'm honest.'

'Then I assume you won't mind if Bodan and I are part of this conversation too? Just to clarify things.'

He could hardly say no; she was well within her rights to toss him out on his ear for the potential danger he'd brought to her family. He looked up when Raina slid a bowl of steaming pear pudding next to his dinner plate.

'You ladies do spoil me,' he mused, and the girl gave him a look.

'Don't make us regret it.' With that, she slipped away to continue serving, and Aleks settled down to his meal, savouring the hot food and trying to figure out how he would explain things. He liked to think that Bodan and Ksenia wouldn't judge him for being a deserter, and wouldn't report him to the authorities, but . . . he couldn't count on anything. Why had Torell opened his big mouth in front of Raina?

Before Aleks could blink, dinner was over and the pub was near empty once more. There were two men still drinking in the corner by the fireplace, but after a few kind words from Ksenia they happily picked up their coats and left, staggering slightly on their way out. With just the five of them in the room, Aleks shrunk under the expectant gazes of his companions. 'I suppose I should start from the beginning, shouldn't I?'

'You can start by telling me why our family are under the impression that you're training in the military down in Rensav,' Torell retorted. Bodan whipped round to look at Aleks.

'The military? Storms, lad. Bu–' He paused, considering. 'You're far too young to have served your four years.'

'Four years?' Torell asked, perplexed. 'He was only down there a week before the postmarks changed.'

'Can I explain?' Aleks cut in. Four faces turned to him. 'I did go to Rensav, at first,' he admitted, keeping his voice quiet and his eyes on the door, knee bouncing anxiously. 'The way I saw it, the army was my way of standing out rather than being compared unfavourably to you lot,' he said to Torell, who flinched at his blunt wording.

'No one was comparing you to us,' he argued weakly, but Aleks knew that was a lie. He'd had people say it to his face almost every day of his childhood, never mind what might have been said about him when he wasn't around.

'We both know they were,' he replied gently, trying to get across that he didn't blame Torell for it. Turning back to the room at large, he sipped at his tankard of water. 'So I enlisted. Mounted infantry, so they'd let me keep Quicksilver with me. Only when I got in, it was nothing like I'd expected it to be.'

He glossed over a lot of the details of his week in cadet training, saying just enough to express how horrible it had been. 'I had a bit of a . . . disagreement with my commander, when I asked him to let me pay my fee and he refused, deciding to have his lieutenant beat it into me that I was stuck there. So I grabbed my horse and I rode as fast as I could. Like Bodan said, I haven't done my four years, and there was no way they'd let me go before then.'

Quite proud of his escape, he went into more detail, and even Raina was on the edge of her seat as he described sneaking Quicksilver out of the stables and making a break for it through the woods. And, well, if he exaggerated a little, who had to know?

'After that, I just rode North as fast as I could,' he admitted. 'I didn't know if they'd be searching for me, or even if they'd care, but I knew I couldn't risk being dragged back there. I went straight to the tunnels, then came up here as soon as I could.'

'I can understand all that,' Torell said, 'but why did you keep writing to us as if you were in the army? We're hardly likely to turn you in, are we?'

'I'd been here for almost a week when your first letter came,' he told his older brother. 'Ma and Da just sounded so *proud* that I'd enlisted, that I'd finally "become a man," as Da put it. And you and the others were just so surprised that I'd done it, I couldn't let you down and admit I hadn't been able to handle it. And I knew if I *did* admit it, Ma would insist I come home and work in the shop. I could hardly tell her how they treated me there. She'd never let me leave the house again!'

'You could never let us down,' Torell insisted gruffly, meeting Aleks's eyes. 'By the sound of it, none of us would've been able to handle it in there. Gods, how do they get away with it?'

'Most who go in at cadet level in Rensav are orphans, criminals, runaways; people with nowhere else to go. Those who actually want to get anywhere in the army pay enlistment fees to get proper training in Pervaya,' Aleks said grimly. 'At least, that's how it's supposed to be. They've become a little . . . lax. But it keeps criminals out of society and people off the streets, so no one's going to complain.' He turned to Bodan and Ksenia. Raina had been awfully quiet since he'd started describing his treatment at the army base, and he wished she hadn't insisted on hearing the full story. 'I'm sorry for deceiving you all,' he said honestly. 'And I'll completely understand if you want me to pack my things and leave – I won't ask you to harbour a criminal.'

'Don't be daft, lad,' Ksenia said immediately, shaking her head at him. 'There's no reason for you to be going anywhere. Storms, boy, they're probably not even looking for you. One cadet is nothing down in Rensav. They'll likely just assume you tried to escape and got eaten by bears or something.'

Aleks clenched his jaw; he wouldn't tell them about Shulga. He didn't want them to worry; he could handle it.

'She has a point, lad,' Bodan agreed. 'And besides, where else can I get a kitchen boy for free around here? Bloody everyone wants payment these days.'

Aleks laughed, smiling widely at the pair. 'Then thank you, very much,' he said sincerely.

'What do you want me to tell the family?' Torell asked, shuffling his chair a little closer to Aleks. 'I said from the start that I was coming to visit you. They assumed I was heading South, but I knew I'd find you in Syvana. I can . . . I can tell them I went to Rensav, if you like. Make up something about how I spent a little time with you there, but you were busy with training. Or I can tell them the truth, and you can stop getting your mail redirected.'

'I think I'd best go and sort the horses for the night,' Bodan declared, getting to his feet.

'Raina, dear, come and help me with the washing-up,' Ksenia urged, nudging her niece to her feet. Aleks hid a smile; they weren't very discreet in their efforts to give Torell and him some privacy, but he appreciated it all the same.

'Do you honestly think they wouldn't make you come back and drag me home if you told them the truth?' Aleks asked Torell. 'They'll think I can't take care of myself.'

167

'I'm of half a mind to bring you back with me right now,' Torell admitted. 'Gods, Aleks, what were you thinking?'

Aleks winced; that was exactly the reaction he'd been dreading. Stupid little Aleks, letting the family down, as per usual. Always making mistakes, unlike his perfect brothers. 'I'm not going home,' he said. 'I'm happy here, even after the rocky start. I've got a job, a life –'

'A broken nose,' Torell cut in, eyes on the bruising. 'You're not exactly reassuring me here, kid.' Bristling at the moniker, Aleks gave his brother a glare.

'It's nothing to worry about. And it's none of your business.' If his older brother forced him home, Aleks would never get to fly a skyship. On top of that, Shulga would follow eventually, and he didn't want that man anywhere near his family. 'I mean it, Tor, if you're going to try and bring me home, you can leave.'

Torell stared at him, eyes unreadable. Finally, he sighed. 'You have grown up, haven't you? Never thought I'd see the day.' Aleks blinked, unexpectedly pleased by the comment. 'I can't force you to do anything. You're an adult, free to make your own decisions. As for what to tell the family . . . I'm sure once I tell them you've got a steady job and a decent place to live they'll be fine with the situation. Honestly, little brother, I think they'll be much happier knowing you're here than they will be thinking you're a cadet. As proud as Da sounded in his letter, he's worried about you. We all are.'

'Didn't think I could cut it, did you?' Aleks asked.

'Well, no,' Torell admitted. 'But to be fair, we were sort of right.' Aleks grinned; he couldn't really argue there. 'Don't worry about their reactions, I'll handle it.'

His words strengthened Aleks's resolve to stay quiet about Shulga; Torell didn't need to know. 'I really am happy here, Tor. Though, of course, I miss all of you.'

'We miss you too, though I do envy you being here. Little Daniil doesn't stop crying, I swear to the Goddess. But listen, maybe if I go home and tell everyone the truth, you'll be able to write us letters with some substance to them rather than just a page of lies?'

Aleks shifted uncomfortably in his seat, then nodded. 'You can tell them the truth,' he relented. 'Or . . . I could write a letter for you to take back with you, explaining things. How long are you staying, anyway?'

'Only another day or two. I'm cutting it a little close as it is, with the baby,' Torell admitted, excitement clear on his face.

'Then why in the name of the gods are you here, man? You know damn well Nadeah will murder you if you miss the arrival of your firstborn!' Aleks exclaimed.

Torell gave him a look that told him he was missing the point. 'You're my brother,' he said simply. Aleks smiled, getting to his feet in order to lean over and hug the older man, feeling arms automatically wind around him in turn.

'Thank you,' he murmured softly into his brother's neck. 'I *am* glad to see you, you know. I don't think I've said so yet.'

Torell squeezed him tighter, dropping a kiss on his younger brother's head.

'I know, brat. I'm glad to see you too.' He pulled away, clearing his throat. 'Anyway, I'd best be off – I need to find lodgings for the night. The last place I was at cost a fortune.'

'Don't be daft, you can stay here. We've got a spare room,' Aleks insisted, jumping to his feet. 'Come on, I'll show you around.'

Torell didn't put up much of a protest, allowing Aleks to lead him towards the stairs, room key in hand. Aleks's lips curved as he failed to fight a smile; it was good to see his brother again, despite everything.

'Now, while you were at work I was chatting to Raina. What's this I hear about a lady friend?' Torell wiggled his eyebrows suggestively, and Aleks groaned. Maybe he hadn't missed him quite so much.

19

Before Aleks knew it, another three weeks had passed in a snow-filled blur, and the city was rife with rumours of the king calling for grounding any day soon, banning all non-emergency skyships from flight.

Torell had only stayed two more days in Syvana. Aleks had persuaded him to take Quicksilver back with him, since he'd walked all the way to Syvana. It wasn't fair to keep the horse stabled constantly, and with his potential adventure to the Stormlands ahead, Aleks wanted to know Quicksilver was safe at home.

A week and a half after Torell left, Aleks received a letter from his family. It was a whole two pages long, and made a lump rise in his throat upon reading.

It was obvious from Nadeah's section of the letter that having Torell there to explain in person had helped far more than Aleks's letter had. He'd have to thank his brother in his next letter; his visit had been just what he'd needed, in more ways than one. It sounded like Torell had returned home just in time too – Nadeah's section also told him of the little girl she'd given birth to, Talya Casmir Vasin, and it made Aleks more homesick than he'd been in a long time. Up until Torell's visit, he'd been far too distracted by his new life to really think about what was going on back home.

Aleks and Saria were practically inseparable during their free time now, usually in whichever quiet courtyard or corner of the city library they could find, talking softly and exchanging kisses, blushing beet-red whenever they were inevitably caught by some unsuspecting member of the public. Sometimes they went to the Compass for dinner, Saria getting on well with his little found family there, but she wasn't allowed in his room, and Aleks was always very aware of the eyes on him when he brought her over; there was definitely no privacy.

Saria occasionally made an offer for Aleks to come over to her house, since it was getting so cold out, but the prospect of being properly introduced to Saria's father after their last meeting terrified him. He couldn't avoid the meeting forever, though.

And so one day he found himself outside Saria's house, wearing a tie for the first time since Torell's wedding. Hesitating for only a few moments before approaching the door and ringing the bell, his back straightened on instinct when Saria's father opened the door, and Aleks plastered what he hoped was a smile on his face. It may have turned out more like a grimace.

'Aleks,' the man greeted him neutrally, holding out a hand. Aleks took it, trying not to wince at the strong grip.

'I, uh, brought you this, sir,' he said hastily, holding out the bottle of mead that Raina had insisted he bring. 'For your table.' Saria's father nodded sharply in approval, stepping aside to allow Aleks entry.

'Come in, you're letting the cold in,' he urged. The house was warm and welcoming, with paintings of landscapes and cityscapes decorating the walls. Some of them Aleks recognised, because he'd seen them in books, but others were unfamiliar to him.

'You have a beautiful home, sir,' he said, taking his hat off and stuffing it in his coat pocket along with his gloves, hoping his hair wasn't completely terrible.

'Call me Evgeny,' Saria's father replied.

'Of course, Evgeny, sir.' The man chuckled quietly, rolling his eyes at the formal address, and Aleks hid a grin; maybe this meal wouldn't be as terrifying as he'd expected it to be.

'Come,' Evgeny directed, gesturing to a door off to the side of the hallway. 'The ladies are waiting.' Aleks followed him into a cosy living room, a fire crackling pleasantly in the hearth. A grin tugged at his lips when he saw Saria sitting on the sofa, and he automatically took a step towards her.

'Don't be rude, boy!' The voice stopped him in his tracks. He turned, spotting a thin, dark-haired woman with a face like a hawk, sitting in a stiff-backed armchair and eyeing him distastefully. 'Where are your manners?'

'My sister, Anastasia,' Evgeny supplied, and Aleks tensed; this was Saria's infamous aunt, then. He hadn't known she'd be present this evening.

'My apologies, ma'am,' he murmured, offering a short bow to the woman. Her lips curled, but it was nowhere near a smile, and she offered him her hand. He obligingly kissed the back of it, mentally running through all the social etiquette lessons his mother had given him, wondering if

173

there was anything else he was meant to do. What if the rules were different in the North? From what Saria had told him, her aunt placed a lot of importance on manners and tradition. 'It's a pleasure to meet you.'

Anastasia huffed, her grey eyes wary as she looked him up and down before turning to her niece. 'Is this really the best you could do, dear?' she asked sceptically. Aleks felt embarrassment squirm in his stomach as Saria flushed red in indignation.

'Aunt Ana!' she hissed, glaring at her aunt. 'Aleks is a lovely man with a good job, and he cares about me! It's not about doing better, it's about wanting *him*.' She glanced up at Aleks, smiling tentatively at him, and he returned the look with a faint grin.

'Why don't we take this into the dining room?' Evgeny suggested, his deep voice ringing out over the tense room, settling any potential argument that may have erupted.

'Oh, I suppose so – no need to let dinner get cold,' Anastasia agreed, getting to her feet. Saria stood, her hand slipping into Aleks's as she darted to his side, leaning up to kiss his cheek.

'I'm sorry about Aunt Ana,' she murmured in his ear, a frown on her face. 'She wasn't best pleased when I turned down lunch with a businessman's son because of you. I think she's determined not to like you, so don't let her bother you.' Aleks made a face, but didn't say anything, merely twining his arm with Saria's and following Evgeny and Anastasia into the dining room. The table was already set, and Aleks waited until the two adults were seated before taking a chair, Saria heading away to what he assumed was the kitchen.

'So, Aleks, was it? That's not a proper name,' Anastasia remarked, raising a thin eyebrow at him.

'It's short for Aleksandr, ma'am. But I have three older brothers, so for Ma to yell for all of us, she had to shorten a few names,' he joked.

'Three older brothers?' Anastasia muttered. 'Storms, the girl couldn't even pick an heir.' Aleks bristled, but didn't say anything; he had to get through this dinner, for Saria's sake. 'And where are you from, Aleksandr?'

'Baysar, out West,' he answered promptly. 'You might not have heard of it, it's only a little village.' He took a small amount of pleasure at the contortions Anastasia's face made at the revelation that he was a country boy. Things could only go downhill from here.

Saria returned with the meal, and Aleks grinned at her. 'It smells delicious,' he said, smile widening when she flushed prettily.

'Thank you.' She served her father first, he being the head of the family, then Aleks, then Anastasia, and finally herself, sitting down beside Aleks once everyone had their food. After Evgeny poured the mead his guest had brought, Anastasia took the bottle from him, reading the label carefully.

'Where did you say this was from, Aleksandr?' she asked.

'I didn't, but it's from the Brass Compass, the inn I'm staying at. The landlord makes his own mead and cider, and they were gracious enough to allow me to bring a bottle for you,' he explained, feeling a small rush of amusement at the way she turned her nose up at the bottle, setting it back down on the table.

'Saria, dear, the boy doesn't even have a house. Have you really thought about what you're getting yourself into?' the woman asked her niece, who smiled sweetly.

'Yes, Aunt Ana. It doesn't bother me in the slightest. Aleks is saving up, and the landlord and his family are lovely people. Shall we begin, Father?' Saria said with a smile, and Evgeny nodded, picking up his cutlery.

As they ate, Aleks was all too aware of Anastasia's gaze on him, making him feel like a field mouse hiding from a bird of prey.

'How is old Luka, Aleks?' Evgeny asked pleasantly, and Aleks swallowed his mouthful before answering.

'He's doing well. Getting a little shaky, though he'd be the last to admit it. I think it's just the season – the cold gets to everyone, you know.'

Evgeny nodded. 'He's lasted harsher winters than this – I'm sure he'll be perfectly fine. Is he teaching you well?'

'Yes, sir,' Aleks replied brightly, smiling. 'It's all so interesting, and he's taking me out with him to the shipyard every now and then to help fit parts.' He figured he'd stick to the story he'd been telling Saria.

'You work for Luka?' Anastasia cut in, making dainty squares of her parsnips before eating them. 'The batty old mechanic who works out of the run-down shop on Cinova?'

'It's hardly run-down,' Aleks protested as politely as he could. 'It just needed a bit of cleaning, which I took care of. It's looking great now.'

'He cleans? That's a refreshing trait in a man your age,' Evgeny joked, the small half-smile on his lips assuring Aleks he approved.

'He cooks too,' Saria piped up, giving Aleks a grin. 'Wonderfully, I might add. And doesn't shy away from washing the dishes after.'

'Honestly, dear, if you wanted someone to do all that you'd get a maid, not a husband,' Anastasia said with a shake of her head.

'I think it's admirable,' Evgeny said, giving his sister a warning look. She huffed, falling silent, though it didn't last long.

'Aleksandr, what are your prospects? Presumably you don't intend to be the old man's dogsbody forever,' she questioned.

'After a year, Luka will sign off on my certificate of trade,' Aleks replied. 'Then I suppose I'll set up a shop of my own.'

'Hmm, I suppose that's a good enough profession,' Anastasia relented, lips pursed. There was a somewhat awkward silence while they all ate, and Aleks tried not to make direct eye contact with Anastasia, not wanting to prompt any more questions from her.

'Saria, dear, you're slouching, it's unattractive,' Anastasia scolded, and Aleks glanced sideways; Saria didn't seem to be slouching to him. Still, she obediently straightened her back, looking uncomfortable as she did so. 'I keep saying this new trend of letting corsets looser is only going to breed poor posture in girls. Tight corsets never hurt anyone, and there's no reason to stop it now!'

'Actually, there have been several instances, all over Tellus, of too tight corsets causing women to faint because they're unable to breathe,' Aleks said, knowing he was antagonising her but not caring, not when she was being rude to Saria.

'A few even died because their corsets were so tight that they crushed their ribs.' Anastasia's eyes were cold as they met his, and he tried not to flinch.

'Yes, well. Clearly they didn't have them on properly,' she sneered. 'If you tighten a corset properly, it won't do anything but fix posture and minimise the waist. Something you could also benefit from, dear,' she added to Saria, casting an appraising glance over her niece.

'I think Saria looks lovely as she is,' Aleks told the woman boldly. 'Her waist is just fine.'

'Well, if you're the type to settle for "fine", I suppose that says everything,' Anastasia retorted without missing a beat.

'So, what do your brothers do, Aleks?' Evgeny cut in loudly, glaring at his sister.

'My eldest brother, Maxim, is all set to take over the family shop once Da retires. He and his wife have just had a son,' said Aleks, glad to be back on solid conversational ground. He doubted Anastasia could find much fault with his brothers; no one ever could. 'The second eldest, Torell, is studying to become a teacher, and his wife just gave birth to a little girl a few weeks ago. Grigori is closest to me in age, and he's a Man of Faith. I think he's hoping to become minister of our temple one day – our current minister is rather elderly.'

'At least the rest of your family seem to be respectable members of society. Even if they are *Westerners.*' Anastasia spat the word as if it were a curse.

'Oh, hush, Ana,' Evgeny soothed. 'We have Western blood in us, you know we do.' Anastasia coloured, glaring at her brother, and Aleks hid a grin.

Conversation paused once more when Saria got up to take the plates, bringing out sweet-smelling apple cake as dessert. Aleks and Evgeny both complimented her cooking, though, of course, Anastasia complained it was too dry, just to be contrary. Aleks wondered how Saria could always be so cheerful when discussing her aunt with him, since clearly the woman was a hag.

Still, he managed to get through dessert without insulting the woman or making a fool of himself – he thought – and when they had finished eating they moved back into the living room, Saria pouring coffee for everyone. She sat on the sofa beside Aleks, and he gently pressed his knee against hers, giving her an encouraging smile. She had an apologetic look on her face, but he shook his head a fraction; Anastasia's attitude was hardly her fault.

'It's getting late,' Anastasia declared, looking at the clock on the wall. 'I think I should be retiring for the night. Saria, we shall be having a discussion in the morning about your . . . choices. After all, you know how much my approval *costs*.' Saria winced at the emphasis on the last word.

'I think you place more worth on your opinion than I do, Aunt Ana. Money isn't everything, and I'd much rather be poor and happy than have all the money in the world but be stuck married to a man I don't love,' she said stubbornly.

Anastasia huffed. 'That's because you're young and don't know any better. But if that's how you feel about the matter, then all I can say is be careful what you wish for, my dear.'

She got to her feet, and Evgeny stood with her, kissing her cheek.

'Goodnight, sister. Sleep well,' he murmured. Anastasia moved to give Saria a kiss goodnight, then stopped in front of Aleks. He wondered if he should stand, then figured that by this point very little he could do was likely to raise her opinion of him. Still, he kissed the back of her hand when she offered it.

'It was lovely to meet you, ma'am,' he said politely, the words sounding false even to him. Her lips curled in distaste, and she took her hand back quickly.

'Indeed,' she drawled in reply, giving Saria a pointed look before leaving. Aleks held his breath while he heard footsteps go up the stairs, releasing it in a sigh when a door banged loudly.

'Well. Your aunt is definitely . . . spirited,' he declared, turning to Saria, who let out a giggle.

'I'm so sorry, Aleks. I really wasn't expecting her to be quite so rude,' she began, but he cut her off with a shake of his head.

'It's fine,' he insisted. 'It was nothing I haven't heard before, I assure you. Though if I might ask, what was all that about just now? The "be careful what you wish for" thing?'

Saria glanced at her father, who frowned at the reminder of his sister's words.

'As the elder sibling, Anastasia is in charge of the family estate, which is . . . not a small amount of money,' Evgeny said.

'She keeps threatening to cut me off,' Saria grumbled. 'Says that if I must disrespect my family by marrying below my status, I don't deserve the money. Basically, if I don't marry one of the men she picks out for me before I turn twenty, I'm on my own. There's only so much Da can do when she controls his money as well.'

Aleks was unsure how to respond. He couldn't ask Saria to do that for him. Even if she didn't want to marry him yet – or at all – her twentieth birthday wasn't far off, and she'd have to make the decision soon. Saria caught his conflicted expression and leaned in to kiss his cheek. 'Don't worry about it,' she urged. 'Like I told her, I don't want her money if it comes at the cost of my own happiness. And I suspect she's all talk, truly. I can't see her actually denying me my inheritance.'

'If you say so,' Aleks said doubtfully. Saria didn't look too confident about her own words, and Aleks doubled his resolve to win Anastasia over. She could make or break his relationship with Saria, regardless of how much Saria pretended not to care about her opinion.

'Still, we must apologise,' Evgeny said. 'My sister isn't usually so open with her opinions. We expected her to be less than pleased with you, given the . . . high hopes she had for Saria's marriage prospects. But she's ordinarily much better at curbing her tongue.'

'Honestly, it didn't bother me,' Aleks lied easily. 'She's just looking out for Saria, I can understand that.'

Saria scoffed. 'There's looking out for me and then there's being downright rude. And that was definitely rude. She wasn't even meant to be here. I specifically chose tonight because she usually has dinner with her prayer group on Thursdays. But apparently this week's host has come down with the flu, so it was cancelled.'

'Well, I was bound to meet her eventually, wasn't I?' Aleks reasoned, shrugging. 'At least now I've got it over and done with. And I'm sure she'll run out of things to disapprove of in the end.'

'Oh, I wouldn't be so sure,' Saria replied with a giggle. She lifted his arm, tucking it around her shoulders, and he let himself relax when Evgeny didn't even blink. He pressed a kiss to Saria's hair, smiling.

'It really wasn't that bad,' he said softly.

'Either way, I don't want her behaviour to reflect poorly on my family,' Evgeny said, draining the last of his coffee. 'And I assure you, you're welcome here whenever you wish.'

'Thank you,' Aleks murmured earnestly, bringing a smile to the tall man's lips. 'I think I should be going, before it's too cold to venture outside.' A glance out of the window showed the snow was falling thick and fast.

'Yes, of course. Wouldn't want you freezing to death before you get home,' Saria said teasingly, seemingly bolstered by her father's words. 'Come on, I'll walk you out.' They both stood, and Aleks moved to shake Evgeny's hand.

'Thank you for inviting me into your home, sir, and for the lovely meal.'

'You are very much welcome, lad. Have a safe journey home.' Aleks bowed quickly to the man, then followed Saria out of the room into the hallway, grabbing his coat off the rack.

'Storms, I'm so sorry,' she murmured, but he cut her off with a kiss.

'I told you, it's fine,' he whispered, cupping her cheek. 'I promise. Your aunt hates me, I can deal with that.' He grinned at her, winking roguishly. 'I'm sure in time she'll learn to love me.' Saria giggled, shaking her head in amusement, and he pulled away to shrug his coat on. 'And because I haven't said it yet, you look beautiful,' he added honestly, resting his hands on her waist.

'Thank you. I must say, I approve of the tie. Very dapper,' she replied, fingers brushing over the silk knot at his throat. His cheeks burned.

'I didn't want to look underdressed.' Saria's grin widened, and as she pulled open the front door she leaned in, kissing him. 'Goodnight, Aleks. I'll see you tomorrow.' She curtseyed, and he bowed, throwing her a jaunty salute as he stepped out into the freezing night.

'I look forward to it.' He turned away, jogging down the road.

He was brushing inches of snow off his shoulders and head when he stopped in front of the door of the Compass, kicking his ice-caked boots against the wall before entering, goosebumps rising at the sudden change from cold to warm. He shut the door quickly to keep the heat in, tugging off his hat and pulling at the tie around his neck, groaning when it only got tighter. 'Oh, come here, you hopeless sod,' Ksenia muttered, edging around a table full of young men and women to reach out and undo his tie for him, getting the top button of his shirt too. 'You'd better get used to them, if you're going to be hanging around with that lass of yours. How did it go, anyway?' She wrapped an arm around his shoulders, bringing him over to the bar as Raina appeared from the kitchen, an expectant look on her face.

'Well, Evgeny – Saria's father – is actually a gentle giant. Looks terrifying, but is very pleasant to talk to,' he said, hopping up on to a bar stool.

'That's good, then? He gave you his blessing?' Raina pressed, shoving a mug of hot cider into his hands. He took it gratefully, keeping his gloves on while the warmth crept back into his fingers.

'Oh, yes, he seemed perfectly happy with me dating Saria.'

'And yet you don't look too happy,' Ksenia observed as Aleks sighed, resting his head on his hand.

'I'm not finished yet. Her father is great. Her aunt, on the other hand, is an absolute *harpy*.'

Aleks was excited when Luka told him he could move on to learning the flight protocols; it was one step closer to actually flying. He needn't have got his hopes up.

It turned out that flight protocols, when devised by Luka, were a long and arduous process involving checking every single piece of equipment on the ship. Twice. And then several more times, without instruction, to see if Aleks had it in his head. One missed item on Luka's mental checklist resulted in him having to go back and start the entire process again.

Still, as painful as it was to keep going over the same checks until he was sure his brain had melted, Aleks was confident by the end of the weekend that he could happily prepare the ship for flight in his sleep. Luka clapped him on the back as he hopped off the end of the ladder on Sunday evening, grinning. 'Keep going like this, lad, and you'll be taking her out by the end of next week.'

'Really? That soon? I can't wait!' Aleks replied eagerly, making Luka laugh.

'Yeah, yeah, don't get too excited now. Taking her out for half an hour doesn't mean you'll be off adventuring any time soon,' the white-haired man pointed out, nudging Aleks's shoulder. Still, things in the warehouse seemed to have more of a sense of urgency to them; despite Luka not yet having set a departure date – nor, technically, agreed to the trip in the first place – Aleks felt now more than ever like a clock was ticking and his days were numbered. It was both exhilarating and terrifying when he thought about it too hard.

Unfortunately, due to Aleks's productivity in the work shop before he'd been shown the skyship, Luka's business had actually started to get customers and couldn't be left alone for days on end. Luka spoke as if it were absurd for people to want to buy things in a shop, but Aleks didn't mind spending the odd day there, especially when he got a percentage of the sales for his trouble. He spent the time catching up on finishing some of Luka's abandoned projects, happily keeping himself occupied in his little corner. He'd stopped working in the basement after Shulga's visit, always wanting a view of the door, just in case.

As he worked he let himself daydream, imagining what it would be like to fly through the Stormlands. It wouldn't be easy, he knew that much – his daydreams didn't include the possibility of crashing to a cold, watery death – but he was certain there had to be something amazing on the other side. A whole country, maybe: flatlands, unlike Siberene's mountains; probably not hot like Mericus or

185

Kasem, but perhaps with warm seasons, like Erova. There might even be animals the likes of which no one had ever seen before. With no one to hunt them, or force them into captivity and regulate breeding, the wildlife there would probably be fantastic and extraordinary.

A grin tugged at his lips as he cracked the casing on a half-finished video recorder; he'd had the idea to finish making it, as well as some audio recorders, for when Luka eventually relented and let him fly through the Stormlands. He'd need to document his adventure, after all.

20

Before Luka even said anything, Aleks could tell the day had arrived. The old man was almost vibrating with energy, foot tapping impatiently as they rode the tram, and almost running towards the warehouse once they got off.

'How you feeling, lad?' he asked as he unlocked the warehouse door, glancing over his shoulder.

'Pretty good,' Aleks responded with a grin. 'Well-rested, well-fed. Weather's good today.' Luka nodded, humming under his breath.

'It is, isn't it?' he agreed. 'I think it's about time we let this bird stretch her wings.'

'Really?' Aleks asked hopefully, excitement flooding his veins. The elderly mechanic nodded again.

'It's a good day for it, and you'll need the practice. We won't take her out long, mind, just a couple of hours. Long enough to give you a feel of being in the air,' he added, warning him not to get too eager. Aleks grinned anyway. Helping with the rig that would allow them to get the ship out of the warehouse and on to the flight deck Luka had built at the back, where the land started to dip down towards the cliffs. It took a lot to move the heavy vehicle, but the rig worked perfectly, and within no time Aleks was hoisting himself up on to the ship's deck, feeling the wind buffet him into the railing. They hurried below deck quickly, and Aleks turned towards the control room, frowning when Luka turned in the opposite direction.

'Aren't you coming?' he asked. The man gave Aleks the look that told him he was being an idiot.

'If you want to get this ship off the ground, you'll need me down in the engine room.' Aleks went chalk-white; he was going to be alone in the control room for his first flight?

'Of course you're right. Go to the engine room, I'll turn on the speakers,' he said, squaring his shoulders. He'd been through the process a hundred times; he didn't need Luka holding his hand. Besides, he would still be able to instruct him through the speakers. Aleks slid into the seat in the control room, flicking the switch on the speakers and running over the preflight checklist in his mind. Start the furnace, raise the sail, extend the wings, tilt the wings, and wait for the updraught to catch. That was the easy part; it was gaining control of the ship once it was airborne that was going to be the challenge.

'Furnace is on and heating up quickly. Ready when you are, lad,' Luka's voice crackled through the speakers, making him jump.

'Right. Right. Raising the sail now.' Aleks reached forward, pulling the stiff lever, and wished he could see the sail spread out as it caught in the fierce wind outside. The ship rocked slightly, and Aleks knew the sail was fully raised. 'Releasing the wings.' With the pull of a different lever, there was a loud creaking sound and the wings began to stretch out. If Aleks turned, he could see the tips in the corner of the viewscreen. Another shudder ran through the body of the ship. 'Ready to tilt?'

'On your mark, boy,' Luka confirmed, practically giggling with excitement. Aleks's grin was wide as he flicked the switch that controlled the gears. Nothing could have prepared him for the lurching jolt that happened the moment the wings tilted, violently launching the ship into the air. He could hear Luka cackling down the speakers, but ignored him, reaching for the steering wheel and turning the two handles that would raise the stabilising propellers before the ship could spiral too far out of control. A whoop escaped his lips as he saw the ground below grow further and further away, his stomach churning with nerves and excitement and adrenalin as he wrestled the ship into obedience. Practising the motions on a stationary ship and actually putting them into use in reality were two vastly different things, and Aleks felt a brief moment of panic when the ship shot up, wondering if he'd be able to regain control.

He gritted his teeth, feet braced firmly on the floor, and spun the wheel as far left as he could, turning the ship away from the coastline and over the water. 'You're doing good, lad! Just get her past the coastal winds and she'll ride out steady, no problem!' Luka encouraged.

'Easier said than done!' Aleks retorted, directing the wings and propellers with one hand as he kept control of the steering wheel with the other. The fight was becoming easier, the resistance against him easing up, until eventually he was able to let the wings settle. He brought the ship round, turning just enough to look at Syvana through the viewscreen, and let out a low whistle. 'The view's beautiful from up here,' he breathed. He could hardly believe he was so far up, flying an actual skyship on his own; well, almost on his own. The city already looked so small, the people like tiny bugs as they went about their business. Compared to the few other skyships in the air around him, he was far too small to be noticed up in the clouds.

'Don't take her out too far, boy, or you'll start hitting stormwake from further West, and we don't want that on your first outing,' Luka warned. Aleks nodded, glancing over at the wall of charcoal clouds from the Stormlands way off in the distance.

'Mind if I have a bit of fun?' he asked, not waiting for a reply before jerking the wheel round sharply to the right. He heard Luka squawk down in the engine room as he was thrown off his feet, judging by the thump. 'Sorry!'

'What in the name of the gods do you think you're doing, boy?' Luka exclaimed, voice slightly strangled.

'Having a look at the Stormlands!' Aleks called back. 'Let's see how bad they really are.'

Aleks snickered as he heard Luka muttering about insane teenagers, steadying the ship as a strong updraught sent them rocketing higher into the sky. 'Bring her down if you value air in your lungs!' the elderly mechanic yelled, voice even louder through the speakers. Aleks winced, obligingly tilting the wings to send them shooting downwards, keeping to the low cloud cover. He knew that, above all else, he couldn't go anywhere near the trade ship flight paths, or they'd be caught and arrested.

It took almost two hours, Aleks getting more comfortable with the controls with every mile he flew, until finally he reached the Stormlands. Aleks felt his breath leave his lungs at the sight of them. They truly were incredible up close; endless swirls of cloud and rain lit up by flashes of lightning, wind tearing them every which way as the hurricanes jostled for space. His throat went dry – maybe they had become too powerful to fly through – but he squared his jaw and flew a little closer. He could manage it. The ship was starting to pull away from his hands, but Aleks was confident he could keep her under control, and Luka's easy chatter meant the mechanic hadn't even noticed how close they were to the Stormlands. Aleks kept at it despite the little voice in his head telling him to stop, insisting he was still on his first flight and shouldn't get too cocky.

'Storms, is that the time?' Luka exclaimed suddenly, startling Aleks into jolting the controls a fraction. 'Looks like we both got a tad carried away. Turn her around, lad, and head on home before it starts to get dark.' Aleks followed the instruction without complaint; he felt comfortable, but he definitely wanted to give it a few more flights before he tried navigating in the dark.

On the way back, Luka gave him a little more leeway when it was proven he wasn't going to crash them into the ocean, only barking instructions when Aleks came close to doing something dangerously incorrect. He surprised himself with how quickly he picked things up;

once he got the hang of it, flying was a lot like riding a horse. You had to respond and react to the slightest movements, acting on instinct. The ship reared, you reared with it; it took a nosedive, you levelled it out smoothly. And when the storm sent you bucking and flailing, all you could do was ride it out and hold on tight. It felt amazing, like he'd been waiting his whole life to get airborne. It was even better than kissing Saria; not that he'd ever say so to her, and he hoped he'd never have to choose between the two.

'About time to bring her down now, lad. It'll get darker and windier before long,' Luka warned. Aleks brought the ship around in a gentle arc, peering through the foggy sky to find their landing spot. This was going to be the hard part; landing the ship smoothly and exactly in the right place.

Spotting the warehouse, he directed the ship further downwards, bringing the propellers in and pressing the button that sent the struts of the wings splaying, enough to buffer the descent so they didn't go crashing to the ground. 'Easy does it, lad. There you go, nice and gentle,' Luka said softly, his voice reassuring in Aleks's ears as he inched the ship down, letting the sail slacken, and exhaling audibly in relief at the soft thump that signalled their landing. 'Very nice, very nice,' Luka said approvingly. Aleks laughed, the sound slightly desperate. He'd done it. He'd flown a skyship. 'Stay there, I'm coming up.' Aleks didn't think he could have got out of the seat if he'd wanted to; his legs had turned to water.

He craned his neck at the sound of footsteps, grinning back at Luka as the white-haired man approached him, beaming. 'Not bad, then,' Aleks said by way of greeting.

Luka laughed, clasping his shoulder. 'No, not bad at all,' he agreed, reaching for the levers to secure the wings away and let the sail loose. 'Though somewhat more ambitious than I'd planned for your first outing.' Luka tried to sound stern but his face gave away his delight. 'How was it for you?'

'Terrifying. Exhilarating. Bloody brilliant,' Aleks replied. Luka hoisted him to his feet with one hand under his armpit, and Aleks felt his knees wobble. 'Give me a minute and I'll be able to walk again.'

'Take your time, take your time,' Luka urged, rubbing his back gently. 'You're not feeling sick, are you?' Aleks shook his head and the mechanic nodded, looking pleased. 'Good. That's one less thing to worry about. I've lost count of the number of first-timers I've seen empty their guts on landing.'

'How often have you seen first-time pilots straight after landing?' Aleks asked with raised eyebrows, earning an odd look.

'Did I never tell you I used to be a flight instructor?' Luka asked, sounding surprised. Aleks shook his head.

'Never mentioned it.'

'Oh.' Luka frowned, then shrugged. 'Well, now you know. I learned to fly when I was younger than you are, with my da. Started training others at the flight school by the ship-yard almost as soon as I was qualified, to earn some extra money so I could save up for my own workshop.'

'Didn't you get an apprenticeship?' Aleks queried, wondering how the man was able to sell his wares if he'd never got his certificate.

'Oh, yes – at the same time I was teaching pilots. It was hardly a full-time job. There were only so many times I could send them up and watch them puke on the way back down before calling it a day,' Luka mused. 'Got your land-legs back yet?' Aleks bit his lip, testing his legs, then nodded in satisfaction when they held his weight.

The pair of them left the ship and used the rig to bring it back inside, bolting the doors tightly shut. Luka wandered over to his satchel, pulling out a thermos of tea and two chipped mugs, and filled them both, passing one to Aleks. He took it gratefully, inhaling the familiar scent. 'Sit down and drink that while you get your head on straight,' Luka ordered, nudging him on to the bench against the wall. Aleks obeyed, letting himself relax now he was on solid ground. Luka dashed over to the ship, checking the wings and sail and even undoing the bolts on the panels covering the propellers so he could check those too. 'I'll teach you how to do this next time,' he called over to Aleks. 'But for now, you'll need a rest. First flight is never easy.'

Aleks's head was spinning a little, and he was quite sure the floor wasn't meant to sway like that. He squeezed his eyes shut, setting his tea down to massage his temples, and leaned back against the wall. 'Definitely an experience, though,' he called back. 'When can I do it again?' Luka laughed, and when Aleks opened his eyes it was to see the man's rheumy brown eyes sparkling as he grinned at him, satisfied with the ship's state.

'Knew you'd enjoy it. You seem like the type to get hooked on flying,' he remarked, running a hand over the broad spine of the nearest wing before coming to join Aleks on the bench. 'Not tomorrow – weather looks terrible. See how it looks on Wednesday, hmm?'

'Wednesday sounds fine by me,' Aleks agreed. 'I want to get as much flight time in as I can before winter truly comes, to prepare myself for the Stormlands.'

'What have I told you about that, lad? Just a pipe dream – it won't happen,' Luka said. 'You felt how it was out there. You did well for your first run – you're a natural – but you barely even touched the Stormlands and they nearly flipped us.'

Aleks shook his head, fixing imploring eyes on his boss. It hadn't been that bad. Of course, Luka didn't have any sort of view of the outside world while in the engine room. He hadn't seen how far Aleks had gone. 'I was in the outer layer of the Stormlands,' he informed the mechanic, watching his jaw drop. 'And that's on my first run. Imagine how good I can be in a month or so! It's not too harsh out there, Luka, you were wrong. I can fly it.'

'You went that close? Are you mad, boy?' Luka exclaimed, grabbing Aleks by the shoulders. 'You could've killed us both!'

'I didn't, though,' Aleks said. 'I kept it safe, kept away from the worst of it. But I'm telling you, Luka, it's achievable. I'm not saying I want to go out tomorrow and fly right through, but . . . teach me with that goal in mind. We'll see how we go.'

'You can't do it on your own, lad. You'd need a crew.'

'Then we'll cross that bridge when we get there,' Aleks insisted. He looked his mentor straight in the eye. 'Please, Luka, trust me. I know you want to see what's on the other side as much as I do. You built an entire ship just to take a look. Now let me take that ship and find out!'

'This really means a lot to you, doesn't it?' Luka asked.

'I've dreamed about it since I was old enough to know what the Stormlands were,' Aleks admitted. That wasn't all of it – barely even the tip of the iceberg – but he didn't think he could adequately explain to the man how much it would mean for him to go on that journey and live to tell the tale. It was worth the risk and then some.

Luka sighed, releasing him and turning away. Aleks's shoulders slumped, sure that was the end of the conversation. But then Luka spoke. 'I'm not saying yes right away,' he started. When he turned back to meet Aleks's gaze he was smiling. 'But I'm not saying no either. Storms' sake, lad, I'd given up on all this nonsense before you came along. I'm not as young as I used to be, y'know!'

Aleks laughed, slinging an arm around the man's frail shoulders. 'Then it's a good thing I turned up when I did, isn't it!' He couldn't shake the smile from his lips as the pair of them started to lock up for the night. He would win Luka over; he would convince the mechanic to let him fly through the Stormlands. He was already halfway there.

21

Aleks was getting addicted to the feeling of flying. Once the terror subsided, of course.

After three weeks of near daily flights, going out for longer and longer each time, Aleks was confident in his abilities. He'd been through some of the smaller storm barriers, and even further in to the edge of the Stormlands, just to test himself. He hadn't died or damaged the ship in any way, and he liked to count that as a win. Luka wouldn't let him go too far in, insisting that if he went closer he might get caught in the drift and end up getting sucked in for hours, or worse.

'Careful now, lad – don't go getting too cocky,' the old mechanic said one day.

'I know, I know, I won't,' he assured him, turning the ship away from the potential updraught, however much he'd have liked to ride it further in. 'But we know I can do this, Luka. Let's be honest – if I were one of your students, back at the flight school, would I have passed my exam by now?' His frustration bled through in his tone; after all the extra time he'd spent at the warehouse – time he could've spent with Saria, who he'd barely seen all week – he just wanted to make some *progress*.

'You passed your exam three days ago. I made you take the test,' Luka told him with a snort. Aleks smiled to himself; he'd wondered what the oddly structured directions had been about. 'But you're not learning to fly a slow old trade ship from here to Erova. You're learning to do something that no one in all of Tellus has ever done before, so excuse me if I want to make sure you're prepared for it. If you lose my ship in those bloody Stormlands, I'll have to start all over again,' he grumbled. Aleks grinned to himself, hearing the hidden concern in the man's voice. He knew full well that Luka was worried about him rather than the ship.

'She's your ship, you built her, you should know she's perfectly capable of this. It's not the pilot that makes the difference, it's the ship,' he pointed out confidently, as he'd done countless times since they'd started this venture. He had no doubt that in Luka's ship, even an idiot could fly to the other side of the infamous storm barrier. Sometimes he wondered how the ship would handle with an expert pilot at the helm, and it made him somewhat jealous and proud at the same time. Proud because Luka had picked him of all people, but jealous at the prospect of how much better a real pilot would be.

'Bring her in, lad. It's starting to get frosty down here, so gods know what the outside of her looks like,' Luka ordered, breaking into his musings. Aleks muttered an affirmation, wishing he had some light to guide him; it was pitch black outside, but a lamp on an illegal skyship was practically painting a target on his head. Still, the city was bright even at the late hour, and it gave him just enough light to find the warehouse.

'Bringing her down now, Luka,' he said, gently pulling the lever to tilt the wings. By now, landing was something he could do in his sleep, but the dark made everything harder. He took it carefully, smiling to himself when the ship bumped down gently on the platform of the rig, then pulled the wings in. Letting the sail slack and making sure everything was in order, he got to his feet and left the control room, meeting Luka in the corridor.

'Nice work, lad. Getting smoother and smoother every time,' the mechanic said, patting him on the back and nudging him towards the ladder. 'I think you're ready to take her out for real.' Aleks nearly fell off the ladder, eyes widening in shock.

'What, you mean like . . . through the Stormlands?' he checked, turning as soon as he was on deck to stare incredulously at the man. Luka nodded, his expression unreadable.

'Exactly that,' he confirmed. 'You can practise all you like, but you'll never know until you try it, and it'll be good to get it over with before the blizzards set in. Unless you're having second thoughts.' His eyes darkened in concern, but Aleks shook his head.

'No, no, I said I'd do it and I will, I just . . . wasn't expecting it to be so soon,' he admitted.

'It's not going to be tomorrow, lad. You've still got to find a crew to go with you,' Luka pointed out.

Aleks looked at him in confusion. 'What? Aren't you coming with me?'

'Don't be daft, lad, of course I'm not coming. I told you when we started that I'm too old for this lark,' he replied.

Aleks frowned; he'd thought Luka would at least come along with him and work the engine room, even if he considered himself too old to fly.

'Well, where in Tellus am I going to find a crew for an illegal, possibly fatal venture?' he asked as they started checking over the outside of the ship, looking for damage as it defrosted, water dripping on to the concrete floor.

'Funny you should mention that,' Luka muttered, a knowing smirk appearing on his face. 'There's a lad about your age, may be a bit older, trained under an ex-colleague of mine about four years ago. He was a reckless idiot then, and is probably a reckless idiot now, but he was bloody good behind the wheel of a ship. This sort of thing is right up his alley, and from what I remember he has a mechanic for a brother.'

'And we can trust him?' Aleks asked cautiously. Luka nodded.

'Boy kept more secrets than a minister when I knew him, and I doubt that's changed. And the potential to make history will tempt him far more than any obligation he feels to report what we're doing,' he assured Aleks, pulling a rag from his coat pocket to buff out a scratch on the ship's hull.

'What about the brother?'

'Cut from the same cloth – don't worry.'

Aleks nodded, binding the wing carefully once more after checking the fabric for tears. 'If you say they're trust-worthy, I believe you. So where can I find them?'

'Go to the flight school and ask for Drazan. That's the younger brother, the pilot; he's more likely to be around. From what I've heard, he's doing lots of teaching in the hope of someone letting him pilot their ship long-term. Sharp lad, good instincts; should pick up the steering on this girl without too many problems if you show him the ropes.'

Aleks nodded. 'I'll go on Saturday,' he promised.

'Good, good. Shouldn't be too hard to find him. Drazan's hardly a common name.' Luka wandered over to pick up his satchel, rummaging through it for the keys to the warehouse. 'I'll start stocking up for the trip. Water, non-perishables, all that. The galley has all the basics in it, but you don't know what you'll find on the other side of the Stormlands. For all we know, there's just empty sea, so you'll need plenty of food, just in case. If you're lucky you'll find land with animals and recognisable plants.' He paused, eyeing Aleks contemplatively. 'Can you hunt, lad?'

'Luka, I grew up in the middle of nowhere out West – of course I can hunt,' Aleks retorted with a roll of his eyes, though in actual fact he was excited by the prospect of hunting in foreign lands. 'I'll need a gun, though, and some wire for traps.'

'Not a problem, not a problem. I know I've got a gun around the shop somewhere. If not, I'll whip you up one, won't take but a few hours,' Luka assured him. Aleks wondered what his life had become when he was hanging around a warehouse with a man who could build a gun in only a few hours. His parents would kill him if they knew.

The pair parted at the tram station in the city centre, Luka heading back to the workshop and Aleks to the Compass.

'Where have you been, then?' Bodan asked when he arrived, eyebrows raised and arms folded over his chest. Aleks frowned; had he promised to work that night?

'Out,' he replied vaguely, making the bearded man scowl.

'I can see that,' Bodan retorted, cuffing Aleks on the shoulder. 'You look half-frozen. Go on, get by the fire before you catch your death of cold.' Aleks obediently went to sit at the table by the kitchen fire, surprised when Bodan followed him.

'Oh, is our dirty stop-out finally home, then?' Ksenia asked when she walked into the kitchen with a tray of used tankards. 'It's about time.' Aleks glanced at his pocket watch, wincing when he saw how late it was.

'I'm sorry, I lost track of time,' he began.

'You seem to be making a habit of it,' cut in Bodan. 'Almost every night this week you've been back late, grinning like a madman. If I didn't know better, I'd say you were up to something.'

'Is Aleks back?' Raina called, appearing in the cellar stairway. As she caught sight of him, she frowned. 'Where have you been, then? You can't have been out with Saria – her da wouldn't let her stay out this late, especially not with a boy.' Aleks sighed, pulling off his hat to run his fingers through his hair.

'I was with Luka,' he said eventually, leaning back against the brick of the hearth, relishing its warmth. 'We've been working on a project and some of it has to be done at night.' That only seemed to make them more curious, and he bit his lip, thinking. He'd have to tell them something sooner or later – sooner, if things were going to go as fast as Luka expected – to explain his absence when he finally left.

'If I tell you, you have to promise not to tell a soul,' he started, voice completely serious. Raina slipped further into the room, shutting the door behind her to close them off to the rest of the pub.

'What's going on, Aleks?' Ksenia asked, a worried frown on her face. 'You're not in trouble, are you?'

'No, no. Well, not yet, anyway,' he added wryly. 'Luka built a skyship. Smaller, faster and better than any skyship ever invented. It's a three-person crew maximum, and he's been teaching me to fly it. We're . . . I'm going to fly it through the Stormlands to see what's on the other side.' He was grinning just at the thought of it. Bodan sighed, shaking his head.

'That man,' he muttered. 'Getting kids caught up in his crazy ideas.'

'It's not crazy!' Aleks protested. 'It was my idea to take on the Stormlands. And I'm not a kid. The ship works astonishingly well. I'm almost ready to set out in her, I just need the other two members of my crew. It might be a bit of a long shot, but if this works . . . we'll go down in history.'

'I didn't think history was something that interested you, lad,' Ksenia remarked, her lips pursed. 'What were you going to tell us, anyway? When the time came, and you had to leave?'

'I hadn't figured that out yet,' Aleks admitted. 'I wanted to tell you the truth, but then I thought . . . if I didn't come back, you might have got Luka into trouble. And at least if I'd told you I was going back home or something, you wouldn't worry about me. Wouldn't mourn me, if the worst happens.' Raina's hand flew to her mouth and Aleks regretted his choice of words.

'You daft boy,' Ksenia murmured, swatting him round the head. 'You don't think we'd worry about you even if you were heading home? I'd insist on a letter as soon as you got there, and at least one a week once you'd settled.' Aleks blinked, surprised at this.

'When are you headed out?' Bodan asked gruffly, leaning against the countertop.

'Not sure yet,' Aleks replied. 'Like I said, I need to find two other crew members, and then there's things like supplies and provisions to get ready. But I promise I'll let you know in advance.'

'Aleks . . . you could die,' Raina breathed, finally speaking. She was pale, her fingers anxiously playing with a loose thread on her dress.

'It's a risk I'm willing to take,' he declared firmly. 'If anything happens, it'll be a problem with my flying skills, not Luka's ship. I don't doubt she'll get me through the Stormlands, nimble little thing that she is. And I swear to the gods I'll do everything in my power to come back.' The girl stared at him for a long moment, before letting out a small squeak and darting across the kitchen, practically falling into his lap to hug him. He held her tightly, kissing the top of her head.

'You had better come back,' she muttered into his shoulder. 'Or I'll make you wash the dishes from now until the end of the world.' He laughed around the lump in his throat.

'I'll come back,' he assured her, hating that it felt like he was lying to her. 'I'll be back before you've even had a chance to miss me.'

'I think we should all go to bed,' Ksenia said softly a few moments later, breaking the tense silence that had settled over them. 'It's late.' Aleks gently eased Raina off his lap, squeezing her hand before letting her go, and she wiped at her cheeks, straightening up.

'Yes, you're right,' she agreed. 'Goodnight, everyone. I'll see you in the morning.' Stopping to kiss her aunt and uncle goodnight, she left the kitchen, and Aleks let out a long breath.

'I hadn't expected her to be so upset. Or anyone else, for that matter,' he admitted quietly.

'That's because you're an idiot,' Ksenia murmured fondly, making him laugh. 'Goodnight, lad. Thank you for being honest with us.'

'Goodnight,' Aleks replied, glancing over to include Bodan, who merely nodded in reply. Grabbing his hat off the table, Aleks trudged up to his bedroom and sank on to his bed. If it was that hard telling them, how hard would it be to explain it to Saria once the time came? But he still didn't regret agreeing to do it, not when he imagined reaching the other side of the Stormlands, seeing parts of the world that no one had ever seen before. He'd be mad to turn the chance down. He snorted to himself, lips curling in a half-smile. Most would probably consider him mad for doing it in the first place.

22

Saturday morning found Aleks leaving the Compass with a shopping list in his hand and a determined expression on his face, his purse weighing heavy in his pocket. He and Luka had methodically gone through everything each of them had thought would be necessary on the trip, and there were still a fair few things Aleks needed to buy. He'd figured that he might as well get his shopping done at the same time as looking for Drazan. Most of the things on his list could be found in or near the shipyard, anyway.

It was strange being near the shipyard; he hadn't been since he'd first arrived in Syvana, and while he'd been amazed then at watching the skyships take off and land, it was a whole new feeling now he'd actually experienced flying himself. He watched enviously as several trade ships rose as if they were made of air themselves and landed without even a single bump. He wished he could do it that seamlessly.

Wandering through the crowd, Aleks kept his eyes peeled for the flight school. He took a minor detour when he spotted a shop that claimed to sell everything you could ever need to fly a skyship, buying a thickly padded brown leather flight coat. It made his wallet significantly lighter, but it was warm and would hold up to the harsh weather.

It wasn't until he'd walked almost from one end of the shipyard to the other that he saw it; a building proclaiming to be the *School of Skyship Mechanics, Engineering and Ownership*.

The building's entrance hall was small, with a desk set up in one corner and a bored-looking woman sitting behind it writing in a notebook. Aleks approached the desk somewhat nervously, and the woman looked up at him. 'If you want to book lessons, I'm going to need to see a signed sponsorship form from your captain or master,' she said in a monotone voice.

'Oh, no,' Aleks replied, shaking his head. 'I'm just looking for someone, actually. His name is Drazan.' The woman pursed her thin lips.

'He's out teaching at the moment, but his session should finish in fifteen minutes or so. You're welcome to wait.' She pointed to a short row of chairs against the opposite wall. Aleks sat down, propping his ankle on his knee and leaning back. Hopefully fifteen minutes would pass quickly; he was unnerved by the silence of the room, after the noise and bustle of the shipyard outside.

Pulling his shopping list from his pocket and crossing off the items he'd bought, he jumped when someone called his name.

'Aleks! Storms, it's you!' He looked up, eyes widening when he saw a face he hadn't seen in months. 'I thought that scruffy hair looked familiar. Gods, I'm glad to see you safe and sound.'

'Zhora!' he cried, jumping to his feet. Zhora crossed the small room in a couple of strides, bundling him in a tight hug. 'Fancy meeting you here.'

The tall man barked out a laugh. 'Yes, well, didn't I tell you we'd meet again?' he pointed out cheerfully. 'You're looking well! A bit better fed than the last time I saw you.' Aleks stifled a grimace, remembering the state he'd been in after escaping the military base.

'Oh, I'm being well and truly spoiled now, I assure you,' he said. 'I'm lodging over at the Brass Compass, and the landlady there is the best cook I've ever met.'

'Oh, aye, I know the place. Bloody good cider too,' Zhora agreed. 'What brings you round this way, then? Not looking to learn to fly, are you?'

'No, I'm looking for someone,' Aleks explained. 'Man named Drazan – do you know him?'

'Know him? He's my little brother,' Zhora replied. 'What do you want that scoundrel for?' Aleks blinked in shock; did that mean Zhora was the mechanic Luka wanted in on their mission?

'I work for Luka now, the mechanic,' Aleks started, mindful of the woman behind the desk who was not so discreetly eavesdropping. 'He's got a bit of a project going that he needs a little help with, and apparently you and your brother are the men for the job. He sent me out here to find Drazan and talk to him. I had no idea you were his brother.'

Zhora's face lit up with a mischievous smile. 'Old Luka's got a project, has he? Sounds awfully mysterious,' he teased.

'Oh, trust me, it is. But it'll be right up your alley, I'm sure. I was told Drazan would be back from a lesson soon, so I was just waiting for him.'

Zhora clapped him on the shoulder. 'Might as well wait for him by the landing deck. He and I were going to head out for lunch together. You're welcome to join us, lad. We can talk over this little project in detail.' Hand on Aleks's shoulder, he led him through a door at the back of the room, into a narrow corridor and through another door, which opened out into a section of the shipyard that was clearly set aside for learner pilots. 'How've you been, anyway? It's been quite a while.'

Aleks and Zhora chatted happily, catching up on what each of them had been up to. Since work on the tunnels had finished, Zhora had come back home and started offering his services at the shipyard to anyone who needed any repairs doing, which then led to the flight school hiring him for maintenance on their ships. He was thinking over an offer to teach one of their mechanics courses, but Zhora assured Aleks that he hadn't taken any permanent position yet.

'Ah, there he is! Watch the little show-off,' Zhora said suddenly, pointing out a small merchant-size ship that was drawing ever nearer to them.

'What if it's the student behind the wheel?' Aleks asked in amusement, but Zhora shook his head.

'Nah, the kid he's taking out today is only three lessons in, so he won't let him land yet. Don't want to break anything.' Aleks smiled to himself, remembering his own first landing.

The ship descended smoothly, settling down as light as a feather on a concrete landing deck. 'OK, that's impressive,' Aleks murmured.

'Little brat's good for something,' agreed Zhora fondly. They waited for Drazan and his student to emerge from the ship, and as soon as Aleks saw him it was obvious he was Zhora's brother. He was practically the spitting image of his older sibling, with the same dark brown hair, square jaw and vibrant blue eyes. When Drazan drew closer, Aleks could see he was almost as tall as Zhora too.

'Zhora!' he called in greeting, shooing away his student with a few words. 'I thought you'd be waiting inside. Who's your friend?' He eyed Aleks curiously, and Aleks smiled back at him.

'This is Aleks, Draz,' Zhora told his brother. 'The traveller I met back in the tunnels – remember I told you about him? Turns out he's working for old Luka now, and the nutter has a project he wants the pair of us in on. Aleks here is his dutiful little messenger boy, come to tell us the details,' he teased, making Aleks scowl. Drazan smiled and held a hand out.

'Pleasure to meet you, Aleks. I hear you're quite the adventurous lad, unless my big brother's been telling tales again,' he joked.

'Depends what he's been telling you,' Aleks replied, shaking Drazan's hand firmly. Drazan was probably two or three years older than him, and at least three inches taller, but seemed friendly enough. If he was anything like his brother, Aleks was sure they'd get on.

'Well, now I'm intrigued.'

'I invited Aleks to join us for lunch,' Zhora cut in. 'Figured he could tell us more about Luka's latest madcap idea.'

'Sounds like an excellent plan,' Drazan agreed as they headed around the side of the building, through to the main shipyard. He fiddled with his flight goggles where they were draped around his neck, glancing at Aleks inquisitively. 'So what's his idea, then? Something fun, I hope.'

Aleks grinned; that depended on his definition of fun. 'Something best discussed in private, especially away from guards,' he replied.

'We'd best find somewhere to eat undisturbed, then,' Drazan said, looking excited. 'I know just the place.' He grabbed Zhora's arm, tugging him down a side street, and Aleks followed quickly. Drazan's place turned out to be a small restaurant squeezed between two shops, and they were given a table in the corner, far away from the other two people in the restaurant. Aleks glanced around suspiciously, checking their area was clear before talking.

'Luka's built a skyship,' he murmured, the two men leaning in close to hear. 'And while he's been teaching me to fly it, we need a qualified pilot and a decent mechanic for what we plan to do with it.'

'And what do you plan to do with it?' Drazan asked, eyes shining eagerly.

'Fly the Stormlands,' Aleks told him. He could say it a hundred times and it would still send shivers of excitement down his spine. 'All the way through to the other side.' Zhora swore, and Drazan let out a low, impressed whistle.

'You really think it'll work?' Zhora asked, and Aleks nodded.

'Definitely. I've flown her about as close to the Stormlands as I can get without getting taken by an updraught right into the centre, and I'm certain that with a good pilot behind her wheel she'll have no problems. You should see her go – she's incredible,' he gushed.

'She sounds amazing,' Drazan murmured.

'She is. But Luka says he's too old to make the journey, so I need two people to join me, and he assured me you two were the right men for the job.'

'By the sound of it, I'd say he's right. I'm in,' Drazan said decisively.

Aleks raised an eyebrow at him, spooning stew into his mouth.' We might not return,' he reasoned, but Drazan merely shrugged.

'Similar risks every time I take a particularly dense student up with me. I quite fancy my chances with the Stormlands.'

Aleks grinned, shaking his hand. 'Good to have you on board. Zhora?'

The older man chuckled, leaning back in his chair. 'Can't let the brat have all the fun without me, can I? Where he goes, I go,' he replied. 'When do we get to see her?'

'Tomorrow, if you like. We can take her up, get you both used to her. She flies a little differently to most ships, so I'm told. But if I picked it up within a month I'm sure you'll have no problem,' he said to Drazan, who grinned, looking excited at the challenge. 'Meet at Luka's workshop at eight; I assume you know where that is?' Both men nodded, Drazan's lips twitching.

'Oh, yeah. Nearly burned it down when I was ten,' he remarked. Zhora laughed, and Aleks blinked in astonishment.

'I don't want to know, do I?' he asked, wondering what he was getting himself into making those two his crewmates.

23

Zhora and Drazan were at Luka's around the same time as Aleks arrived, both wearing thick leather flight coats. Drazan had a pair of battered black flight goggles hanging around his neck, and he grinned brightly when he saw Aleks approaching. 'Good morning for flying,' he said by way of greeting. Aleks let them into Luka's workshop, shaking his coat a little to get the snow off before entering; Luka would make him mop the floors if he tracked snow in.

'We've got company,' he called. Leading the pair to the end of the row of shelves, he smiled to himself, seeing Luka bent over at his workbench working on the promised gun. It was looking good already, and Aleks didn't doubt it would fire like a dream when Luka was finished with it. He couldn't wait. Clearing his throat, Aleks waited for the white-haired man to look up, smiling at the mildly disgruntled expression he wore.

'Yes, what?'

'Long time no see, Luka,' Drazan announced. Luka whipped his head round, smiling when he spotted the pair of brothers.

'Oh, good, you found them,' he said to Aleks, jumping to his feet and grabbing his coat from the hook on the wall. 'Shall we get going, then? You're wasting time, lads. Get a move on. I assume Aleks has filled you in?'

'He told us about everything he could in a semi-public place,' Zhora confirmed. 'Apparently the details are best seen for ourselves.' Luka grinned, setting off down the street towards the nearest tram station.

'Yes, I don't doubt that. You're working on skyships now, aren't you? Branik mentioned they'd snapped you up at the flight school.' Zhora nodded.

'Yes, sir. They keep trying to persuade me to teach, but... I like to keep myself free for interesting opportunities,' he replied, winking at Aleks.

'Good, good. You don't want them roping you in there – they'll never let you go. Only reason they let me leave was because they thought I'd cracked.'

'I'll keep that in mind for when I want out,' Drazan joked, only for Luka to turn around and give him a pointed look.

'Don't be daft, lad. They won't fall for the same thing twice. You'll have to find your own escape route.' They waited for the tram, and bundled into the carriage with the other commuters.

'Where are we headed, anyway?' Zhora asked, voice low in Aleks's ear.

'Just outside the city limits, by the cliffs. It's a decent taking-off spot, and well-hidden,' he replied quietly.

Luka practically dragged them off the tram when they reached their stop, leading the way down the path Aleks could probably walk in his sleep by now.

'Oh, I've never been out this way before. Ma always warned us that heading out Northwest would only end in falling off cliffs,' Drazan remarked cheerily as they left the city walls, boots crunching on the icy path.

'Your Ma was a smart woman,' Luka replied. Aleks raised an eyebrow – was their mother not around any more? His silent question was confirmed by Zhora's half-smile.

'Aye, that she was,' he agreed softly. 'Is this the place, then?' The warehouse was in sight by now, and Aleks nodded.

'That's it. You wait till you see what's inside.' Luka's half-frozen fingers fumbled with the keys but he managed to unlock the door, shoving it open with his shoulder. Aleks wandered over to the light switch, flicking it so Drazan and Zhora could get a good view of the ship. He grinned to himself when he heard Drazan's gasp, turning to see matching wide-eyed expressions on the brothers' faces.

'Bloody hell, she's gorgeous,' Drazan murmured. 'When can I fly her?'

Aleks laughed, sharing an amused look with Luka. 'Help us check her over, then we'll take her out straight away,' he said, dropping his satchel by the bench and getting to work. Zhora and Drazan seemed to understand the ship's mechanics a lot quicker than he had, no doubt because of their previous experience. Luka happily bragged about his design, glad for a fresh audience who had a better idea than Aleks of the work that had gone in to creating such a machine. The two brothers were full of questions, taking in everything eagerly, and Aleks was surprised to find that he could answer a lot of their queries. Obviously Luka's nattering had sunk in more than he'd thought.

With the ship checked over and pulled out on to the deck outside, Aleks led the way up the ladder, heaving the trapdoor open and dropping below deck with ease. Giving the brothers a quick tour of the ship, which would be their home for however long the voyage took, Aleks showed Drazan to the control room while Zhora followed Luka to the engine room downstairs.

Sitting in the seat in the control room, Aleks let Drazan explore a little. He flicked on the speakers, waiting for Luka to give him the go-ahead, peering out of the viewscreen to see where the wind was heading. It looked to be a very strong Northerly wind, but not the worst he'd dealt with. 'Ready when you are, lad. Best way for them to learn is to watch,' Luka's voice called over the speakers, making Drazan jump. Aleks nodded, grinning to himself.

'Yes, sir. Sail,' he checked off aloud. 'Wings.' He extended the wings, catching Drazan's eye in his reflection in the glass screen. 'You might want to hold on to something, Drazan. This part gets a bit bumpy.' Drazan grinned, planting his feet wide and gripping the back of Aleks's seat. 'Tilting now, prepare for take-off.' With a turn of the handle he tilted the wings and the ship shot into the air like a bullet, nearly sending Drazan sprawling across the floor.

'Oh, she's feisty!' the young man crowed happily.

'She is that,' Aleks agreed. 'How are you doing, Luka?'

'Just fine, lad, just fine. Zhora here is a kid in a sweet shop. Take her as far out as you like, just keep an eye on the height.' Aleks rolled his eyes, smoothly turning the ship towards the Stormlands.

'I know, I know. Storms, man, I've done this plenty, I know how high she can go,' he muttered under his breath, making Drazan snigger.

'Luka's just worried about his baby – leave him be,' Drazan teased softly, too quiet for the speakers to pick up. 'She flies like nothing I've ever seen before, though. How does she work?' Drazan shuffled closer, perching on the arm of Aleks's seat.

'It's more instinct than anything else,' he admitted, flying daringly close to the tall columns of rain-filled cloud that had torn away from the Stormlands on their own wind currents. As much as he wanted to dive straight into one and see what would happen, he knew doing so would be a move he couldn't easily reverse. 'A ship this small, you can feel even the lightest of breezes nudging you.'

'It looks much more fun than flying a regular skyship,' Drazan murmured. He turned to the speaker's microphone, a grin on his face. 'Hey, Zhora, can we keep her?' Aleks smiled, hearing Zhora's bark of laughter in response.

'I'll be having words with Luka if we can't – she's amazing. True work of genius.'

'Oh, don't say that in front of him – his ego's big enough as it is,' Aleks mock-complained, reaching out to tilt the left wing to avoid sending them soaring into the heart of a whirlwind, feeling the steering wheel straining in his hand against the force of the storm. Edging the ship into safer skies, he turned to look at Drazan. 'Fancy a go?'

Aleks didn't need to ask twice, and the man eagerly slipped into the seat as Aleks vacated it, a look of intense concentration taking over his features as he set one hand on the steering wheel, the other over the wing controls. 'Drazan's at the helm now,' Aleks said loudly. 'So if we crash, it's not my fault.' Drazan made a whine of offence, which turned into a yelp of surprise as they were blindsided by a particularly strong gust of wind, his hand scrabbling to right them. Things were wobbly for a while as Drazan got the hang of the controls, but soon they were flying almost as smoothly as they had been with Aleks at the wheel.

'She's definitely got some life in her, hasn't she?' Drazan remarked brightly, showing off a little by winding through a series of thin storm columns.

'And then some. How does she feel?' Aleks asked, leaning on the back of the seat and swaying with the movement of the ship. 'You're good at this.'

'She makes it so easy. It's definitely different to what I'm used to, but you're right about it being mostly instinct. I wish more ships handled like this.' It was obvious how passionate about flying he was; Luka had definitely made the right choice there. 'How did you end up here, anyway? I haven't seen you around at the flight school.' Aleks shrugged, explaining how he'd stumbled into Luka's shop and everything had escalated from there.

'I've only ever had lessons from Luka,' he finished, watching as Drazan's gaze changed to a look of astonishment.

'You're not formally trained and you're that good? Storms, the old man hasn't lost his touch with newbies. But this is a big undertaking for such a green pilot. Are you sure you're up for it? You have a family . . . not like Zhora and me. You have people to miss you if you don't come back. We can find another pilot, if needed.' Aleks swallowed thickly at the reminder of what might happen, but didn't get the chance to reply.

'No, we can't,' Luka's voice snapped over the speakers, making both men jump. They'd forgotten the connection was live. 'The ship won't make it across without him, lad, even with you at the wheel. Aleks has the instinct for her – you can't train that into a pilot, especially one that's already used to regular ships. You need him. He's a big boy, he understands the decision he's made.' Aleks couldn't stop himself from grinning at Luka's words, surprised at the man's show of faith. Drazan didn't seem put out, nodding in acceptance with a smile on his face.

'I look forward to working with you, then, Captain.'

They spent hours in the air. At one point, Zhora left Luka in the engine room and came up to join his brother and friend in the control room, marvelling at the ease with which Drazan flew the ship. 'She looks a darn sight less complicated than your average skyship, I'll tell you that now,' he remarked.

'Smoother too, for such a tiny little thing,' said Drazan. 'If she had the controls of a larger ship we'd be halfway to the bottom of the ocean by now,' he mused, pulling a worryingly tight turn through the centre of a storm cloud.

As much as he wanted to stay out until the sun set, Aleks had to meet Saria for dinner, and a glance at his pocket watch told him they'd better bring her in soon or he'd be late. 'Luka, as much as I hate to say it, we need to wind this up. I've got somewhere to be, and you know what happens when I'm late.' Drazan frowned in confusion, but gently urged the ship in a slow arc, bringing her back to face Siberene.

'Have you told your girl yet, lad?' Luka queried, making Aleks wince.

'Not yet, no. I was going to do it tonight,' he admitted.

'You've got a girl?' Zhora asked, surprised. 'You didn't mention that little detail!' Aleks flushed.

'Her name's Saria,' he told his friend, unable to stop the smile that tugged at his lips at her mere name. Storms, he was done for. 'She's the daughter of the man who owns the jewellery shop in the courtyard.' Zhora smirked, reaching out to ruffle his hair.

'Aww, you look so smitten just talking about her. Do I get to meet her?'

'Storms, no, I want her to like me,' Aleks retorted easily, making Drazan laugh and send the ship dropping a good ten feet.

Trying to ignore Zhora's teasing as they descended, Aleks took the controls back from Drazan when they got close enough to land, wanting to show how to land such a small ship before allowing Drazan to attempt it himself. It wasn't as smooth as he'd seen Drazan land the day before, but it was gentle enough, and he looked up at the two brothers with a grin on his face when he stood from the seat. 'What do you think, then?'

'When can we leave?' Drazan returned instantly, making him laugh. Zhora smiled, nodding.

'I'm definitely in too. Though I'd like a few more trips out in her before I'm truly comfortable working without Luka there,' he admitted.

'That can easily be done,' Luka assured him, popping up from the trapdoor at the other end of the corridor. 'I can take both of you out any time this week; Aleks doesn't even have to be here. I might leave him to keep an eye on the shop – he's making a few things for you to take on your venture.' Aleks sighed at the prospect of being left in the shop, but knew it would be good for Drazan especially to get a chance at being the only person in the control room. Besides, he deserved to experience Luka's unique brand of teaching.

Aleks began checking the ship over, but Luka cuffed him over the head, giving him an impatient look. 'Go on, lad, go and see your girl. And good luck,' he added, meeting his gaze. 'I hope she takes it well.'

Aleks smiled wryly. 'So do I.' Heading over to pick up his satchel, he turned to Zhora and Drazan. 'I'll see you both soon.'

'See you soon, lad. Good luck,' said Zhora with a hug.

Aleks left the three of them to put the ship away for the night, heading out into the cold and jogging back to the tram station.

Nerves curling uncomfortably in his stomach the entire ride into the city centre, he tried to push them away when he got to the courtyard, seeing Saria waiting for him at her usual spot by the fountain.

'Hi,' he greeted her breathlessly, leaning in for a kiss.

She smiled at him, taking his gloved hand in her own.

'Hello, you. Busy day? You look terribly worn down.' Her eyes were concerned.

'I'm fine, just had a bit of a long day. I bumped into a friend of mine yesterday, though, which was unexpected.' They started off walking aimlessly, not really caring where they ended up, and Saria gave him an amused look.

'I didn't know you had any friends up North,' she remarked lightly. He grinned, shrugging as he wrapped an arm around her waist, pulling her closer.

'He was working in the tunnels when I passed through on my way here,' he explained. 'I saw him at the shipyard yesterday when on an errand for Luka. He's been working there since the tunnel work finished, apparently. It was good catching up with him – he's a great bloke.'

'That's lovely,' Saria replied, sounding happy. 'You could do with a few more friends around here. Though if he starts monopolising your time, I'll have to have words with him,' she teased.

They ended up at the winter-blooming park, though the flowers were hardly visible through the thick layer of snow; obviously no one bothered to shovel it like they did in the streets. It was the perfect place to have a conversation without being overheard. 'Listen, Saria,' Aleks started, coming to an immediate halt. She eyed him curiously, but when he tried to open his mouth again it felt like his throat was made of sandpaper.

'Is everything all right?' she queried, brow furrowing in concern. Taking a deep breath, Aleks squared his shoulders. It was like pulling out a splinter; best done quickly and in one go.

'Saria –'

'I knew I'd find you again eventually.' The unexpected voice cut him off and Aleks froze in horror. Crossing the small bridge over the nearby stream was Shulga, looking no worse for wear after their last encounter. He was out of uniform this time, wearing a plain black greatcoat that almost brushed the snow. He looked amused at the expression on Aleks's face. 'You didn't really think I'd just let you go, did you? Especially not after your little woman there brained me with a flowerpot.'

'Why do you care so much?' Saria asked boldly, stepping up to face him, jaw set despite the way her hands were shaking at her sides. 'Aleks is just one cadet. He's never done anything to you, or to anyone else. He's not a criminal serving a sentence, just a man that you tricked into a horrible life. Would it really kill you to let him go and get back to terrorising other people?'

Shulga laughed coldly. 'Is that what he's told you? That he's never done anything to me? Oh, sweetheart, I'm sorry to say your boy's been telling tales again.' Saria's determined expression faltered. Aleks cursed silently; surely Shulga wouldn't dare tell her about the journal. He'd incriminate himself far more than he would Aleks.

'You're lying to me,' Saria insisted, tucking a stray lock of blonde hair behind her ear. 'Aleks told me all about Rensav, and why he had to escape. He told me how much of a monster you are. If he did do anything to you, you probably deserved it.'

'Did he tell you about how he stole from the Crown on his way out?' His tone was mocking, and Aleks saw red.

'I never stole from the Crown!' he argued. 'You stole from the Crown, and I stole from you! I didn't even realise what I had until after I'd left. I was looking for my enlistment papers. I figured since I signed them under false pretences, you wouldn't mind me taking them back.' Shulga's eyes narrowed as they met Aleks's, Saria forgotten for the moment as the two men stared each other down.

'You've read it, then?' Shulga asked, not looking as panicked as Aleks had imagined he would.

'Of course I read it. You're disgusting, keeping something like that for yourself when it needs to be in an evidence locker. I bet you're just waiting for the day you can start repeating those tests on cadets.' The smirk on the lieutenant's face was all the answer Aleks needed.

'Aleks, what are you talking about? What did you steal?' Saria cut in sharply.

'Nothing important,' he insisted, which turned out to be the wrong answer.

'Clearly it is if this lunatic wants to kill you over it!'

'Lunatic? My dear, you insult me,' Shulga said, shaking his head. 'And I don't want him dead, I want him serving – it's a far worse punishment. But if dead is my only option, I'll take what I can get.' He stepped off the bridge, now only a few feet away from Aleks and Saria. 'But neither can happen until you give me back my bloody journal!'

'You're never getting it back!' Aleks roared, ducking the punch the taller man threw his way. 'The world is better off with that knowledge lost. I should throw the bloody thing into the storms.' Shulga grabbed Aleks's shoulder, wrenching him close and kneeing him in the stomach.

'You wouldn't dare,' he hissed, eyes flashing. 'You're too curious – I can see it in your eyes. You've not finished the journal yet, have you, brat? You want to know how it ends. Now tell me where it is!'

'I know how it ends, the whole world does,' Aleks spat in reply, face turning red as Shulga's grip moved to his throat. Wrestling the man off him, he kicked out, catching Shulga's thigh. 'And I won't tell you where I've put it!' Shulga growled in rage, lurching forward to try and choke Aleks a second time. 'Go ahead and kill me, but it won't get you any closer to finding it! You're not getting that journal back, and if you come after me again I'll go to the newscasts, show the whole country what you've been keeping from them. Perhaps it'll prompt the king to have a closer look at how things are run at the Rensav base, hmm?' He grinned viciously, expecting Shulga to retreat at the threat, but the lieutenant just laughed.

'Oh, you're so naive it's almost adorable.' He stepped away from Aleks, brushing off his coat. 'As tempting as it is, if I kill you now I'll never get my journal back. Just be aware that I'm watching you, Vasin, and your little girl-friend too. I'll find where you've hidden it, and when I do I'll drag your sorry arse back to Rensav. I have plans for that journal, boy, and you've been in my way for far too long now.' He glanced at Saria, gaze turning predatory. 'Maybe I'll bring her too. The boys could use a little fun at the base – half of them haven't seen a female in years.' He barked out a laugh as Aleks went chalk white. 'You'll slip up eventually, brat. Get ready to see your barracks mates again soon – I know they've missed you *ever* so much.' Spitting in Aleks's face, Shulga turned sharply and crossed back over the bridge, his footprints quickly covered by falling snow.

Rubbing at his bruised neck, Aleks turned to Saria, opening his mouth and then closing it again abruptly. She was shaking and looked about ready to faint, but her hazel eyes were full of anger. 'I don't want to know,' she snapped, arms folded over her chest. 'Whatever that journal is, whatever it is you stole from him, I'm not interested. All I know is, he wants it back, and he's *never* going to leave you alone. I just . . . I can't, Aleks, I mean it.' She began to well up, two fat tears streaking down her cold-flushed cheeks. 'I love you. But all this, just being *around* you, it's too dangerous. He'll kill us both!'

'Saria, wait, I promise, he won't find us again!' Aleks stuttered, still reeling from her words. Why was it that the first time she said she loved him was when she was trying to break up with him?

'You said that the last time, and now look!' Saria shook her head, taking one step closer and leaning up to press her lips to Aleks's. 'I'm sorry, but I can't do this. I can't live my life constantly looking over my shoulder, which is exactly what you're doing. I hope you stay safe, I really do, but I have my family to think of. Clearly you aren't thinking of yours.' She paused, choking back a sob. 'This is over, Aleks. Don't talk to me, don't come after me – I don't want to get involved in whatever gods-forsaken mess you've got yourself into.'

They were both crying by the time she finished, and Aleks reached out, grasping her shoulder. 'Wait! I can fix this, please!' he begged, but she shook him off.

'You can't fix everything, Aleks! You can't undo what you've done. You might be stuck in your situation, and I hate that you are, but I'm not. And as much as I love you, I can't stay and put myself in danger. Just let it go. Let *me* go.'

The lump in Aleks's throat was so big he couldn't speak, so he merely nodded, blinking away a fresh wave of tears. Saria was right; he'd be selfish to keep her with him when he was a dead man walking. Shulga would catch up with him eventually, and he didn't want Saria to be around when he did. This was twice now, and he doubted the next time he'd get so lucky. Shulga may have left, but Aleks didn't doubt the man was watching him still. He'd follow Aleks home, follow him everywhere, until he found out where the journal was. Aleks wouldn't be free of him until he left for the Stormlands, and he couldn't risk Saria's life like that. Part of him wanted to just give back the journal and be done with it, barter for his freedom and keep his relationship, but he couldn't do that. He couldn't live with the awful things Shulga would do with that journal on his conscience.

'Goodbye, Saria,' he managed finally, voice hoarse. She nodded, biting her lip, then turned to walk away. Aleks couldn't bear to watch her go. It was better this way, he reminded himself. After all, it was one less person to miss him if he never came back from the Stormlands.

24

Luka gave the crew a six-day deadline. Six days, and the weather would be as perfect as they could hope for, according to the forecasts. Six days before they left Syvana and Siberene altogether, potentially for the last time. Aleks spent a lot of the first day hiding in his corner of the workshop under the pretence of finishing the last audio recorder, though really he'd finished it days before. Anything to keep his mind off Saria, and Shulga, and his impending journey. It was hard to be as excited as he wanted to be when he was acutely aware of everything that could go wrong over the coming days.

By the second day, Aleks had more of a handle on himself, and he stayed at the Compass while Luka took Zhora and Drazan out in the ship, helping behind the bar and in the kitchen. He kept himself busy, and none of the three needed to ask why he'd decided to spend the whole day with them for once. Raina had hugged him tightly at the end of the day, before imperiously telling him that he was going to spend the next day in the city with her. It was a Saturday, and Saria would be with her aunt and therefore unlikely to bump into them, so Aleks had no reason to say no.

Bundled up in coats, hats and scarves, the pair of them left for the market first thing in the morning, Raina happily dragging him through the stalls, occasionally stopping to look at a pretty trinket or item of clothing. Aleks was content to go along with what she wanted to do, making sure they stuck to the back alleys and less popular roads. He'd managed to keep the lieutenant away from his new family at the Compass thus far; he only had a couple more days left.

'Do you mind if we go to the courtyard?' Aleks asked when they finally left the market, Raina's arm in his and her shopping in his satchel; he'd insisted on carrying it for her. It was a risk, but he had one last errand to do before he left.

'Not at all,' Raina agreed, giving him a knowing look. 'Stopping in to see Saria, are we?' He'd told her about the break-up, and she was insistent they'd sort it out eventually. She didn't know the real reason, however, so her optimism was flawed.

'No, she's out with her family today,' he replied, grimacing. He hadn't seen Saria since the night in the park, and quite honestly he wasn't sure if he was ready yet. 'There was something else I wanted to look at.'

The walk from the market to the courtyard was short, and as expected the open area was half packed with people by the time they got there. Most of them were clearly tourists, shivering in coats far too thin for the time of year, bright smiles on their faces despite that. Aleks led Raina through the throng of people towards a familiar shopfront. He tried to ignore his paranoia, sure he was imagining the feeling of someone's gaze on him.

'I thought you weren't going to see Saria?' Raina asked, confused, as they stepped into the jewellery shop.

'I'm not.' Aleks took off his hat upon entry, relieved to see Evgeny's apprentice standing behind the counter. He'd only guessed that Evgeny would be with his daughter. He'd never met the apprentice, and he eyed the long-limbed Kaseman teenager carefully. He looked fairly meek, his coffee-brown eyes only half raising at their entrance, his shoulders hunched anxiously.

'Welcome, sir and madam. How may I help you?' he stuttered, attempting a smile. Aleks half smiled back, edging towards a display in the corner of the room. A display that had caught his eye every time he'd been inside the shop.

'I'd like to buy an engagement ring,' Aleks declared, voice only catching slightly. Beside him, Raina gasped.

'Aleks, you can't be serious!' She whispered, eyes wide. 'You two aren't even together any more!' He shrugged, looking down at the case of rings.

'When . . . if I get back, I hope she'll have had enough time without me to maybe give me another chance,' he replied. 'And if I don't come back, then, well . . . I want her to know how I felt. Even if she doesn't return my feelings.' Aleks glanced up from the rings, giving Raina a smile that was definitely more of a grimace. 'The worst she can do is say no, right?' He knew that Saria was the girl he wanted to marry, and if he survived the whole adventure he wanted to do so as quickly as possible, if she was willing. He'd be a free man once he got home, and if he could just win her aunt over she'd have no reason to stay away. Unless her feelings had changed, of course, but he'd handle that if the

231

situation arose. If Shulga kept chasing Aleks when he returned home, Aleks could report him to the kingsguard without fear of being dragged back to Rensav. By then, Aleks's arrest warrant would have been dealt with.

Raina sighed, winding her arm around his and leaning into his shoulder. 'Oh, Aleks,' she murmured. 'Don't talk like that. You *are* coming back.' She straightened up, facing the apprentice jeweller and folding her arms over her chest. 'He wants to buy an engagement ring, he said. Are these all the ones you've got?'

The apprentice froze, looking nervous. He clearly wasn't used to serving customers by himself yet. 'Y-yes, madam. Unless sir would like a custom design.'

'I don't have time to custom order, but thank you. Raina, stop it, you're scaring him,' Aleks added offhandedly, paying closer attention to a small selection of sapphire and amethyst rings. They were Saria's favourite. He knew that traditionally engagement rings were meant to hold diamonds, but the symbol of wealth wasn't quite so prized in Siberene where diamonds came by the thousands from the mountains, and tradition was starting to make way to modernisation as other stones became more and more popular. Aleks knew Saria wouldn't want a traditional ring; she was hardly a traditional sort of woman. The fact that someone of her class was even giving him the time of day proved that.

His gaze landed on a ring that held a bright sapphire in the middle with two small amethysts on either side. The silver band crept up the sides of the stones like tendrils of vines, holding them in place. 'How much is this one?' he asked.

'Ooh, pretty,' Raina murmured in approval.

The jeweller's apprentice bit his lip. 'I . . . I shouldn't, really,' he started.

Aleks raised an eyebrow. 'Has it been reserved for someone already?' he asked. The apprentice shook his head.

'No, sir, but . . . it's the boss's daughter's favourite. I think he was always hoping, well, y'know.' The apprentice tugged at the cuff of his shirt, clearly uncomfortable. Aleks turned, catching Raina's eye as they shared matching grins.

'How much is it?' Aleks repeated, feeling somewhat sorry for the poor apprentice.

'Thirty golds, sir.'

'I'll take it.' It would clear out a good amount of his savings, but it was worth it. Besides, he thought to himself, should he not return, he'd have no use for money. 'Your boss can always make another for his daughter, should he so choose.' If things went Aleks's way, Evgeny wouldn't have to. 'However, it is, perhaps, in both our best interests if you don't mention who bought it. Just so your boss can't track me down and demand it back,' he added wryly, leaning on the counter and putting on his best friendly smile. The apprentice hesitantly returned it, nodding.

'Perhaps you're right, sir. Maybe if I don't mention it he won't notice for a while. You'll be paying in coin, then?' Aleks pulled his large money purse from his satchel, counting out the coins as the apprentice boxed up the ring for him.

'Pleasure doing business with you,' he declared once the exchange had been made. 'Now, I'd better make myself scarce before your boss comes back.'

'Thank you, sir,' the apprentice sighed in relief. 'And I hope the Goddess smiles on your upcoming proposal.'

Aleks nodded in thanks at the blessing, leaving the shop with Raina.

'Any other secret errands to run while we're out?' Raina asked, reaching to dust snow off his collar as it settled.

'No, that was the only one. Listen, Raina, I need you to do me a favour,' he said abruptly.

'Of course,' she agreed easily. 'What?' Aleks reached into his pocket, pulling out the box holding the ring.

'I want you to look after this for me,' he requested quietly. 'While I'm gone. If . . . if a month passes and I don't come back, give it to Saria. Tell her I love her, and I'm sorry, and I want her to have it.' Raina's lower lip wobbled, but she took the box from him.

'I'll look after it,' she promised. 'But only because you're likely to lose it if you keep it with you.' He snorted and she smiled. 'You're coming back, Aleks. You said you would.'

'I know, I know. But just in case.'

Raina huffed, tucking the box into her inner coat pocket, but didn't say anything more. Aleks wisely ignored the stray tears she couldn't keep at bay.

Aleks and Raina didn't get to talk much about their little shopping trip once they got back to the Compass as Ksenia quickly put them both to work. Aleks was glad of the distraction; the lump in his throat was prone to rising at odd moments, and he was finding it harder and harder to push the emotion aside.

After he'd eaten, Aleks went upstairs to his room, looking at the small space. Most of his clothes were already in the ship, and everything he was leaving behind was stored in the trunk at the foot of the bed; Luka had told them all to only bring what they couldn't do without.

He sat down at his desk, flipped his notebook open to a clean page and picked up his pen, ignoring how the ink leaked on to his fingers when he held it. Pulling his bottom lip between his teeth as he thought about what he wanted to write, he put pen to paper and let the words come.

Aleks wrote two letters, both to his family. One that he would send in the morning, explaining to them that he was doing a bit of travelling for work, and that they probably wouldn't hear from him for a few weeks. The second letter was one he was planning to ask Raina to keep for him, to send in the event that he didn't return, explaining the truth of everything. This one proved significantly harder to write, and he wasn't surprised to find himself crying before he'd even finished it. He started at a knock on the door, turning to see Raina poking her head in. 'Oh,' she murmured when she saw the state he was in. 'Never mind, it can wait.'

'No, no, come in,' he urged, wiping furiously at his cheeks. Ksenia wouldn't mind them bending the rules a little, under the circumstances. Raina giggled.

'You've just smeared ink all over your face, you daft idiot,' she said fondly. He groaned, glancing down at his ink-stained fingers.

'I'll wash it off in the morning. Is everything all right?' Raina shrugged, moving to perch on the edge of his bed, and revealed a striped bundle from behind her back, handing it wordlessly to him. Aleks took it, holding it out, a surprised smile on his face when he realised it was a knitted jumper. It had stripes of black, white and blue in varying widths; the colours of Siberene.

'Aunt Ksenia made it for you,' Raina explained, watching him run the soft wool between his fingers. 'It'll be cold out there in the Stormlands, and, well . . . she thought it might remind you of home. Give you more determination to come back.' Aleks smiled, setting the jumper down carefully and then sitting beside Raina and slinging an arm around her shoulders.

'I couldn't possibly have more determination to come back than I do already,' he assured her quietly. 'But thank you, and Ksenia. It'll be nice to have something from here to take with me.'

'Are you all right?' Raina asked tentatively.

'Yes,' he lied. 'I'm fine. Just writing letters to my family. I hate to ask more favours of you, but I was wondering if you would look after one of the letters, to send to them in case I don't make it back. It explains what will have really happened to me, and . . . I know I can trust you to send it.' He felt guilty, using her as his messenger like that, but he knew that he could trust her.

'OK. OK, I can do that. I pray I don't have to, but . . . I can do that,' Raina agreed, and he kissed her cheek in gratitude.

'Thank you.' They sat together for several minutes, just enjoying the silence. Eventually, Raina pulled away from him, getting to her feet.

'I'll leave you to your evening, then. Still a couple more days left, right?' She attempted a smile, but it fell flat. Aleks reached out to grab her hand, squeezing gently.

'Yeah, I'm not leaving just yet.' He paused, biting his lip. 'But in case I don't get the chance to say it later . . . thank you. And your family. You've made me feel so at home, these past few months have been some of the best of my life . . . I can't even begin to think of the words to tell you how grateful I am for that.'

'Don't be stupid, you don't need to thank us. We've loved having you here. It's been nice, especially as my cousins moved out a few years ago. Like having a sibling.'

'I always wanted a sister,' Aleks admitted with a half-smile. 'I guess you'll have to do.' Raina cuffed him lightly around the ear.

'And I suppose I'm stuck with you as a big brother, then.' Her expression was brighter now, and she left his room looking a little less like the world was ending. Aleks's good cheer lasted only until she'd left the room, however; her words had reminded him of his blood siblings, his own big brothers. He may never see them again, may never meet Torell's daughter. But going back would only lead to his eventual capture, and then his life would be so much worse. If he could successfully make it back from the Stormlands, Luka could get his record wiped, and he'd be a free man. He had little to lose, and so much to gain.

25

Aleks decided to spend one of his last free days alone, wandering the city. He was careful to avoid the courtyard, not wanting to come across Saria, but instead took a lazy stroll through some of his favourite places in Syvana.

He didn't notice when someone started to follow him until he started back towards the Compass via a series of random roads and turnings, as was becoming the norm for him. He heard footsteps, too closely matching his own to be a coincidence. Aleks turned down a street that led away from the Compass, towards the shipyard, cursing under his breath when the footsteps continued. Three more unnecessary turns proved that the stranger was definitely trailing him.

Too tired to bother trying to lose his tail before he got to the Compass, Aleks turned on the spot, startling the stranger – who wasn't much of a stranger at all. Shulga had a nasty smirk on his face, and Aleks's heart sank. 'What now?' He'd expected the man to stay in the shadows until Aleks slipped up and gave away the location of the journal, now stowed safely in his room on the ship. Did he want to threaten Aleks some more, or had he finally given up waiting and just wanted to kill him?

'Trouble in paradise, brat?' Shulga asked, folding his arms across his chest. Aleks's brow furrowed in confusion. 'Your little girlfriend isn't as stupid as I thought. She at least has morals.' The sinking feeling grew.

'What have you done to Saria?' His voice was low but Shulga merely grinned.

'I've done nothing. It's what *she's* done to *you* that you should be worrying about.' The lieutenant reached into his breast pocket and pulled out a whistle, blowing two sharp blasts. Out of nowhere a pair of guards emerged, flanking Shulga. Aleks instinctively took a step back. What was going on? 'Your bitch turned you in, boy,' Shulga declared smugly. 'Clearly decided she'd had enough of your criminal self. Imagine my surprise when I received a message from the Syvana kingsguard commander, telling me a young lady had come in with information on where to find my missing cadet, and I had best make my way over. Of course, under the circumstances, I'd been keeping my search for you somewhat quiet until I found what I was looking for; I didn't want to get banned from the entire city, after all. But I can work this in my favour.' Shulga smirked wider at the horrified look on Aleks's face.

'She told us all about where you've been working. Only thing she wouldn't tell was who'd been hiding you through all this. But that's no matter, we'll find that out in due time. And then I'll find what I've been looking for.'

'Aleksandr Vasin, you're under arrest for desertion and theft of military property,' the guard on the left declared. A quick glance at his shoulder stripes confirmed he was low-ranking, as was his partner.

'Theft of military property?' Aleks yelped, eyes wide. What had Saria told them? 'I didn't steal anything belonging to the military!'

'That's not what we've been told,' the guard on the right snarled, his bushy black eyebrows so close together they were practically one straight line. Aleks glanced at Shulga. Surely, if Shulga had told the entire truth, he would also be in trouble for having the journal? Either way, he had to get out; if he could escape them, he could get to Luka's and leave tonight, go to the one place Shulga could never follow him.

As the monobrowed guard reached out to grab him, Aleks ducked away, turning on his heel and sprinting in the direction of the shipyard. Even at this late hour, there would still be plenty of chaos going on. Enough for him to lose the guards, he hoped.

The three soldiers raced after him, but Aleks was faster and knew the paths better, bobbing and weaving through people and down small alleyways. Finally, he burst into the shipyard through a side street, the lights and noise assaulting him. He pushed on. He could still hear his aggressors, their heavy military boots pounding the concrete, but they were slowed behind a group of crewmen carrying large crates.

Aleks made a beeline for the flight school, praying to any god that might listen that Drazan was on shift. The pilot kept all sorts of odd hours, and could usually be found there when not with Zhora. Startled yells followed Aleks as he ran, and a glance over his shoulder showed that Shulga and his two henchmen were pushing people out of the way and barging through the crowd.

Using the back entrance to the flight school instead of the main front one, Aleks managed a half-wave to the secretary and headed for Drazan's office. The door was open and the light was on. 'Thank you, Goddess,' Aleks breathed, skidding to a halt in the doorway.

Drazan looked up, eyebrows rising at Aleks's panicked state. 'Storms, man, what's the matter with you?'

'They've come for me,' Aleks breathed, keeping his ears alert for any sound that might be Shulga entering the flight school. 'The guards, Saria turned me in, it's a long story, no time to explain. But they're coming to arrest me, and I can't evade them this time. I don't have two days, we need to leave tonight.'

As he spoke, Drazan stood, expression serious. He tidied away the papers he was grading, tucking them in a desk drawer. 'Gods. Right. OK. Gods.' He ran a hand through his hair, shaking his head. 'Good thing Zhora and I are mostly packed up, anyway. Are they following you now?' At Aleks's nod, he cursed softly. 'OK. I'll get Zhora, grab the last of our things and head over to Luka's. We'll meet you at the warehouse, just get there whenever you can, all right?' Drazan crossed the room in three long strides, placing a hand on Aleks's shoulder. 'Stay safe, man. See you in a few hours. Gods be with you.'

'Thanks, I'll need them,' Aleks replied with a grim smile. He left through the front door, eyes darting around the shipyard, and the barest grin slipped across his lips at the sight of Shulga interrogating a burly crewman about fifteen feet away. Creeping away in the opposite direction, Aleks breathed a sigh of relief and hared off towards the

Compass. All he had to do was grab his bag and say his good-byes, then get to the warehouse without being caught. Drazan would take care of the rest.

Heart racing, it didn't take long for Aleks to get to the Compass, slowing just enough not to break the door as he burst through.

Raina's dark eyes were concerned as he made his way over to the bar. 'What's the matter?' she asked quietly. Aleks shook his head, gesturing towards the kitchen.

'Not here,' he murmured, slipping behind the bar and leading the way through. Ksenia was in there washing dishes, and her cheerful expression fell at Aleks's demeanour. 'I need to leave tonight,' he declared bluntly, and Ksenia dropped the bowl she was holding into the sink with a clatter.

'What? But you said you had two more days!' Raina protested.

'I did, but things have changed. Saria turned me in to the guards – they're on the hunt for me as we speak. I need to leave tonight, or they'll catch up with me and put all of you in danger.'

'We can take them.' Bodan's voice made Aleks jump, and he spun round to see the bearded man standing in the doorway. 'We'll keep you hidden.'

'I appreciate the sentiment, but it's no use. If I go now, you'll be safe. I won't put you at risk. I'm sorry. It's only two days earlier, anyway. I just need to pack my bag, then I'll be off.' Raina let out a small noise, rushing forward to hug him.

'Be careful. Don't do anything stupid. And . . . enjoy yourself.'

She pulled back with a tearful smile. Ksenia and Bodan had both come closer, and Ksenia bundled him in a suffocatingly tight hug, which he returned tenfold.

'Don't tempt fate,' she instructed firmly. 'Stay on the Goddess's good side and she'll keep you safe, even past her reach. Be a good lad, and come home soon.'

'I will,' he assured her, kissing her cheek. 'Look after yourself. I'll see you soon.' Her lips pursed at that, but she didn't say anything more, letting him go.

'You know what you're doing?' Bodan asked, and Aleks nodded. 'You trust these two men you're flying with?' Again, Aleks nodded, and Bodan smiled, reaching out to grab him by the shoulder and pull him into a rough hug. 'Then best of luck to you, lad. May the winds blow your way and the ice stay off your sails.'

'And may your hearth and heart stay warm, and the Goddess bless your home,' Aleks returned, choking up a little as he spoke.

'Stay safe, Aleks,' Ksenia urged, her husband's arm coming around her waist as his other hand rested on Raina's shoulder. Aleks nodded, hand resting on the door handle.

'I'll stay as safe as I can,' he swore, knowing he couldn't promise much more. Reluctantly tearing his gaze from them, he glanced to the doorway out to the bar. 'I'll go and grab my things. You should all get back to work – don't want anything looking suspicious.' Aleks made for the staircase, jogging up to his room. It didn't take long to shove the last of his belongings in a bag, and he forced himself to leave the room again, satchel slung over his shoulder. He wished he could say goodbye to Saria, see her one last time, but clearly she wanted nothing to do with him now. The betrayal hurt, and he forced his thoughts away from her, focusing on the task at hand.

When he got back downstairs, it was to find the trio working as normal, though Ksenia's smile was more strained than usual. They looked up from behind the bar, and Bodan nodded to him; they'd said their goodbyes.

Before he knew it he was walking away from the Compass, scarf pulled up over his face and coat hood low over his eyes. It was snowing, but only lightly; good enough weather for take-off. Not the best, but it would do, under the circumstances.

The tram was almost empty when he boarded, taking a seat in the corner and leaning against the carriage wall. There were two men in suits who were absorbed in whispered discussion, and another man who looked like he might possibly have spent the night there. When they stopped about halfway through the journey, a smartly dressed woman boarded and sat a few seats down from Aleks, immediately pulling a book from her handbag and opening it. Aleks's knee bounced the entire journey, his pulse jumping every time the doors opened, half expecting Shulga to step in.

He arrived to find the warehouse unlocked, and he nudged the door open, blinking at the bright lights.

'Oh, good, you made it!' Drazan called, peering out over the railing on deck. 'We're just about ready if you are – get on up here!' Aleks wasted no time, hitching his satchel further up his shoulder and scrambling on deck. 'Zhora and

Luka are in the engine room, making last-minute flight checks. Supplies are loaded, everything's bolted down, we are clear to fly.'

'Brilliant,' Aleks breathed, pulse beginning to return to normal. As soon as they were airborne he'd be safe.

The pair went below deck, parting ways as Aleks made for his tiny room. He set his satchel down on the bed, flipping it open and letting the contents spill out on to the narrow mattress. Hurriedly folding the last of his clothes to put in the trunk, he placed his notebook and pen carefully in the desk drawer, trying to ignore the shiny gun sitting beside them in the compartment. There was a lamp bolted to the desk, and a smaller box inside the trunk containing all the audio and video recorders. Those were the only mechanical items Aleks had in his room; the rest were down in storage.

Making sure everything was either locked away or bolted down, he made his way to the engine room where the other three were gathered, Luka and Zhora just closing up a panel. 'We all set?' Aleks asked, and Zhora nodded.

'Good to go. I hear you've had an eventful afternoon,' he replied. Aleks grimaced, shaking his head.

'Don't worry about it. The sooner we leave, the better,' he insisted. Zhora's lips pursed, but he didn't say anything, and Luka moved to stand by Aleks as the two brothers started conversing in low tones. The old mechanic turned to him, eyes concerned.

'You ready for this, lad?'

'As I'll ever be. Sure you don't want to come with us?' Aleks asked with a grin that he knew didn't reach his eyes. Luka shook his head.

'No, no, I'll leave the adventures to you crazy brats,' he teased lightly. 'Besides, someone needs to stay here to keep an eye on things. I'll watch out for that lieutenant of yours, lad – make sure he stays away from the Compass. They're fine folk there, they don't need your trouble at their door.' Aleks shot Luka a grateful look. The man might be old and frail-looking, but Aleks knew what he was capable of, and trusted him to keep his word.

'Much appreciated. We'll try and make it back quickly. There's only a month's worth of rations, anyway.' The implication lingered heavily between them; if they didn't return in a month, they weren't likely to be returning at all.

'You'll be fine, lad. But I swear to the gods, if my ship has the slightest scratch on her when you get back, I'll have all three of your hides.' Aleks couldn't help but laugh, wrapping his arms tightly around the white-haired man before he could protest at the embrace.

'She'll be good as new, I promise,' he assured Luka with a grin. Luka scowled, struggling away from him.

'She'd better be,' he muttered, face softening as he clapped Aleks on the shoulder. 'Good luck, lad. I have every bit of faith that you'll be home within the month.' The four of them got to work moving the ship out on to the landing deck. Aleks's heart was once again beating frantically in his chest, his blood racing and a grin tugging at his lips as he got the ship ready for take-off. This was something he was good at; this was something he could do. And he was going to do something that no one in the world had ever done before.

'Wait!' Drazan said abruptly, startling them. Aleks's gaze immediately flicked to the door; had he been followed? 'She doesn't have a name. We can't fly a ship without a name, it's bad luck.'

'A load of superstitious bull! She doesn't need a name, she's unique enough as it is,' Luka insisted.

'No, he's right,' Zhora said. 'She has to have a name. We're chancing the gods enough as it is. We don't want to risk it any more with bad luck, superstitious bull or not.'

Aleks hummed thoughtfully. 'What to call her, though? Special girl like her deserves an equally special name.' And the clock was ticking faster than he'd like.

'*Thunderbug!*' Zhora declared, breaking the silence that had fallen. 'Because she's tiny and fast, a little light in the storm.' There had been a lot of the tiny insects around recently; they only came out after a hard rainstorm, lighting up the evenings with their luminescent bodies and rumbling quietly like thunder as they called to their fellows. Aleks liked to watch them dart around the stable block from his bedroom window.

Drazan turned to Aleks, grinning, and the pair looked at Luka. It was his baby, after all.

'It fits,' the old man agreed, patting the ship on the side. '*Thunderbug* it is. Now get going, you're wasting daylight!'

Following the two older members of his crew – *his* crew, he was captain of a *skyship* – up the ladder, Aleks went straight to the control room with Drazan, while Zhora headed for the engine room. It was the first time the three of them had been on board without Luka, and the eccentric man's absence was more tangible than Aleks had expected it to be. As he and Drazan worked on the take-off preparations he half expected to hear Luka's fondly scathing remarks through the speakers about how long they were taking. Still, Drazan did his best to fill the silence with aimless nattering, though it stopped when Aleks tilted the wings, sending them shooting up into the air.

For once, Aleks didn't mess about with drifting turns and slaloms through powerful updraughts. They had a destination, and a fuel limit, and the more light in the sky by the time they got to the Stormlands, the better. 'This is it, then,' Drazan murmured, leaning on the back of Aleks's seat. 'No turning back now.'

'This is it,' Aleks agreed, his tone a mix of excitement and apprehension. 'Aren't you supposed to be asleep?' They'd worked out a schedule, allowing them to take turns resting. They would always need one person in the control room and one in the engine room keeping an eye on things. It was, Luka had told them, one of the downsides of such an intricately designed ship. In contrast to a regular skyship, where the engine room could be left to its own devices for hours at a time if the weather was steady, the engines and mechanics of their ship needed near constant monitoring.

'You think I can sleep now? Nah, I'm fine. Besides, we've got plenty of coffee in the galley.' Aleks wondered if giving Drazan coffee was a smart idea; he was perky enough without it. Sometimes it was hard to believe the man was two and a half years older than he was.

'If you're sure.' Aleks relaxed in the seat, knowing it would take several hours of flying before they hit the dangerous part of the Stormlands. 'How's everything down your end, Zhora?'

'Running smoothly, no problems here,' Zhora responded. 'Bloody boring down here without the old man for company. I'm wishing I'd brought a book.'

'Hopefully once we get a little further in, you won't want that book,' Aleks pointed out, swerving them around a particularly fierce-looking swirl of wind and rain. The wall of black cloud up ahead was drawing ever nearer, though was still far away enough for them not to worry about it yet. Trying to imagine spending hours among the terrifying storms was impossible.

When it got to the point that Drazan was playing noughts and crosses with himself in the condensation on the view-screen, Aleks sent him to make dinner. He wasn't completely sure what time it was, not wanting to take either of his hands off the controls to check, and wished they'd thought of bolting down a timepiece somewhere in the control room.

Later, Drazan dropped off a pasty and a full skin of water, taking over the controls so Aleks could eat. 'Zhora's fine downstairs,' he said, smiling as they caught the edge of a small tornado and rocketed up several feet. 'I took him down a book, so he's occupied now.'

'Good, good. How you feeling?' Aleks took the opportunity to shed his coat and check his pocket watch. He ate quickly, wanting to make sure he was in the pilot's seat for the first leg of the crossing. While Drazan was a more experienced pilot in general, Aleks still had more experience with the *Thunderbug*, and he wanted to be in charge when they first entered the Stormlands to see how she handled.

'Oh, I'm just fine,' Drazan assured him brightly, relinquishing the pilot's seat. 'Ready to get to the main event.'

Aleks began to feel the ship resist him, the steering wheel trying to move itself, and the levers straining under his fingers. He glanced over at Drazan, whose smile had been replaced by an expression of intense concentration, and braced himself once the other man had firmly strapped himself into the harness they'd attached to the wall for this very purpose.

'Hold on tight, Zhora,' he said over the speakers. 'The fun is just about to begin.'

26

Of all the things Aleks had anticipated about flying through the Stormlands, he hadn't expected it to be quite so quick.

The entire ship jerked the moment Aleks plunged them into a dark cloud, further in than he'd ever been before. Almost immediately they were swept away in the curl of a hurricane, launching further into the storm with more power than the ship ever could have managed on her own. 'Ride with her, Aleks!' Drazan shouted, whooping with delight as he leaned right out in his harness with his feet bracing him to the floor, his body swinging round and slamming against the wall every time they changed direction. He didn't seem to mind, keeping his hands on the video recorder he was directing towards the viewscreen.

'I don't think I can do anything but!' Aleks shouted back, keeping a guiding hand on the steering wheel even as it spun furiously this way and that under his grip. He knew the ship could handle it; with the amount of steel running through the supports and the strength of the bracers keeping them attached it would take a lot more than a fierce storm to snap her wings. Concentrating mostly on just staying in his seat, Aleks wondered why they had added a harness for Drazan but neglected a seatbelt for him; that seemed like a serious oversight now.

Eventually, he managed to acclimatise to the movement enough to try and attempt a change in direction, wrenching the steering wheel under the force of the wind. It was almost pitch black inside the cloud, occasionally lit up by a flash of lightning, and Aleks winced at the size of the hailstones pelting the viewscreen. 'Everything all right down below, Zhora?' he called in concern, not having heard a thing from the mechanic since they'd entered the Stormlands.

'Bit bumpy, but everything's still working just fine!' Zhora's voice crackled back through the speakers. 'How's she handling, lad?'

'About as well as we expected,' Aleks replied, which was to say, with very little input from him. Their plan from the start had been to ride it out and hope the storm eventually spat them out the other side. Unlike plenty of other skyships that had made the attempt, they were small enough not to have to worry about conflicting wind directions tearing them apart, or being too heavy to ride the storm. All they had to do was pray they didn't get struck by lightning and try to keep the ship going in a vaguely westerly direction. The compass on the control panel in front of Aleks was spinning and jerking madly with every twist and turn, and couldn't have given them the right direction if it tried. 'Are you even getting any footage, Drazan?' he asked, glancing aside at the reckless young man who was still leaning out as far as he could, attempting to hold the recorder steady.

'Not a clue, but it's worth a shot, right? No one will believe us without proof. Ow, gods!' he exclaimed as the ship lurched, sending him slamming backwards and causing his head to hit the wall.

Gritting his teeth, Aleks kept at it, grateful for Drazan's shouts of warning each time he noticed a wind that would blow them off course, or a particularly lethal-looking thundercloud. The hail seemed to have stopped, at least in their area of the storm, but rain still lashed down at them from all angles, making Aleks worry for the state of the deck. Thankfully the ship wasn't built for beauty; she'd probably be a mess by the time they made it out of the Stormlands. If they made it out.

'So much for the plan of switching shifts halfway,' Aleks muttered to himself. 'I don't think either of us will be able to move until we're in the clear.' With his own watch out of reach the only references he had to the outside world were the pocket watch attached to Drazan's waistcoat and the compass on the control panel. If not for them, Aleks would have believed they were lost in the endless cloud, flying themselves in circles for hours on end. He could barely feel his hands by this point, his vision a blur of cloud and lightning flashes.

'That's all right – you can let me have a go on the way back,' Drazan pointed out brightly, making Aleks laugh.

'She's all yours,' he promised; he never wanted to do this again. His heart was racing, his whole body on edge, just waiting for the moment everything started to go wrong. He wondered what Saria would think if he never returned, if she'd care enough to find out what had happened to him, but he pushed the thought away forcefully. Now wasn't the time. 'Storms, I'm going to murder Luka when we get back. Why in the name of the gods did he think this could possibly be a good idea?' Aleks didn't need to look at Drazan to know he was grinning.

'Oh, lighten up,' said Drazan. 'Don't tell me you're not having fun.' Aleks opened his mouth to state exactly that, only to close it again, grinning as they soared through a jet black cloud and into a lighter charcoal-coloured one.

'I can't,' he admitted honestly. 'I'm still going to kill him, though. He should be the one getting us through this nightmare.'

'We both know that if Luka were our pilot we'd be halfway to the ocean floor by now,' Drazan pointed out bluntly. 'The man was good, back in the day, and he's still a bloody genius, but . . . he's not got your reflexes.' Aleks's eyebrows rose briefly in admission of the roundabout compliment, but his attention was still focused on the ship.

'I need to switch out fuel, so if the power goes off for a second or two, don't be alarmed,' Zhora told them from below. Aleks and Drazan shared an uneasy look; to have burned through one tyrium cube already wasn't good. They'd have to be conservative with the rest of their fuel; apparently being dragged in ten different directions and trying to stay upright was very draining on the ship's mechanics.

'Do it quickly, then, while we're in a relatively calm spot,' Aleks urged. A few moments later he felt the tension in the controls slacken and the ship abruptly dropped several feet. Trying to keep the contents of his stomach where they were, Aleks was grateful when the controls came back online and he slammed further down in his seat, immediately bringing them back on course. His breath came in gasps and he couldn't be completely sure he wouldn't vomit, but he ignored his gag reflex and kept them flying. With a full tyrium cube in the furnace the ship seemed to have far more power, twisting and turning gracefully on command.

'How far in are we, do you think?' Drazan queried, finally lowering the video recorder.

'A mile or so, I'd like to say. Give or take,' Aleks guessed, shrugging. 'But for all I know, we're barely ten feet from where we started.'

'Nah – ten feet in wasn't nearly this bad,' Drazan insisted. 'I just wish we knew how wide the Stormlands are, so we could at least guess when we get to the middle.'

'The middle hardly matters – the end is the only bit I care about,' Aleks muttered, yelping at the sudden jerk to the left which was accompanied by the thud of a hailstone that sounded as large as a horse.

'It's getting really nasty out there,' Zhora remarked, sounding almost pleased. Aleks could imagine him darting about the engine room, turning cogs and realigning pipes. Zhora probably had the hardest job of the three of them, and Aleks dreaded his shift down there, even though it would take place when they were – hopefully – in the clear. He'd only worked the engine room once during flight, when Drazan had the controls, and that had been with Luka looking over his shoulder, proving that once again the theory was vastly different from the reality. Zhora and Drazan were both more capable of working the engine room than he was, but in order for their shift system to work, all three of them had to be able to do both jobs. Even Zhora had been taught how to fly the ship, just in case.

'Is it just me, or do the clouds seem to be getting lighter?' Drazan asked optimistically, squinting at the horizon. Aleks frowned; it all looked the same to him. He could barely tell where one storm cloud overlapped with another, let alone whether they were getting lighter or not.

'We can only hope,' he replied, starting at the unexpected rumble of thunder that accompanied the flashes of lightning. Aleks was amazed they hadn't been hit by any yet; it seemed to be all around them. He prayed it meant the gods were on their side.

'What time is it?' Aleks asked, and Drazan juggled with the recorder to try and dig his pocket watch out. Flipping it open, his eyebrows shot up and he looked at Aleks.

'It's quarter past eleven!' They'd been in the Stormlands for over five hours.

'Maybe we really are coming out the other side, then,' Aleks said, grinning at Drazan.

'It's about bloody time!' Zhora remarked, and they jumped at the sound of his voice. 'My arms are about to fall off.'

'Want me to come down and relieve you?' Drazan asked, concern in his voice.

Aleks gave him a look. 'Do you really think you can get out of that harness without falling flat on your arse?' he asked.

Drazan paused. 'That could be a problem,' he agreed. They could both hear Zhora sniggering through the speakers.

'Don't worry about it, lad. I can last another hour or two, and, gods willing, by then we should be out of the worst of it,' the elder brother said. 'But if we're still in this bloody storm in two hours' time, I'll take you up on that offer.'

'If we're still in this storm in two hours' time, you won't be the only one needing a rest,' Aleks cut in, disgruntled. He was steering almost without realising it, and his arms were beginning to cramp. He'd been flying for almost seven hours solid.

As they rode out the worst of the storm, Aleks let the ship pick up a little speed, bolstered by the high winds catching the sail. His stomach churned in anticipation when he realised they were definitely on their way out; they were being carried as quickly as they had on the way in. He just hoped that they were coming out the other side. For all he knew, they could be somewhere near Erova. 'I think this is it,' he told Drazan excitedly, and the dark-haired man fumbled to turn the video recorder back on, leaning out once more to capture the footage of them emerging through the edge of the storm. It was hard to believe they'd actually lasted the whole way, when every ship before them had failed – it just showed how incredible the *Thunderbug* was.

'Are we nearly out?' Zhora asked, sounding as exhausted as Aleks felt.

'Seem to be,' Aleks confirmed. They powered forward, the clouds around them getting paler and paler, the lightning waning and the rain easing up. Aleks kept his eyes peeled for any glimpse of land, sea or open sky.

'Look! There!' Drazan exclaimed, almost falling over as he bounced on the balls of his feet, pointing with the hand that wasn't holding the recorder. 'I see sky!' Aleks tried to figure out where the man was pointing, and his eyes widened when he saw the sliver of dark blue-grey that definitely wasn't part of any storm cloud.

'Oh, thank the gods,' Zhora murmured, barely audible. Aleks urged the ship forward, wishing he could give her more speed, despite the fact that she was already going twice as fast as the average skyship.

The storm released them into relatively clear skies, the wind from the Stormlands pushing them clear by over twenty feet before Aleks could even consider doing anything with the controls. When he heard Drazan gasp softly behind him, he looked up from where he was hastily righting the wings, his jaw dropping.

That solved the mystery of whether there was land on the other side of the Stormlands, at least.

27

Aleks wasn't sure how long they drifted aimlessly, pushed in all directions from the smaller storms breaking away from the Stormlands; he was too busy staring incredulously at the enormous expanse of land in front of them. The only light was that of the moon, but it was enough to see the land was stunning.

It seemed to be flat for the most part. The woodland area in the centre was so thick he couldn't really tell what the topography was like. On the side closest to them, the occasional field of grassland broke up the thick forestry, and the outlying land was sand and rock right up until the cliffs. To his amazement, it looked like the other side of the forest was just an endless stretch of sand and rock too, going on for miles until it met the ocean. 'It's beautiful,' Drazan murmured, his recorder held steady as their flight evened out. Aleks gathered himself, regaining his concentration enough to bring the ship under his control, turning them towards the land.

'It's huge,' he replied. 'How could all this possibly be here and no one ever knew?' It seemed bigger than Siberene, though that could have been because of the absence of mountains interrupting his view.

'What is it?' Zhora asked from the engine room. 'What does it look like?'

'It's incredible,' Drazan told him. 'There's land, a lot of it. Flat, with forests, and even a desert.' Aleks's brow furrowed at the word. He'd heard of deserts before, in Kasem and Mericus, but not so close to home.

'Gods,' Zhora breathed. 'I'll have to come up and see it.' Drazan released himself from his harness.

'Definitely. Shall I come down and take over so you can have a look and then get some sleep?' One glance at the pocket watch told them that it had barely been three quarters of an hour since their last time check; it was just after midnight.

'If you're sure?' Zhora checked, a yawn interrupting his words. 'I wouldn't normally be this tired, but . . . storms, getting through that was hard work. I'm not looking forward to doing it again.'

'I don't think any of us are,' Aleks agreed sympathetically. 'Come and have a look, then go to bed, Zhora. You've more than earned it.'

Drazan finally lowered his recorder, turning it off and pocketing it. 'See you later,' he said, clapping Aleks on the shoulder. Aleks nodded, taking the opportunity of fairly calm skies to let one hand off the controls, stretching out his arm. He wished he could stand up and stretch his legs; they were beginning to go a little numb.

Zhora knocked lightly on the doorway before entering, and Aleks could hear the breath catch in his throat when he got his first glimpse of the land in front of them. 'Storms,' he muttered, edging in closer. 'That's definitely worth the journey, wouldn't you say so?'

'And more,' Aleks agreed – the country really was beautiful. He couldn't wait to see it in daylight.

'How are you holding up?'

'I'm sore,' Aleks admitted with a faint grimace. 'Losing the feeling in my limbs. Hungry. Other than that, I'm just fantastic.' Zhora laughed, gently ruffling Aleks's hair.

'Keep going, lad. By the look of things, we can land her on that island in about an hour. It looks safe enough to me.' Aleks glanced at the flat area of sand he'd been planning on using as a landing deck.

'Yeah, should manage that without too much trouble. Then we can all go to bed.'

'Oh, that sounds like a wonderful plan,' Zhora mused. He looked back over at the viewscreen, letting out a quiet whistle. 'Quite a sight, isn't it?'

Aleks nodded. 'It's so strange, seeing all that wild land. Makes you wonder if that's what everywhere else used to look like before people settled there,' he said thoughtfully, trying to imagine Siberene without its cities and roads and villages. It was hard; all he could picture was endless white snow and grey rock.

'It probably is,' Zhora agreed, shrugging. 'There are rumours that Anglya used to have a lot of forests and green space, but, well, once they found the tyrium deposits . . .' He trailed off, not needing to say more. Once tyrium had been discovered, Anglya had become the mining capital of Tellus, practically gutting itself in order to get to the precious purple mineral that fuelled the whole world. He didn't know what the Anglyans would do if they ever ran out of it; dig them-selves hollow trying to find more, probably. There were protesters, he'd heard, complaining that if they kept mining they'd damage the structure of the land so much they'd sink into the ocean, but most people regarded them as lunatics for saying so.

'Imagine if this place were rich in tyrium,' Aleks said with a wry grin, gesturing towards the land ahead. 'Think of how many people would kill themselves trying to get here.'

Zhora hummed in agreement, stretching his long arms up to the ceiling. 'If you'll excuse me, I'm off to get some sleep – it's far, far past my bedtime.'

'Sleep well, Zhora,' Aleks replied, smiling. Settling as comfortably as he could in his seat, he guided the ship towards the edge of the country below, trying to judge the distance until they hit land. It was fairly far, but Zhora's estimate of an hour looked to be about spot on. He hoped it was, at least; he didn't know how much longer he could stay awake without food in his stomach. He was beginning to feel a little light-headed, and wished he'd thought to ask Drazan to bring him something to snack on before going down to the engine room.

'How are we doing up there, Aleks?' The voice made him jump, and it took a few moments to remember that the speakers were still on.

'Pretty good so far. Give me an hour, should have her down safely. Think you can stay awake that long?'

'Shouldn't be a problem,' Drazan replied. 'How about you? Starting to feel it yet?'

'More than,' he said emphatically. 'But another hour won't kill me. It's just a shame we couldn't have come out during daylight. That would've been one hell of a sight.'

'Wouldn't it just?' Drazan agreed, somewhat wistfully. 'But in the morning we can take her up and get a proper look around from the sky. Get some decent footage and all that. I think what I've got is going to be a bit too dark to be of use.'

'We'll see.' Luka had assured them that he could get whatever film they brought back made into a proper newscast video, so they could show everyone what they'd found on the other side of the Stormlands. But Aleks doubted Luka had ever imagined something like this.

It was strange, landing somewhere other than the deck behind Luka's warehouse. Easier in some regards, as he didn't have to land exactly on top of the rig, but harder because trying to spot a flat area of land in the dark was no small feat. Eventually, he decided on an area far enough back from the cliff edge to be safe, landing gently with a soft thump. He slumped in his seat and groaned loudly after turning everything off and pulling the wings and sail in. He let out out a long breath. They'd done it. They had flown through the Stormlands and discovered a whole new country on the other side.

Aleks craned his neck when he heard someone approaching and smiled wearily at Drazan. 'Evening,' he drawled.

'You look terrible,' Drazan said. Aleks snorted, standing up with wobbly legs. Drazan's arm slid under his, holding him upright, and Aleks shot him a grateful look.

'Not had jelly-legs since my first few days learning to fly,' he admitted sheepishly. Drazan laughed, releasing him once he was sure he could stand.

'Spend any longer than seven hours in the pilot's seat, you'll find your legs going. I once did a sixteen-hour flight; I had to be carried to my bunk afterwards,' he told Aleks, leading the way out of the control room. The trap to the engine room was shut, and Aleks made a mental note to head down in the morning and turn on the furnace before attempting to shower. 'We did it, though.' Drazan was grinning, and Aleks couldn't help but grin back.

'We did. Thought we wouldn't a few times back there,' he admitted, somewhat relieved when Drazan nodded in agreement. 'And I have to say, I wasn't expecting to find this.'

'I know what you mean. I thought there'd be an island or two at most. Nothing like this place.' Aleks opened his mouth to answer, only to be cut off by a yawn.

'We should both get some sleep,' he declared, heading for his bedroom door. 'Will it be safe?'

'We'll have to hope so,' Drazan replied with a shrug. 'Not like either of us are in any state to sit up and guard for the night. But I'm sure it'll be fine – things look fairly quiet out there.'

After bidding Drazan goodnight, Aleks nudged his door open, barely managing to shed his clothes before falling into bed, asleep almost as soon as his head hit the pillow.

28

Aleks woke unseasonably early the next morning, despite his exhaustion and the late hour he'd gone to bed, eager to get moving. Delicious smells were wafting through the ship. When he wandered into the galley, he found Zhora and Drazan already up. 'Morning, Aleks,' Drazan greeted him brightly, none the worse for his long day. Zhora still looked a little weary, but Aleks was sure he'd be better after he'd eaten.

'Morning,' Aleks returned, sliding into the chair opposite Drazan. 'Sleep well?'

'Well enough, but I could've done with a few more hours,' Zhora replied, bringing a plate of bacon and toast to the table. 'I wasn't going to have a lie-in with all that outside to explore, though.'

Aleks piled bacon between two slices of toast before Drazan could snatch it all up, smiling gratefully when Zhora returned to the table with three mugs of water.

'What's the plan for today, then?' Drazan queried, cheeks bulging with bread and meat. They were all eating quickly, impatient to get out and explore their strange new surroundings.

'Have a look around on foot first, I think. Then we should fly out again and get some video footage in daylight of just how big this place is,' Aleks said thoughtfully. 'Maybe try and get to the other side of the island and see what it's like.' They wanted to gather as much information about the land as they could. Perhaps one day there would be people here, a whole new country in Tellus.

'Sounds good to me. Storms, I can't wait to see it.'

Not wanting to waste any more time, the three of them were almost vibrating with excitement as they headed up on to the deck, Aleks in the lead. He squinted at the bright sunlight. 'Gods,' he murmured, moving away from the trapdoor so Drazan and Zhora could join him. In daylight, the sand was a rusty copper colour and the forest a lush green like Aleks had never seen before. It was far warmer than he was used to, and he shrugged off his coat.

'Well, would you look at that,' Zhora said softly.

'I've never seen anything like it,' Drazan added, eyes wide as he looked around.

Finding the tough rope netting in a locked cubbyhole on deck, Aleks brought it out and tossed it over the side of the ship, securing his end in place. They didn't have a ladder or gangplank, so rigging rope would have to do. He looked at Zhora and Drazan, but they both urged him forward silently, so he took a deep breath, starting the climb down.

His boots sank into the soft sand when he stepped to the ground. Aleks walked round to have a look on the other side of the ship, towards the cliffs, and when he heard footsteps behind him he stopped, turning. Drazan jogged up to him, a grin on his face. 'All hail, King Aleks,' he exclaimed, offering an elaborate bow.

'What are you talking about?' Aleks asked, bemused. Drazan straightened up, still grinning.

'Laws of undiscovered country, isn't it?' he pointed out. 'Captain of the first ship to land on previously undiscovered territory becomes ruler and regent of that territory. Old laws, mostly forgotten by now, but they're still valid.' Aleks remembered learning about the old laws at school, and the old story of how King Marten had first discovered Siberene. He was a young Anglyan lord, determined to explore the whole of Tellus, but as soon as he'd landed in what would become Siberene he'd fallen in love with the place, declared it his own and started a small settlement that eventually grew to be Syvana. He went on to explore more of the land and founded the other three main Siberene cities as well, choosing Rensav to build his palace.

'Bloody hell,' Aleks muttered, stunned. 'Do the old laws still apply, though? I thought there were regulations about the definition of a ship's crew, and I'm sure three people aren't enough.'

'The brat's right, lad,' Zhora assured him, smiling. 'So long as the entire crew agree that their captain is their captain, it counts. And, well, Drazan and I have no argument.' Aleks stood dumbfounded as he stared at the two brothers.

'Wow,' he said, more to himself than the other two. Drazan chuckled.

'How about we have a look around, hmm?' he suggested. Aleks nodded, glad of the change of subject. He took both recorders from his jacket pockets, and Drazan revealed his own one from the night before.

'Will she be safe?' Zhora asked, patting the ship's side.

'What's likely to happen to her?' Drazan retorted with raised eyebrows, flicking his recorder around to capture the view of the cliffs.

'I don't know – animals, fierce winds? Could be anything around here. Just think of the beasts you find in forests in other lands,' Zhora pointed out. Aleks didn't know what kinds of animal could be found in other countries, but the ones in the forests in Siberene were not the kind he'd like to get up close and personal with.

'Should I get my gun?' Aleks offered, seeing the others didn't have theirs on them.

Zhora nodded. 'It can't hurt to take it just in case.'

Aleks scrambled back up the rigging rope and hurried to his room, digging the gun out of his desk drawer. While he was there he exchanged his thick jumper for a thinner one, shrugging his jacket back on over the top; he would have left that behind but he needed the pockets.

Outside, Zhora and Drazan were waiting by a large protruding rock several feet away from the ship. Drazan was running his hand over it experimentally, frowning when his fingers came back covered in chalky orange-red dust. 'It's so strange, having a place like this between the Stormlands,' he mused when Aleks drew closer. 'I was expecting somewhere similar to Siberene, or even Anglya. This is . . .'

'A lot warmer than anticipated,' Zhora finished for him. 'Maybe it's the difference between cold and hot that makes the Stormlands.'

'What's Dalivia's excuse, then? It's fairly warm there too,' Drazan pointed out, leading the way towards the edge of the forest, video recorder out. Aleks glanced over to the Dalivian side of the Stormlands; until now, most people had just assumed the Stormlands were one enormous storm barrier. They now had proof that there were actually two of them, with clear skies in the middle.

'Not a clue,' Zhora admitted. 'But there probably is a reason. Hopefully some brainiac will be able to figure it out once we take all our discoveries home.' Aleks hadn't thought about what their voyage would mean scientifically. When he had agreed to pilot the *Thunderbug*, he'd merely thought of it as an adventure. But seeing this place, he was beginning to understand the magnitude of what they were doing.

Their heavy boots crunched on the undergrowth of the forest. He could see several brightly coloured birds flitting among the trees, calling out to each other in musical tones. These were smaller, less vicious-looking than the eagles and falcons that populated the area around his village. Drazan tried his best to capture them on his video recorder, and Aleks took out his own recorder in the hope of catching anything his friend missed.

'Look, there!' Zhora murmured, pointing to a thick tree nearby. Aleks whirled round, spotting a strange furry animal hanging lazily from one of the tree's outstretched branches. It was a greyish brown, with long arms and legs and sharp-looking claws that dug into the wood to hold it in place. Its slightly squashed-looking face was half turned away from them, and if Aleks wasn't mistaken the animal was asleep.

'Well, that answers one question,' Drazan said softly, bright eyes darting around. 'Definitely life around here, despite the isolation.'

They ventured in deeper, trying to stay as quiet as possible to avoid disturbing anything, and while Drazan was fascinated by the animals, Aleks was on the lookout for exotic plants. He'd grown up wandering the forest near his village, learning to identify all the trees and flowers native to Siberene; seeing such vastly different plant life here amazed him. The plants came in all shapes and sizes and colours, explosions of red and yellow and purple. Some of the trees had leaves the size of his head, thick and waxy, while others had branches covered in tiny spines instead of leaves.

Walking further into the forest, Aleks's gaze was drawn to a cluster of blue and purple wildflowers, his thoughts turning to Saria; if only he could take some back to her. She loved flowers. He carefully unearthed a few, wishing he'd brought his satchel, and made a mental note to come back later with some jars. He knew they wouldn't survive the journey back to Siberene, but surely dead plants were better than nothing; there was bound to be someone who would find them interesting, even if Saria wouldn't want to accept them from him. The Academy, maybe. While Luka hadn't said anything about taking samples, Aleks wanted some sort of solid proof of their adventure.

They tried to follow their tracks back to the ship, getting lost twice before finally emerging in the rocky flatlands, only a few feet from where they'd entered. Back at the *Thunderbug*, Aleks dug out some empty jars to store his plant samples in, adding a little of the rusty red soil and some water in the hope that they might survive a while longer.

'How long do you think we should stay for?' Aleks asked once they were having a quick lunch, getting some respite from the hot sun before they went out again. They still had plenty of time and supplies, but Aleks knew he could easily spend weeks exploring the new land. It was so different to what he was used to, so full of new things to discover, and he wanted to examine every inch. He was very aware that it was likely to be their only trip to the country, even if he was technically its king – *king!* There was no guarantee that their survival of the Stormlands hadn't been a total fluke, and he wasn't sure if they would make the journey again.

'See how long it takes us to get a proper look around, I suppose,' Zhora replied. A 'proper look around', Aleks thought, could take them the full month. They needed something more than that if they were to see as much as they could in as little time as possible. They needed a plan. That was the captain's job, he supposed.

'Right. Let me get my notebook.'

29

Fed and in high spirits from their earlier adventure, the three prepared to take off once more, Aleks and Drazan trying to work out the logistics of getting airborne so far away from a strong updraught and on such soft sand. Aleks had decided that they should fly over and document as much of the land from above as they could, then divide it into sections to explore on foot, limiting how many days they spent in each section.

'You might have to get the propellers involved,' Drazan suggested. 'It's not the best way to take off, but it's doable. Just have to hope we don't create a sandstorm in the process.' Aleks nodded, sitting down in the pilot's seat and starting everything up. He raised the sail, extending the wings, and kept his fingers crossed as he tilted the ship in an attempt to catch an updraught. Nothing. Cursing under his breath, he shared an annoyed glance with Drazan. Reaching out, he pulled both levers to get the side propellers up, warning Zhora down in the engine room. Almost as soon as the propellers set they started up, sending a gust of sand past the viewscreen. Still, it did the trick, and the ship rose steadily into the air. Aleks steered straight for the cliff line, surprised at how quiet the air was around the island. They caught a feeble updraught near the edge of the cliffs, giving them a little boost upwards to get to better winds, and finally they rocketed away from the land.

'Well, that definitely isn't a selling point,' Aleks murmured. If people were ever to settle in this country, it would take some serious manpower to build a shipyard far enough out to get the draughts necessary to raise a ship. Any ship larger than theirs wouldn't stand a chance.

'This place has very few practical selling points, beyond the fact that it exists,' Drazan said, leaning on the back of Aleks's seat.

Drazan pulled his video recorder out, awed as he recorded the view. The colours of the country were more vibrant than anything he'd ever seen before. Siberene was dreary, full of muted colours and practically monochrome in its landscape; here, there wasn't a single shade of grey in sight. Even the bare earth was a rich rust-red colour, glittering in the sunlight. The land had one enormous forest in the centre, with desert around the edges right up to the cliffs. In some places, Aleks could see the land meeting sea at a much more gentle slope, the water as calm as any lake – he'd never seen the ocean so still!

'Are we heading back, or finding somewhere else to stay for the night?' Zhora asked after they'd been airborne for almost two hours, though he guessed they'd barely covered a third of the length of the country. By Aleks's estimate, they still had a good four or five hours of proper daylight. Drazan was drawing lines on a rough map of the island in order to split it into sections for them to tackle one at a time. Each section would take them two days – they hoped.

'I think we can make it across to the other desert. Might as well while we're up here. If we start at that end and work back, we'll be closer to our Stormlands by the time we want to leave,' Aleks said, eyeing the distance to the far end of the island.

Aleks let Drazan take over in the pilot's seat for a while, shoulders aching from the long flight the day before. 'The air is so still around here,' Drazan remarked, struggling a little to get hold of the propellers to keep them upright.

'You're telling me – the furnace is burning out like nobody's business. It's sweltering down here,' Zhora complained. Aleks winced; maybe flying out so far hadn't been the best idea. Still, they were over halfway, it was too late to back out now.

'Note for the future – the middle of the gap between Stormlands is a dead zone,' Drazan muttered, grimacing.

The further they got out over the centre of the area between the Stormlands, the harder the ship had to work to stay aloft. Aleks went down below to join Zhora in the engine room. 'How's it going?' he asked, stripping off his jacket and jumper in the sweltering heat.

'Not a complete catastrophe so far, so about as well as expected,' Zhora replied drily, wiping at his sweaty forehead. He was already down to his white undershirt, braces hanging around his hips. 'Just keep an eye on the left propeller gears, would you? I swear, any minute now, one of them's gonna go flying.' Aleks instantly saw what he meant. Every single gear was spinning so fast they all seemed to blur into one, and the chains were visibly straining at the effort.

'Ease up on her a bit, Drazan, if you can!' he called in the direction of the speaker's microphone. 'Or we'll have a real problem on our hands.'

'I'm trying my best, but if we want to reach the desert she's going to have to give it all she's got,' Drazan replied, sounding grim. Aleks frowned deeply. It was too late to turn back now; they were closer to the desert than they were to their previous landing spot. Getting back in one piece would be the real challenge.

'This area of the world is definitely not designed for skyships,' Zhora muttered, carefully switching out a gear on one of the back propeller's plates.

'You're telling me,' agreed Aleks. 'If you look down from here, the sea's completely calm.' Zhora's eyebrows rose in astonishment; there was nowhere in Tellus that had calm seas. The only people who had actual water-faring ships were the Erovans with their many rivers and coves, and the few Mericans who lived in lake-land areas. But from the look of the water below them, ships would probably handle just fine.

'We're picking up wind!' Drazan crowed, interrupting them. 'Not much, but enough for me to ease off on the propellers a bit. I'm just hoping the further out we go the more things will pick up.' The mechanism beside Aleks slowed drastically, and he saw that heavy black residue was covering the gears from their frantic overworking.

'Even if it takes us longer, just try and stick to the updraughts,' Aleks instructed. 'We've got all the time in the world but we haven't got all the spare parts.'

'Well, I wouldn't call it all the time in the world,' Zhora argued lightly. 'I want to get her down and turned off as soon as possible, just to be safe. But if getting wind power means going out of our way, then by all means go ahead.'

Aleks wished they had a porthole down in the engine room, just so he could see what was going on around them. He felt caged in the cramped, overheated room, but Zhora needed the help. 'Trying to cool this place down is going to be a challenge,' he mused, pushing his damp hair off his forehead.

'It'll cool down overnight, I hope, or we'll have a few issues. Have to tell Luka to install better ventilation in his next model,' Zhora joked. Aleks chuckled, smiling to himself.

'He's probably started it already, now his warehouse is empty. We'll get back and there'll be no room to land this one.' He hoped Luka did have some sort of insane, brilliant project to keep him occupied while they were away; he'd seen how out of sorts the man got when there was nothing around to challenge him.

As they flew, Aleks noticed the mechanisms moving less and less. 'We're nearly there,' Drazan assured them through the speakers. 'Give me twenty minutes or so to bring her down gently. Half this sand looks like we'd sink in it if I landed wrong.' Aleks imagined trying to dig the ship out of sand, and winced. Was there any part of this place that was skyship-friendly?

'If we're going to be landing, you might want to sit down, lad,' Zhora suggested.

'Is landing really that rough down here?' Aleks asked, sitting down.

'In a ship this small, you bet it is. If I hadn't had Luka with me the first time, I'd have gone arse over elbows the moment we touched ground,' he confided with a laugh. Aleks grinned, trying to imagine Zhora falling over so spectacularly.

Within twenty minutes they were on the ground, and despite a fairly smooth landing, Aleks was still glad of Zhora's warning. Clambering to his feet, he went back up to the control room, where Drazan was stretching out his legs. The sun was just setting on the horizon, edging the treetops with a gold-purple glow and leaving it too dark to see much of anything else.

Walking with Drazan through to their tiny galley, Aleks noted Zhora had left both traps open to air out the engine room.

'We're going to have to be careful when we head back over that way,' Zhora told them. 'The furnace has nearly overheated down there, it's been working so hard. I've turned everything off for now to let it cool overnight.'

'Duly noted.' Aleks downed a mug of water and rummaged through the cupboards, looking for something he could cook for dinner.

A comfortable silence settled over them as they ate, only broken by laughter when the lights finally gave out, having used the last of the ship's stored power. The three of them stumbled around in the dark until Drazan found and lit the lamp bolted to the counter, giving them enough light to dig a hand-lamp out of one of the cupboards. Zhora took it downstairs to find a few more lamps, leaving Aleks and Drazan in the dimly lit galley.

'We should probably think about going to bed in a little while, anyway,' said Aleks.

'Nah, not just yet. I want to get up on deck once it's properly dark and see if anything interesting makes an appearance. There could be a whole load of nocturnal wildlife out there. Not that I can film it in the dark, but it'd be nice to see,' Drazan said, shadows flickering across his face as he paced in and out of the lamp's pool of light.

'Want some company?' Aleks offered.

Drazan shrugged. 'Only if you want to. I'm happy to stay out on my own. Or maybe bug Zhora into staying up a few hours with me.'

'Nah, let him sleep, he's earned it. I'll stay up with you,' Aleks promised. The conversation halted when Zhora returned with two more lamps for his companions.

'You staying up, then?'

'Drazan wants to see what the nightlife is like around here,' Aleks explained. 'I said I'd keep him company.'

Zhora let out a wide yawn. 'I'm off to bed. Be careful out there – we don't know what could be in those woods.'

'I know, I know,' Drazan assured him. 'We'll be perfectly safe. I've got my gun, so stop being such a worrywart.' Zhora cuffed his brother's shoulder, and Aleks and Drazan went up on deck, taking their lamps and a flask of water between them. Even in the evening air it was still warmer than most days in Siberene.

'Whole different world out here, isn't it?' Aleks mused, keeping his voice low as they perched on the edge of the deck, leaning against the railings. Drazan set his lamp between them and Aleks turned his own off, not needing it. The moon was just as bright as it had been the night before, and the stars shone as clear as diamonds, making their little lamp near useless. The forest was still rustling with life despite the late hour, resonating with the occasional screech and bird call.

'Completely,' Drazan agreed. 'Seems closest to Kasem, from what I've heard, but they don't have nearly as much greenery. Makes you wonder, though, what they'd think if they suddenly ended up in Siberene.' Aleks snorted softly, imagining a sun-drenched Kasem native turning up in icy Siberene unexpectedly. They'd probably die of shock.

'What do you think will happen once we get back and people know about this place?' Aleks asked.

'I don't know, but every time I think about it I start wondering if maybe we shouldn't just keep it all to ourselves,' Drazan replied, a slight frown tugging at his brows. 'I can just imagine what would happen when people finally have the ships capable of getting over here, and how they'd desperately try to colonise it and make it part of the rest of the world and, well . . . maybe it's in the middle of the Stormlands for a reason. Maybe it was put here so that people wouldn't destroy it like we've destroyed everywhere else. Like you said, imagine what would happen if tyrium was found here. The whole place would be gutted quicker than Anglya was.'

Aleks bit his lip. He agreed with Drazan; the land was far too beautiful to be marred by human presence, but to go home and pretend nothing had happened . . . all their efforts would be wasted.

'We won't be the only ones who find a way out here,' he pointed out. 'Eventually, someone else will have the same idea, be it two months from now, two years, or even twenty years. We can't keep this place a secret forever. Surely if we tell people about it now, we'll at least give them a chance to do right by it.'

'And what happens when someone finally does get through?' Drazan asked.

'Then good luck to them trying to get anything through the Stormlands big enough to colonise this place. They'd have to be packing a lot of manpower and some heavy-duty equipment.' Enormous ships full of building equipment and workmen would never survive the journey.

'You have a point, I suppose,' Drazan relented, watching as a large bird soared out over the treetops before disappearing once more. 'I just wish we could make sure this place is protected.'

'So do I, but I think with the Stormlands either side it's about as protected as it's going to get,' Aleks reasoned, shrugging his shoulders. Drazan hummed in agreement, and they went back to watching for wildlife.

After a while, Aleks voiced the thought that neither of them wanted to acknowledge. 'What if we don't make it home, though?' he asked softly, eyes meeting Drazan's in the dim light.

'We will,' insisted Drazan. 'We have to, we've got too much waiting for us. You especially – all that family of yours, and Saria.' Aleks opened his mouth, but Drazan cut him off. 'Don't start! We both know how much you love her. You didn't even let a little thing like her trying to get you arrested affect your feelings,' he said with a knowing grin. Aleks blushed, but didn't deny it. Even in a place as incredible as this, Saria was constantly on his mind.

'How about you?' he asked. 'And Zhora. Surely you've got friends to get back to?'

Drazan shrugged. 'Not really. Sure, there're people at the flight school I get on with, but . . . no one who'd really miss me if I didn't come back. Or Zhora. We just sort of keep ourselves to ourselves.' Aleks could tell there was more to it than that, but didn't get the chance to ask, for the next second Drazan was clapping him on the shoulder. 'So tell me more about your girl, Saria, then. Clearly she's got to be something special to have this effect on you, even after everything that's happened.'

Aleks couldn't help but grin as he started to talk, finding it a little difficult to stop once he got going. It was nice, talking about her to someone who was neither related to him nor a girl. Drazan was an excellent listener, happily letting him ramble on about how much Saria's aunt hated him, and his fears that she'd have moved on by the time he got home.

'I wish I'd had the chance to tell her the truth,' Aleks admitted quietly. 'But, well, things didn't exactly go as planned.' It made his chest ache to consider the possibility that he might not return, that Saria would never know what had happened to him. She'd probably just assume he'd been taken back to Rensav – where she thought he belonged, if her turning him in was any indication.

'You can tell her the truth when we get home,' Drazan said. 'She'll have had a chance to miss you by then. Should give you a warm welcome, and an apology for calling the guards on you.' He gave him a grin, which Aleks tentatively returned. He hoped Drazan was right, that Saria would have missed him.

Eventually, they decided to call it a night, picking up their things and heading below deck, locking up behind them. Once in bed, Aleks was asleep within minutes, too tired to dwell on how far away from home he was, or the possibility of never making it back.

30

The next morning, Aleks was the first one on deck, and when he looked around his jaw dropped.

All he could see was sand. Miles and miles of rust-red sand, the occasional rock spearing the surface. He saw small shrub-like plants poking up through the sand, and some taller, strange-looking specimens. 'Gods,' he breathed. How were the plants even alive? Did it ever rain out here? Behind the ship was the forest; the thick shade looked welcoming in the face of the heat, which made Aleks's skin prickle and his lungs burn. He felt like it was sucking all the moisture from his body.

He undid the top three buttons of his shirt as he moved aside for the others to climb up, throwing the rigging net over the edge and clambering down to the sand.

'This is ridiculous,' Drazan said, awed. 'You wouldn't think places like this existed.'

'Maybe if we take back footage of this, people won't want to try and colonise it,' Aleks joked. Drazan chuckled, smiling as he joined him on the sand.

'That might work, especially in Siberene. If it's not covered in snow, we're not interested.' Both Aleks and Zhora snorted.

Drazan had a leather satchel slung over one shoulder, and he reached into it, pulling out a strange wide-brimmed hat. 'What on Tellus is that?' Aleks asked with raised eyebrows. Drazan grinned, setting it on his head at a jaunty angle.

'Hat I picked up in Mericus once. I forget what they call them. Keeps the sun off your face,' he explained. 'I packed for all weathers — there's a full snowsuit in my room too.'

'How far out do we want to go?' asked Aleks. Neither of the others had a waistcoat on, and Aleks was beginning to feel a little overdressed. He stripped his off, tossing it down the trapdoor hole.

'I don't fancy going out so far in that desert,' Drazan said. 'We stray too far from the ship and we'll get lost for sure.'

'I remember seeing a field or something not too far in to the centre, when we were flying over, maybe we could head for that via the forest,' Drazan suggested.

'Sounds good to me,' Aleks agreed. The forest meant shade, and shade meant not boiling to death. 'And if we find water, even better — if it's going to be this hot the whole time our supplies won't last nearly as long as we need them to.'

They set off towards the forest, leaving tracks in the sand. It became more compacted and clay-like the closer they got to the trees, until it was the same sort of red earth they had encountered at the other end of the country.

Aleks was grateful for the shade once they got into the forest, though the temperature was hardly any cooler. All it meant was things were a little more humid instead of bone-dry, and Aleks wondered where the water source was.

He hadn't seen a lake or river from the sky, but with the trees so thick it was probably hidden. Or maybe it was underground, like the rivers and streams in the Kholar Mountains.

Branches and undergrowth snapping under their heavy boots, Aleks undid a few more buttons of his shirt, feeling his vest stick to his back with sweat. 'Storms, I don't understand how people live in hot places,' Drazan grumbled, shifting his satchel to the other shoulder. 'Give me a blizzard and potential frostbite any day.' Aleks nodded emphatically in agreement, and Zhora laughed.

They walked for what felt like hours – but by Aleks's watch was only about forty-five minutes – before they finally stumbled across a wide open stretch of lush, green grass. It came up to their knees in some places and was dotted with bright red and purple wildflowers, entirely unlike the ones at the other end of the forest. Aleks had never seen anything like them before, and carefully unearthed a few small ones to put in a jar while Drazan recorded some video footage. It was only when they heard him speaking softly to himself that Zhora and Aleks realised he was recording audio too, though he had walked too far away for them to properly hear what he was saying. They found a small mound where the grass was shortest and sat down on top of it, Aleks unlacing his boots and sighing when his feet were free. 'I think I'm getting blisters,' he muttered.

Drazan joined them when he was finished with his filming, happily dropping down between them. A few rabbit-like animals dared to venture into the field while they were there, but none came close enough to get a good look at; all Aleks could see was that while they looked vaguely similar to the rabbits at home, they were about three times larger and looked far more lethal. He was rather glad they didn't decide to come close; he didn't fancy his chances against them.

'I quite fancy having a little wander around the desert,' Drazan announced. 'Not too far out,' he added hastily at the look on his brother's face. 'Just far enough to maybe have a look at some of those odd plants, and see if we can reach the end of the desert.'

'If we must,' Zhora agreed reluctantly, before reaching for his water skin and drinking thirstily. 'I don't think we should stay out too long, though – all this heat can't be good for us.'

'We'll head to the desert today, then tomorrow try and look properly for water. If we don't find it here, we'll move on to the next section, but we need to be careful,' Aleks said decisively. As much as he wanted to explore, water was their priority at the moment.

'As you wish, Your Majesty,' Drazan returned with a playful bow, earning a glare.

After they'd rested enough, they put their boots on and set off once more, tracing their footprints back to where they'd come from. Aleks winced when they emerged from the forest, the sun immediately near blinding him. It was, thankfully, not as hot as it had been earlier, but it was still far hotter than he was comfortable with. Even though the three of them had now stripped to their sleeveless undershirts, they were all soaked through with sweat.

After making a brief stop back in the ship to eat lunch and take a little refuge in the shade, Drazan led them out into the sandy landscape, compass in hand to keep them on track. Aleks wished he had different shoes, his heavy boots sinking inches deep with every step, making his legs ache with the effort to keep moving.

The further they went, the more it became clear that there was nothing new to see in the desert, and the more Zhora and Aleks wanted to strangle Drazan for bringing them out there. But Drazan happily wandered through the sand, occasionally stopping to examine a patch of dry-looking shrubbery. To his annoyance, the strange, tall plants in the distance were too far away to go and examine up close; Aleks and Zhora threatened mutiny when Drazan tried to convince them to walk further.

Feeling a headache brewing from the glaring sunlight, Aleks stumbled a little in the sand, drawing a concerned glance from Zhora. 'I'm fine,' he insisted, voice scratchy from his dry throat. 'I'll just need to sit down for a while when we get back.'

'If you're sure, lad,' Zhora replied, though Aleks couldn't ignore the man's gaze on him the entire way back. Even Drazan seemed to be feeling the exhaustion by now, feet dragging and limbs sluggish when he finally climbed up the rigging rope to get on deck, cursing when his foot tangled in the netting. Zhora laughed, reaching over and grasping his brother's arm, hoisting him the rest of the way up. Climbing below deck, Aleks let out a blissful sigh in the dark, cool hallway. It was nowhere near as cold as he'd like it to be, but anything was better than the inferno that was the outside world.

'I think I'm going to go lie down for a bit,' he said softly.

'Are you sure you're all right?' Drazan asked, worried. 'You look terrible.' Aleks managed a wry half-smile.

'Thanks,' he muttered, rubbing his eyes. 'I'm fine, just a bit light-headed.' He shuffled off towards his room.

Stripping down to his underwear, he collapsed on top of the blankets on the bed, relishing the cool air on his over-heated skin. Gods, he wanted to be home. This place was extraordinary, and exploring it was amazing, even though it was so hot, but he missed the Compass, and Saria most of all. Every day spent here was a day more for Anastasia to introduce her to a man she approved of, a day more for Saria to fall for someone else before Aleks had a chance to make amends.

Eyes closing, he wished he had some sort of cold compress to put on his forehead to soothe his headache, but it really wasn't worth getting up for. He didn't have much time to think on it, though, falling asleep despite the pain in his skull.

'Oh, Aleks . . .' Blearily coming to consciousness, Aleks scowled at the voice, his head pounding. He cracked an eye open, seeing Zhora leaning in his doorway, a frown tugging at his brows. The clock on his desk said it was morning; how had he slept for so long? He'd missed dinner!

'What's the matter?' he asked, wondering why he felt both cold and hot at the same time. Surely that wasn't possible?

'You've got sunburn,' Zhora told him. 'Bad sunburn, by the looks of things.' Aleks squinted up at him, puzzled.

'What's sunburn?' His face itched, so he brought a hand up to scratch at his cheek, hissing at the unexpected burst of pain it caused.

'That's sunburn.' Zhora strode into the room, pulling a small mirror from his pocket and handing it to Aleks, who sat up, groaning as the room spun around him. Holding the mirror up to his face, his eyes widened when he saw the bright pink hue of his skin. Glancing down, he saw his arms and part of his chest had suffered the same fate, and by the feel of his neck it was also just as tender. Every part of his skin that hadn't been covered by fabric yesterday now felt like it was on fire.

'Why has this happened? You're all right,' he murmured somewhat enviously, eyeing Zhora's arms and face. They looked a few shades darker than usual, but tanned rather than burned.

'I've spent time in hot places before, I'm used to it. Also, my da was Merican, and Drazan and I inherited his skin colouring. I'll bet you're Siberene through and through,' Zhora presumed, folding his arms over his chest. Aleks nodded.

'As far back as we can trace. What does that have to do with anything?'

'People who aren't used to the sun are more likely to get bad sunburn – you have to build up a resistance to it. Gods, I'm sorry, lad. We should've known you'd burn – you're as pale as snow.' Aleks scowled, looking down at himself; where he wasn't bright pink from the sunburn, his skin was practically transparent in its whiteness.

'How do I get rid of it? I feel awful,' he asked, wincing with every movement as he got to his feet and pulled on his sleep trousers. Just standing up made his head pound, and he thought he was going to be sick.

'You look awful,' Zhora said wryly. 'All you can do is stay hydrated and wait for it to go away. Give it a week or so, and the burned skin will peel off and you'll be as good as new.'

'And what about the headache? I feel like I've been hit by a merchant ship.'

Zhora frowned. 'You've got a headache? That doesn't sound good. Anything else? Nausea, maybe?'

'Definitely nausea,' Aleks confirmed. 'I ache all over. I'm dizzy, I feel feverish . . . am I sick?' he asked, panicked; had he caught some strange disease native to hot places? A wave of light-headedness overcame him, and he sat back down on the bed, biting his lip to stop himself from vomiting. 'Zhora, what's wrong with me?'

'Sounds like sunstroke to me,' Zhora said. 'Gods, we should've known. Lie back down, lad, and I'll get you some water.'

He did as he was told, eyes squeezing shut as the world spun once more.

'Ouch.' The voice was Drazan's, and Aleks tentatively opened his eyes again, seeing both brothers standing in his doorway, Zhora with a tankard in one hand. 'Definitely looks like sunstroke. That's you off-duty, for sure.'

'It might be worth all of us staying in today,' Zhora suggested as he passed the tankard to Aleks, helping him sit up to drink it. 'Little sips, lad.'

'But we need to find water,' Aleks protested, once he'd quenched his thirst. 'Now more than ever, if the heat is going to leave me feeling like this.'

'We have time, Aleks.' Zhora's voice was firm. 'You need to rest, and we don't want to get sunstroke ourselves. Drazan and I can clean up the engine room today – it'll do the girl good.'

Aleks sighed, aware he'd lost the battle and too exhausted to argue further. 'All right, fine. But just today. If I'm still like this tomorrow, you two need to keep going regardless. We can't afford to waste time.'

'It's not wasting time, it's looking out for our captain! Sunstroke isn't something to brush off, Aleks. You could get seriously ill if it gets any worse.'

'OK,' he relented; they knew more about this than he did.

'Drazan, you start breakfast while I carry on downstairs. Aleks needs salt, and lots of it, so a broth of some kind would be good,' Zhora instructed. 'You just get some sleep, lad.' Aleks didn't need to be told twice; he already felt his foggy mind drifting off, his eyes falling shut.

By the time Zhora and Drazan stopped for an early dinner, Aleks was feeling well enough to venture out of his room and join his crewmates in the galley. He'd drunk nearly his entire bodyweight in water – despite his protests about rationing it – and downed several bowls of broth at Zhora's instruction. It seemed to be working.

As they ate, Zhora reported back on the state of the engine room, assuring them that now things had cooled down and he'd cleaned up a little, only three parts had needed replacing, and they were fairly small. They'd been lucky, but another large dead zone might be the end of them.

'How will we get back, then?' Aleks asked, frowning.

'Well, we've been talking about that,' Zhora replied, leaning back in his chair once his plate was clean. 'Drazan and I thought it might be best to just skip the central sections near the dead zone and then head out further West, get as close to the other Stormlands as possible so there's something to carry us out, and maybe fly up a while to see if there's any other land around here.'

Aleks perked up at this. 'Sounds like a good plan to me. Can she withstand it?' he asked, patting the wall of the ship. Flying out that far and then alongside the entire length of the Stormlands would be a long trip.

'If the wind is as good as we hope it'll be at the Stormlands, she'll be just fine,' Zhora said confidently. 'A trip back to colder air should do her some good. Even just sitting here is heating things up.'

Aleks zoned out through the rest of the conversation during dinner. 'I think I'm going to go back to bed, if that's all right with you,' he declared when he was finished. 'I'm still exhausted.'

Zhora nodded, gently ruffling his hair. 'Take some water with you, lad. The more you drink, the better your skin will get.'

'Sleep well, Aleks. I'm sorry we didn't think about sunstroke yesterday,' Drazan added, but Aleks waved him off.

'It wasn't your fault,' he insisted, smiling. He opened his mouth to say goodnight but was drowned out by loud noises from outside the ship. All three of them froze. It sounded like shouting.

31

Aleks looked up in alarm, meeting the equally panicked gazes of his crewmates. 'That's a weird-sounding animal,' Drazan said with a weak chuckle. The noise continued, growing louder.

'That's no animal,' Zhora replied, a grim look on his face. They could hear the shouting more clearly now; whatever was out there was drawing closer. It sounded like words; not words that Aleks recognised by any means, but words nonetheless.

'Do we go out there?' he asked tentatively, looking to Zhora, who scratched at his stubbled chin.

'Sounds like we're going to have to. Grab your guns – we have no idea what it is.' His face betrayed the lie; they knew exactly what was out there, they just didn't believe it.

Ducking back to his room, Aleks shrugged on a loose shirt, ignoring the pain it caused, and dug through his satchel for his gun. The adrenalin in his system kept the worst of his symptoms at bay, but he still felt like he'd been run over by an entire stampede of horses. Meeting Drazan and Zhora back in the narrow hallway, he found the brothers equally armed. Zhora was preparing to climb out of the open trap. The shouting was deafening, and as Aleks made his way up on deck, he couldn't believe his eyes. They were surrounded.

The people of the land beyond the Stormlands were darkly tanned, dressed in loose shorts and very little else, their skin gleaming in the sunlight. Even the women, to Aleks's embarrassment, wore nothing but shorts and sandals, their chests freely exposed. Some wore their frizzy black hair loose, others in tight braids, and all of them were staring at the three Siberene men with wide eyes. Every single person seemed to be holding some sort of weapon.

'We are peaceful!' Zhora exclaimed, holding his hands up in the universal sign of peace. The people didn't seem to recognise the guns tucked in their belts, or they probably would have contested that statement.

'Yes, we don't mean you any harm,' Aleks piped up nervously. Their gazes were blank; of course, there was no reason for any of them to speak Siberene. That was going to make things difficult.

The crowd facing them began to part, everyone stepping aside for a young, muscular woman with bright-coloured fabrics draped around her waist in a sort of skirt, her braided hair threaded with wooden beads. Aleks averted his eyes from her chest on instinct, feeling his already pink cheeks flush brighter. The woman looked up at them, her eyes a vivid amber colour. 'Halt,' she said slowly. Aleks gasped; she had just spoken Siberene!

'Do you ... understand us?' he asked tentatively, flinching as the woman's intense gaze focused on him. She nodded once, her posture regal.

'Yes, but slow. Old tongue,' she answered. 'Grandfather tongue.'

'Grandfather?' Drazan asked, speaking for the first time. 'You mean, your grandfather spoke like us? Our language?' She nodded again, and Aleks didn't think it was possible to be any more stunned than he was.

'A ship got through,' he breathed. One day, many decades ago, a ship had made it through the Stormlands. He felt an irrational spike of anger – they weren't the first ones after all – but pushed it aside. Clearly whoever had come through before hadn't done so with their ship in one piece. He couldn't imagine anyone willingly staying in such a hot wasteland, especially someone from Siberene. They must have been stranded.

'Come,' the woman ordered, her tone sharp. 'Follow.' Aleks opened his mouth to protest, but Zhora silenced him with a look, watching the crowd of people step back far enough to let the three climb down the rigging net. Aleks was unnerved by the number of people staring at him. He could hear them murmuring in their strange language; now that he listened more carefully it sounded both famil- iar and foreign to him, like it had once upon a time been Siberene but had changed and evolved over the years. How long ago had the ship landed, for the language to have changed so much?

'Follow,' the woman said again, turning towards the forest. Two young men with biceps the size of Aleks's head flanked the woman, glaring at the three foreigners. Was the woman their queen? She certainly seemed important, the way everyone was deferring to her.

As they walked through the forest the woman turned to them, curiosity in her eyes. 'You came in wooden box?' she asked.

'It's a ship,' Aleks explained. 'A flying machine.'

'Ship,' the woman repeated, sounding out the word. 'Flying. Like bird?'

'Yes,' Aleks confirmed, smiling faintly. 'We flew in our ship, from the other side of the storms.' At that, the woman gasped aloud.

'Other side?' she breathed in astonishment. 'Goddess Land?'

'Yes, yes, that's right!' Drazan said, enthusiasm growing. 'We come from the Goddess Land, beyond the storms. You know it?' Glancing away from the woman for a brief moment, Aleks almost stumbled in his shock. They had reached what seemed to be a village, with small wooden huts dotting the grass. He looked up, amazed to see more huts built in the trees, with bridges and ladders of vines connecting them. It was ingenious.

'Legend,' the woman explained, 'says many-great-grand-father was from Goddess Land. Came with wife and friends, got stuck.'

'How many years ago?' Zhora asked. The woman shrugged helplessly.

'Many many years,' she replied. 'I am fourteenth captain. Many-great-grandfather was first captain.' Aleks let out a long breath; fourteen generations. It had to have been a long, long time ago that the ship came out here. How on Tellus had they managed that?

When they stopped in what Aleks assumed was the centre of the village, the crowd seemed to grow impatient, calling out to their captain. As she replied, more people emerged from the wooden huts; half-naked children were among them, listening attentively. When she was finished she turned back to the crew, her eyes landing on Aleks. He squared his shoulders, offering her a smile, heart racing. 'My name is Aleks.'

'Kara,' she replied, pointing to herself. 'Captain.'

'This is Zhora, and Drazan,' Aleks introduced them slowly, pointing to each man in turn. 'I am captain,' he added, pointing back to himself. Kara seemed to brighten at that, taking a step closer to him.

'Well met, captain. Sit,' she added, gesturing to several long wooden benches around what seemed to be a fire pit, though there was no fire. Aleks supposed they didn't need one during the day. He, Zhora and Drazan obligingly sat on a bench, and Kara sat opposite them, still flanked by her hulking bodyguards. The crowd moved with them, gathering in a circle around the benches, and the hair on the back of Aleks's neck stood on end. 'You flew from Goddess Land,' Kara declared, her gaze meeting his. 'Explain, how?'

Taking a deep breath, Aleks explained their journey, Zhora and Drazan occasionally chipping in. He tried to speak slowly and simply, and to ignore the dozens of people hanging on to his every word, despite not fully understanding them. When he was finished he paused. 'Could you tell me how you came here? How your many-great-grandfather came from the Goddess Land?'

'No one knows,' Kara replied sadly. 'Used to know, many captains ago. Not any more. Long, long time ago. We move on.' Aleks held back a sigh of frustration; of course, if it had been fourteen generations, the story probably hadn't survived in any reliable form. The same way the story of the First Men changed depending on where you learned it. 'We thought it myth, until you.'

'No, there is definitely a world outside the storms,' Zhora assured her. 'Thousands and thousands of people, six countries, and plenty more flying machines.' Kara gasped, reeling back in shock.

'Thousands and thousands?' she repeated, as if such a number were absurd. Aleks smiled slightly.

'Millions,' he told her, not sure if the word would mean anything. In a society this small, what need would they have to count so high?

'More fly here from Goddess Land?' Kara asked suddenly, alarmed, and Aleks hastened to placate her.

'No, no, we come alone. Our people think it impossible to travel through storms.'

'But you flew,' she said reproachfully, making him grin.

'We are unusual.' His gaze softened. 'No one else is coming. I swear.' Kara didn't look convinced, but she nodded, relaxing a little.

'Tell me of the Goddess Land,' she half requested, half ordered. Aleks let Zhora do most of the talking, the eldest of their trio having seen more of the world than him and Drazan combined. Trying to keep the vocabulary simple, he told her first of Siberene, and then a little of the other countries, explaining how they travelled and traded and fought, and of how cold Siberene was in comparison to her homeland. She was enraptured, though many of her people grew bored and wandered off when it became clear nothing interesting was going to happen.

Aleks couldn't have said how long they sat there talking to the strange woman. Long enough that when she stood abruptly, he realised he had completely forgotten the fact that she was shirtless. 'Full dark come soon,' she declared. 'You must return to flying machine. Forest full of danger in the dark.'

'Can we come back tomorrow?' Drazan asked. Aleks had to admit, he too was curious to see how the people lived so primitively. But at the same time they set him on edge, and he didn't want to stay any longer than necessary.

Aleks stood, offering Kara a nod, worried he'd fall over if he tried to bow. 'It has been nice talking to you,' he told her, making her smile, and she bowed slightly clumsily in return.

'And nice talking to you,' she replied, offering the same gesture to Drazan and Zhora. She called out in her own language and two young men came running up. Kara gave a hurried command, and they saluted before turning to the three foreigners. 'Go with boys, they will return you to flying machine.'

That seemed to be the end of their meeting, as Kara left with her ever present guards, immediately being swept into conversation with some of the elder members of the community. It seemed like everyone wanted to hear about the mysterious visitors. Their two escorts jerked their heads in a clear gesture for them to follow, then set off into the forest. With one glance back at the strange village, Aleks took off after them, his crewmates at his side.

★ ★ ★

The three men didn't speak until they were safely back in their ship with the trap closed, their two escorts having retreated back to the forest. 'Well,' Drazan breathed, 'that was unexpected.'

'It's insane,' Zhora murmured, shaking his head incredulously. 'For a ship that old to have survived the journey through the Stormlands, and to have made it to land . . . a one in a million chance.'

'Well, if you think about it, over the years there have probably been thousands of ships sent into the Stormlands,' Aleks reasoned. 'One of them was bound to have made it before ours. I'm just amazed there were women on board.' Things back then had been even less progressive than they were now; he was surprised a woman had even been allowed to set foot on an expedition ship.

'I guess it answers the question of whether the land is habitable, though,' Drazan said, leading the way through to the galley. He poured three mugs of cider; none of them would be going to bed just yet.

'We can't tell anyone about them,' Zhora said abruptly. 'When we get back. You saw the panic on her face at the thought of other outsiders coming. Could you imagine if we went back home and told everyone that there's a group of people living beyond the Stormlands? They'd invade their homes, make them slaves in their own country, replace their village with concrete and stone.'

Aleks grimaced. 'We didn't have our video recorders on us,' he pointed out. 'And we won't take them tomorrow either. We have enough footage of this land looking empty . . . no one has to know it's inhabited.' He somewhat envied Kara and her people; they clearly lived a far simpler life than he was used to. But when he imagined living without modern comforts, and in such blazing heat, he knew he could never join them. Especially not if it meant leaving behind everyone he knew and loved.

'But what happens when other outsiders get through? You said that it'll be hard for them to do it without Luka's ship, but . . . it will no doubt happen eventually. Luka can't be the only person to design such a thing. What happens when they stumble across Kara's people, and find out we lied?' Drazan asked, brow furrowed.

'We deal with that if it comes to it,' Zhora said. 'For now, I think all of us should go to bed. Aleks needs to rest.'

The three said their goodnights, retreating to their rooms. Despite his exhaustion it took Aleks longer than usual to get to sleep, his brain still back in the forest with Kara and her people. He still had so many questions; how long could they stay before they had to go home? Would that be enough time for him to learn everything he wanted to about their society and their land? He sighed, rolling over and squeezing his eyes shut. He'd ask Zhora in the morning.

Morning found Aleks in the ship's tiny bathroom, trying to convince himself to leave the shower. He was still feeling the effects of his sunstroke, but the water helped immensely. Still, he needed to step out and join his crew before he wasted too much water. 'Stop hogging the shower!' Drazan shouted, banging on the bathroom door.

Dressed and feeling slightly more human again, he wandered through to the galley, Drazan on his heel. Zhora was up and dressed with breakfast nearly finished. He grinned playfully at his brother. 'About time you got your lazy arse up! I thought you'd sleep through till noon,' he teased.

'What's the plan for today, then?' Aleks asked once he was halfway through his breakfast.

'Your plan is you leave.' Aleks's heart skipped a beat at the interruption. He turned towards the doorway to see Kara standing there, her hands on her hips. Today she had a length of dark grey fabric draped over her shoulders and chest; was it slightly colder outside?

'How did you get in?' Zhora asked. The woman laughed.

'Door was open,' she explained, pointing up towards the trap topside. Of course, they'd left it open to give the engine room a bit of cool air overnight. 'You leave now.'

'Excuse me?' Aleks frowned, perplexed. Had they done something to offend her?

'Go back to Goddess Land, and do not come here again. We do not want you,' Kara declared, her amber eyes cold. 'My people, they talk of you. Some still have know-ledge of old tongue, they hear you. They talk of Goddess Land, of machines, of flying. We do not need flying.' Aleks's frown deepened; some of her people had been able to understand them? Why was that such a bad thing?

'So they're curious,' he said with a shrug. 'We don't mind answering questions.' Kara glared, taking a step further into the room.

'I said we do not need flying,' she insisted angrily. 'Your people, your life, in the Goddess Land, you are too . . .' she trailed off, saying a long word in her own language with a

302

frustrated look on her face, clearly trying to find the Siberene equivalent, . . . 'wanting for power,' she settled on eventually. 'You want, want, want. You trade metal for things just to own them, you fight to take from others. You take and do not give, and my people do not need that. Leave now before you taint them, and do not send more of your people here.'

'Hold on a minute!' Drazan exclaimed, jumping to his feet. 'We have been polite, we did nothing to harm you. All we want to do is learn about you and your people – we never said anything about imposing our culture on you.'

'You impose enough being here,' Kara snapped. 'You talk of your home and my people listen. They wonder why we do not have those things, and when I say we do not need them they ask why. They did not ask why before you came.'

'So you're angry at us for opening their eyes to the world outside?' Aleks asked. The woman nodded sharply.

'The world outside will not be kind to us. I do not need my people wanting to be kind to the world,' she told him, finality in her tone. 'There is plan, to collect you when sun is highest, bring you back to village, talk more. I want you gone before that. If you are still here, I will kill you.' Aleks flinched; there was no hesitation in her tone. 'You come back? I kill you. Any people from the Goddess Land come back, they are dead. Go back to your home, and leave mine to be free of wanting and flying.' She slipped a hand into a fold in her shorts, taking it out to reveal a sharp knife that glinted in the low lamplight.

Aleks held up his hands to placate her, eyes wide. 'OK, OK,' he said hurriedly. 'We'll leave. We won't tell our people of you. But when they learn that this land is here, they will some day make it through like we did. You cannot hide forever.'

'When that happens, my people will be prepared,' Kara said, lips curled in a snarl. 'You are nice people, but your land is not. Leave, or I will make you.'

'We're leaving,' Zhora promised. 'We'll fly as soon as you leave the ship. There's no need for violence.'

'That is funny, coming from men of Goddess Land,' Kara scoffed, raising one dark eyebrow at him. Still, she put her knife back in her shorts, then turned to Aleks and offered a short bow. 'Well met, captain.' He could hardly say the same after her threats, but he bowed anyway, and before he even straightened up she turned on her heel and left.

The three men were motionless for several moments, stunned at what had just happened. Zhora was the first to speak. 'We'd best prepare for flight, then,' he said quietly, shaking his head. 'Shame, shame.'

'I would've liked to stay longer,' Aleks agreed. 'But if she doesn't want us here . . . this is her land, by the old laws.' Aleks wasn't a king; she was the sovereign here. They couldn't go against her word. Especially not when she had brandished a knife at them, and her people vastly outnumbered them.

'I'll go and start bolting things down,' Drazan declared, getting to his feet. 'Aleks, don't even think about getting in that pilot's seat – you're still on rest. For now, at least. Come on, we'd best be quick about things.'

Kara's threat at the forefront of their minds, the three prepared their ship for flight as quickly as they could, Zhora meticulously checking over everything in the engine room. The trip back would be tough, and Aleks only hoped the ship could make it.

32

With Drazan in the pilot's seat, they managed to get the ship off the ground and far enough out to start catching the stronger air currents. Getting in the air had been a challenge, but there was just enough of a wind to lift them a couple of feet – enough to start the propellers to get them the rest of the way. Their plan was to skirt around the edge of the country itself, hoping to avoid the dead zone in the centre.

They'd only been flying for a couple of hours before disaster struck. 'Turning the propellers on now,' the pilot declared. Their shift system had been altered so that Zhora was in the engine room for this part, and though Aleks was meant to be sleeping, he chose to stay with Drazan. It was a shame they were leaving so abruptly; Aleks had wanted to fly out a little closer to the Dalivian side of the Stormlands, and maybe further North to see if there was any other land. But without a safe landing place, it was out of the question; the ship couldn't keep going that long in this heat.

'Come on, girl, don't fail us now,' Drazan murmured softly as the propellers whirred and whirred, the sails useless without a strong wind. Halfway to the other side of the island and they were beginning to feel the heat even in the control room.

'Getting a bit warm in here, lads!' Zhora warned them.

'Not much I can do about it, big brother,' Drazan retorted, voice wavering slightly. Even in a ship as small as theirs, the propellers were designed to aid in changing directions, not to support the ship completely in lieu of any wind.

'Come on, come on, please,' Aleks breathed. It didn't work. The whining of the propellers grew louder and there was a loud banging noise. The ship jolted harshly to the left, almost sending Aleks to the floor. 'What was that?'

There was no response through the speakers, and suddenly the smell of burning caught Aleks's nose, making him gag. 'Zhora, what's happened down there?' Drazan called, sounding alarmed as he attempted to stop the ship from dropping like a stone. 'The propellers aren't working – we've got nothing to keep us airborne,' he muttered. When he turned to face the open doorway he could see thick black smoke drifting up from the engine room.

'Zhora!' Aleks shouted, loud enough to be heard down below even without the speakers, in case they'd just blown offline. 'Talk to us, Zhora!' There was no reply. Drazan glanced over, fear on his face.

'If I bring her down at this speed, we'll crash,' he said, frantically working the controls to find some way of slowing their descent. They were still over the sea, but land was drawing ever closer.

'Right,' Aleks muttered. 'I'm going downstairs.' His heart was pounding as he rushed towards the ladder. He pulled his shirt up over his mouth and nose to block out the smoke, tugging his flight goggles over his eyes. 'Zhora?' he called hesitantly, stepping into the engine room. He could hardly see anything, but there didn't seem to be any movement. Dread curled in his stomach. 'Zhora, where are you?'

The ship was dropping faster by the minute. Hurrying to the left propeller – the source of the smoke – Aleks wished he'd brought a scarf to tie around his face as the smell was making him choke. He pushed through, waving his hands in front of his face to clear the black smog and get a better look. The entire mechanism was twisted and gnarled, melted beyond all recognition. No wonder it wasn't turning. 'I can't fix this!' he shouted up to Drazan, panicked. 'Not before we hit the ground!' He heard the pilot curse loudly.

'Can't Zhora help you?' Drazan called back, and Aleks frowned. Wherever Zhora was in the room, he wasn't making any noise. That didn't bode well.

'Just try and bring her down safely!' Aleks said, ignoring the question. Darting over to the right propeller, he let out a huff of relief; this one was intact, just knocked out of place. 'I can get the right propeller back online – will that be enough?'

'It's going to have to be!' At Drazan's response, Aleks quickly realigned the propeller's mechanism, relieved when it began to turn as it was supposed to. The ship jolted, seeming to slow down a fraction; it wasn't going to make for a smooth landing by any means, but it might just be enough to save them.

'Just bring her down wherever you can!' Aleks yelled.

Coughing, trying to avoid inhaling lungfuls of smoke in the process, he turned to look around the rest of the engine room, squinting through the smoke to get a glimpse of Zhora. He had to get him out quickly, before the smoke suffocated him. 'Zhora,' he called, not quite loud enough for Drazan to hear. He didn't want the pilot to worry, not when he needed to concentrate on landing them safely. 'Zhora, where are you?'

He paused as he accidentally kicked something both soft and solid. His eyes stung as he waved the smoke away and looked down at the floor. Zhora lay there, skin blackened with soot, his face a mass of burns and his eyes staring up, unseeing. Aleks dropped to his knees. He shook the man's shoulder and checked his pulse, but he knew what he would find: nothing.

Aleks lurched forward as the ship came to an abrupt halt, bouncing twice before landing. When it was still, he looked down at Zhora's unmoving body, a lump in his throat. Gods, he couldn't be . . . how?

'Aleks? Zhora?' Drazan's voice broke through Aleks's daze. The boy scrambled to his feet, hurrying to the ladder.

'Don't come down!' he shouted hastily, standing at the foot of the ladder just as Drazan peered over the edge. The pilot looked confused and tired, coughing as he accidentally inhaled a lungful of smoke.

'What is it?' he asked. 'Gods, this smoke is awful! Are you all right? Hang on.' He got to his feet, moving to open the trap to the outside world, letting the smoke drift out. 'How bad is it down there?' He looked grim, and Aleks swallowed harshly. His eyes watered behind his goggles, but he knew it wasn't due to the smoke. 'Storms, I'm going to kill Luka when we get back. Indestructible, my arse! It's going to take Zhora days to fix this! Where is he? Already started?'

'Drazan . . .' Aleks started, the words refusing to form in his throat. Drazan's frown grew deeper.

'Aleks, what's happened? Where's Zhora?'

'I don't know what happened,' Aleks said. 'It looks like the propeller blew and Zhora got caught, but . . . it's not good, Draz.' Drazan paled, practically throwing himself down the ladder, pushing past Aleks. Now that the smoke had cleared slightly, it was easy to see Zhora lying on the floor. Drazan let out an anguished cry at the sight of his brother.

'No!' He dropped to the ground at Zhora's side, gripping his shoulder. 'No! Zhora, come on, don't do this to me, you can't! Come on, big brother, just wake up!'

'Drazan,' Aleks murmured, taking a tentative step closer. 'He's gone.' Drazan choked out a sob, head bowed, hand still gripping the front of Zhora's shirt.

'He can't,' he said, suddenly sounding very young.

Aleks crouched at his friend's side, resting a hand on his shoulder. 'I'm so sorry, Drazan. Gods, this is all my fault.' If he hadn't convinced them to come in the first place, Zhora would still be alive.

'Don't you dare,' Drazan growled, startling Aleks as he looked up sharply. 'Don't you *dare* blame yourself. This is Luka's fault for not building a better bloody ship, and Kara's fault for making us leave so quickly, and bloody *Zhora's* fault for agreeing to come to this blasted place, but it's *not yours*, all right?' The pilot was crying by the time he finished speaking, and Aleks didn't hesitate to pull him into a tight hug. He wished he could believe his words.

'Come on,' he murmured, after they'd been sitting there for a while. 'We should go up on deck, before we get smoke-sick.'

'But what about . . .' Drazan trailed off, eyes darting to his brother, and Aleks squeezed his shoulder.

'We can come back down for him when the smoke's cleared,' he promised. 'Get him out, clean him up a bit. Find somewhere to . . . to lay him to rest.' Drazan flinched. Still, he didn't resist when Aleks urged him to his feet, directing him towards the ladder.

When they emerged on deck, Aleks couldn't help but take great lungfuls of fresh air, looking up to see the wispy black cloud that had formed above them from the smoke. It was a huge giveaway, but he could only hope Kara's reach didn't extend to the other end of the country.

'We should check the rest of the ship,' Drazan announced, voice hollow. 'I didn't bring her down gently. If there's external damage . . . we might have a bigger problem than we thought.' If the structure of the ship was damaged in any way they wouldn't be able to fix it. They had spare mechanical parts, but little else.

Aleks moved to throw the rigging rope over the side, climbing down with ease. The ship was slightly unstable, but hopefully that wasn't a serious problem. Not waiting for Drazan, Aleks started walking around the ship, carefully checking the wood and metal holding everything together.

They had left the wings extended, and he checked over one while Drazan went around the other side and checked the other, looking for any rips or tears. There was a small scorch mark on Aleks's, but it was on the very edge and didn't look like it was going to be a problem. It didn't bode well for the propeller though, and he swore when he manually tucked the wing away in order to pull up the hatch covering the propeller. It had blown spectacularly. 'We've got a problem, Draz!'

The propeller was mangled, the blades warped through overheating and covered in black dust from sparking, which explained the small burn on the wing. They were lucky it hadn't caught alight; then they would have been in real trouble. Drazan jogged around to meet him, letting out a low whistle at the sight of the propeller. 'Gods,' he muttered, shaking his head. 'Can we fix it?'

Aleks bit his lip, doing a mental inventory of the spare parts in the storage room. 'In theory,' he said eventually. 'If we can straighten the blades out ourselves and clean it up a bit, I should have enough to replace the innards. It's – it's not pretty in there.' Aleks prayed that was all the damage. If the furnace or engine had problems too, he didn't know if they'd have enough parts to replace it all.

'How long do you think it'll take?' Drazan asked quietly, eyes still focused on the broken propeller. Aleks hummed.

'A day, maybe two?' he guessed. 'It all depends on how bad things are inside once it's cleared. Luka taught me a lot about the ship, but . . . I'm no mechanic, not really.' Neither of them said what they were thinking. Zhora would have known. Zhora would have had them back to rights in no time.

'You can fix it,' Drazan said confidently. 'You know this ship almost as well as Luka himself. And I'll help where I can.' It wasn't like they had any other choice; the ship was their only way home, and Aleks refused to sit back and accept they were stranded.

'Let's get this unhooked so we can start shaping the blades,' he suggested, 'while we're still stuck out here.' It was baking hot but Aleks ignored his sunburn, directing Drazan so the two of them could remove the propeller from the ship. Neither of them spoke but for instructions, and Aleks tried to force his attention away from the plume of black smoke still trailing from the ship, and from what awaited them when they went back inside.

'How far do you think Kara's territory reaches?' Drazan asked, startling Aleks.

He glanced over at the forest. 'Let's just work as quickly as we can,' he said. 'We'll deal with things as they come.' There was no use worrying about it yet. They had bigger things to think about. If they couldn't fix the ship, they were stranded.

33

By the time the pair had the propeller removed and lying on the sand, Aleks was in desperate need of water. 'We should go back inside,' he suggested. 'Get out of the sun, have a break.'

'Get Zhora,' Drazan finished quietly. 'OK.' He let Aleks lead the way back up the rigging rope.

Everything smelled of smoke, and there was some still lingering in the air, but Aleks found he could breathe comfortably without his shirt over his face.

He went to the galley first, filled a glass with water and drank it thirstily, urging Drazan to do the same. The pilot seemed dazed, his eyes constantly straying to the doorway. Part of Aleks wanted to go down to the engine room immediately, to get everything over with, but another part wanted to avoid the room forever and just hide away in ignorance. It was too late for that.

Soon, they had no excuse, and Drazan looked up to meet Aleks's gaze head on. 'It's time,' he declared. 'We . . . we shouldn't leave him waiting any longer.' Swallowing thickly, Aleks nodded, and Drazan turned for the door.

He froze at the top of the ladder, hands clenched so tight that his knuckles were white. 'I can go first, if you want?' Aleks offered, but Drazan shook his head.

'No, no. I can do it,' he insisted. He took a deep breath and climbed down the ladder, his palms clammy on the warm metal. Aleks followed, grimacing at the grit still in the air, and felt the breath leave his lungs when he reached the bottom. Zhora's face was blistered and bloodied, his limbs askew and his clothing charred. From the look of things, he'd been right up close to the propeller mechanism when it had exploded. No wonder he hadn't made it out alive. 'Gods,' Drazan breathed, closing his eyes tightly. Aleks stood close behind, hand on his shoulder in silent support. 'I always thought it'd be me, y'know? We both did, I think. I was always so reckless, so irresponsible with my own safety, right from when I was a sprog. I always thought if one of us was going to get killed in an accident, it would be me, without a doubt.'

Aleks didn't know what to say to that. 'I'm sorry I got you both into this mess. If I'd known –' He was cut off as Drazan whirled round to face him, glaring.

'I already told you not to blame yourself!' he argued. 'We both made our choice. Don't cheapen what he did by pretending you forced him into it. He – he was a grown man. He knew what he was doing. These things happen.'

'I'm still sorry.'

Drazan sighed, shaking his head and turning away from Aleks, moving closer to his brother. He kneeled, stroking Zhora's sweat-drenched hair.

'We should bury him in the forest,' he said softly. 'He would have liked that.'

'Let's do it, then,' Aleks agreed. 'Today, before we have to start fixing the ship.' As much as the pair would have liked to send Zhora off in the way he deserved, they didn't have time for that. Kara's people could find them at any moment, and the longer they stayed the greater the chance of something else happening to the ship. They needed to get home, and quickly.

'Storms, why didn't he *say* anything?' Drazan breathed. 'If he'd said how bad it was getting down here, I would have landed us in a heartbeat. Idiot.'

'He probably thought he could handle it,' Aleks said. 'Probably didn't want to risk landing somewhere Kara would catch us.'

'Let's get him outside,' Drazan urged, getting to his feet.

Pushing away any discomfort at handling a dead body, Aleks moved to stand by Zhora's feet, Drazan at his shoulders. He glanced over at the ladder and the trapdoor above it. This wasn't going to be easy.

It took a while, but between the two of them they managed to carry Zhora up to the deck and carefully lower him to the ground. Both men were sweating with exertion by the end of it, Drazan rolling his shoulders with a wince. 'Gods, if I'd known he was that heavy, I'd have banned him from the bakery round the corner back home,' he muttered drily. Aleks couldn't help but snort. The sun was high in the sky, and he glanced towards the shade of the forest.

'Did we bring a shovel?' he asked suddenly. Drazan paused, frowning.

'You know what, I don't think we did.' In all their planning, needing to dig a hole hadn't come up as a possibility. 'This is going to take a while. I can . . . I can do it myself, if you want to get started in the engine room,' he offered.

'Don't be daft,' Aleks said. 'I'm not letting you do that on your own. We do it together.' Drazan smiled, looking relieved.

The pair carried Zhora over to the trees, walking until they found a small section of grassland that looked fairly undisturbed by animals. While they didn't have shovels, they did have knives, and Drazan marked out a rectangle in the grass, cutting through the turf easily and pulling it up with his hands until they were left with exposed earth. 'Storms, why did he have to be so bloody tall?' he remarked, wasting no time in kneeling down and digging with his hands. 'This is going to take hours.'

Aleks helped him dig, not caring about the mud caking his fingers. He was a country boy; he was used to getting his hands dirty. 'Zhora practically raised me, y'know,' Drazan said abruptly, not pausing in his rhythm. 'Ma died birthing me, and our da passed when I was about eleven. Even before that, he was working all the time. Zhora was in charge of getting me fed, making sure I went to school, all that. There was only five years between us, but . . . he would've made a good father.'

Drazan was alone now. He had no one. Except Aleks, of course. 'Zhora was a good man,' Aleks said. 'I was so lost when I came through the tunnels that second time. Hardly a coin to my name, bruised from head to foot – anyone else would have ignored me, or turned me in for my own good. Zhora didn't even question my situation – just cleaned me up and offered to lie to the kingsguard for me when they came through. It's not often you meet a man like that.' A memory rose in the forefront of his mind and he smiled faintly. 'He said I reminded him of you. At first, I didn't think it was a compliment, but n– now I know better.' Drazan glanced up, grinning, though the smile was some-what wooden. 'He loved you, you know.'

'Never doubted it,' Drazan replied with complete convic-tion, smile growing a little more sincere. 'He never let me. Even when I hated him for bossing me around.'

As they dug, Drazan began to tell Aleks stories of his and Zhora's childhood, the tightness in his shoulders easing with every word. Aleks listened, letting the man grieve through his stories, wishing he could have heard them while Zhora was alive. No doubt the older brother would have been constantly correcting the younger, making little remarks about how foolish Drazan had been as a sprog. In return, Aleks shared a few stories of his own childhood, speaking fondly of his three brothers. He missed them more than he'd expected, suddenly longing to go back and visit them once he was home safe. He still hadn't met Torell's daughter. His chest hurt a little, thinking how eager he'd been to leave his family behind – both biological and the family he'd made for himself in Syvana, and the family he'd hoped to build with Saria in the future. How certain he'd been that he had hardly anything left. He'd been so stupid, so quick to dismiss all the great things in his life and focus on the negatives.

'That should do it, I think,' Drazan declared, leaning back on his heels. They were both filthy and sweating, staring at the hole they'd created. It wasn't perfect, but it looked deep enough for their purposes. Standing wearily, the pair moved to where they had left Zhora's body, preparing to lift him into the makeshift grave. 'Wait!' Drazan blurted out just as Aleks bent to grip Zhora's legs. 'I . . . I don't know any funeral rites.' He looked distressed, and Aleks mentally thanked Grigori for being so serious in his study habits. Aleks knew almost every religious rite off by heart.

'I can do them,' he assured Drazan, watching him let out a breath of relief. As they lifted, Aleks began to murmur the words quietly, surprised at how easily they came to him. He hadn't heard them in a long while, but his speech didn't falter for a second. 'May the Goddess guide your spirit to your ancestors, and return your body to the earth it came from. Life does not fade, only alter, and may yours be blessed in its future journey,' he finished, just as they lowered Zhora into the grave.

'Goodbye, brother. I know you'll be watching over me, wherever the Goddess takes you. I only hope you'll be proud of what you see,' Drazan whispered, voice choked as he scattered dirt over Zhora's form, starting to fill in the hole. Aleks kept his face turned away as he shifted the earth, not wanting to watch Zhora be obscured from them forever. 'She will find him, right? Even through the Stormlands?'

'All land belongs to her,' Aleks said. 'She'll find him.' Dying in flight was the one that always caused problems, when bodies could never be returned to the land they came from. But Aleks was confident the Goddess extended as far as this place, even though Kara referred to everything outside the Stormlands as 'Goddess Land'. Any land was the Goddess's land.

'Good. That – that's good,' Drazan murmured in relief.

When the grave was filled, the two men stared down at it, finding it hard to believe their third crewmate was in there, lost to them forever. There would be no one to visit his grave, no one to even know where he was buried, except them. It didn't even look much like a grave.

Pulling his knife from where he'd stuck it in the ground, Aleks strode over to a nearby tree, easily cutting off a long branch. He cut the branch into three roughly equal pieces and one shorter piece, then looked up at Drazan. 'Have you got any string? Rope, wire, anything like that?' Digging into his pocket, Drazan pulled out a coil of copper wire, tossing it to the younger pilot. Within minutes, Aleks had tied the wood pieces together, creating a triangle with a short stick protruding from one side. Drazan's eyes widened in understanding, and he moved aside to let Aleks push the short stick into the earth at the head of the grave, leaving only the triangle visible. The sign of the gods. It wasn't much – nothing compared to the carved headstones that were commonly used – but it was better than nothing.

'*Thank you*,' Drazan breathed, pulling Aleks into a rib-crushing hug. He buried his face in Aleks's neck, and the younger man could feel tears wet his skin. 'Thank you, Aleks.'

'The Goddess can't miss him now,' Aleks said quietly, hugging back. 'She'll keep him safe.'

He didn't know how long they stood there embracing at the side of Zhora's grave, but they both jumped at a loud screeching noise from deeper in the forest; a bird of some sort.

'We should get back to the ship,' Drazan murmured, reluctance on his face. 'See if we can get some work done before nightfall.'

Stepping back from his friend, Aleks nodded. They needed all the daylight they could get. 'Right, yeah.' Drazan paused, turning to the wooden triangle. Kissing his fingers, he pressed them to the top corner; the Goddess's corner.

'Look after him.' Aleks moved to copy him, saying a silent prayer, begging for forgiveness and safe passage home. As much as Drazan said it wasn't Aleks's fault . . . he had to take at least part of the responsibility.

Tearing themselves away, they gathered their things, leaving Zhora behind in the peaceful little corner of the forest. The Goddess had him now.

34

Instructing Drazan to take a welding flame and hammer and attempt to bend the propeller blades back into shape, Aleks began the much more delicate process of rebuilding the propeller's mechanism.

'Storms, what was Luka thinking when he put this together?' Aleks growled to himself, trying to figure out how to connect a tiny gear on one plate to a much larger gear on the other using only one chain. Even though he'd spent a lot of time working on the ship, he wasn't a mechanic. 'Think, Aleks, think!' Luka had shown him how to identify, disassemble and reassemble everything in the engine room. Why couldn't he remember it? He tried to cast his mind back to being in the engine room with the old man in the beginning, but all his memory gave him was thoughts of Saria and getting home from work early to see her. He should have paid more attention!

Taking a deep breath, Aleks attempted to focus, looking critically at the mechanism. He'd finished countless machines in the workshop without any real knowledge of the mechanics behind them. The propeller was on a whole different scale, but surely the basics were the same?

Making sure he'd cleared every piece of broken machinery from the inside of the propeller, he stared at his pile of replacement parts. He could do this.

Being inside, Aleks didn't notice when the sun set. He did, however, notice when footsteps overhead signalled Drazan's return from fixing the propeller. His head poked down through the trapdoor, his face covered with soot but for two rings where his goggles had been. 'How's it going?' he asked, and Aleks grimaced.

'Slowly, but surely. It took me a while to figure things out, but I think I'm getting the hang of it now. Old Luka is mad as a bag of cats – I should've known things wouldn't make logical sense.' Drazan's lips quirked into the barest of smiles. 'How about you?'

'The propeller is all back to rights,' Drazan reported. 'The blades aren't perfect, but it should do enough to get us out by the Stormlands. The natural wind will take us from that point.' It was going to be hard, going through the Stormlands with their propellers hardly functioning, but they could do it. 'I was going to start dinner. We skipped lunch.' Aleks's stomach rumbled loudly, expressing his agreement for him, and the pair laughed in spite of everything.

'Sounds good. I'll keep working here. The sooner the mechanism's sorted, the sooner we can fly.' He was definitely making progress; if he was lucky, they might even be ready to leave by mid-afternoon the next day. He didn't want to spend any more time than necessary where they were. They should have taken the enormous dead zone as a sign to leave well alone; the country was not meant for those who relied so much on technology.

When Drazan called him for dinner, Aleks went to wash first, his hands still covered in dirt and engine oil up to the elbows. Storms, he needed a shower.

The galley seemed quiet without Zhora there, humming as he cooked and cracking the occasional joke. Aleks noticed Drazan's hands clenched around his cutlery, and knew he wasn't the only one feeling the loss in the room. 'What are you going to do, when we get back?' he asked tentatively. He knew the two brothers had lived together, and doubted Drazan could afford their house on his own.

'Hadn't thought much about it,' Drazan replied with a shrug. 'Go back to teaching at the flight school, try and save up for a little place of my own. Sell the house, I suppose.'

'You'd be welcome to stay at the Compass,' Aleks offered. 'Ksenia wouldn't mind, nor would Bodan. Just until you can find somewhere affordable.' The last thing he wanted was for Drazan to disappear after everything was over, with no one but himself for company. Drazan paused, smiling around a mouthful of peas.

'Yeah. Yeah, maybe.'

Knowing they wouldn't be away much longer, Aleks rifled through the cupboards for the last bottle of Bodan's cider. He'd been saving it for their final meal before home, but . . . he thought the occasion called for it. Pouring two mugs, he passed one over to Drazan, raising his own. 'To Zhora,' he murmured. 'We wouldn't have got here without him.' Drazan smiled, tapping his mug against Aleks's.

'And it's still debatable whether we'll get home without him,' he added drily. 'To Zhora. Gods bless, big brother.'

Drinking deeply, Aleks closed his eyes, wishing the ship would just fix itself and they could go home. He was done with adventuring. He was done with being scared for his life, and the lives of his friends. He was done with not knowing what the next few hours would hold, let alone the next few days. He wanted to be home.

They drank to Zhora's memory, and dragged themselves to bed when they could hardly keep their eyes open any longer. When Aleks went to the bathroom in the middle of the night, he found Drazan asleep in the corridor; of course, he had shared his room with Zhora. No one wanted to sleep with ghosts.

35

It took all of the morning and most of the afternoon, but eventually Aleks had the left propeller back to rights, sort of. The ship was full of nervous energy as the pair began to prepare it for flight, locking everything away in cupboards and bolting down anything that might move when storms rocked the ship. Breakfast was a veritable feast, now that there was no need to ration the food. Besides, neither man wanted to take to the Stormlands on an empty stomach.

When Aleks wandered up to join Drazan outside, it was to find him leaning against the railing, watching birds fly over the treetops, video recorder in hand. 'Just getting a last look,' he explained.

Aleks smiled. 'I know. I came up to do the same. It may not have treated us well, but I'd be an idiot not to come up and say goodbye to this beautiful place.' Propping his forearms on the railing, his shoulder bumped Drazan's gently, and the blue-eyed man smiled.

'Makes you feel a bit special, doesn't it? Knowing we'll be the only people in Siberene who have seen this place in person. I wonder how long it'll be before we're not,' he mused.

'Oh, years, I expect. It'll take a while before someone's able to replicate Luka's particular brand of genius,' Aleks said.

'I suppose you're right.' A comfortable silence fell between them, both their minds on the third member of their crew. 'What do we do when we get home?' Drazan asked eventually. 'I know the plan was to give the video to Luka and show the world, but . . . things are different now.' Zhora was dead, and this country was home to people who didn't want to be disturbed. Showing the video could do more harm than good at this point.

'We show it,' Aleks decided. 'We cut out any signs of Kara and her people, we don't even tell Luka about them, but the rest of it . . . we just have to make sure we make it clear this place isn't fit for people or for flight. If we don't show it, people will still be killing themselves trying to fly the Stormlands and discover what's on the other side. And if anyone does get through, they'll only provoke Kara, and who knows what problems that'll cause? Besides, if we don't show it, all this will have been for nothing.' Zhora's sacrifice would have been for nothing, if they didn't show the world what he'd died for. 'Maybe knowing what happened to Zhora will discourage people from looking for it.' He felt sick as he spoke, hating the thought of his friend's death becoming one of many cautionary tales about the Stormlands.

His mind drifted to home, heart aching at how close they were, yet still so far away. Everything would be different; he would hopefully be free in the eyes of the law.

Saria . . . Saria still probably wanted him arrested. Shulga would still be after him, and after the journal. Pausing, Aleks bit his lip, an idea forming. 'I'll be right back.'

Ducking down to his bedroom, he opened the trunk at the foot of his bed, digging through it until he found Hunter's journal at the bottom where he'd hidden it. He ran back up on deck, seeing Drazan looking at him in confusion. Aleks ignored him and made for the rigging rope, clambering down to the ground. 'Aleks, what are you doing?' Drazan asked.

Making a beeline for the nearest cliff, Aleks started to run, anger bubbling up inside him. 'This bloody journal is why everything went wrong,' he spat. 'I never should've taken it – I was too nosy for my own good.' He stopped just before the edge of the cliff, staring down into the deep blue water thirty feet below.

'What is it?' Drazan jogged up beside him, brows furrowed.

'Nathaniel Hunter's private journal,' Aleks declared, staring at the thing in disgust. 'One of them, at least. My lieutenant had *reclaimed* it from evidence, and I found it in his office when I was searching for my enlistment forms before I escaped.' Taking it had been the worst decision he'd ever made, not that he'd known that at the time. Though if he had left it in Shulga's hands, gods only knew what could have come of it. 'This is the reason I can't live free. If I'd just deserted . . . they would've given up on me eventually. But since I have this, and Shulga *knows* I have this, he won't rest until he has it back. He won't leave me alone.'

'What's in it?' Drazan asked. Of course, he'd been slightly older than Aleks when the Anglyan government had fallen. He would have been more aware of Hunter and his despicable deeds at the time.

'It's bad. There's enough information in here for someone to recreate Hunter's soldiers. Not that I knew that when I took it. I could've left it well alone, but no, I had to be curious and steal the damn thing.'

'Surely that's good, right? This lieutenant of yours sounds like the worst sort of person; it can't be a bad thing that you got it away from him. Who knows what he was planning on doing with that information,' Drazan said.

'It's still caused me more trouble than it's worth.' Aleks tried to think what his life would have been like if he hadn't taken the journal. Shulga probably wouldn't have tracked him so doggedly; he wouldn't have caused problems with Saria by lying and putting her in danger. He'd have kept his past secret from everyone.

He looked down at the leather-bound book in his hands, flipping through the pages. He still hadn't read it cover to cover. Clenching his jaw, he looked up, pitching the journal over the edge with one solid throw, watching several pages come loose as it plummeted towards the ocean. It floated for a moment, surrounded by dampening pages, then began to sink, leaving a dark swirl where the ink bled into the water. There: now no one could use that knowledge, ever again. It felt like a weight had been lifted off his shoulders, though his heart was still heavy with guilt. Drazan stood silently at his side, face blank.

It was almost ten minutes before Aleks turned away from the cliff, clearing his throat. 'Come on,' he urged, 'we need to get going.' They walked back to the ship in silence.

With little other choice, Aleks went down to the engine room and Drazan turned to the control room. Aleks had promised to let him fly the Stormlands on the way home, not particularly wanting to do so again. Although, after what had happened with Zhora, he wasn't feeling too confident about the engine room either.

'You ready?' he asked, looking over the mechanisms in front of him.

'Whenever you are,' Drazan said through the speakers. Together they ran through take-off procedure as they had done a hundred times, though the absence of Zhora was palpable. They both still expected the man to cut in, telling them to stop chattering over the speakers and pay attention, even as he himself cracked jokes in the quiet moments.

Aleks hated being down in the engine room, unable to see what was going on outside or how the storms were looking. He didn't know how Zhora had been able to stand it.

'Any minute now,' Drazan called through the speakers, sounding exhilarated. Aleks could feel the ship lurching as they drew closer to the raging storm. 'Oh, and Aleks? You might want to sit down.'

The Stormlands seemed to pass far quicker, and far less eventfully than the first time round. Drazan was clearly enjoying the challenge, and having a bit more fun with things than Aleks had – all he'd been thinking about at the time was getting them through in one piece – but he kept them on course easily, and they emerged while it was still light outside, if only just. The Stormlands threw them out several miles further North than they had anticipated, leaving them closer to Anglya than Siberene.

'Are we through?' Aleks asked when the ride had become smoother.

'Completely. Just below Hebris, but I've turned us in the right direction – shouldn't take long to get back on track. I'd almost forgotten what it was like to fly with real wind under your sails,' Drazan remarked. 'Storms, I never want to see another dead zone in my life.' Aleks laughed.

'You and me both. How are you feeling?'

'Honestly?' Drazan replied. 'Bloody awful. My arms are on fire.' Aleks grimaced, then glanced around the engine room.

'Things are pretty quiet down here, if you wanted to switch,' he offered, before biting his lip. Of course, Drazan wouldn't want to come and work in the engine room, the room that killed his brother. 'No, never mind, it was a stupid thought. I'm sorry.'

'No, actually I think I might like that,' Drazan said tentatively. 'Besides, I've done the bit I wanted to do, and it's only right you bring us home.'

'Are you sure?' Aleks asked.

'Aleks, just get up here,' Drazan sighed. Aleks nodded, hurrying up the ladder through to the control room. Drazan looked awful, sweat on his brow and his eyes bloodshot from concentration. 'Thanks,' he murmured, sliding from the pilot's seat to let Aleks take his place. 'Just don't use the propellers and we'll be fine.' Turning to the viewscreen,

Aleks couldn't help but grin, seeing the lights of Syvana twinkling in the distance up ahead. They were so close he could taste it.

With home in sight, their course steady, Aleks allowed himself a few moments to daydream about getting back, wondering how his friends would react. They'd hardly been gone a few days. Raina would probably hit him for worrying her needlessly, while Ksenia would no doubt cry and then feed him to death. Saria . . . Saria would hopefully be willing to hear him out. Even if she turned down his ring, he needed to clear the air with her. He'd missed her more than he'd ever thought possible.

Pulling around towards the edge of Siberene, as he'd done every time when landing the ship at the warehouse, he felt a warmth in his chest at the sight of the familiar spires and peaks in the city, now well lit for the dark evening.

'Coming in to land,' he warned Drazan, eyes fixed on the landing platform ahead. It was odd, having to land in a specific place after several days of landing wherever they wanted, and for a brief moment Aleks worried he would miss.

But they touched down gently on the rig, Aleks automatically pulling in the wings and sails. He was glad to be home but, still, it felt wrong. They had left a man behind.

Hearing footsteps, Aleks turned, smiling at a weary-looking Drazan. He leaned against the back of the pilot's seat, giving Aleks a tentative smile. 'Home sweet home,' he murmured, the cheer in his voice utterly false. Aleks reached up, squeezing his forearm briefly, staying silent. What could you say to a man who had lost his last remaining family member?

36

They were both surprised when they found the warehouse unlocked and wondered if they would find Luka inside. As they moved the doors to bring the rig in, they saw that the large room was completely empty. They heaved the rig inside and shut the back doors behind them, Aleks reaching for the rigging rope to get back on deck. 'You know there's a ladder now, right?' Drazan pointed out, gesturing to the ladder leaning against the wall, but Aleks shrugged.

'Nothing wrong with the rope,' he replied, making his way up. Drazan followed him, and they went to their respective bedrooms to pack the necessary items. They could come back for the rest of their things later. Aleks layered up in undershirts, jumpers and a thick coat, feeling strange in the many layers after days of wearing just a shirt. He looked up when he heard a knock on the door.

'Should I bring the recorders out with me?' Drazan asked. 'Or should we leave them here until we come back with Luka?'

'Leave them here, I think. At least then we know they're safe,' Aleks replied, glancing over to where he'd kept his recorders in the desk drawer. 'It's not like we can do anything with them without Luka.' Drazan nodded, turning back to his own room, and Aleks checked over for anything he might have missed that couldn't wait until the next day. Satisfied, he shouldered his satchel and went back out on deck to wait for his crewmate. When Drazan emerged, it was with a frown on his face.

'I'm going to leave Zhora's stuff here, for now,' he declared, his own bag over his shoulder. 'It's too soon to go looking through his things.'

'Yeah, of course,' Aleks agreed. 'Let's get out of here.' Leading the way out of the warehouse, he shut the doors firmly behind them. Aleks shivered, the harsh cold both familiar and unfamiliar after all his time in the sunshine.

'Blimey, I'd forgotten how chilly it could get around here,' Drazan murmured, rubbing his arms through his thick coat. His breath turned to fog, and Aleks could feel the still tender skin on his face being soothed by the cold, even through his scarf.

Riding the tram back towards the city centre, there seemed to be a wordless agreement between the pair to go to Luka's first.

Drazan rang the doorbell, and Aleks waited on the step with bated breath, unable to quell his grin when the door opened and a familiar grumpy face peered out. Luka's foggy eyes widened in surprise when he saw them.

'By the gods, you made it,' he breathed, reaching out to drag Drazan inside, giving Aleks no choice but to follow. 'How was it? Did you find anything? Did she make the journey all right? I assume the Stormlands weren't a problem since you're here, but what was the rest of it like? Don't stand there like statues, come and tell me everything!' He paused, eyeing them with a frown. 'You're one short.' Aleks swallowed harshly and saw Drazan flinch.

'There was a malfunction,' Drazan said, looking the old mechanic dead in the eye. 'The left propeller blew. Zhora didn't make it.' Luka stared, his face paper-white.

'What?' he croaked. Aleks had never seen the man look so shocked, so off guard.

'The whole place was a giant dead zone,' Aleks informed him. 'Things got a little heated in the engine room. We didn't know until it was too late.' Luka's mouth opened and closed like a fish and he shook his head slowly.

'Of all the things ... I never imagined it would be a dead zone. Gods, I never prepared her for that.'

'Evidently,' Drazan muttered.

'If I'd known, I swear, I never would have let you go. I would have prepared her better.'

'It's too late for would-haves,' Drazan pointed out. 'You didn't know, none of us did. We had terrible luck, Zhora the worst of all, but there's nothing that can be done.'

'Come in. I'll put the kettle on,' Luka urged, directing the two men towards the stairs up to his apartment above the workshop. 'You can tell me everything.' As they followed him, Aleks and Drazan shared a look, one thing clear between them: they wouldn't be telling him *everything*.

They were there for at least two hours, going over their journey in detail. They made up some feeble story about exploring the forest to cover the truth about Kara, but Luka didn't seem to notice, still shell-shocked by the news about

Zhora. He was silent for a long while after they finished, then turned to Aleks with a half-smile.

'How does it feel to be a king, then?' he asked impishly. Aleks groaned, shaking his head, and Drazan laughed. Of course, with everyone under the impression that there were no people on the land, they would believe Aleks to be king by right. Aleks felt a little bad about lying to Luka, despite the man being the reason he'd discovered Kara's community in the first place, but he and Drazan had agreed that the fewer people who knew, the better.

'We are never speaking of that again,' Aleks declared vehemently. 'Besides, surely I can't be a king until I colonise it?'

'That's not how the old laws work, lad,' Luka replied with an amused look. 'Captain of the first ship to land on uncharted territory is king of that territory, regardless of colonisation. And you'd better get used to speaking of it – that's all anyone's going to want to talk about once this goes public. The Peasant King, they'll call you, or something equally ridiculous. You'll be a story for the ages – boy from the arse-end-of-nowhere out West travels to Syvana and ends up a king. Breed a whole new generation of adventurers.' Aleks bit his lip, knowing Luka was right but not wanting to admit it.

'Those new adventurers will be wasting their time if they're looking to become kings themselves,' Drazan pointed out. 'We checked every inch of the gap between the Stormlands, and Aleks's country is the only one there. Unless there's another part of Tellus people are keeping secret, every bit of land has now been discovered. Besides, after what happened to Zhora, I don't doubt people will think twice about flying there.'

'Aleks's country?' Luka asked with raised eyebrows. 'Storms, lad, haven't you named it yet?'

'That wasn't really on my list of priorities,' Aleks admitted.

'Hmm, fair point. Think of a name, lad. We'll need something to tell the authorities when we take the footage to them.' He glanced up at the clock on the wall. 'It's getting late now and no doubt you both want to go home and sleep in your own beds, hug your friends and all that. Come back here tomorrow afternoon – we can go and get the rest of your things and pick up the recorders.'

Luka walked them towards the door, pausing. 'I'm glad you're back, lads,' he said solemnly. 'And I'm sorry about Zhora. He was a bloody good mechanic.' Drazan smiled weakly, nodding.

'Goodnight, Luka. It's good to see you too,' Aleks replied.

Walking with Drazan until the point where they would usually part ways, Aleks wasn't surprised when he hesitated. 'I . . . would your landlady mind if I booked in for the night?' he asked tentatively. 'I know it's short notice, but . . . I don't think I can face going home yet.' A pang of sympathy in his chest, Aleks nodded.

'You're welcome at the Compass,' he promised. 'Even if it's just sleeping on my floor. But we're bound to have a spare room.' Drazan smiled, shoulder bumping Aleks's as they both continued towards the Compass. Aleks briefly considered taking a detour to see Saria, but knew that was better left for when he'd had more sleep and time to think through what he wanted to say to her. He'd only get one chance at that reunion.

A grin tugged at Aleks's lips when they rounded the corner and ended up on the street behind the Compass, seeing the lights on and hearing the bustle inside from several feet away. He realised belatedly that he had no idea what day it was, but he suspected it was close to the weekend, judging by how many people seemed to be inside at the late hour. Leading Drazan in through the back alley, he detoured towards the stables, surprised to see a small, somewhat rotund pack pony nibbling away happily at the hay in the corner of its stable. That was new. After a quick scratch of the pony's mane Aleks went around to the front door so as not to startle anyone in the kitchen, heart pounding like a hammer against his ribs. Taking a deep breath to steady himself, he pushed open the door and removed his hat, the familiar warmth flooding over him.

'Aleks!' Raina's cry could be heard over the noise, and he stumbled back into the door as she appeared out of nowhere, throwing her arms around his neck. 'You're home! You're home!' she exclaimed into his coat lapel, hugging him tightly. He hugged back, kissing the top of her head.

'I'm home,' he agreed, chuckling. 'And people are staring.' He tried to ease Raina towards the bar, where Ksenia and Bodan were also staring at him, gobsmacked.

'You brute, we were so worried about you!' Raina declared fiercely, pulling away to smack his shoulder. 'Let me look at you.' She grasped his shoulders in her hands, keeping him at arm's length as she studied him. 'What happened to your face?'

'Sunburn,' he said with a wry smile. 'It's a lot better now. You should have seen what I looked like on the first day – it was awful.'

'How on Tellus did you get sunburn?' she asked incredulously. He winked at her.

'I'll tell you later. It's good to see you, brat.'

He allowed Ksenia to smother him in a hug, laughing as he wrapped his arms around her. 'You missed me, then?' That earned him a gentle swat to the back of his head, and the woman kissed his cheek before releasing him.

'Of course we missed you! Oh, storms, you did get burned, didn't you?' she said with a frown, running gentle fingers over his forehead and cheeks. She glanced over his shoulder, seeing Drazan standing awkwardly in front of the door. 'Who's your friend?'

'That's Drazan,' Aleks said. 'My, uh, crewmate. He was wondering if he could stay here for the night.'

'Didn't you say there were three of you out there?' Ksenia asked. 'You and two brothers.'

Aleks winced. 'There were,' he confirmed. The look on his face clearly said it all, and Ksenia gasped, hand going to her mouth.

'Gods,' she breathed. 'The poor lad. Of course he can stay, as long as he likes. The least we can do for a man who kept you safe while you were away.' Aleks turned and gave Drazan a thumbs up. Drazan smiled at the confirmation, relaxing somewhat. 'Go and sit down. I'll get you both some dinner, as I'm sure you've not eaten yet.' Aleks admitted he hadn't, and Ksenia disappeared into the kitchen. Aleks glanced over at Bodan, who was pouring cider. The bearded man looked up, offering a gruff smile.

'Good to have you back, lad,' he declared, reaching out to clap Aleks firmly on the shoulder.

'Good to be back.' Beckoning Drazan over, he walked up to the other end of the bar, perching on his usual stool. He tugged off his gloves and shed his coat, dropping it neatly on top of his satchel by his feet. Raina leaned over the bar, giving him a pointed look.

'How long have you been home?' she asked. He pulled out his pocket watch, checking the time.

'About two hours. I would've been here sooner but we had to check in with Luka first,' he replied, scratching at his flaky forehead and making her grimace.

'Other than the sunburn, are you hurt?'

'I'm perfectly fine.'

'Did you find anything?' The stern expression on her face gave way to eager curiosity, and he grinned, leaning forward to tug at her ponytail.

'Wait until we're all locked up and I'll tell you everything,' he promised, bringing a grin to her lips. She was shooed away to get back to work when Ksenia emerged from the kitchen with two hot slices of pie and vegetables and two equally large tankards of hot cider. Aleks's mouth watered as she set it in front of him and Drazan. 'Oh, gods, I've missed your cooking,' he declared, making her smile. 'I said I'd tell Raina everything once the pub empties for the night – you're welcome to join us,' he told her.

'I'll take you up on that,' she agreed, getting back to work.

Every bite of Aleks's meal tasted like heaven in his mouth, and he couldn't help but notice that the three of them – Raina in particular – kept glancing over at him every few minutes, like they couldn't quite believe he was back. He felt a pang of guilt, sipping at his cider. He wouldn't be going away again any time soon if he could help it.

'You're lucky, you know,' Drazan said, startling him. Aleks raised a querying eyebrow. 'You've got your family out West, and you've got these people here. They obviously care about you like one of their own.' He sounded wistful, and Aleks reached over to clasp his forearm.

'There's always room for one more, you know. Don't think I'm letting you just bugger off to the flight school and that's that.' Drazan's hollow eyes creased at the corners as he smiled gently.

The pub cleared out soon after they had finished eating. Aleks grabbed a damp rag from the kitchen without prompting, going to help Raina wipe down tables. 'Get talking, then,' the girl urged, and Ksenia clucked her tongue.

'Raina, don't be rude,' she scolded.

'Aleks, won't you please tell me the tale of your intrepid adventures?' Raina asked with exaggerated sweetness, making him laugh.

'Oh, I suppose I could.' Talking as he wiped down the tables was almost therapeutic, and Raina proved to be a brilliant audience. He knew Ksenia and Bodan were listening in too, but they were silent, getting on with their work as he talked. Raina, on the other hand, 'ooh'ed and 'ahh'ed, listening intently and sporadically interrupting with a question. Occasionally, Drazan chimed in from his seat at the bar, getting more involved as the story went on.

Aleks didn't tell her everything, of course, and glossed over some of the more dangerous parts of the journey, exaggerating others that he thought might amuse or interest her. Raina seemed captivated by his description of the forest and its wildlife.

'It sounds incredible,' she breathed, her eyes round with wonder. 'And it's yours?'

'Technically, yes,' he lied, 'as in, it doesn't belong to anyone else.' That was the story he was stuck with, he supposed. 'But we're not going back. That place isn't meant for people — if the Stormlands aren't warning enough, the heat is overwhelming and most of the sky is a dead zone.'

'Good,' Raina said firmly. He raised an eyebrow at her, and she blushed. 'It all sounds so pretty. People never appreciate pretty things unless they made them themselves. Colonising would be the worst thing to happen to it.'

'That's what we thought,' Aleks replied, making her smile. 'Anyway, if you'll all excuse me, I'm absolutely exhausted, but . . . it's really, really good to be back,' he said honestly, meeting each of their gazes in turn. Bodan's lips twitched in a smile behind his beard, and he reached up to the board of room keys behind the bar, tossing Aleks a familiar key.

'Everything's just as you left it. Well, a bit cleaner than you left it; the missus went round with the duster,' he added. He took a second key off the board, placing it on the bar in front of Drazan. 'You can have room four, it's just below Aleks's. If you need anything at all, just give us a shout, or pester Aleks. He's been here long enough by now to know where we keep most things.' Drazan's smile was genuine, and he offered the man a short bow.

'Thank you for your hospitality at such short notice, sir,' he said, only to be waved off.

'It's the least I can do, lad. Any friend of Aleks's is welcome here, and it sounds like you could use a good night's sleep,' Bodan added. Aleks smiled to himself, hugging Raina goodnight. It was good to be home.

37

The light of the sun through his window woke Aleks the next morning, and he lay in bed for several minutes, just basking in the pale daylight. Eventually, however, he heard movement from the rest of the inn's inhabitants and sluggishly got out of bed, gathering some clothes and heading over to the bathroom. They were the nicest work clothes he had, and he left them in a pile on the bench while he showered.

Drazan was already awake when Aleks went downstairs, a mug of tea in his hands and dark circles under his bloodshot eyes, but he managed a small smile of greeting. Raina was behind the bar stacking glasses, and he tapped her on the shoulder. 'Morning, bratling,' he greeted fondly, offering her a smile.

'Morning, you. Breakfast?'

'Please,' he responded, sliding into a seat beside Drazan.

'Any plans for the day, boys?' she asked, and Aleks bit his lip. There was one thing he wanted to do . . . but he didn't know how well it would go down.

'We need to be at Luka's before noon,' Drazan piped up. His voice was hoarse, and Aleks wondered if he'd been crying in the night. 'To talk things over.'

'I might go for a walk before then. Clear my head a bit. Maybe ... maybe swing by the courtyard,' Aleks said, watching as Raina's hand faltered in plating up scrambled eggs.

'You're still going to see her? After what she did to you?' she asked, voice icy. Aleks shrugged.

'We need to talk. She needs to know I'm not in jail, and ... I still love her, Raina. Even after everything, I still love her. I still want to marry her,' he admitted, thinking of the engagement ring.

'She nearly got you arrested,' Raina pointed out. 'That doesn't exactly seem like the basis of a happy relationship.'

'She only did that because I lied to her about the journal,' Aleks argued. 'She thought I'd stolen military property.'

'What journal?' Raina asked, perplexed. Aleks shook his head.

'It doesn't matter any more. I need to talk to her, Raina. I can't just leave it like this.' He'd come too close to death to let Saria go without a fight. Sure, they had issues to work out, and he didn't exactly trust her just yet, but he still loved her.

'You're a grown man – it's your decision,' Raina said with a shrug. 'Just don't expect the conversation to go well.'

Aleks laughed ruefully. 'Oh, trust me, I'm not.' He was well aware that it would probably be a train wreck. But that wasn't going to stop him from trying.

Finishing his breakfast, Aleks bid goodbye to his two companions, promising to meet Drazan at Luka's at noon.

The walk to the courtyard went by in a flash, his mind occupied by thoughts of his upcoming conversation. Aleks tried to plan it out in his head, imagining any number of reactions she might have, but all it did was make him more anxious.

It was strange, being in the city again after a week of no one but Drazan and Zhora for company. Everything was much louder than he remembered, but after the vibrance of the land beyond the Stormlands he felt like he was watching everything through a terrible video recorder, like the colours had all bled out and faded. That was Siberene, he supposed.

When he reached the courtyard, his eyes immediately zeroed in on the familiar table set up near the fountain, a blonde-haired figure wrapped in a heavy navy coat standing behind it. Saria was smiling at a pair of girls buying bracelets, though it didn't reach her eyes. She looked paler than usual, and as if she hadn't been sleeping well.

He watched for a few minutes, stomach curling with nerves, until he couldn't wait any longer. He had to talk to her. Hood pulled up over his head, Saria didn't recognise him until he was right in front of her table, a tentative smile on his face. 'Hi.'

She gasped, hazel eyes widening. 'Aleks,' she breathed. 'But . . . the lieutenant . . .'

'Nearly got me. I've been . . . out of the country for a while, keeping my head down. Look, Saria, can we talk? Privately?'

Saria bit her lip, glancing down at her table of wares. 'I suppose. Let me just pack up.'

Soon she had everything boxed up and her table folded, and Aleks watched as she quickly ran them back to her father's shop. They both agreed it was best if Evgeny didn't see Aleks.

When she emerged again, she nodded to him, following his lead to a quiet courtyard a few streets away. Last time they'd been there it was to sneak some time alone, and Aleks's heart clenched unexpectedly at the memory. That felt like aeons ago now. 'I'm sorry,' Saria blurted out as soon as they were alone. 'I'm so sorry, Aleks, gods! I shouldn't have done it, I shouldn't have gone to the kingsguard. I was just so *hurt*, so angry. I started to think maybe that lieutenant was right, perhaps you *had* done something wrong. Surely there had to be a reason he was so determined to get you?'

'You believed that bastard over me?' Aleks asked incredulously.

'What was I supposed to think?' Saria retorted. 'You were on the run from the military, and had lied to me several times over! For all I knew, you were an escaped criminal and he was coming to bring you back in.'

'I only lied to keep you safe,' Aleks insisted. 'Shulga is a monster, Saria. He was on my trail because I stole something that he himself stole from the Crown.' He explained briefly about the journal, not going into too much detail – Saria was two and a half years older than him, so she knew who Nathaniel Hunter was and what he was responsible for. Her expression was horrified, her face chalk-white.

'And I led him straight to you, giving him valid reason to have you arrested. Oh, gods, Aleks, what have I done?' She blinked away tears, and he couldn't help but bring her into his arms, kissing her hair.

'It's OK, it's fine now,' he soothed.

'But I nearly got you arrested!' Saria exclaimed.

'The night Shulga found us in the park, remember I was going to tell you something?' Aleks said, changing the subject abruptly. Saria nodded. 'I was planning on leaving, even then. I can't tell you right now where I was going, but I promise I will later. The point is, I was going somewhere I wasn't entirely sure I'd return from. And I wanted to tell you before I left. But then the Shulga thing happened, and you broke up with me, and . . . well, I thought it was a sign from the gods that I needed to go, that I had nothing to stop me. Still, a few days before I was supposed to leave, I went by your father's shop and bought a ring from his apprentice. An engagement ring.'

Saria gasped, her hand flying to her mouth, and Aleks smiled briefly.

'Raina thought I was mad. You and I weren't even together any more. But I knew I wanted to marry you, even if you never wanted to speak to me again. I *still* want to marry you, even though I lied and put you at risk and you dumped me and almost got me arrested.' Saria let out a laugh at his words, wiping her eyes. 'I love you, Saria. I'm not expecting things to go back to the way they were, and I'm not saying we should get married right now, but . . . I think we can work through this. If you want to.' Aleks could feel his pulse racing.

'No more lies,' Saria said after a long silence. 'No more hiding things to protect me. We've both made some mistakes here, Aleks.'

'No more lies,' he agreed instantly. 'I'll tell you everything, I swear.' The clock struck noon, and Aleks swore. 'But I'm late for work. Look, can we maybe continue this later? Say, at the Compass, tonight after work?' That was the safest environment he could think of to divulge his secrets without being overheard. Saria nodded, making him grin with relief.

He made to stand, but Saria reached out and grabbed him by the coat front, pulling him into a firm kiss. Surprised, he kissed her back, overwhelmed by how amazing it felt to be able to do so. He'd thought he'd never get to kiss Saria again. 'The Compass, after work,' Saria confirmed once they eventually parted, a blush coming to her cheek. 'I still love you, Aleks, even though I tried my hardest not to. We can work this out.'

'I love you too,' he murmured, kissing her softly once more. As much as he would have loved to stay with her, Luka and Drazan were waiting for him. He stepped away, reluctantly turning to start running towards the tram station, a grin on his face. That had gone far, far better than he'd imagined.

Luka and Drazan didn't comment on his late arrival, or his flushed cheeks, but Drazan did clap him on the back with a smirk. The pair had been in the warehouse for a while, Luka checking over the external repairs to the ship, but they'd waited for Aleks before going up to get everything they'd brought back from the country they'd discovered.

'I got a bunch of plant samples and things too,' Aleks said as he handed over his video and audio recorders to the elderly mechanic, Drazan doing the same. 'In case you were interested – I figured since it was likely to be the only chance we'd ever get to research those things, we'd better bring back as much information as possible.'

The excuse they'd given to Luka to explain why they'd left so early, and in such a hurry, was their inability to find fresh water before their supplies got too low, and Aleks's sunstroke, which had made him too ill to go outside. Aleks wasn't entirely sure the old man believed them, but he didn't question their story, which was the important thing.

'Good work, lad,' Luka said, putting the recorders in his satchel with a satisfied smile. 'I know a couple of scientist types who would kill for those samples. I'll write some letters tonight. And I'll get this footage over to a friend of mine who works with newscast development, get him to piece everything together into something usable.'

'So we're taking this to the newscasts, then?' Drazan asked.

'Of course, lad! People need to know what's out there, for research purposes. Now that the only land past the Stormlands has been claimed, all those idiots flying for the glory of discovering and claiming a new country will go and find their glory somewhere a little less deadly. And as for the academic types, well, they'll have plenty to study from what you boys brought back before they start sending their own expedition ships out again,' Luka said. 'It's the only bit of the Goddess's green land that hasn't been ruined by man, and I think you can agree it should stay that way as long as possible. We'll get the footage up, make it look as inhospitable as possible to stop any thoughts about colonising the place, and wait for the hype to die down. That, unfortunately, is the easy part.'

350

'What do you mean?' Drazan asked, and Luka turned to him.

'You don't really think people will just leave you alone after learning about all this, do you? The moment that broadcast goes public, everyone's going to be all over you. They'll want interviews and all sorts! Especially you, Aleks,' he added. The boy scowled, folding his arms over his chest.

'Why me? Drazan did just as much as I did!' he protested.

'Yes, but as you're the captain, you're the king, and you're the only one anyone's going to want to talk about.'

A thought came to Aleks. 'Have you done what you promised you would?' he asked Luka. 'Talked to your friends in the records department? Because if I'm still enlisted, the last thing I want is to be in the public eye.' What if the guards came after him, even with his record clean, and arrested him? What if Shulga caught him again? Just because he'd destroyed the journal it didn't mean the lieutenant would leave him be. He'd hoped with a clean record he could report the lieutenant for harassment, but that might not work out in his favour.

'I talked to my contact while you were away,' Luka said. 'The deed should be done by now. Don't worry, lad – with your files gone, they've got nothing against you. And you'll be too much of a public figure for them to make you accidentally disappear.' That didn't make Aleks feel any better, but he let the subject drop. 'Besides, you think you have problems. If people take this the wrong way, I'll end up in jail for starting the whole bloody thing.' He patted the side of the ship to emphasise his point, and Aleks's stomach turned to lead.

'They wouldn't, would they? Not once they know what we found?'

'They have every right to,' Luka replied calmly. 'I sent out an unregistered ship, and a crewman died because of it. That's enough to land me in prison for the rest of my days.'

'Then we don't say how Zhora died,' Drazan told him, surprising them both. 'We'll say it was an animal attack, or something. We all made our choices, Luka. Zhora wouldn't have wanted you to get in trouble for it – you didn't know what would happen.'

'No, but I should have,' Luka muttered. 'If that's what you want to do, then I won't argue. But don't do it to spare me, lad. It's my invention that did the damage.'

'It's the dead zone that did the damage,' Drazan argued. 'Both of you, for storms' sake, stop blaming yourselves! It's not going to help any, and it's not going to bring him back, so just stop bloody apologising and deal with what happened!'

'Drazan, it's OK,' Aleks murmured. 'We'll stop blaming ourselves, we'll lie on the newscasts. We didn't mean to upset you.' Drazan sniffed, blinking back the tears forming in his eyes.

'No, no, I'm fine. I just . . . it was an accident, a horrible one, but getting in trouble for it won't do anything but harm. I'd rather just lie and move on.'

'Then that's what we'll do,' Luka declared, nodding. 'Which means we need to get our stories straight. We need to know exactly what we're going to tell them, and how to do this in a way that will make it all blow over as quickly as possible. I'm sure it can be done, if we think hard enough about it.'

* * *

The three of them plotted until Aleks had to go and meet Saria, at which point he and Drazan bid Luka goodnight and headed towards the Compass.

Saria was already there when the two men arrived, having what looked like a rather serious conversation with Raina. The pair looked up when the door opened, and Aleks raised an eyebrow at Raina, who put on an innocent expression. 'I didn't say anything,' she insisted. Saria laughed, standing to greet Aleks.

'Raina was merely defending your character,' she told him. 'Something I probably should have done more of myself recently.' Aleks leaned down to kiss her.

'Not your fault,' he murmured. Glancing aside, he tried not to blush at the look on Drazan's face. 'Saria, this is my friend, Drazan. Drazan, meet Saria.' Drazan offered the woman a bow, smiling.

'It's a pleasure. I feel like I know you already, Aleks talks about you so much,' Drazan added playfully, making Aleks's cheeks redden.

'After the last week, I'm not entirely sure that's a good thing,' Saria replied, curtseying. Drazan chuckled.

'All wonderful things, I promise. Now I'll leave you two to, uh, talk. Raina, do you need help in the kitchen?'

'Always. Aleks, Aunt Ksenia says you have permission to take Saria up to your room in order to speak privately, but *just this once*, and the door stays unlocked,' she said, wagging a stern finger in his direction. That only made Aleks blush even more, but Raina dragged Drazan away to the kitchen before he could comment. Turning to Saria, Aleks gestured feebly towards the stairs.

'Shall we?' Saria nodded, letting him lead the way up to his bedroom. It felt strange, bringing Saria up there. He forced himself to focus, taking the desk chair as Saria perched on the edge of the bed. 'OK,' he started, letting out a long breath. 'I've got a lot to tell you. Jus– don't interrupt until I'm finished, OK? I want to get it all out first.'

Saria's expression was serious as she reached across the gap between them to take his hand, squeezing it tightly. 'Take your time,' she urged softly.

Eyes fixed firmly on the floor, unable to say what he needed to say face to face, Aleks began to talk – going right back to the beginning, when he'd first left Baysar. He owed Saria the truth, all of it.

38

Over an hour later, Aleks finally stopped talking, a lump high in his throat from having described Zhora's death. He hadn't left anything out: the journal, Kara and her people, he'd told Saria all of it. True to her word, she'd listened without comment, though tears had come to her eyes at several points in his story. Aleks had moved to sit beside her on the bed, he wasn't sure when, and Saria had an arm around his waist, her head on his shoulder to comfort him as he spoke.

'Holy gods,' she murmured when he was finished. 'You really did get yourself into some situations, didn't you?'

Aleks laughed. 'You could say that, yeah.' He turned to face her, finally meeting her tearful gaze. 'I wanted to tell you, but it wasn't safe. I didn't want to put you at risk any more than I had already, but I told you what I could.'

'And then I went and betrayed your trust by going to the kingsguard,' Saria finished, angry at herself. 'Aleks –'

'Stop,' he cut in, 'you've already apologised plenty. It's over. No need to keep feeling guilty about it and bringing it up.'

'Then you need to stop apologising for keeping secrets,' she insisted. 'Make it even. From this point on, the past is forgiven, and we'll move on.'

'Deal,' Aleks agreed, even though he knew it wouldn't be easy. It would take more than one conversation for them to forgive each other and learn to trust one another again. But it was a start. 'So now you know everything. And soon, the rest of the country will too, to an extent.' He'd told her that they were keeping Kara a secret, and she agreed with their reasoning, promising not to say a word.

'How long have you got before things go public?' Saria asked, and Aleks shrugged.

'Depends on how long it takes Luka to contact his various people. I'm just going to keep my head down and get on with things, to be honest. I finally have the chance of a normal life again – marriage, an apprenticeship, kids. I want to make a start on that as soon as possible.' Saria's expression changed at the word 'marriage', and she bit her lip.

'You said this morning . . . you bought a ring, before you left?' she reminded him tentatively. Aleks blushed.

'Raina's looking after it for me,' he confirmed. 'I wanted her to be able to give it to you if I never . . . if I didn't make it back.' He wasn't sure what to do with it – he didn't want to take it back, but he doubted it would be the best idea to propose right now, under the circumstances. He said as much to Saria, who gave a small half-smile.

'Give it a month,' she suggested. 'I do want to marry you, but you're right, we'd be fools to jump back into where we were so quickly, after everything. Have Raina keep it a little longer. Then . . . then we'll see where we are. But Aunt Ana's been at me now more than ever to find a husband, since I said I'd broken it off with you. I'll be twenty in three months, that's far too old for a lady like me to be unmarried, as far as she's concerned. Maybe if you proposed it would actually shut her up.' Aleks snorted – Anastasia had far too many opinions on Saria's love life.

'Won't she cut off your inheritance if I propose?'

'I already told you, I don't care if she does,' Saria said, squeezing his knee. 'She can throw me out on the street – I'm not going to keep quiet and marry some rich man just to make her happy.' She leaned her head against Aleks's shoulder for a brief moment. 'But that doesn't mean I want you to rush a proposal just to spite her. So . . . a month.'

'A month sounds good,' he agreed, breathing a silent sigh of relief that she was even willing to consider the idea. 'We'll just shelve the subject for a while.'

Silence fell between them, and Saria glanced at the time-piece on the wall. 'Dinner service will be ending soon,' she said. 'We should go downstairs.'

'Well,' Aleks started, shifting on the bed to face her properly, a playful glint in his eyes. 'Ksenia will leave leftovers out for us if we miss service. And while they think we're up here talking . . . maybe we should take advantage of the privacy. It's likely to be all we'll get for a long while, once the newscasts go out.'

Saria's cheeks went pink, even as a coy smile crossed her lips. Gods, it felt like far too long since he'd last been able to kiss her properly. 'And here you told me you were a gentle-man,' she teased, before leaning in to press her lips to his.

It was four days later that everything went to hell.

The day the news finally broke was just like any other. Luka had warned Aleks and Drazan that he'd handed the footage to his friend, but they didn't know how long the process might take. Aleks barely paid attention to the newscast screen in the middle of the junction as he walked the familiar journey to Luka's warehouse, but when a flash of bright green trees and rust-red dirt crossed the screen, he stopped dead in his tracks. '*This incredible discovery was made by the crew of a small ship named the* Thunderbug, *captained by young Aleks Vasin,*' the reporter declared, and a still from one of the videos flashed up on screen, clearly showing Aleks's face, thankfully sunburn-free. '*He and two crewmates flew the ship through the Stormlands, finding the country of Karana on the other side.*'

Aleks watched in a mix of awe and horror as their video footage played out, with audio both from them and the anonymous reporter. He flinched at the sight of Zhora on screen, grinning widely as they walked through the forest. Gods, he hoped Drazan wasn't watching this alone.

After the video ended, the reporter went on to speculate about the future of the country, referring to it by the name that Aleks had eventually given it, with Drazan's help. When it became clear nothing else of use was going to be said, Aleks slipped out of the crowd that had gathered around the newscast screen, keeping his head ducked in the hope of not being recognised. Unfortunately, luck was not on his side.

'It's him! It's the Stormlands boy!' a man exclaimed, pointing a finger. Aleks froze like a deer in a spotlight, before darting away as fast as he could, slipping down several side alleys as people began to chase him, shouting questions.

All his experience avoiding Shulga came in handy, and he managed to lose the group within about fifteen minutes.

Ducking into a rarely used public lavatory, he dug his scarf out of his satchel, winding it around his neck and face. He was glad Luka wasn't expecting him at the workshop that day; the mechanic had been mentioned several times in the newscast, and plenty of people knew where to find him. At least the warehouse was secret.

He spent the entire tram ride looking about nervously, but, luckily, he remained anonymous. Breaking away from a group of people departing the tram, he headed towards the warehouse.

Luka was already there, carefully polishing some smaller scratches out of the ship's woodwork. He looked up at Aleks's harassed expression. 'So it's out, then?' he presumed, and Aleks growled under his breath.

'A little warning would have been nice,' he grumbled. 'I had to spend fifteen minutes running away from crazy people all wanting to talk to me.'

'It'll only get worse, lad,' Luka assured him, probably thinking he was being helpful. He wasn't.

Aleks spent the entire day hiding in Luka's warehouse. Drazan turned up too, claiming he'd almost been barricaded inside the tram by people who'd recognised him. Luka didn't seem to mind the company, putting Drazan to work on polishing, and taking Aleks into the engine room to dismantle the repairs he'd made. 'You're lucky you didn't kill yourselves,' the old mechanic muttered, removing gears and chains all over the place. 'One wrong move and the entire ship would have gone down.'

'I'm not as hopeless as you think I am, Luka,' Aleks said brightly, silently vowing never to admit how close he'd come to getting the mechanism wrong. Some things were best kept secret.

When the hour grew late and Luka said that they were free to go if they wanted, the two men hesitated, unsure of whether they'd be able to make it home safely. Luka looked pointedly at Aleks. 'You can't stay here forever, lads. Might as well get it over with.' Aleks sighed, running a hand through his hair.

'I suppose you're right,' Drazan replied, gathering his things. 'But if we get kidnapped or something, I'm blaming you.'

Luka rolled his eyes. 'Goodnight, lads.'

No one looked twice at them as they walked through the streets, all too busy going about their own business. Aleks caught several snippets of conversations about the new country, his name involved in plenty of them, and while he was tempted to eavesdrop and hear what people thought about the news, he didn't dare risk being seen.

Letting his shoulders slump in relief as they rounded the corner towards the inn, he heard someone scream his name. Looking up, his eyes went wide at the sight that greeted him; the Compass was surrounded by people, all of whom were now staring at him and Drazan with eager expressions on their faces, several calling out to them. Both of them cursed, ducking back around the corner, then between two other buildings to get to the back of the inn, hiding in the stables for a breather.

'We'll have to make a run for it,' Drazan declared. Bracing himself, Aleks darted across the short stretch of concrete towards the kitchen door, reaching for the handle. To his surprise it was locked, and he cursed again, pounding on the door. 'Raina, it's me! Let me in!' he called as loud as he dared, hoping she could hear him through the thick wood. After several moments the door opened a crack and a suspicious brown eye stared out at him, widening when it landed on his face. The door opened fully and Raina ushered the pair in quickly, slamming it shut and locking it behind them.

'Oh, thank the gods! We thought you'd never get home in all this madness!' she whispered, brushing the snow off Drazan's shoulders. Aleks tugged his hat off his head, stuffing it into his coat pocket.

'What on Tellus is going on? How long have all those people been here?' he asked, kicking off his snow-caked boots and leaving them by the kitchen door. Hanging up his coat, he headed towards the fire, welcoming the warmth.

'Since shortly after the video was first broadcast,' Raina replied, practically forcing them into chairs at the table. 'Stay there, I'll grab your dinner.' She ducked away to the other end of the kitchen, returning with two bowls of chunky stew and a basket of warm bread rolls. 'They've been asking all sorts of questions about you both and trying to get inside. It's been a nightmare – our regulars can hardly get past! Some of the crowd are coming in and paying for drinks – probably hoping you'll come home and they'll get to talk to you – but most of them are just lurking outside. Uncle Bo said that if they didn't leave soon he'd alert the kingsguard to take care of them.'

'Storms, I knew this was a bad idea,' muttered Aleks, and Raina squeezed his shoulders comfortingly.

'It'll all blow over,' she said, leaving the pair to their dinner and getting back to work. Had Aleks known it would encroach on his personal life in such a way, he'd have had second thoughts about releasing the video. How long before someone who knew him from Rensav got wind of where he was?

After dinner, Aleks and Drazan started washing dishes, wanting to do something to help out. When Ksenia came in to grab more food, she let out a sigh of relief when she saw them. 'You don't have to do that, dears,' she insisted.

'It's the least we can do for causing all this drama,' Aleks replied.

Ksenia tutted. 'This isn't your fault – you didn't force them to start behaving like imbeciles,' she said.

Aleks smiled at her, reaching out to hug her briefly. The noise outside had eased up a little; hopefully the crowd had got bored waiting and gone home. 'Is it safe for us to go upstairs?' he asked Ksenia.

'Not quite, but give me two minutes,' she assured him, the smallest smirk on her face. Aleks grinned back, grabbing his coat and edging towards the door, Drazan on his tail. He saw Ksenia move behind the bar, chatting amicably with one of their regulars, and handing him a pint of ale. The man went back to his table, the sway in his walk making Aleks frown; he wasn't usually drunk this early. He stumbled as he squeezed between two chairs, knocking his entire pint into the lap of a ruddy-faced man with a bristly black moustache. Aleks recognised him too; they were friends, he thought. The man's face went even

362

redder, and he stood up, reaching out to grab the drunken man by the collar.

'I'm terribly sorry,' the man started, before he was cut off by a firm shove. The drunk man shouted something unintelligible, throwing a hard punch at his companion's jaw, and then all hell broke loose. Aleks stood in the doorway, watching in shock, and was startled when a hand smacked his arm.

'What are you waiting for?' Ksenia hissed, pushing them both towards the stairs. 'They can't keep this up much longer – we'll have to throw them out!' Aleks grinned, catching on, and kissed the woman's cheek before sprinting up the stairs, coat in hand, Drazan's footsteps close behind. He owed both of those men a pint.

39

Aleks was starting to go spare when two days later he still couldn't leave the inn, and nor could Drazan. He'd heard from Raina that Luka was having similar problems leaving his shop. Apparently, the first video about Karana was just the beginning, and since then there had been interviews with scientists, mechanics and weather experts about the land beyond the Stormlands. Everyone seemed to want to get their point of view heard, though the three people whose views the public actually wanted to hear were notably absent; himself, Drazan and Luka. There was some amusing footage of interviewers turning up at Luka's workshop, only to be threatened with what the old mechanic claimed to be a deadly weapon, but Aleks knew was merely a partially completed toaster.

Most of the news was speculation, though Aleks was surprised to hear that three expeditions to the Stormlands had already been sent out to confirm their findings. Surely they didn't think they'd have much luck in normal-sized skyships? Even in Luka's ship they hadn't all survived the journey. Guilt curled in Aleks's stomach, but he pushed it away; the people going out there did so by their own choice.

It wasn't his fault. And if they did get through, well . . . he could only hope they didn't run into Kara, or they certainly wouldn't be making it back.

He and Drazan couldn't stay hiding forever, he knew. The public were hungry for more news, and he worried they'd start getting impatient if he left them waiting much longer. Saria managed to visit occasionally, but most of his time was spent playing chess in his room with Drazan and wishing everything would go back to normal. Raina, his ever faithful messenger, brought them reports on the latest from the newscasts, and at last check they were calling Aleks the Common King. Drazan's predictions were right, to an extent. Several people were insisting he be given some measure of power along with his title, despite having no one under his rule and no land to base his kingdom in. It was a nice gesture of support, but Aleks wished they would settle down and leave him be.

Having been in his room most of the day, Aleks frowned at Drazan when they both heard yelling from downstairs. He glanced at the pocket watch resting on the corner of his desk; it was far too early in the evening for the drunks to be rowdy. Getting to his feet when the noise got louder, he dared to venture downstairs. Drazan followed curiously, staying back several paces. Aleks's eyes widened when he saw three uniformed guardsmen in the middle of the pub, directing everyone to stand against the wall.

He hesitated at the bottom of the stairs, wondering if the guards were just there on Bodan's behest to clear the rabble outside. Then one of them turned and spotted him. 'There he is, sir!' the guard exclaimed, and the man beside him turned, his gaze narrowing when he saw Aleks. Shulga.

'Long time no see, brat,' the lieutenant spat. Aleks flinched. 'You foolish boy, becoming such a celebrity. Did you really think I would let things go?' He paused, drawing a pair of handcuffs from his belt. 'Aleksandr Vasin, you're under arrest for the unauthorised flight of an illegal vehicle, desertion from the military, theft, and destruction of government property.' Aleks froze, swallowing thickly. Drazan drew closer behind him, but Aleks shook his head a fraction. He didn't want his friend getting involved.

'Destruction of government property?' he asked with raised brows, sounding far calmer than he felt. Shulga smirked.

'That fence you broke,' he pointed out. 'Yes, we found it eventually. Fixed it up nice and new, so no one else will be getting through there in future.' Aleks snorted under his breath; they really were trying to pin everything they could on him, weren't they? He could see Raina standing wide-eyed in fright behind the bar, her face pale, and he wished they had cornered him at Luka's.

'It'll be best if you come quietly,' Shulga told him, looking positively delighted as he wrenched Aleks's arms behind his back, cuffing him far too tightly. Bodan moved to protest, but his wife held him back, her hand on his arm. Aleks was glad; they didn't need to pay the price for his mistakes.

'I want to talk to Luka,' Aleks said, tugging against the cuffs. His files had been destroyed; they had no proof of his desertion. They couldn't hold him.

'We'll make sure to let him know,' one of the other guards sneered. Eventually, Aleks gave in, allowing them to drag him out of the inn. The crowd was still gathered outside, but not one of them spoke as he was marched out towards the blue-painted guard's carriage. He felt his face burn as hundreds of eyes watched him being shoved into the back of the carriage, almost falling on his face before he regained his balance and managed to shift into a seated position in the corner, arms pressing uncomfortably against the wood once the carriage began to move.

He couldn't hear what the guards were saying, their words drowned out by the rattling of wheels over the cobblestones and the rhythmic whirr of the carriage's motor, but even more so by the pounding of his own blood in his ears. How could he have been so stupid? He had told Luka it wouldn't be enough to get his record wiped; Shulga was out for blood! Storms, he was going to strangle the old mechanic. How the gods was he going to get out of this one?

He couldn't help but run scenarios in his mind, trying to determine what would become of him. If the worst came to the worst, he'd be back at the base in Rensav, or in jail somewhere. The best he could probably hope for would be serving out his four years as a guard in Syvana, or even Pervaya. He could handle that.

His thinking – which had quickly become panicking – was brought to an abrupt halt as the carriage stopped suddenly, causing him to hit his head against the hard wood. Moments later the carriage doors swung open, and Shulga stood there sneering at him. 'Come on, then,' he urged, stepping up into the carriage to force Aleks to his feet, clearly aware he wouldn't be able to do so on his own. He then proceeded to drag him out, and when Aleks stumbled to his knees Shulga just hoisted him back up again. 'No dawdling,' he growled, shoving him forward.

In front of them was the tall, imposing building of the city prison. It was made of jet black rock, the windows barred and the perimeter fence high and barbed at the top. It looked like the kind of place that could steal a man's soul, and Aleks desperately hoped he wouldn't be there long. He tried to deal with the rough handling by his guards the best he could; if anything, Shulga was making sure to cause him as much pain as possible. There was another guard at the door, who was at least twice the width of any man Aleks had ever seen, nothing but muscle to speak of. His head was shaved and a tattoo curled up the side of his neck and on to his cheek. Aleks couldn't tell what it depicted, but whatever it was, it had a set of lethal-looking fangs.

One of the guards pulled an ID badge from his pocket, showing it to the door guard, who grunted and scowled but eventually pulled the heavy lever on the door lock. There was a series of clicks and then the door swung open, revealing a dark, dank corridor. Aleks shivered as he went in. They hadn't allowed him to grab his coat or hat, and there was no heating. Teeth chattering, he was dragged through the corridor, the door slamming shut behind them. They turned a corner and reached another door with another heavy-duty lock, where one of the guards roughly patted Aleks down. They confiscated the pen in his pocket, his watch and the buckled straps on his jacket, making him wonder what previous prisoners had attempted to do with such items. The thought wasn't comforting.

Aleks was marched through the next door towards a row of identical barred cells. He was directed to a small one at the very end of the row, which contained nothing but a wooden cot, a bucket in the corner, a basin of water and a tiny window allowing slats of light to enter the cell. 'Welcome home,' Shulga drawled as he finally released the handcuffs, his satisfied tone making Aleks's skin crawl.

'I won't be here for long,' Aleks retorted confidently. Shulga snorted, while his two flunkies laughed aloud.

'You're awfully sure of yourself for someone with the charges you're facing,' the man remarked. 'Not looking forward to seeing all your old friends back in barracks? They've missed you terribly.' Aleks felt physically sick at the prospect of going back to Rensav. He wouldn't let that happen. 'You get one visitor,' the guard on the left told him, earning a glare from Shulga. 'Choose wisely.'

'Luka,' Aleks answered immediately. 'My employer.'

'Very well. A message will be sent.' With that, Shulga and the guards left, and Aleks sat on the edge of the cot, running a hand through his hair. He was relieved they hadn't brought Drazan in too. The man had suffered enough as it was.

The damp, bone-deep cold of the cell began to get to him, and he shifted further back on the cot, tucking his knees up to his chest. Why couldn't they have grabbed him off the street? It might have been more worrying, but at least he'd be warmer. Sighing to himself, Aleks began to count down the minutes, wondering when Luka would be allowed to visit. When they said that a message would be sent, surely they didn't mean a letter? That could take days to get to him!

As he waited, his imagination began to take over, providing scenario after scenario, each more grim than the last. He'd rather stay in prison than go back to Rensav, but he doubted they would give him the choice. The army didn't let people escape before they paid their dues.

Left alone with nothing but his thoughts and the silence, Aleks nearly fell off his cot in alarm when footsteps echoed through the corridor hours later. His eyes widened when a stocky, unfamiliar guard appeared leading a figure with a familiar shock of white hair. Aleks couldn't help but grin at Luka, who seemed completely unperturbed by their surroundings, his expression unchanging as he looked around as though everyone in the building was a complete idiot, Aleks included. The man could be so predictable sometimes.

'You have half an hour,' the guard informed them, unlocking the cell door long enough for Luka to enter, then locking it again. Thankfully he left instead of standing watch over their conversation, and Aleks fixed the mechanic with a hopeful look. Luka walked over to him, perching on the other end of the cot.

'I thought you said I'd be safe? You told me your friend had it covered,' Aleks said accusingly. Luka frowned.

'I thought he did. I haven't heard from him since, though, which worries me. I apologise, lad – if I'd held up my end of our deal, you wouldn't be in this mess.'

'It's not your fault,' Aleks sighed, as much as he would like to blame someone other than himself. He'd made the decision to fly the ship, it was his responsibility. As was

370

everything else he was in trouble for. 'Just please say you can help me.' Luka scratched thoughtfully at his chin.

'I don't doubt I can,' he said, and Aleks's heart skipped a beat. 'It'll take me a little while, though. And it all depends on how fast I can get an audience with the guard captain. And how susceptible that captain is to bribery.' Wide-eyed, Aleks shook his head.

'You can't bribe the guard captain, Luka! You'd need inordinate amounts of money for something like that.' Luka grinned, winking.

'Don't be daft, lad. Of course I won't bribe him with money,' he assured Aleks, a hint of mischief in his tone. 'Just leave it to me. I'll do my best to get you out in good time. And *don't do anything stupid.*' His dark eyes bore into Aleks's as he spoke, and the boy was mildly offended.

'What do you think I'm going to do, punch a guard?' he asked sarcastically. Luka raised a bushy eyebrow at him.

'If Shulga annoys you enough, I wouldn't put it past you,' he muttered. 'Just stay quiet, do what they tell you, and try not to antagonise anyone. Even if they start insulting you and your loved ones. I mean it, lad.' His expression was more serious than Aleks had ever seen before, and it made him nervous. 'They'll try everything to get you to act out, and then nothing I do will be worth anything. As soon as they can slap another set of charges on you, it's out of my power. I only have so much to barter with,' he pointed out. Aleks sighed, nodding to show he understood.

'I'll be good,' he promised, cowed by the prospect of having to go back to Rensav. 'Just . . . hurry, please.' He heard footsteps further up the corridor and knew it was the guard coming back to retrieve Luka; their half hour was up. 'And tell Saria – tell Saria I love her.' Luka's lips twitched in a small smile, and he got to his feet, clasping Aleks's shoulder.

'Tell her yourself, lad – you'll see her soon enough. Remember what I told you, and leave everything to me.' The guard unlocked the cell, clearing his throat pointedly, and Luka made for the exit.

'Thank you,' Aleks called after him. 'For helping me.' Luka turned.

'It's my fault you're in here, lad,' he reasoned. 'Least I can do is help where I can.' With that, he left, escorted by the guard, and Aleks was alone once more. Most people would probably think him foolish for putting his life in the hands of a certifiably insane, geriatric mechanic, but Aleks trusted Luka to keep his word. All it would take was time.

40

Luka hadn't been wrong about how the guards would treat him; they jeered and mocked him whenever they came to check on him or bring him food. Shulga was the worst, finding any excuse to pass his cell and attack him. When he had returned to give Aleks his evening meal, he'd accompanied it with a sharp kick to Aleks's ribs, his steel-toed boots knocking the wind from his lungs. 'Your little girlfriend will never see you again, y'know,' he said. 'And I'll find my journal sooner or later, so all your work will be for nought.'

'The journal's gone,' Aleks sighed, having already told Shulga as much the last time he'd been in to interrogate him. 'I threw it off a cliff back in the Stormlands.'

'So you say,' Shulga retorted. 'But would you really destroy such an important piece of . . . history?' The glint in his eyes sent shivers down Aleks's spine.

'If it meant it stayed out of your filthy hands, yes,' he snapped in reply. 'But by all means, go ahead and check. You know where I live, and legally there's nothing stopping you from going through my room now I'm in custody. Look for yourself, if you don't believe me.' It wasn't like he had much to hide now the journal was gone, and it was bound to happen eventually if Luka didn't manage to get him out of jail.

'I might just do that.' Shulga turned, leaving the cell and locking it behind him. It was clear from his face that he hadn't expected Aleks to be so forthcoming on the matter. The lieutenant lurked outside the cell, taunting him about all the horrible things that might happen to him now he'd been caught, while Aleks stared at the bland-looking mess he had been given for dinner. He clenched his jaw, trying to block out Shulga's words. Luka had told him not to get into trouble, and that meant staying completely silent, even when he wished the man had stayed inside the cell so he could punch his smarmy face in.

To Aleks's relief, the lieutenant left fairly soon, obviously bored of getting no response. Aleks forced himself to eat the lukewarm slop, washing it down with water that tasted vaguely of mildew. He hoped he didn't catch anything. Shoving the empty tray towards the edge of the bars, he retreated to his cot. He had no blanket or pillow, but he didn't mind all that much, resting his head on his arms. He was cold and kept his boots on as he tried to sleep, not wanting to wake up to numb toes, or worse. The bucket in the corner of the cell was mocking him; his bladder was uncomfortably full, but he hated the thought of degrading himself by using the bucket.

Eventually, it became a non-issue. Choosing a moment when he thought the corridor was empty, he was as quick as possible, then washed his hands in the ice-cold water stagnating in the basin. The water probably made his hands dirtier than before, and the cold sank right into his bones as he tucked his hands under his armpits, curling up on the cot once more. 'No rush or anything, Luka,' he murmured to himself, jaw clenched to stop his teeth chattering. 'But if you could hurry things up a bit, it'd be much appreciated.' He tacked on a silent prayer to any of the three gods that might be listening, urging them for a reprieve. They had served him well so far; hopefully they wouldn't let him down now.

Morning dawned with a loud klaxon going off throughout the building, though Aleks hardly reacted; it sounded the same as the klaxon from the barracks in Rensav. For a moment he was back there, curled up in his cot with Jarek mocking him from the next bed, about to start a day of pain and physical exhaustion. He shook it off, reminding himself where he was, even though the reality was hardly better.

Sitting up, wincing at the ache in his back and shoulders from the hard wooden bed, he stretched the best he could and looked around. The faint light of early morning filtered through his barred window, and he knew it was probably obscenely early to be awake. He wished they hadn't taken his pocket watch, if only so he could keep track of how many hours he'd spent in this dreary place. He supposed it was all part of their tactics, though; leave someone oblivious of the time, and an hour could seem like ten.

Waiting on his cot for someone to come past his cell – preferably with breakfast – he was sorely disappointed by the tiny portion of bland porridge eventually offered to him. It was gone in barely four mouthfuls. He was still hungry, but he had bigger things to worry about. When Shulga came he was flanked by three other guards, and Aleks's eyes widened as one of them brought out the key to his cell, unlocking the door. 'Stand up and face the wall,' Shulga ordered harshly. His face was unreadable, and it made Aleks anxious. He was grabbed by the arms and manhandled into a pair of handcuffs before being yanked around to face the cell doors. 'You're coming with us.'

'Where are you taking me?' Aleks asked in alarm.

'Never you mind. Now shut up and walk,' Shulga told him sharply, pushing him out of the cell. One of the guards walked off with his breakfast tray, while the other two stayed close to Aleks's sides. He obeyed, trying to keep up despite the pain in his shoulders, sure that the next grab of his arm would wrench it out of place. He was led back to the heavy locked door, and hope rose in his chest when he was directed down the narrow corridor he'd walked through on his way in.

The grey sunlight made him squint as he went outside, and it took him a few moments to notice he was being pushed towards a carriage. This one was solid steel, more heavy-duty than the one he'd arrived in, and it made him wonder; this was usually the type of carriage they used to cart off dangerous killers and people they thought would break out of the wooden ones. Did they really think that highly of him?

'Get in,' Shulga grunted, swinging the door open. There was a bench on the wall of this carriage, and Aleks settled on it, feet planted firmly on the floor and leaning forward slightly so as not to crush his hands. The door was slammed shut, and after a few moments they were on the move.

They definitely weren't releasing him, but as far as he knew there was no other jail in the city. His pulse quickened; were they taking him back down to Rensav already?

He straightened up when the carriage came to a halt, wishing there was a window for him to look out of to know where he was. He'd just have to wait for the doors to open. He didn't have to wait long, and tried not to look like a startled rabbit when Shulga came to retrieve him, wrestling him out of the back of the carriage. He looked around, confusion growing. They were parked in front of a nondescript grey building, somewhere in the city centre by the look of things.

The guard shoved him forward, another one going ahead to open the door, and Aleks tried not to show his shock once he was inside. For all its plain appearance on the outside, the building was lavishly decorated inside, making Aleks feel sorely out of place in his dirty jacket and trousers. He hadn't even been given the chance to wash that morning. They ended up in a reception room, painted light blue with dark wood furnishings and portraits on the walls, each of a different king or queen of Siberene. A tall, wiry man was sitting behind a desk, dressed in a sharp suit and eyeing him warily. 'Is this him?' he asked, and Shulga nodded.

'Where should we take him?' The tall man pointed towards a door on the left, a frown on his face.

'Through there – they're waiting for him. *Don't* leave him alone with them,' he warned, making Shulga raise an eyebrow.

'Do I look like I'm stupid?' he retorted, shoving Aleks by the shoulder. 'Come on, you're wasting time.'

Aleks didn't know whether to be scared or excited at this abrupt turn of events. Stomach churning, he walked with his guard escort towards the door in question. The guard in front unlocked the door, which had an absurdly complicated mechanism. Aleks suddenly wondered if he was in some sort of psychiatric hospital, but quickly put that thought aside; even the nicest hospitals weren't this well-decorated.

Door open, Aleks felt two hands gripping his shoulders to stop him from doing anything other than walk forward. He froze in his tracks as soon as he saw who else was in the room. Sitting on a plush velvet armchair with a politely interested expression on his face was none other than King Andrei Rudavin himself. On either side of him in chairs of their own, making no attempt to disguise their boredom, were his sons, Toma and Erik. Aleks tried not to gape, belatedly dropping into a bow, and was unable to stifle the hiss of pain as the movement tugged on his already sore shoulders. 'Your Majesties,' he murmured, trying to regain his composure. What in the name of the gods were *they* doing here?

'Please, sit,' the king requested, gesturing to the free chair opposite him. Aleks wondered exactly what he'd got himself into now.

41

'I've wanted to meet you for a while,' the king remarked, lips curling in what was almost amusement. 'Oh gentlemen, don't be ridiculous – he's a deserter, not a murderer. Cuff him at the front so the poor brat can sit down without dislocating something.' Shulga hastened to obey, though he didn't look too happy about it. Aleks was shoved unceremoniously into the chair opposite the king, and he tried to appear calm. Inside, he was screaming: what on Tellus had Luka done now?

With a guard either side of his chair and another standing halfway between him and the royal family, it truly did look like he was some sort of murderer. 'Good, now we can get down to business,' the king declared, clasping his ring-adorned hands under his chin. 'You've caused quite a stir recently, Aleksandr. You and your merry band of adventurers.'

'I'm sorry, Your Majesty –' Aleks cut himself off; there wasn't really much he could say to explain himself. He shook his head, and the man chuckled.

'Don't, don't. I'm rather impressed, to be honest. You've got guts,' he replied. 'How did you do it?'

'It wasn't anything to do with my skills,' Aleks insisted. 'It was all Luka's ship. We wouldn't have been able to make it without him.' The king nodded, looking thoughtful.

'Yes, I've heard of this famed ship. Like nothing else anyone's ever seen, so I'm told – though since you landed no one has *actually* seen it,' he remarked.

Aleks shrugged, leaning back in his chair a little, his shoulders aching. 'Luka is very protective towards his inventions.'

The king raised an eyebrow, and even Prince Erik smirked a little.

'Not just his inventions, by the look of things. I don't know if you know, but a man was caught attempting to destroy your enlistment papers and arrest warrant, shortly after you returned from your expedition. He claimed to be doing it on your employer's orders. He was, of course . . . dealt with.' Aleks flinched; that didn't sound good.

'Was that really necessary?' he asked.

'Oh, absolutely. I can't have men in such a sensitive department willing to do *favours* for friends. Besides, you caused quite some trouble down in Rensav. Tell me, Aleksandr, was my cadet training not to your liking?' Aleks looked the man in the eye and shivered. The king knew exactly what happened in Rensav. Suddenly, Aleks started to question everything he'd heard about the king, everything he'd thought to be true – he was supposed to be loving and just, striving to make this country the best it could be. He was the one who had gained them independence, freed them from Anglya's iron fist. How much of that persona was a lie?

'No, sire,' he replied simply, 'the training seems to be an acquired taste.' Toma snorted softly and Erik's blue eyes flickered in amusement.

'Evidently. I suppose not everyone has the strength to handle such rigorous training.'

'Rigorous training?' Aleks scoffed, ignoring the way all three of his guards growled at him for interrupting the king. 'Torture is more like it! It's hideous, what the commanders get away with down there. You should be ashamed of yourself! The military is supposed to be a noble institution, and all you've done is debase and belittle every-thing it stands for by allowing your men to act in such a way.'

Shulga reached out, backhanding Aleks across the face, and while both princes flinched and gasped, Aleks merely looked his attacker in the eye. 'You can do better than that,' he taunted, feeling reckless. Aleks was in front of the king, he was probably set for death, anyway. 'We both know it.' He was tempted to tell the king about the journal Shulga had stolen, but he had the feeling the man would be inter-ested in it for all the wrong reasons. Perhaps it would be better to let the matter lie. The thing was at the bottom of the ocean now.

'You insult me by questioning my practices,' King Andrei snapped. 'The base in Rensav is necessary for this country's good fortune. Without it, we would have far more criminals on the streets and in our prisons, and a far smaller army. The . . . corrective treatment is a small price to pay.'

'Corrective, my arse,' Aleks muttered, and Shulga raised his fist in warning.

'Father, what's he talking about?' Prince Erik asked quietly, earning a sharp look for speaking out of turn.

'Enough,' the king hissed, losing all his earlier false warmth. 'Your opinion of the Rensav base matters little, Mr Vasin. With the recent increase in tourism, the base is being moved to the island of Ropastal. Everything shall continue as it always has.' Aleks grimaced, disgusted, and even the two princes looked unsettled, despite clearly having no idea what was being discussed. Still, at least if the base was situated on an island, no one would accidentally walk into it like Aleks had. Though it would make escaping near impossible.

'We've gone off track,' King Andrei said eventually, lips twitching in a brief smile as he calmed down. 'This Luka of yours, Mr Vasin, has offered his skyship in return for your release. It will be taken to the Academy to be studied and replicated, should you decide to sign the papers.'

Aleks gaped; Luka had done *what?* 'But . . . I'm not worth that ship!' he protested, earning a raised eyebrow from Erik.

'He obviously thinks you are,' the prince retorted. He was barely a year older than Aleks, but he already looked every part the future king, a confidence on his face that was just the right side of arrogance.

'That doesn't settle everything, however,' King Andrei interrupted, giving his son a mild chiding look. Aleks wondered why he'd brought them if he didn't expect them to talk. Intimidation, maybe? 'The point still stands – you owe me four years' service. The old mechanic said nothing about negating that charge when he made the deal for your release.'

'Please, Your Majesty,' Aleks blurted out. 'I'll do anything to free myself of the commitment. I'm getting married and . . . I don't want to make her wait four years for me.' While he hadn't actually proposed to Saria yet, he was feeling fairly confident that he'd get to it sooner or later, and wasn't above using it to tug on the king's heartstrings. If he had any.

'Married? Who to? The newscasts never mentioned a bride?' Erik asked curiously. Aleks smiled just thinking about Saria.

'The daughter of the owner of the jewellery shop in the fountain courtyard,' he replied. 'I never gave them any reason to mention her – she doesn't need to be in the spotlight.'

'A jeweller's daughter?' The king gave Aleks a look that held a measure of respect. 'You're marrying up.' Aleks laughed, a wry twist to his lips.

'Believe me, sire, I know,' he assured him. 'But I mean it. I don't want to serve and, well, I'd hate to be interviewed about my discovery and accidentally let slip how things really are in Rensav. That would defeat the purpose of you moving that base, don't you think?' His voice was almost innocent, and the king's eyes narrowed.

'You play a dangerous game, boy. Rest assured I could have your throat slit before you could utter one word of the truth about Rensav. Any time, anywhere. I am king, after all. My people are everywhere, and this is not Anglya. I am not so foolish as to let a rebellion happen right under my nose.' He smiled cruelly, and Aleks was reminded that the man in front of him was the one who had declared war on Anglya, and had fought for his country's independence with every resource available to him. King Andrei was a king for wartime, but Aleks was beginning to doubt his ability to be a king for peace. Rensav was proof of that.

'They're calling you the Common King, have you heard?' King Andrei asked, surprising Aleks with the abrupt change in conversation. 'Some suggest that being the first captain to land on that nice country of yours gives you the same measure of power as myself!' He sounded mildly scandalised at the notion. 'Ridiculous, really. But the people are all about the underdog, and they love a good story of turning rags to riches.'

'Hardly riches,' Aleks argued, but the king shook his head.

'Not yet, lad, but give them time. I don't doubt you've heard but a fraction of what people are wishing for you. If the public had their way, you'd have a throne next to mine and your own court of lords before the turn of the season.' Aleks's eyebrows shot up incredulously at the news. He didn't want any of that! 'Now, of course, I can hardly have a young upstart like you jeopardising my rule,' the king continued. 'Especially when your land consists of merely trees, sand and animals. However, the newscasts are ignorant of one vital piece of information. You are, technically, still a cadet of the Siberene military. Everything you own, every title you have, belongs to your commanding officers until the time you graduate from cadet training.' He paused, smiling wolfishly. 'And, as the king, everything belonging to your commanding officers belongs to me. I believe you'll find that makes your land and title mine.' Even his sons looked surprised, Toma actually letting his jaw drop a fraction, and Aleks was hard pressed not to do the same. He opened his mouth to protest, then shut it again; he was sure that if he read his enlistment contract, it would only prove the king correct. And he couldn't tell him that the land wasn't even his; if he said a word about Kara, there would be expedition ships out there based on Luka's design, ready to invade the peaceful forest village.

'Why are you telling me this?' he asked.

'I'm a kind man, Aleksandr,' the king told him, his words contradicting the cold smile on his face, 'and a fair ruler. But, more importantly, I'm not an idiot. I know there would be a revolt if I were to claim your land from you, even if it is rightfully mine. However, should it be reported that, upon your release from prison due to my gracious intervention, you were so overcome with gratitude and patriotism that you offered me your land and title as a gesture of fealty – why, people would be celebrating in the streets at the increased power of their country and their kingdom.'

'You want Karana?' Aleks clarified. 'In exchange for a complete discharge from the military?' King Andrei nodded once.

'Exactly that, lad. You have no use for the land, and if I have the old mechanic's ship, it'll only be a matter of time before I have a fleet of identical ships to command as I please. You have nothing with which to make that country worth something. Give me fifteen years and it will be as prosperous as Siberene itself,' he boasted, sending unease through Aleks's stomach. Would he really be able to do so? If he had Luka's ship . . . but Aleks didn't have much of a choice. Kara would have to defend her own people, if it came down to it.

'I'll give you the country,' he agreed reluctantly. 'But I warn you, sire, that land is not meant to be ruined through colonisation. It is so beautiful, so incredible in its development away from civilisation. To alter that would be to take away the last piece of true Goddess-owned land this world has left.' He eyed the king intently as he spoke, long past caring if he was offending the man. It had to be said, and the worst the king could do was scold him; he wouldn't put Aleks back in prison or he'd lose Luka's ship. 'My crewmate died, not because of an animal attack, but because the dead zone was so harsh it blew our propeller while he was in the engine room. Karana is not meant for us.' Maybe Zhora would still be alive if they'd realised that earlier.

'How dare you!' King Andrei said angrily. 'How dare you presume to tell me what I can and can't do! You know nothing of the Goddess's purpose, nor the building of a colony – the beauty of nature can be sacrificed for the good of the people. If I didn't believe that, I'd never get anywhere.'

'Is Siberene itself not enough?' Aleks argued earnestly. 'Siberene has prospered plenty without the knowledge of land beyond the Stormlands, and to believe we cannot thrive without it would reflect rather poorly on your ability as king, sire.' He knew he had overstepped the mark when the king's dark brows furrowed and his eyes became icy as he stared at the boy in front of him.

'Our deal still stands,' he snapped. 'You will have your freedom, both from my prison and my military, and in return I will have the ship and your country. Do not *dare* to lecture me on my ability as king when you have nothing of worth to your name.' Aleks stood, and Shulga took a half-step forward.

'There was no lecturing involved, sire, and no offence meant,' Aleks insisted. 'Merely a warning, and perhaps a word of advice. Nothing good will come of staining the beauty of that land, and you're likely to lose more than you gain in attempting to do so.'

King Andrei glared at him and Aleks bowed low, the position more comfortable now his hands weren't cuffed behind his back. As he rose, he caught Prince Erik's eye. When he noticed Aleks staring, he froze, then nodded once, slowly, where his father couldn't see. Surprised, Aleks nodded back; hopefully that meant at least one member of the royal family had been listening to his words. Perhaps the future of Siberene was in better hands than the present.

'It was a pleasure to meet you all,' he said politely. 'Though forgive me if I say I shan't make a habit of it.' Erik smiled before he could hide it, while King Andrei's glare merely darkened.

'See that you don't,' he replied sharply. Aleks glanced at a furious-looking Shulga, wondering if he was free to leave, and began backing up towards the door, keeping his face directed at his monarch. It was rude to turn your back on a king.

'My condolences on the loss of your crewmate,' Erik said just as Aleks reached the door. 'He was a brave man to undertake such an adventure.' The king turned to glare at his son, but Erik didn't flinch. Seeing them together, Aleks could only hope that King Andrei wasn't given a further fifteen years on the throne in which to implement his plan.

'Thank you, Your Highness,' Aleks murmured sincerely. 'I shall pass your kindness on to his brother.' Erik smiled, nodding towards him, and Aleks ignored Shulga's icy glare as he was led from the room, hoping vehemently that he never crossed paths with King Andrei Rudavin again. It had turned out well enough for him this time, but he had the feeling that should there be a next time, he wouldn't be nearly so lucky.

42

Aleks could hardly believe what had happened. His handcuffs were removed as soon as the door was shut behind him. All three of his guards were scowling, clearly annoyed by his freedom, and he grinned at them smugly, giving Shulga in particular a sarcastic little wave. The tall man behind the desk in the reception room raised his eyebrows at them, and the faintest smile flickered across his lips when he saw Aleks being released. 'He accepted the offer, then?' he presumed, and Aleks stepped forward, resisting the urge to roll his eyes when his guards all tensed, prepared to restrain him.

'I did,' he confirmed, figuring that now he wasn't a prisoner, the man would be willing to talk to him instead of over him. 'Where do I sign?' All he wanted was to go home, shower, get warm and see his friends. The man reached into a drawer in his desk, pulling out two sets of stapled papers.

'Here, and here,' he instructed, handing over a pen and gesturing to the dotted lines at the bottom of each paper. 'This one to release you of all charges, and this one to forfeit your commitment to the military.' Aleks took the pen, a wide smile on his face as he scrawled his signature twice.

He got a dizzying amount of pleasure from signing the second one, secure in the knowledge that he would never again have to see the cold, grim inside of Rensav's military base. He could get an apprenticeship, he could go home and see his family, he could get *married*.

'Congratulations, you're free to go.'

'Thank you,' Aleks replied, grinning and shaking the man's hand. He was almost giddy with excitement as he walked towards the door, refraining from sticking his tongue out childishly at the guards when they didn't follow him. The door unlocked easily from that side, and almost as soon as he stepped out a black blur came flying at him. He held his hands up automatically, frowning when he caught his coat.

'Thought you might need it,' a familiar voice called, and when he moved the thick leather off his face he saw Luka standing a few feet in front of him, smirking. 'Happy now?' Aleks laughed, dashing forward and grabbing the old man in a tight hug.

'Thank you,' he said heartily, feeling a lump rise in his throat. 'You gave up your ship for my freedom . . . you gave up everything. I can never repay you for that.' Luka struggled out of the hug, tutting even as he fought a smile.

'Don't be daft, lad. I didn't give up everything!' he insisted. Aleks shrugged his coat on, giving the man a perplexed look.

'But you gave up the *Thunderbug*. Eight years of your work, and it'll be dismantled and replicated a hundred times over at the Academy. There'll be ships like it travelling through the Stormlands within a few years,' he pointed out, frowning. As much as he hated it, he still knew that all the small ships in the world couldn't make Karana a viable colony, and people would see that for themselves as soon as they reached it. Besides, he thought he'd got through to Prince Erik.

'Gods, you're an idiot sometimes,' Luka muttered, shaking his head. 'I can build a new ship without too many problems. I've sod all else to do with my time. And I'll tell you this – the greatest mechanical minds at the Academy could spend ten years dismantling and studying that ship, but not a single one will be able to rebuild anything even remotely similar without my input.' From anyone else it would have sounded arrogant, but Aleks knew that if Luka believed it then it was probably true.

'Did you finish fixing her left propeller?' he asked suddenly.

'Not exactly,' he drawled in reply. 'Like I said, none of them will even come close to figuring out how it works. The Academy teaches people to copy, not to create, and you know damn well you need plenty of creativity to understand my girl.' His voice was proud, and Aleks laughed.

'They'll come after you when they realise they can't get her to work. Beg for your help, bribe you, everything.'

'And I still won't give them a word,' Luka promised. 'Until they can finally churn out someone who isn't a mindless idiot doomed to make timepieces for the rest of his life, I have nothing to say to the Academy.' He clapped Aleks on the shoulder, urging him forward. 'Now, let's get you home. I know a lot of people are awfully worried about you. That poor Raina girl seems to think they'll cart you off to Rensav as soon as we turn our backs.' Aleks remembered the look on Raina's face as the guards had dragged him handcuffed from the inn, guilt curling in his stomach at causing so much stress.

'How has everyone been? Was there anything in the newscasts about it?' he asked worriedly, turning a corner with Luka at his side. It would take them a while to get back to the Compass from where they were, but Aleks was glad for the walk; it would give him time to get his head straight.

'No, but there were enough people there that night for things to spread through word of mouth. Most seem to believe the arrest is just for captaining the ship; they all think it's grossly unfair and have been petitioning for your release since you were arrested. The whole desertion charge seems to have been kept quiet.'

'That's good,' Aleks said softly, relieved. 'No doubt the newscasts reporters will be all over the most recent development in good time. I had no idea the king was even in the city.'

'He wasn't, until the first newscast about Karana. Apparently he hightailed it here with his eldest as soon as he was available, and covered it by saying they were visiting the younger lad,' Luka informed him knowledgeably.

'Well, I'm sure while he's here he'll be happy to do interviews about taking over the rule of Karana on behalf of the Siberene royal family,' Aleks remarked with irony. Luka stopped, turning to look at him in shock.

'Rule? They took it from you?' he asked, and Aleks frowned, nodding. Not that it was really his in the first place, but no one needed to know that.

The conversation halted when they stopped outside the Compass. Aleks grinned, pushing the door open. Expecting Raina, Ksenia and Bodan, his eyes widened when he also saw Saria and Drazan sitting by the bar, smiling broadly at him. Saria practically flew into his arms, bringing him into a firm kiss. 'Oh, thank the gods you're OK,' she breathed, her cheek against his as she hugged him. 'I was so worried they'd find a way to keep you in there, or worse.'

'I'm fine,' he whispered, fingers tangling in her hair. 'I'm home and they have nothing to keep me there any more. I signed release papers, I'm cleared of all charges, and my enlistment papers are gone,' he promised. She smiled, letting him go so he could greet the others. Raina hugged him, pulling back to meet his gaze seriously.

'Is everything all right now?' she asked pointedly, and he nodded, tugging her ponytail gently. She looked worried, clearly still expecting someone to drag him off for four years of military service.

'Everything is just fine,' he confirmed. 'I'm cleared of all offence charges and obligations. I'm a completely free man.' The girl beamed, hugging him again.

'Thank the gods,' she murmured vehemently. 'And don't you ever scare me like that again!' Instead of arguing that it was hardly his fault, he nodded, managing a grin.

'I won't, I promise,' he assured her. Drazan hugged him in greeting, hustling him onto his stool at the bar, where Ksenia presented him with a large, home-cooked dinner.

'How did old Luka manage it, then?' Drazan asked, looking from Aleks to the mechanic. 'We thought for sure there must be military secrets involved, for him to bribe the guard captain. What does he know?' Aleks smirked to himself, wondering how to break it to the pilot that Luka hadn't just bribed the guard captain but the king too.

'Let the man eat first, storms!' Ksenia interrupted. 'He's had one hell of a weekend, no doubt.' Aleks smiled wryly; that was one way of putting it.

After he'd eaten, Bodan brought out the good cider, and together he and Luka recounted everything that had happened from the moment Aleks had been arrested, one filling in details where the other couldn't. Aleks grinned at his captive audience as he revealed the meeting he'd had earlier in the day, repeating almost every word that had transpired, and watching their amazed faces as they digested it all.

'Expect a newscast soon giving some concocted story about how I offered the land to my king in fealty or something. No doubt they'll make me look awfully meek and spineless while they do so,' Aleks mused, shrugging.

'That's a shame,' Drazan remarked. 'I was starting to like the idea of being friends with a king.' The pilot winked conspiratorially, making Aleks snort.

'Leave off,' he muttered, rolling his eyes. 'I didn't want the title in the first place. I just hope he won't end up doing anything with it.' He hadn't mentioned the look he'd shared with Prince Erik, not wanting to raise any hopes if it turned out the man had similar opinions to his father. Still, Aleks liked to think he had got through to him. 'No, I'm just glad to be free. It's more than I ever expected.' He paused, frowning. 'I just wish we hadn't had to go through so much to get there.' Drazan reached over to touch his shoulder, a knowing look on his face.

'You can't predict the future, Aleks. None of this would have happened if you could. But . . . it could have gone worse.' He swallowed and Aleks offered a half-smile. He was right; it could have gone a lot worse. All of them could have died out there, or two of them, leaving the third stranded and alone. Or Aleks could have died in Rensav before any of that even happened.

'Just thank the gods it's over,' he mused. 'Albeit not quite in one piece.' Drazan nodded, then raised his tankard.

'To Aleks's freedom, the end of a journey, and the beginning of a new one,' he added with a faint smile.

'And to Zhora, who helped me when I needed it most, and made all of this possible, even if he can't be here to see it,' Aleks said, raising his tankard. A murmur of 'To Zhora' went round the group, followed by the tap of tankards and then silence as everyone drank.

'I wish I could've met Zhora,' Saria said. 'I have a lot to thank him for.' Aleks's arm tightened around her shoulders and he kissed her temple.

'He wouldn't have let you,' he told her fondly, making Drazan smile. Surrounded by people who had become as close as family, Aleks couldn't help but glance at Drazan, thinking of the man who should have been occupying the space between him and Luka. Plenty of amazing things had resulted from Aleks leaving home, and he would never forget them: flying through the Stormlands and meeting Kara and her people; seeing the beauty of the land there; meeting so many wonderful people in Syvana, people who he knew would be in his life for decades to come; finding Saria and falling in love – none of it would have been possible if he'd stayed in his tiny village and done what was expected of him. But, despite all that, those things would never be worth Zhora's life.